PULSE

BOLT SAGA: VOLUME THREE
PARTS 7 - 8 - 9

ANGEL PAYNE

PULSE

BOLT SAGA: VOLUME THREE
PARTS 7 - 8 - 9

ANGEL PAYNE

WATERHOUSE PRESS

TABLE OF CONTENTS

For my incredible Thomas,

and the Parisian adventures that inspire

PULSE

PART 7

CHAPTER ONE

EMMA

Riddle me this...

Is it possible to drown in agony and soar in ecstasy at the same time?

And could I get *any* cornier about swooning over my secret fiancé?

"Don't answer that," I mumble to my libido—because the struggle gets even more real, surpassing all clichés and hashtags—as I watch my man, standing on a ridge close to the driveway of our freshly built canyon home, helping a construction crew drill a tunnel into the side of a mountain. The other guys are clad in jeans, T-shirts, and hardhats. Reece Andrew Richards is wearing nothing but his shit-kicker boots, tight leather pants, and a whole lot of sweat. The crew members are using a couple of jackhammers and lots of other loud equipment. My shit-hot fiancé is using only the bright-blue lightning erupting from his fingertips. And every jolt reveals new definition in the tantalizing muscles of his tall, rippled body...

Blatantly reminding me of the excess energy he'll need to burn off after the excavation...

Ecstasy.

But then agony. I tear my gaze away from Reece as I

remember the two extra members in his audience today.

So I plaster on an awkward smile for my future mother-in-law. *And* his.

Kill. Me. Now.

Before I get the chance to consider doing the deed myself, the man takes a break from his labors to glance over, flashing a grin of his own. Correction. *The grin*. The Reece Andrew Richards special, a twist of carnality and arrogance so potent, the tabloid media has all but built shrines in its honor. I admit to falling prey to its spell myself on more than a few occasions—though not this one. Right now, all I can do is narrow a glower back that's filled with one message alone. The next time he invites both our mothers to lunch, while *he* looks like *that*, he'd better be prepared to deal with the consequences. Exactly *what* consequences? I haven't gotten that far yet, but if there's anything I've learned from loving this man, it's to have a huge imagination...

"Well, honey. You weren't kidding when you said to have a big imagination."

My mother proves, yet again, her uncanny karmic timing—and her ability to take in a view as amazing as this and find it lacking. The acres of land around us, rolling hills carpeted with spring wildflowers, stretch all the way to the tiny ribbon of PCH below. Just past the highway is the sparkling band of the Pacific, gleaming a rich sapphire that blends with the clear Southern California sky. From up here, in the hills just north of Malibu, it's impossible to fathom that the bustle of downtown LA is only an hour away. The rustle of wind across the bluff is a balmy symphony, its perfect harmony rising from the coastal birds in the shrubs. The air is clean and crisp, smelling of rosemary and eucalyptus and tinged with a hint of sea spray...

And lunch.

Thank *God* for lunch.

"Who's hungry?" I sidestep Mother's snip with one of the best excuses on earth. I already can't wait for the meal ahead. Anya, my favorite salad creator from the little country mart down in Malibu Village, finally succumbed to the ungodly amount of money Reece offered her to come up a couple of times a week to prep dishes for the construction crews when I can't. From time to time—actually, on more occasions than I want to admit—she keeps me fueled and going as well. Though we're finally putting finishing touches on the main residence of the complex, Reece and I won't be able to completely call it home until the rest is built out, meaning our time is still split between downtown and up here.

So yeah, Anya has been a gift from the gods—and never more so than now, as I escort Mother and Trixie Richards into the house through the Mediterranean-influenced front door with baby bougainvillea bushes planted at either side. We cross the polished Italianate tiles of the front foyer to stop at the top of the wide, curved staircase leading down to the main living room area.

Since Reece had the vision to build the house down, embedding it into the side of the mountain, the grandeur of the place unfolds before us in terraced layers, with iron and wood furniture complementing the arched doorways, stone walls, and native flowers in huge urns painted in swirls of burgundy and blue. The wall tapestries copy that color theme, though are woven in modern swirled designs.

Today, the room's massive glass doors are swiveled to let in the balmy afternoon breeze, lightly teasing at the glass table Anya has set with white linen and trendy-shaped china. In the center of the table is a vase of freshly picked wildflowers and an ice bucket supporting a bottle of Dom Pérignon.

"Oh, my goodness." Trixie's comment is nearly a gasp. "It's..."

"A little better than the outside," Mother concedes, adding a delicate sniff.

Trixie flashes a subtle side-eye at her. "I was going to say palatial," she comments while wrapping a gentle hand into mine. "But *not* a stuffy palace." She adds hastily, "It's regal but relaxed. And very beautiful."

"Of course." Mother approaches from my other side, hooking her elbow through mine in a strange show of possessiveness. While the moment has me bumbling for a second, I welcome the awkwardness. Mother has never been the fuss-and-kiss type, but maybe today's the day we *both* break out of a few comfort zones. "And the house is stunning too." She dots that with a quick squeeze to my elbow, succeeding in robbing me of words for several seconds as I'm too busy gulping back emotion.

Trixie, thinking we're only sharing another sweet mother-daughter moment instead of our *only* mother-daughter moment, remarks, "Lunch smells divine. What are we having?"

"Smells like Anya's specialty," I reply as the three of us descend the stairs. "So something gooey, Italian, and perfect."

Anya, appearing from the kitchen that takes up a few thousand feet of the house's next level, responds to my theory with her graceful laugh. The woman, with her long fiery curls, cute broomstick skirt, and pink pointy-toed boots, literally looks like she just walked off some fantasy movie set, but this is Anya in everyday mode. "Emma is right. You ladies will enjoy a kale Caesar salad with fresh avocados and chickpeas; then, whole wheat lasagna with zucchini, spinach, and goat cheese, dashed with truffle oil. I also whipped up some oven-roasted green beans and sprinkled them with aged goat cheese and fresh parmesan."

Mother's eyes light up. "Magnificent."

Nearly at the same time, Trixie mutters, "Was that even in English?"

A giggle bursts off my lips. As in, a real laugh. *Wait.* Is this me, *enjoying* lunch between the only two women on the planet capable of making me capitalize the word *Stress*?

That's not true either. One more name belongs on that list.

Faline.

But today isn't for dwelling on the bitch who still haunts my nightmares. It's for building on the dream of forever with the man who helped me survive her. Who literally swooped in and saved me from her.

Who strides in like a modern-day Errol Flynn now, rocking those incredible leather pants, a billowy black shirt he's just thrown on, and even a black scarf of some sort tied around his head to keep his gorgeous but sweaty hair off his face.

And stealing my breath all over again.

Damn.

Reece is delicious even without his rugged boots. He likely kicked off the filthy things at the front door when he came in. His bare feet hit the tiles with undeniable strength as he approaches, and the air practically shudders from the impact of his presence. I'm not the only one who feels it. I can see how his energy impacts both Trixie and Mother—though clearly, their intimate parts aren't as swept away as mine...

Or Anya's.

It's impossible to ignore how the woman is affected by my pirate stud, with the pulse in her throat quickening and the roses in her cheeks growing, but it's not like poor Anya—or nearly any other woman who comes in this close contact with him—can help herself. It is what it *is*, and I deal with it in new forms every day. Short of ordering Reece to turn the new tunnel into a prison cell instead of Team Bolt's high-tech command center—and chaining him inside for the rest of his life—there's nothing I can do but deal with the discomfort and trust our connection. That inexplicable, incomparable bond that seems to strengthen between us every day.

That ignites anew in his silver-gray eyes as he walks straight toward me...

And kisses me...

And floors me all over again.

It's not a tonsillectomy. To everyone here, it's probably no more than a fast, casual peck. But to him and me, it's everything. Fresh fire. Perfect energy. A storm of two souls and an awed awareness we acknowledge with the quick connection of our stares.

Just like that, I don't care about lunch.

Just that easily, I could jump on him like a hot, horny bunny. Yeah, even if he *does* keep regarding me like a wolf who wants to eat me alive.

Just that quickly, his gaze flares, indicating he's read every nasty thought in my head as clearly as his own. Perhaps because they're so similar...

"Reece." His mother's scold is a wedge of ice in the middle of our lusty fire. "Stop crowding in on her like a cretin."

With barely a falter to his stare or a hitch in his stance, he murmurs, "Hi, Mom. Great to see you too."

"Yes, yes." She sounds distracted but betrays her pride as he reaches back, clasping her hand with his glove-covered one. "And that's all you get for now, until you smell better."

"Which won't be until tomorrow night at the Griffith Observatory's ball," he returns, to be answered by her instant huff.

"All right, fine. Come here, then." After she tugs him into a fast hug, the woman pushes back with a sniff only a mother could get away with. "*Lord*, son."

"It's warm outside, Mom." He swings his gaze back to me with the blatant but silent follow-up. *And it's damn* hot *in here...*

"Well, at least I stopped you from hulking over poor Emma for a moment."

I can't help giggling.

Reece can't stop scowling.

"Mother, I'm her fi—" he falters and draws the word out— "fiii-reaking boyfriend."

As he murders the words, I tilt my head and feign enough of a light laugh to disguise my study of Trixie's face. Is she wise to Reece's near catastrophe of a slip? Yes, he's my fiancé—in all the ways that matter, in my heart and his—but no way in hell does that mean our mothers need to know too. Not yet.

Because as soon as they know, the rest of the world will know too.

And when the rest of the world knows, so will the Consortium.

And once those bastards get their hands on that kind of information...

It won't be information anymore.

It'll be their weapon.

But stressing out over our evil scientist enemies isn't an inch of help right now, especially when it looks like Reece yanked the "big reveal" in time. I help him out with a charming shrug, telling Trixie, "To be honest, I like him in Neanderthal mode."

"Not in that dress, you don't." Mother keeps her tone light but goes full Anna Wintour with her face, looking panicked at Reece's proximity to my flowery A-line tea dress. "*Princess and the Pirate* works in the world of romance novels and nowhere else, missy."

"Amen," Trixie murmurs, prompting Reece and me to trade a secret glance. Correction: a hurried look of horror. While we'd conceived this lunch with a larger goal in mind, to warm up both sets of our parents to the concept of our wedding taking place here sometime in the next couple of years, the subject of them *getting along* had never been broached— probably because it was too surreal.

"But I like romance novels..." My mumble is a caterpillar of sound beneath Mother and Trixie's fresh chatter, which jumps from the virtues of the A-line silhouette, to every gown the royals have worn in the last three weeks, to the latest TV bio-drama *about* the royals, to the scandal surrounding some British actor not even related to the royals, to said actor's love child now topping the charts with her pop-hip-hop-rasta-rap song about it...

"Holy shit." Reece dares to push a little closer in order to mutter it for my ears alone. "They're already comparing notes on pop divas?"

I drag in a deep breath. I don't know whether it's sad or hilarious that his aroma of mud and sweat is actually guiding my senses back to a semblance of Zen. "This is either really good or really bad."

He nuzzles his lips against my cheek. "Well, let me know how it goes."

I jerk away by a few inches, gawk already in place. "Where the hell are *you* going?"

A shrug of his sculpted shoulders. "You want the command center excavated in a few weeks?" Then a glance of heated intent to my lips. "Besides, if I keep standing this close to you, all I'll want to do is fuck you."

"Mr. Richards." I feign a scandalized whisper, sliding a surreptitious hand beneath his shirt and against his bare abdomen. "With your own mother one room over?"

"Keep touching me like that, Bunny, and I won't even wait until the bedroom." Despite his all-but-a-promise growl, the kiss he lowers to my nose is chaste. "Can't wait to hear about the fun. Take notes so you can fill me in later."

My soft groan trails in the wake of his backward step. "You're such a bastard."

"The bastard you love."

"Regrettably, yes."

"Lucky for *me*, yes."

And just like that, I'm a puddle of smitten for him once more. "Lucky for me too," I murmur, squeezing his fingers. More than anything, I wish we didn't have to be touching through the barrier of his gloves. I yearn for the tingling heat of his bared, glowing fingertips along my naked, vulnerable skin, corresponding to his wicked, whispered words in my ear...

A heavy gulp vibrates the rugged column of his neck, indicating he's still on the same mental page. But he breaks our contact with a rough grunt, long enough to jog his sights out toward the patio, where Trixie and Mother have wandered with glasses of champagne offered by Anya. Thankfully, having gotten her hormones under control, the pink-booted one has wandered back to the kitchen.

"Hey, Mom?" Reece shouts. "I've got to go back to work— but in no universe is that permission to yank out the baby album for Em, okay?"

Trixie displays her stylish purse, which probably couldn't fit *half* a good romance novel. "And where, exactly, would I be stowing said album, my son?"

"On the Swarovski-covered brick you fondly call your phone?" When all he receives to that is his mother's dismissive wave, he mumbles to me, "Seriously, don't let her go there."

"But whhhyyyy?" I take advantage of the fact that my own maternal unit has wandered out to gawk at the negative edge pool and steal a quick snuggle against his chest. "Baby Reece? Sounds like fun."

There's a dark rumble from the middle of that chest. "There is nothing *fun* about you seeing my penis in a diaper, sweetheart." But the new tension in his body belies a different story. Though his chest is always the texture of a muscled wall, the mien now defines every inch of him—even the angles of the gorgeous face I look back up to.

"Okay. Got it. No diapers." I rub the center of his sternum. "Now you going to tell me what *else* is going on?"

For a heartbeat that feels like an eternity, he doesn't return my gaze. Finally, with a violent jerk of his head, he forces out a tight smile. "Nothing, baby. Really."

Sharp arch—of *both* brows. "You know what a girl thinks when she hears that, right?"

The humor beneath his chuff is a little more authentic. "Okay, then nothing *important*." He busses my nose again. "I mean it. Now go have fun."

Yet another pointed glare. "I'm getting you a dictionary for your birthday, mister. *Nothing?* And now *fun?* You know the rest of the world has different definitions for those, yeah?"

As his well-calculated answer, I receive only the slow curve of his knowing grin and a perfect view of his incredible backside before he clears the stairs with a couple of electric-fueled bounds and disappears back out the front door.

"Reece Andrew, you really *are* a bastard."

My grumble isn't even a tiny consolation as I steel my nerves for what the next couple of hours may bring—especially as I rejoin Mother and Trixie in the middle of a debate about whether the newest "it" film couple used camera angles and cock socks or really "did the deed" in their hottest love scene. How the hell is a girl supposed to eat a full meal, even the incredible one before me, after hearing her mother use the term *cock sock?*

Somehow, I get in a few bites of everything. It's delicious, meaning I can't wait to enjoy some leftovers tonight with Reece—preferably after indulging the horny bunny temptation a little more fully with him. I use the fantasy as mental fortification during a conversation that covers every subject from the hot Hollywood couple's PDA during their Mexican Riviera vacation, to butt injections and clitoral jewelry and the newest workout trend, ironically called primal scream therapy. Which is sounding like a better and better idea by the minute...

Until, miracle of miracles, Mother's cell phone rings. Though she apologizes for the interruption, I glance at the screen and urge her to answer. Since it's a doctor's office and not either of the romantic "side dishes" I still suspect her of keeping, it must be important. With any luck, it's actually the right kind of physician—one who can help her see that a bank account full of zeroes isn't a permission slip for a morality code brimming with the same. But I only take tiny bites of that hope—just as I have for fourteen years and counting now.

As soon as Mother walks away, face pressed to her phone, I lift a smile at Trixie—and am pleased that the expression comes from my heart. Despite the woman's ability to banter about every trending socialite subject there is, I've spent enough time with her now to discern there are deeper waters to the woman as well. Thank God.

"So don't faint," I joke while refilling her champagne. "I got domestic last night and attempted a new tiramisu recipe for our dessert. As soon as I grab it, I'll join you and Mother out by the pool."

"Hmmm. I have a better idea." She rises gracefully, looking stunning in her coral linen sheath. "Why don't I give you a hand? I was hoping I'd get you all to myself for a few minutes."

She's not even finished with the statement, and my chest thuds with six kinds of anxiety. *All to herself?* Why? What does she want to tell me? What secret might she expose to me? Or likelier, what kind of ultimatum does she want to give me? Is this the stay-away-from-my-son-you-California-tramp talk? Or worse, the he's-been-engaged-since-he-was-seven talk? Is that why Reece tensed up about the baby album? Is his relationship with me just as dark a stain on their family as his string of European models and actresses—or is there an even grander plan I'm not aware of, like a hidden heiress that Reece considered "off the table" in the shadows of his estrangement from his dad? Only now they're not so estranged anymore, thanks to a not-so-small miracle called the Richards Reaches

Out organization. Amazing what men can accomplish when the small shit gets set aside for the good of so many.

A nonprofit arm is a great addition for an empire's public image.

A girl—who hasn't been handpicked for the succession of the family legacy—shacking up with their son in a luxury commune in the California hills?

Not so much, kiddies.

And now I'm thinking like my sister and not like me. Writing, casting, and orchestrating a tragedy that isn't there.

Not yet, at least.

Stop. It.

The castigation is overruled by the voice of the woman beside me, flooded with the same intense concern as her gaze. "Emmalina? Are you feeling all right, dear?"

At once, I straighten my posture. "Of...of course." Then peer harder at her, desperately battling to read those ocean-green depths. "Why do you ask?"

"You're shaking like a leaf." She states it as if commenting that the sky is blue. "Come here." After pushing up onto one of the stools in front of the high granite bar, she pats the cushion of the chair beside her. "Let's have a little chat."

I oblige like a kid being directed into the dentist's chair. *Just a little chat.* Okay, I can cope with that. That's a lot like *just a little filling*, right? Until the x-rays show that a root canal is needed instead?

"What...do you want to chat...about...?"

I stumble it out as Trixie reaches over and scoops her left hand beneath my right. The tanzanite stone on my ring finger, as well as the diamonds surrounding it, ignites to the shade of blue fire beneath the recessed kitchen lights. Looking at it now prompts the same flood of emotions I felt when Reece dropped to a knee on the ridge outside and presented it to me. Excitement. Anticipation. A little apprehension. A lot of happiness.

And love.

Always, with him, such love.

At last, after angling and tipping my hand in a few different ways, Trixie murmurs, "It's stunning."

"It is." I state it with every ounce of confidence I feel in this moment—born from a love that she'll never be able to truly take from me, no matter what her end game is here.

"And Reece didn't just give it to you as a *yay, we survived the New York City gala catastrophe* thing, did he?"

At once, I avert my gaze and dip into conflicted silence. It would be easy enough to white lie out of this and say the ring actually *was* a token to commemorate how we came through that night last fall, when RRO's first fundraiser was made into a truly "memorable" affair by a gang of hoodlums who—to most outside eyes—held up the crowd for money and jewelry. And yeah, I could easily smoke her with the "just a bauble" deception. Thanks to Mother and Father, I've had lots of experience with playing casual when everything isn't.

But I don't know if I want to try.

Not with this woman with the sincerity that still isn't faltering. Who just keeps smiling at me with such open patience...

"No," I admit, giving in fast to the pull of my instinct—just as I did when first falling for her son. "He didn't."

Her grip tightens by a slight degree. "Then why is it on your *right* hand?"

This answer is easier for me to give. "Because we know

what'll happen as soon as it goes on my left. And right now, we just want—*need*—some space."

I lift my head and search her face, relieved to see the beginnings of understanding.

"Space is okay," she murmurs. "As long as it's for the right reasons."

"Meaning?"

"That it's clear you two have already begun an extraordinary journey together." As she tilts her head, her expression becomes contemplative. "More extraordinary than most, it would seem."

"And that troubles you?" I can't stand having to ask it but haul my big-girl panties on and get it out anyway.

"Of course not." Trixie's snort is so prim, it's cute. "Let me be clear, my dear. It would have been easier to learn that my son-who-isn't-a-superhero actually *is* a superhero in a manner other than watching him take down seven criminals at once, but the actual truth itself—"

"I know." I hold up my free hand. "It's a little crazy..."

"Crazy?" She's scoffing. No, really. *Scoffing.* "But this *is* Reece you're talking about, my dear."

And now, she's actually laughing—to which I'm clueless about how to react. "Errrr..."

"*Emma.*" The second I lower my hand, she grabs it in hers once more. "I'll say this once and then deny it if you ever repeat it." She leans so close, our kneecaps are touching. "God blessed Lawson and me with three incredible sons. And while I love Chase and Tyce for everything that makes them unique and amazing, the angels definitely broke their molds when they sent me Reece Andrew."

Now, it's all too easy to lean forward and settle my other

hand against hers. "Well, *now* you've hooked me."

She spreads her smile a little wider, and it's filled with warm affection. "Since Reece was four years old and declared he was going on a 'turtle diet' in order to grow a shell like the mutant ninja ones, I knew that kid was bound for a unique existence." She lets the smile go to join me in a full laugh. Once I've mellowed, she goes on, "And yes, I knew it would make his teen and college years more challenging." And then surrenders her laugh for an audible, purposeful sigh. "*Much* more challenging."

"Don't tell me he tried to convince the girls he had a turtle shell hidden somewhere."

"If it'd only been so easy." She gazes across the kitchen, through the bay windows of the breakfast nook, with a gaze now gone pinched and sad. "But I'm afraid that following in his brothers' footsteps was a more difficult path than I'd originally anticipated."

"Than *you'd* anticipated?" I push on the emphasis, once more just going on sheer gut instinct. Considering that before six months ago Reece could barely mention his father without twitching an eye, I'm feeling clear about my probe. "Did Lawson not share your view, then?"

Ding, ding, ding. From the looks of the woman's fresh tension, I've hit the grand prize gong. "Reece was just fourteen when my husband took advantage of some prime opportunities to expand Richards Resorts. Reece's grandfather had passed, leaving Lawson with some sizable income to reinvest, and Asian destinations were just starting to open up. Lawson was traveling a great deal to Singapore and Hong Kong. When he did come home, for maybe a few days at a time, he was usually focused on Tyce's lacrosse games or Chase's international business studies. That left Reece fighting for his dad's attention however he could. Acting out was what he chose."

I nod, picking up the regret in her expression after just a few seconds. "And that was likely what worked the best."

"Despite how many times I tried telling my husband that the incidents were just shouts for attention?" She copies my nod, though her version is heavier. "Yes." She quirks a grateful smile as I pull on her hand, surrounding it with understanding pressure. "The cycle seemed never-ending. Every crazy stunt from Reece was answered by Lawson's fury and discipline." She shakes her head fast as soon as I bulge my eyes. "Oh, my husband never touched Reece, though sometimes I wonder if that was what Reece was ultimately after." An odd smirk flits across her lips. "The stunts that boy could pull off..."

With exaggeration, I get more comfortable on my stool. "Which you're going to spill in lieu of the baby pictures?"

Her head falls back as she submits to a new, heartier laugh. "I think my *blood* would be spilled for that—but let's just say that if you ever want to get under his skin, just bring up two gallons of baby oil and Randall Getty's skateboard ramp."

"Oh, *my*." A chuckle sneaks out of me too. "Were there any broken bones involved?"

"Thankfully, no—though I can't say the same about our guy's ego." She slips into a quieter mien after noticing that I do. "Emma? Dearheart?"

"Ummm." It tumbles from me on a rasp while I attempt to gulp down sudden tears. Damn it. I wasn't ready for this—or how so much of it would move me. "Sorry. I'm...I'm okay."

"No, you're not." And yet more of that forthright tenderness, which throws me for a complete loop. Not that Mother never did the same. Her method involved calling me on the BS and then rattling off statistics about how better-educated women landed better boyfriends, fiancés, and finally husbands. "Your turn to spill now." Trixie squeezes one of my knees. "Was it something I said?"

I imply the *yes* by attempting to laugh my tears off. "'Our guy,'" I finally reiterate. "That sounds...nice."

"Oh, *Emma*." She bypasses any more affectionate touches by standing and hauling me into a huge hug. "It was supposed to."

Fervently, I return her embrace. "Simple as that, huh?"

"Simple as that." As she steps away, she transitions from effortless cheer to meaningful focus with Carol Brady ease. "Though things *aren't* that simple with you and Reece, are they? Which is why the ring is here and not here?" In sync with her words, she lifts my right and then left hands.

I pull away, using the guise of moving toward the refrigerator for the tiramisu. "It's a long story."

"Ah," the woman answers softly. "I figured so."

I shift from foot to foot. "I'm sorry, Trixie. I really am, But—"

"If you told me, you'd have to kill me?"

I freeze with my hand around the fridge handle—though feeling more like I've painted myself into a corner. I'm pretty sure Reece encouraged me to invite Mother and Trixie out here so we could exchange recipes and talk about poolside landscaping, not have a mini seminar about the crackpots known as the Consortium.

But she's his *mother*.

She gave him life.

Which means she damn well deserves to know about the assholes trying to take it away.

So no more corner for me.

I stand taller, meeting her gaze directly. "If that comment was a dart, you've darn near hit bull's-eye," I tell her.

"Meaning what?"

"Meaning that *I'd* never kill you, Trixie."

She pushes back to her feet. Eyes me steadily for a long pause. Another. When I barely move, even after the fridge cycles off and shudders into silence, she purses her lips and hauls in a long breath. Then finally breathes, "Whoa."

"Yeah." I try to look at least a little apologetic. After all, the White Rabbit was surely a *little* sorry after yanking Alice down the black hole. "Whoa."

"So the mass robbery attempt by those men at the gala..." She starts to slowly pace. "They weren't a random group of thugs, were they?"

I finally remember to open the refrigerator. After pulling out the big dish with my halfway-decent-looking dessert— shock of shocks—I slide the Pyrex to the counter with a determined *thunk*. "No, they weren't."

Her nostrils flare. "I was afraid of that." Then a heavy sigh. "They were involved somehow...with bad people. *Really* bad people." Her shoulders stiffen when I don't deny it. "The same bastards who...who *changed* my son." She kneads anxious fingers along the back of the chair she just vacated. "Who made him that way." Her fingertips go white. "Who hurt him to do it."

The tears to which I've relented because of her kindness are doubly fierce because of her maternal fury. "Please don't make me answer that, Trixie."

She pushes out a harsh breath. "It's all right, Emma. You already have."

I splay my hands atop the counter, hoping my silent

apology reaches her. "Maybe one day, Reece will be able to explain it all himself," I offer. "But right now, things are so... complicated."

The word is a spot-on fit, but still doesn't feel adequate—even when it sparks a full chuckle from Trixie in response. "What?" I prompt, unable to keep my own lips from twitching.

"Emma," she chides. "You speak as if *complicated* is a new thing for that boy." She shakes her head. "Lawson and I should've just given the word to him as a middle name."

My smirk becomes a full snicker. "Oh, that would've made things too easy."

She regards me with new intensity. "And you've never been happy with easy."

"I've never been happy with complacent." I push off the counter. "Because one's corner of the world is comfortable doesn't mean everyone else's is." Like sun breaking through clouds, my words bring me to a fresh understanding. "That truth has always followed me. Even haunted me, I guess. Like a little storm always threatening to break in the back of my senses. It ensured that I kept...pushing, I suppose." Though even as I say it, I wince. "No. That's not the right word. I wasn't pushing. Or even rebelling. I was..."

"Seeking?"

How can a person so opposite from green and wrinkled suddenly be turning into my Yoda? "Yeah," I rasp, swallowing down deep emotions. "Seeking." And while the word fills in the blank perfectly, it opens another question I can't quite vocalize—so I ask instead with my eyes.

How did you know?

Trixie lifts a slow and knowing smile. Like her son, the woman has the power to read right into me. Through me.

And then knows exactly what to say to me...

"Seekers are special people, my dear. Diamonds that need their cutters. Magnets that need their chargers." The smile rises to her eyes, both softening and strengthening their misty green light. "Lightning that needs their storm."

Now, I just let the tears spill. Just a few but making up in weight what they lack in number. "Lightning and its storm," I whisper as my mind fills with the glory of Reece's silver gaze, electric kisses, and transformative passion. "Yes. Of course..."

I have no idea when Trixie skirted around the counter next to me, but suddenly I'm wrapped back in the woman's arms, held close to her warmth and comfort and acceptance, as she again feeds my heart with the perfect Yoda blend of wisdom, affection, and sincerity.

"Dear God, creator of all that is right in this world, thank you for bringing this perfect storm to my beautiful bolt of a boy. Now watch over them both as they change the world together."

Her words are so fervent and heartfelt, I almost add an *amen*. Instead, I reply with all the affection and gratitude in my heart, "We're sure as hell going to try."

CHAPTER TWO

REECE

Now that I've moved half a mountain, I'm ready to change the world.

But right now, that starts with rocking hers.

The resolve surges through me from the moment all the guys on the crew look up, halting our work for a noticeable second. Since returning from our lunch break, the eight of us have kicked ass carving into the mountain, widening the fissure that will eventually contain the full Team Bolt command center.

Team Bolt.

I seriously try not to laugh myself sick about that shit.

In the end, it's only a label. And one thing I *do* know about labels is that they seldom sum up the truth of what they've been slapped on.

Because this team sure as *hell* isn't all about me. Thank fuck.

I'm jolted back to the moment by a shift in the wind that reminds me I'm standing in a musky tunnel that smells worse than every NFL locker room combined. I follow the dumbstruck stares of the other guys to the entrance of this dirty cave—to where an angel is silhouetted by the late-afternoon sun.

Ohhhh, yeah.

She possesses everything but the wings. The high breasts. The gently flared hips. The long, elegant legs, shown off even more as the hilltop breeze wraps her skirt against her knees. Then, as the wind strengthens, her blond waves escape the shadows, their bright-gold ribbons tying around us all.

"Okay, everyone." Brent, the crew foreman, edges his low growl with impatience, breaking the group fixation. Astute man. As hard as every guy here is working, I can all but hear every thought and fantasy forming in their heads. Visions starring *my* girl. "I know the dirt's complete yums today, but pick your jaws back up and let's get back to it."

As the guys nod and turn, clearly thankful their foreman saved their ball sacks from my backlash, I clap a hand over the top of Brent's shoulder. "I have a better idea." After relishing a second of their skittish stares, I finish, "Let's call it a day." I send a gruff nod Brent's way. "There's only a couple more hours, but we cut lunch short. Mark everyone for a full shift and get home to your families early."

In the midst of the celebratory grunts and hearty thanks from the guys, there's just one creature-from-the-dick-lagoon—Jerry, the token choad of the bunch, smirks and then sneers. "Well, we *know* you'll still be getting in a *full shift*, boss."

"Jesus wept." Brent looks tempted to head-butt the guy. "Jerry, are you fucking kidding—"

"It's cool, man." I add a sound smack to the center of my foreman's chest. Brent bears more than a passing resemblance to any of the brothers in an Aussie-based movie idol family, but his demeanor is all about the Detroit streets where he grew up. "We're all tired, and it's starting to smell like ass in here. Let's all grab showers and then our women. And Jerry?" I cock a brow at the lanky guy with his hands jabbed into his opposing armpits. "Just remember to take off your tool belt first so you don't puncture your dolly at first thrust."

The sound of seven guys at full laughter inside a twenty-foot-long tunnel is kind of cool. Yeah, even when there's one not-so-subtle snarl as their chaser. I ignore Jerry and all but strut out of the tunnel, reminded of the days I used to leave night clubs after dawn—with a number of key modifications. One, I'm stone-cold sober. Two, I haven't just slipped out of a back room after screwing a handful of women. Three, there's only one bed and one woman I can't wait to get to now.

One smoking *hot* woman.

No. Not even that description hits a fraction of the justice due my Emmalina, who's still standing in the main courtyard with an expectant smile on her lips and incredible skies in her eyes. The wind, still stealing in across the bluff, now blows her dress the other direction so the fabric molds across the fronts of her thighs. And into the V that's formed near their top...

Everyone on the crew, including Jerry, knows better than to gawk now.

And I do nothing but gawk. Openly. Unashamedly. Thanking-the-fuck-out-of-God-edly.

Just before my bloodstream brims with fire. And my muscles race with electrons. And every functioning synapse in my skull concentrates on nothing but getting myself to her side without falling on my face—because, honest to God, that gentle breeze could probably plow me over right now. I'm not sure I'd care. No. *Fuck.* I would care. Any delay in getting nearer to her gorgeousness is definitely going to set me the hell off.

My torment, the physical and the mental, only worsens as I close in on her. And her lips part. And her gaze darkens.

And her breaths pump faster, straining her breasts against her bodice. *Faster...*

Finally, finally, I'm able to push in close and lower my face just inches over hers. After a slow smirk and a teasing wink, I grate, "Hi, honey. I'm home."

Her giggle is a gentle caress across my raw senses—which of course ignites an instant blaze in my blood. At once, there's nothing tender or sweet about my raw lust. "Perfect timing," she murmurs, tugging at the sweaty ends of my hair. "Our moms just left."

"Bolt is my name; timing's my game." I issue the joke in response to her first sentence before the context of the second sinks in. "Wait. *What?* They left just *now*?"

Her shrug is as perplexing as it is adorable. "Yeah. So?"

"You know that's three hours for lunch, right?"

"We're women. We had a lot to talk about."

"A lot? About what?"

"Whoa, cowboy." She pulls harder on the ends of my hair. "Slow that roll and don't freak. At no point did your mom dig out her phone and scroll through the pictures app."

"Thank fuck."

"Though there *might* have been a teeny-weeny mention of turtle shells." The twinges at the corners of her mouth get more pronounced. "And a skateboard ramp with baby oil..."

"*Shit.*" If my snarl doesn't clarify my point, I make sure to let my backward stumble do the trick. And yeah, the way I wrench from her, even when she grips my shoulder tighter, silently pleading for me to stay. The moment feels surreal. I can practically see it as if I'm standing outside myself, watching all my asshole glory, a faithful chip off the old block who taught it to me to begin with. But I can't control it. This is how the anger rolls with every new visit to my past, despite Dad's recent efforts to make up for it. The holes in the dam are still there. Maybe they always will be.

I know I promised to play ball with you today, little buddy, but I really have to take this conference call.

I'll listen to your song after Tyce's lacrosse match, I promise.

I suppose you think dying a blue dick into the dog's fur is cute, young man?

I'm guessing by that smirk that you're proud *of the asinine cartoon you doodled onto Chase's homework?*

I don't understand how you dare to laugh at me after the cops dropped you off at the front door.

I don't want to hear about you screwing any more models until those fucking grades are brought back up.

I'm not going to take your calls until you earn them.

Until you prove you can truly be my son.

I wheel away, loathing how facing her has somehow transformed from leaving my work day into confronting my demons. No. Not demons. That's giving the fuckers—and their sire—too much power. Admitting they have that much control over me. Conceding they still govern me like that.

But don't they?

"No." It's more a sound than a word, spewing in as much air from my nostrils as my lips, as I lock my hands at the back of my head and stomp back into the cave, which thankfully smells a little better now.

The dimness engulfs me again. I tell myself that should feel good—well, better than it does—because isn't that why I've even trudged back? To escape a few simple, even silly, memories? Pathology I should be way the hell over now? Hatchets even Dad wants to bury and scars he clearly wants to help heal?

So what's *my* goddamned problem?

The answer is so fucking clear, I'm nauseated. I stop after a couple of steps inside the tunnel, dropping my head between my slumping shoulders as I park both hands against the rock wall.

"Reece?"

Did I really think she wouldn't follow me? Maybe I did, in the flash of a stupid moment that I forgot she's not like any other woman I've ever known. Sure enough, she's picking her way in with steps that are soft and sketchy, since she's still wearing the strappy pumps that go with her gauzy tea dress. *Hell.* Only in edgy music videos and high-fashion editorials does demolished rock and spongy mud go well with flimsy shoes and ladies-who-lunch-wear. "What the hell? What's wrong?"

"You shouldn't be in here."

"Well, neither should you." She steps closer until she's filling my periphery. My body sizzles, in good and bad ways, with the awareness of her nearness. "Early quitting time, remember? What everyone on the crew just thanked you for— and we were about to celebrate too?"

The silky turn of her tone comes with a corresponding caress to my back—which I answer with a fresh flinch. I add a jerk of my head before gritting, "I...can't."

She moves in closer. Mixes her gorgeous scent in with the freshly torn earth. *Soleil Blanc* has always smelled good on her, but now? All I want to do is jerk my head over and inhale the lemon and coconut on her skin mixed with the mud and musk in the air...

"Oh, I'll bet you *can*, Mr. Richards. Just let me show you..."

I capture her hand beneath mine before she can graze

it from my hip to my fly. "No. *Velvet.* I mean, I can't do *this.* The cute-share shit. The turtle shells and the bedtime stories and the throwing-spaghetti-on-the-walls stuff..." Before the bewilderment in her eyes turns into pain, I plunge on. "My memories aren't funny or cuddly, no matter how my mother presented the scenario. I love the woman, as well as those rose-colored glasses of hers, but things *weren't* rosy, okay?"

"Right." She's cut me off on purpose, flipping around to fall back against the wall—her face tautening by matching degrees. "Because *mine* was, yeah?"

I drop the shoulder closest to her. Damn it, I'm not a complete prick. Not yet, anyway. With the physical space between us reopened, I attempt to meet her gaze while murmuring, "I know it wasn't."

"Of course you do. Because I *told* you."

"And I'm thankful you did—"

"But not enough to even try to do the same for me."

"Goddamnit."

"No." She bats away the hand I've raised to her cheek. "Don't bring him into this. The damning here is all mine." She brings her hand back over, shoving so hard at my shoulder that I rock back—but so does she. "Who the *hell* do you think you are, declaring your pain off-limits after I willingly gave you mine?" Her rant cranks harder despite how I yank her close and prevent the ass-over-elbows tumble for which she was clearly headed. As I grip her closer, she squirms harder—firing hot friction between all of our most sensitive places. *Fuck. Me.* "You don't get to raise the drawbridge here, pal. You don't even get to call the archers to the ramparts."

For a long second, I'm not capable of any answer but a deep groan. "*Damn it.*" Despite how my mind and spirit yearn to forfeit this game, my cock is absolutely all-in for the play.

"I thought we'd already covered that."

She utters it half an inch over my lips. There's a husk underlining her voice now, and she's circled her arms back around my neck.

"Emma." My throat is a collection of crags now too. My breath, rasping across the gorgeous curves of her mouth, is shaky. "I...I don't even know *how*..."

"That's why I'm here." She closes the distance between our mouths but only for a sensual slide of a second. "To help you, my love. To—"

I'm not sure what she was preparing to utter next. I'm not sure it matters. Right now, I just know I need more of her than a tertiary taste. I need the full, wet, hot smash of mouths that I take without prelude or permission or apology. I need her. Kissing her. Pushing into her. Dancing my tongue with hers. Melding my desire to hers.

Drowning my pain with her.

Yeah. Good. This is *really* good. The deeper I explore her, the more blurred the lines get—and if she's none the wiser, then what's the harm? And the trade-off is so much better anyhow. Heartache to hard-on. Anger to lust. Needing no one...to needing her.

Only her.

Always her.

And that's when I realize how flawed my thinking is. Needing her means I really *do* have to open all this shit up to her. To expose her to all the vulnerability. Let her see all the loneliness. Give her a flashlight into parts of my soul that I swore, so damn long ago, would never be revisited by anyone in my life. Yeah, including myself.

But here they all are, pouring into my kiss. Burning through my touch. Scraping back my mental layers as Emma peels away the tight black leather encasing my torso...and then unbuttons and unzips the plackets covering my cock.

I moan but hardly recognize the sound. Is that me sounding so desperate and feral? Is this my choice, to be so raw and unmasked?

Am I letting this happen...as she drops to her knees and then, practically in the same motion, pulls my erection all the way into her mouth?

Fuuuuuck.

But out loud, all I can get out is a strangled, "*Unnnhhhh.*" Nothing else develops. Her heat feels too fucking good. In ten seconds, she's demolished me. Paralyzed me. There's cold stone at my back, invisible shackles around my wrists. I'm not tethered, but I feel like I am. She's sucking the resistance from me. Demanding my surrender...

A moan writhes in my chest before searing up my throat. It bursts out, echoing against the cave's walls, which are hard and ruthless enough to be...

Dad's office.

Or a laboratory hell.

Which, in the mud of my mind, are suddenly mashed...as one...

When are you going to live up to how extraordinary you are, Reece?

When are you going to face how extraordinary you are, Alpha Two?

"No," I hear myself stammer. "*No.*"

One voice is the bastard who gave me DNA. The other is the bitch who raped it. The walls of one imprisoned my mind.

The walls of the other enslaved my will.

Different. *Different.*

Then the word is tumbling out of me, over and over, a desperate litany to battle the memories of my youth and the nightmares of my adulthood, still stirring together in a sickening, disgusting brew...

Flooding me.

Frying me.

Crumbling me.

EMMA

"Reece? *Reece!*"

One second, his flesh is hard and huge and perfect in my mouth. The next, he's buckling against the wall before sliding all the way down it, his legs shooting out like the mud floor has become a sheet of ice. A shudder claims his body. He throws his head back so hard, it *thunks* audibly against the dirt.

"Shit, shit, shit. Reece." My logic races for the most obvious explanations. Has he had a seizure? A blood sugar drop? Did he eat lunch? Does he even have to worry about shit like blood sugar? If not, then does he need to plug back in? Or *un*plug?

I thought I was starting to read him better. To know, just by looking at him, what his biological charge is or isn't and exactly what ways I could help him get back to baseline.

This isn't baseline.

I have no damn idea what this is.

I'm plunged even deeper into the dark when he jerks his head up, piercing me with eyes that glow with a texture I've never seen in them before. This is different than how he looked after the showdown with Angelique, when the Consortium first came after him—and even after the skirmish with Faline and her henchmen in New York, when those assholes decided to come after *me*. As he gouges me deeper with those dark-silver blades, I begin to fathom the reason why.

There are layers to his pain now.

Bruises covering scars. Incisions leading straight to veins. Tears blended with blood.

Vulnerabilities hidden by his fury.

And his vehemence.

And his dominance.

As he reaches beneath my skirt, clamping his big hands over my thighs and spreading them until I'm straddling him.

As he jerks me forward, fitting my body more fully over his.

As he rolls his hips up, ensuring every inch of my pussy starts to thrum and pulse and weep, fully aware of his hardness and heat and need.

As he does it again and again and again, wordless in his purpose and relentless in his lust, until my panties are soaked and my whole body is quivering. "Ahhhhhh," I finally spill, the groan mixed of my pleasure and pain, which instantly tightens his hold and intensifies his thrusts. His force is so fierce, I have to grip his neck with one hand and brace the wall with my other. The jagged rock bites into my palm, adding to the wounds he's bringing along with the ecstasy, but I accept it. I accept *him*. The second I realign my stare with his, I know it's exactly what he needs too. To see that his pain won't scare me away. That its ugliness only makes him more beautiful to me.

I rock more feverishly against him. Work my soaked labia up and down his pulsing shaft, savoring the extra texture from the veins that fight his tight, swollen skin. My underwear has been sidelined, rolled into the seam between my crotch and thigh. With one shift in our movements, his incredible cock will be deep inside my shivering sheath.

But not yet.

Not until he knows, beyond doubt, what I want from him now.

More than his sex. More than his desire. Even more than his anger and pain.

"Give." I issue the order in a smoky whisper while shifting my hold from his nape to his jaw, fastening his attention on me. "Give them all to me."

His face turns as jagged as the walls around us.

Because he knows exactly what I'm demanding from him.

I want his ghosts.

Every last wraith that's gotten a free ride on his soul since he was a kid, without the awareness or army to fight them off.

Well, he has an army now. And its commander is here. And ready to fight for him with everything I have. Everything I am.

And I show him so, by lowering until my mouth is at his ear...as I slide the slick tightness of my entrance against his cockhead.

"Give them to me," I exhort again. "All of it. All of them." I dip my head, cradling his so my promise goes nowhere but in his ear. "You're safe. You're perfect. You're mine. You always... will...be..."

The last three words are closer to shudders. As if anyone on the planet could fault me, considering the magic of the long, swollen erection he surges up into me. He's so full and hard and throbbing, filling every corner of my womb while not being enough. *Not. Enough.* He's still fighting my ultimate request. Perhaps even thinks that by fucking me, he'll make me forget...

But his cock only reminds me of everything else I need from him.

Everything else *he* needs to surrender...

The everything I remind him of, as I purposely resist how he feeds our combustion by gripping my legs harder, lunging up into me deeper. The completion I deny us both by twisting my fingers into his hair, yanking on the thick, dark strands until he grimaces and returns his gaze to mine.

"It's all right," I whisper.

"I know." Both of his syllables are taut tremors.

"No, you don't." I grab him tighter. "Look at me. Feel me. Believe in me."

"Christ." He bares his teeth. The war of his soul and his body still rages in the depths of his eyes. "Just take my cock, Emmalina. It's always good enough for everyone else, for fuck's sake."

"I'm not everyone else." I practically spit it back at him. If he really wants a war right now, I'll bring that shit to his doorstep. "And I'm *not* going anywhere."

Silver fire flares in his glower. "And if I just choose to let you ride me for hours with that pretty cunt?"

"Then call me Cowgirl Jane."

"Fuck. Me." His voice is nearly a croak, probably because his cock has instantly swelled. Naturally, he attempts to thrust up again. I resist, using my hold on the wall as leverage, preventing him from parking my pussy all the way down on his erection. Despite all my bravado, it's torment. Our wrestling is spiking the adrenaline in my system, the sprint of my heartbeat, and every damn cell of the blood pumping to my clutching, yearning sex. If he succeeds in just a few full strikes, my body is liable to declare a coup and explode every resistance I have left.

Whether Reece has detected exactly that or has capitulated to the rebels in his own blood, I'll probably never know or care—because a lot of coherent thought flees me from the second he grips my waist and rolls me backward, reversing our positions in one explosive move. Suddenly, my head's in the dirt, my legs are in the air, and my gaze is flooded with all this man's heartache, bared in full to me at last. As he wraps his sizzling fingers in the fabric of my dress, he peels back more layers of his soul, stripping himself for me—as he releases his orgasm into me. His face is breathtaking, and I savor every inch of the sight. His teeth locked. His nostrils flared. His forehead crunched. His gaze ignited. He's a mixture of surrender, strain, sexuality, and pain...and I'll never ever forget the perfection of getting to see him like this. Utterly exposed for me like this...

I fling a hand down and grip hard into his coiled shoulder. Somehow, I've kept my other hand locked against his face and use my hold to make sure he stays with me, looking at all of me as I take in every inch of his body and every part of his soul.

All of him.

His passion. His completion. His burden. His storm.

The terrible beauty of it is too much to bear. I'm washed in emotion, brimming with the tears he's given up on ever shedding for himself—so I let him see every one of them, heavy in my eyes and then pouring down my face, as words flow up from my heart as accompaniment.

"I see you, Reece."

"I know." It's half breath and half growl as he continues pouring himself into me. Filling me with his electric magic...

"I love you, Reece."

"I know."

"*All* of you, Reece."

His face tautens and his lunges deepen, and more of his liquid heat spills into me. "Then do it for me, Emma," he snarls softly against my lips. "Fall apart for me, Velvet." With the slightest roll of his hips, he changes the angle of his thick, thrumming length against the quivering walls of my body. "Come for me. *Come...*"

His mandate is like a dark wizard seducing a virgin to a sacrificial pyre—and every part of my consciousness is that hypnotized maid ready to be devoured by the beast...devoured in the fire of his hunger. I cry out as the first flames hit. In return, the animal bites hard, puncturing the juices from the darkest reaches of my core. I'm consumed and claimed, eviscerated and engulfed, swallowed but set free. I'm demolished but have never been so restored. Drained but never more filled. My pussy keeps convulsing, needing more of his lightning heat. My body keeps clenching, needing more of his stretching salvation. My heart keeps bursting, craving more of the surrender of his.

We could be doing this in a luxury bed on thousand-thread-count sheets, and I wouldn't feel more intimate with him. I maintain the union of our stares, hoping he sees that. Praying he knows in every fiber of his being, as I know in mine, that he's stolen more than my libido and my heart.

He's the storm that's changed the landscape...

Of my life, of my soul, of my existence.

Forever.

The certainty clings to the back of my mind despite the fuzz of the sexual hangover that persists after Reece slows and then stills inside me, finally withdrawing and then wordlessly carrying me into the house. I don't speak either, choosing to let his thoughtful aura settle over me as well. There've been times when we're like this after coming together as we just did, though this occurrence of the quiet—like the stillness after a choir has belted the "Alleluia" chorus—feels much more profound. Somewhere during that music, we recomposed some key stanzas for the song called "Us"—and now we're picking our way carefully back through the new melody, note by precious note.

After showering together, again in peaceful but mindful silence, we towel off and change into nighttime comfies. While we still don't spend every night of the week up here, it's nice to get away for a sleepover or two when we can swing it—and right now, with both of us still in a mode of exhausted contemplation, a drive back to the city feels as doable as a hayride in an ice storm.

In my Stay Shiny T-shirt and cotton yoga pants, I yank my freshly washed hair into a ponytail, leave the master bathroom, and head for the office downstairs for a quick check on emails from anyone in the LA or New York offices of Richards Reaches Out. Other than filling in for vacationing or sick members of the Hotel Brocade's executive team, mostly to thank Karma for the job that brought me to Reece in the first place, my very full-time employment is now with the nonprofit arm of the Richards Resorts empire—which means the afternoon I've just taken off has likely resulted in a huge stack of messages and an even taller stack of emails. Running a growing organization like this is a lot like managing a hotel. Lots of moving parts, little downtime, and miniscule room for error. It'd be a good time to check in, leaving Reece with some physical and mental room of his own.

Only, I don't get more than two steps into the hall before the man loops an arm around my middle and tugs me back against him. At once, my default reaction to his embrace kicks in. I melt into his heat. Revel in his massive muscles. Readily succumb to the way he alters the air itself, like a human blast range. Though he's gotten better about controlling the shockwaves in public, he never holds it back with me—and my entire body tingles in gratitude, especially when realizing his idea of comfies is simply his nylon workout shorts. As he turns me in his hold, I'm given the treat of being pressed against his gladiator's thighs and warrior's torso, with all their sinewy striations still gleaming with post-shower dew...

"Stay." He spreads the command, underlined with a hefty dose of appeal, along my forehead. My reply gushes without second thought—nor much volume.

"Okay."

As he steps back, his lips curve up like an arrogant rogue from a Regency romance. Of course, that makes it easy for him to tug me toward the bed and then under the covers with him. The cool, luxurious linens surround us, inspiring a near orgasmic groan from deep in my throat. I'm so damn happy the man doesn't scrimp on his bedding selections.

Once more, Reece wraps me from behind, securing his tree branch of one forearm around my waist while propping his other arm beneath a pillow, raising his head enough to watch the sun dip over the ocean along with me.

For a long collection of minutes, we simply savor the moment. The glory of the peach and gold sky. The rustlings of the wind through the olive and pepper trees outside. The sturdy peace of each other's presence. It's all so perfect...

Until I ruin it with a soft giggle.

"Do I dare ask what that was for?" There's a grumble beneath his murmur, but only a small one. Mostly, he's still in Regency rogue mode, meaning I can be his glib heroine without worry.

"We're a dating app commercial," I finally giggle out. "Spooning? Gazing at the sunset? Just add wine, and we're every cliché in the book."

"You want some wine?" He grunts and laughs as I backhand his shoulder, though he twists his head fast enough to tag my knuckles with a couple of quick kisses. "Being a cliché sounds damn nice."

"Says the guy who used his hands as jackhammers for most of the day." And, as his steady caresses on my belly prove, is none the worse for wear, either. I lower my hand over his, encouraging him to keep up the TLC. Though I don't care to know where he learned how to stroke a woman's skin like this, I'm damn glad it's in the man's wheelhouse.

"Didn't say it was possible," Reece rebuts. "Just said it sounded nice."

Despite his mini massage, I stiffen. Regency Rogue is gone—replaced by Get-Me-Out-Of-My-Own-Skin Superhero. "You okay?" I back up the query with a matching graze over his fingers—firmly ordering my deeper worries to stay out of the words but knowing he'll sense them anyway.

After a longer-than-normal pause, he utters, "Yeah." Bestows a firm kiss on my neck. "Sure."

"Then why don't I believe you?"

With his chin still fitted against my shoulder, he lets out a huff. "Be patient with me, Emmalina. This is..." A new sigh. His tighter embrace. "This is just all a lot of new for me."

I lift his hand and press an answering kiss to his palm.

"That's fair. It's a lot of new for me too." And I use the adjective as a noun because it's another one of our special things, and in this moment, all of them feel especially important to acknowledge.

"Like getting screwed in the mud?"

I snicker softly. "And *that's* the one you went for first?" Though I wriggle a little, enjoying what the memory just did to the part of him nestled against my ass. "But for the record, yes. Definitely a new. And an enjoyable one at that."

"Noted."

"I'd expect nothing less."

"'Less' certainly wasn't what you got."

Deciding his quip will spawn more with encouragement, I sideswipe another smack into his bicep instead. After his chuckle fades and I'm settled back in, I murmur, "Okay, your turn."

"My turn for what?"

"Ohhhh, no you don't." I secure both hands atop his forearm, keeping him locked in place. "The drill here is clear, mister. Sharing is caring. *Your turn.*"

He *mmmphs* and growls as if I've just awakened him for work and even attempts the same tactic to distract me. Yep, with practiced ease, he works his thigh between mine and starts to drag that perfect log of muscle up and down the sensitive crevice at my center...

"But technically, you didn't 'share.'"

"Excuse me?" I manage the forceful blurt but barely. Holy shit, does the man know how to use that freaking thigh.

"I shared for you." He supplies it with another knowing move—the tuck of his lips against the shell of my ear brings exquisite, erotic torment. "Then you just agreed with embellishment."

"All right, then." I wield my down-to-business tone as fortification. "So *I'll* share for *you* now."

A new growl, not so ready this time. "Should've seen that one coming."

"You were distracted." I provide more evidence by grinding my crotch more wantonly against his quadriceps, savoring the scrape of his wiry leg hair against the soft cotton of my pants.

"Now it seems you are too."

"Not enough to forget I've got to share." The statement sparks fresh tension through Reece's form, but before he can funnel that into seducing me more, I forge forward with the rest. "That I know it was new for you to expose the scars of your past. That you're so used to covering them, you had no idea they still existed. And that they probably hurt as if you've torn them all back open again."

I have a lot more to add but force myself to clamp it at that, cued by the discernible energy rolling through him as a reaction. It's more than agitation but not quite anger...a notch past loneliness yet not all the way to desolation.

In short, I've hit the nail on the head, but now he's debating how to diminish the dents.

And losing the battle.

A fact to which he bears blatant testament, all but snarling out his retort into my ear.

"Re-exposing wounds only infects them, Velvet." He bites down, dragging my lobe between his teeth and layering his triumphant hiss over my sudden outcry. "So don't expect my blood every time you come knocking now."

He keeps his mouth open while leaning in farther, scoring the line of my jaw and the hollow of my neck. At the same time, he shoves his hand beneath my shirt, not stopping until he reaches my breast...and twists relentless fingers around my pointed nipple.

I don't cry this time.

I scream.

He doesn't snarl this time.

He rumbles.

"Okay," I finally gasp. This time, it's not easy. With my breast throbbing and my pulse racing, words are rapidly becoming close to impossible. "Got it. D-Don't...expect...b-blood."

"Not unless you're willing to shed a little in return."

Oh, God.

I'm vaguely aware of the expression actually tumbling off my lips just as the impact of his ultimatum hits my senses...

In the form of the rogue that's returned to his voice.

And the stiffness that swells again in his cock.

And the purpose that guides his hand down my pants.

To the crevice between my buttocks.

And the sensitive entrance he begins to finger there.

CHAPTER THREE

REECE

"Oh...*God.*"

She repeats it, with a higher pitch and a heavier breath, as I work the tip of my index finger inside the rim of her pretty asshole. And fuck *yes*, it's pretty. And hell *yes*, I know that even though my gaze is currently fixed on her mesmerizing profile—and the effect of my penetration on the perfect slit between her gorgeous back cheeks.

The fantasy that's never far from my mind...

But in so many ways has never been further.

Because entertaining it for too long would mean an instantaneous climax.

Holy fuck.

I've always enjoyed the act with other lovers—I may be a mutant, but damn it, I'm still a *guy*—but none of those past occasions even comes close to the turn-on of just *thinking* about my cock there with Emma. *Inside* Emma. The woman who's changed my life. The lover who's changed my desires. All of them now about her...so much better and brighter and hotter because of her.

She proves it all over again now, with her fluttering eyelashes and parted lips and addicting sighs, pulsing out in time to my rhythmic circles of her tiny pucker, urging her forbidden flesh to yield for me. *Christ.* Just watching the effect it has on her is intoxicating. I drink in every inch of her face as I stretch her...and open her...

Fuck.

Fuck.

But I shut my eyes to cancel out that vision because even now I'm spurting precome inside my shorts. If I cared to look down there—and I really fucking don't—I'm sure the edges of the nylon would be aglow with brilliant cobalt light from my happy Smurf Daddy of a dick.

"Happy" being relative.

Really relative.

"Well..." The last of it trails off my tongue as I lick the backside of her ear with lusty languor. As a shiver takes over her skin, her intimate muscles suck at my fingertip. "I'm an equitable man. The trade-off doesn't *have* to be in blood."

To make that message clear—and who am I kidding? I need to and want to make it perfectly clear—I prod her ass a little deeper. I'm past the point of all my previous playful teases and into the realm of showing her exactly what I'm craving here and now. What I might even need, beyond the physical urgency of my body. Baring her like this, conquering her in this primal way, gives the chance to swing our pendulum back to center. Fear for fear. Nakedness for nakedness. Revelation for revelation. And yeah...reward for reward. Emma just doesn't know that part yet.

But if she says yes, I sure as fuck promise that she will.

"Wh-What do you have in mind?"

I smile against her shoulder. That's a *very* good sign—and a damn good question.

"What do *you* have in mind, my velvet cowgirl?" I tilt my

head, knowing she catches my smirk in her periphery, at least. "What special commodities do you have to trade?"

The sexy slopes of her lips purse tight but open right back up as I insert a second finger into her tight, tantalizing hole. "Let's...ummm...let's see..."

"Oh, yes." With one easy flip, I roll her onto her stomach. "Let's." With another, I've tugged her yoga pants to her knees. One deft grab of my toe, and they're off her completely.

"I...I assume my boot collection and guacamole recipe are off the table."

"I'd look great in your Vaccarellos, and your guacamole is the nectar of the gods..." My growl, dark and primal, inserts itself from the second I push apart the sweet valentine of her ass. "But I want the nectar of a *goddess*."

And not just that. As I spread her wider with my free hand, I work a third finger inside her forbidden entrance. As soon as she accepts my invasion, filling the air with her succulent sighs and mewls, I curl my touch around and then in so I can caress into all the wet, fascinating folds of her pussy.

She's captivating.

Breathtaking.

Glistening and shining and coming alive for me in ways I haven't ever anticipated.

There's the shiny arousal just inside the V of her thighs. The dewdrops of sweat trailing the focused furrows in her forehead. The kiss of early twilight, reflecting from the open hills and the distant sea, in the elegant valley of her lower back. She's a collection of light and liquid, of pale-amber skin and gleaming electric reflections—especially as I reach for the nightstand and my fingers start to pulse brighter.

Emma's breaths pump faster as she watches me sheath all

my digits in thick latex gloves. They're a special pair, created and sterilized for electrical laboratory engineers, and I've been saving them just for this occasion.

She breathes even harder when I reach back into the drawer and pull out a new tube of lube. I'm steady about the movements, needing to make sure she sees them and comprehends them but also needing to watch her as she does. *Shit.* I must be a sick fuck. Just witnessing her apprehension jacks my lust by discernible degrees. But I talk myself out of complete remorse by reminding myself of one key fact.

The pendulum is swinging. The scales are balancing.

Or so I fucking hope.

"That's some interesting...nectar."

And even dare to inch beyond hope when she mixes sarcasm into her uneasy snip.

"It's definitely going to help," I ensure, flipping the lid up before squirting a little on my fingers. "But it's not the whole commodity. If this is going to work, I need your buy-in, Velvet. Your trust, your acceptance, your willingness."

Though she's flat against the bed, I watch her swallow heavily. Her flaxen waves are turned to gold by the sun as her gaze turns to storm clouds from trepidation. But after a long moment, a pulse vibrates through her as if she's been punched through the gut with new resolve.

"I'm...I'm willing." She turns her face up so all of its open, expressive curves are visible to me. "And I trust you. And I want to accept you, Reece. To have you claim me...*there.*"

I want to kiss her. Hard.

But I hold back, needing something else more.

"So you want me to take you in your ass."

"Y-Yes."

I need *that*.

"With my cock."

"Y-Yes."

Damn. *Damn*. That too.

I lunge over, bending to her. Pulling her up until she's on her knees on the bed, one hand at her nape and the other in her hair, securing her in place for the bruising passion of my kiss. I work at her lips until she parts with a groan, letting me invade her with my mouth again and again, working her tongue in unfiltered, undaunted gratitude for the gift of her trust—and the treasure I'm about to take.

When I pull my lips from hers at last, I tell her the exact same thing with my eyes, letting the impact of my gratitude sink into her psyche just as my cock's about to take her most carnal tunnel. "Position yourself for me," I dictate firmly. "Raise your ass and drop your head."

She nods, looking a little hesitant. And goddamnit, with that tiny second of intrigue, yanks every molecule of air right out of my chest again. It's not an original theory—the woman stops my heartbeat dozens of times a day in just as many ways—but right now, in her ultimate submission, offering her most vulnerable entrance to me, I forget what breath even is. At the same time, my heart's never felt larger, clamoring like a stallion at the corral of my ribs, surpassed in pain only by the surging bull between my thighs.

Now it's time to let that beast run free.

"*Fuck...*" My groan gives way to a hiss as soon as I drop my shorts and set my dick free. Thanks to my earlier orgasm, at least my damn lightsaber isn't turning the whole room into a spacy cantina. While the veins of my cock are aglow, the flesh between them actually matches that of my thighs, which I press against the back of hers while squeezing an ample quantity of lube over her perfect back hole.

Then inside it as well...

Grunting as her walls close in over my fingers.

Loving how her moans correspond to my deeper thrusts.

Holding my breath as I position my cockhead at her opening.

"Oh! *Unnnhhh.*"

"Ssshhhh, Velvet." I brace a hand to the small of her back, securing her in place. "Relax. Breathe." Though I can't, it's important that *she* does. "Stay pliant for me. Stay perfect..."

Perfect.

The word doesn't begin to touch what it's like to breach her walls, the tightest and sweetest paradise my dick has ever experienced.

Perfect.

Not even half the praise that she deserves for the aria of her rapid sighs filling my senses like a song as I slide deeper into her. Then deeper...

"Oh, *God.*"

"Almost there, sweetheart."

"I— I can't..."

"You can. Just *breathe.*"

"It's...it's so full."

"Yeah. And so good."

So fucking good.

And so goddamned *perfect.*

And yet, still barely enough to describe what it's like to sink myself fully into her, heart thundering and cock throbbing and balls swelling, a crashing celebration of knowing I'm the only one to invade her like this. To see her unravel, raw and wrecked and clutching at the sheets, because of how thoroughly I've raided her virgin recesses.

And I'm not even done yet.

Because now it's time to take the rest of her into the light with me.

She screams into the pillows as I begin to move again, but only in subtle increments. In the next moment, I feel like joining her. It's hell, telling my body to spill just a portion of my come, but thank God for my curious foray into Tantric techniques a few years ago. The little I do remember comes in handy now, along with a brutal twist of my balls, to keep the bulk of my climax at bay.

So worth it.

And, once again, so *perfect*, as the electrons of my ejaculate start working their magic against the inner corners of her body...at the same moment I strip my left hand free of the glove and hold the center of her body, stimulating all the bared nerves in her quivering pussy.

"*Oh!*" Her cry pings through the room as she twists her head against the pillow. As if fucking her ass isn't enough to turn my dick into a surging thunder stick, the new sight of her features takes my inner storm into a new category of torment. *Remember this. Remember this. All of it.* The arousal staining her cheeks. The gasps escaping her lips. The wild Chardonnay and Champagne splash of her hair, tangling more as I lengthen my lunges.

"Good girl." I use my right hand to add another sluice of lube while seeking her most tender button with my left. "Stay with me, Emma. Stay...with...me." The emphasis pounds out along with my defined stabs into her backside, pummeling the crevice that's now so open and ready for me. But as I risk a look down, needing to watch the juncture where my cock takes her with such carnal consummation, she mewls again in blatant protest.

"Can't," she rasps. "*Reece.* Wh-What are you *doing* to me..."

"Bringing you the world, baby." After my next plunge, I keep my dick buried inside her, giving us both new sensations by rolling my hips instead. "The sun. The moon. The stars. The storms. They're all yours, Emma. They're all yours because you've brought them all to me already."

"Oh...*God*..."

She whimpers it this time. The sound, so full of submission and adoration, pulls me over—in more than just the obvious way. I drop my body over hers, rushing my right arm and hand up the length of hers. While I keep taking her ass with my cock and igniting her clit with my other hand, I form my lips to her neck, cherishing the wild cadence of her pulse beneath my mouth.

Knowing now is the time.

"Give."

To take back my trade for the blood.

"All of it, Emmalina. Give it all to me. *Now.*"

The significance of the words isn't lost on her. I see her recognition in the sob that crunches her exquisite face and then bursts from her passion-stung lips. But most of all, I feel it in the orgasm that takes over the sex I'm caressing and the ass I'm fucking. The hot, tight grotto that I flood with my own release, giving her my electric white ropes as she gifts me with her ultimate, shivering surrender.

Taking the innocence she's given in place of her blood, with the certainty that I've come out ahead on the deal.

Way ahead.

No way do I slough off the conclusion, even after our rhythm finally slows and my cock at last softens. "Stay put," I direct, bestowing a soft kiss between her shoulder blades before scrambling into the bathroom and fishing some newly bought hand towels out of the box in which they're still sitting. Taking back one with suds, one for rinsing, and one for drying, I make short work of cleaning us both up before settling back into the pillows and gathering her close to me.

Twilight has taken over the sunset now, casting pewter and plum shadows across the room. They're apt envoys for our sated peace—an accord from the strangest skirmish I've ever had with a lover before. Then again, Emmalina Crist isn't like any woman I've ever known. She didn't fight against me today. She fought *for* me—but best of all, she led me to the place where I could fight for myself. Where I could stab a sword through the memories that have been defining me for too damn long.

Before realizing they don't have to define me anymore.

Holy God.

Does she know what she's really given me today? What she's really done for me? How much I owe her? How thoroughly I love her?

"Reece?"

"Hmmm?"

"Can we do that again sometime?"

Okay, what's the step that comes after *Holy God, I love her*?

"Anytime you'd like, Bunny." I thread my fingers through her mussed hair and kiss the top of her head. "And yeah, that even means slicing open a few veins for you again."

Her soft laugh ripples across my chest. She runs a couple

of fingertips up and down the indent between my pecs. "You know you could've gotten the offer even without that, right?"

"Yeah. I know." I thread my fingers with hers. "But you would've gotten *my* offer, even if you'd hated that."

"Oh, I didn't hate it!"

My turn to chuckle. She riposted as if I'd just banned her from ever having guacamole again. "Glad we got that cleared up."

With a content smile twinging her gorgeous lips, she settles back against me. "See? It feels good to get things cleared out every once in a while. Admit it, Richards. You feel better."

As I tug her closer, I feign a reluctant grunt. No way am I going to point out that just about any guy on the planet would feel like a god after taking their woman in several erotic ways in just two hours. Instead, I just utter, "I've admitted a lot of new things since falling in love with you, Emma Crist."

"Hmmm." But the silken sigh is threaded more with satisfaction than question. "That's a perfect answer, Reece Richards."

"Perfect, eh?"

"As if you didn't know that already?"

Snort. "Maybe I did. A little."

She gives up another sigh before a yawn takes over. I can't blame her for the exhaustion, despite the fact that we haven't even talked about dinner. Maybe after a nap, she'll be open to the idea of me turning *her* into dinner. Now there's another version of *perfect* I can get into...

And making her world perfect, at least for today, is all the perfection I need too.

⚡

Twenty-four hours later, nearly to the minute, I'm silently pleading with the universe for a retroactive time machine. Or the ability to add backward quantum leaping to my skillset. If science can figure out how to turn a guy into a lightning rod, what's a little time-jumping on top of the mix?

Because even though Hollywood and Los Angeles are literally spread at my feet, all I really want is my legs tangled in bedsheets and Emmalina back in my arms. Naked. Definitely that too. If I'm going to go through the hassle—and potential pain—of throwing myself back in time, then my naked woman isn't a negotiable item.

Not happening.

As my brain clangs with the dismal reminder, it also orders me to be grateful for what the moment *has* brought. A rare chance for a fast escape from the black-tie grind going on behind me. While I happily agreed to be the guest of honor for the city's event, a grand ball serving as an early birthday party for the Griffith Park Observatory due to tonight's lunar eclipse, an hour and a half of the perpetual grip-and-grin has sent me outside for a necessary recharge of the shit I can't plug in for— my high society smile and fake-but-you-wouldn't-know-it laugh.

I couldn't have timed the getaway any better. It's just after sunset, an occasion filled with the daily magic of why people come to Southern California and never leave. The heat of the day is threaded with the ocean-borne breezes of the night, and the freeway haze makes itself useful in the lingering glow of a spectacular sunset. There are few better locations in the city from which to take in all this as well. The Griffith

Observatory was an early discovery for me after moving here, being one of the few places with a light show more dazzling than my fingertips. As I stand on the terrace, hands in my pockets, the downtown skyline glimmers like a star at the center of an urban galaxy, and the sky darkens from pink to lavender.

"Earth to Richards."

The crack is accompanied by a heartier laugh than it deserves, so I don't bother with the middle finger I'm used to giving Sawyer Foley. I *do* give him a cocked eyebrow and a double-take, considering I rarely see him out of Tommy Bahama wear and flip flops. His dark-blue dress suit is a notable shocker. Not that I care what the guy wears most of the time, even though he's officially been on my "unofficial" payroll for almost eight months now. As long as he brings his shrewd ex-FBI side to the table, he can go as surf-bum chic as he wants—a style choice presently confined to his lime-green socks emblazoned with parrots as purple as the sunset.

"Sorry, Goldie," I mutter while turning toward him with scuffing steps. "Already bought my Girl Scout cookies at the grocery store."

"Yeah? If you're hoarding the Thin Mints, I quit."

"Thin Mints, huh?" I wheel my sights back out over the city. "Yeah, we're going to have problems."

"Problems?" The interjection comes from one of the three men who have separated from the throng that's poured out of the elevator bay to our left. At most parties, a trio consisting of a guy in astrological steampunk regalia, a dark and exotic god with purple spiked hair, and a brooding six-six hulk would cause a few cases of whiplash, but most of this crowd probably saw weirder during their morning smoothie stops. "What do we have problems about?" the steampunk professor asks, embellishing his first query as he glances at the view like he's seen it a thousand times. And probably has.

"Cool your rockets, Trestle," the exotic one soothes. "I'm fairly sure these two honchos were just getting ready to throw down about which sister is the prettiest."

Mitch's crack, delivered with a good-natured grin, still slams Foley into popsicle mode. And no, stiff and frozen isn't the norm for a guy getting reminded about the girl he's pursuing, but I'll be the last one to call attention to it. Foley's never been secretive about his appreciation of women—at least between the time it takes him to find and fuck one—meaning that since he's moved his sights from Emma onto her sister instead, I no longer want to tear off the guy's testicles. That's a good thing, since it's a crappy idea to castrate the guy who's taken point on our campaign to learn as much as we can, as fast as we can, about the Consortium—who aren't the little nest of "fringe" lunatics I'd once assumed. Thanks to the help of Angelique La Salle, who'd helped the psychotic bastards turn me into a walking isotope in the first place, we'd been ready for the stunt they pulled back in November when they'd attempted to recapture me using Emma as bait...

Or so we'd thought.

Now, we're not so sure about the Consortium's actual purpose that night. Each day of the last six months has brought us closer to actually finding the truth—by pushing ourselves to ask some tough questions.

One: If the Consortium had really been after simply getting me back, why bother with hiring a band of merry men, bad-guy style, to ruin the Richards Reaches Out fundraiser event? What was their ultimate purpose in staging that drama—and re-outing me as a superhero to the world?

Two: If Faline, the bitch mistress on high who led the whole operation, had really desired to punish me by killing Emma, why hadn't Faline just done that? Again, the woman's actions that night don't add up—unless the Consortium had secondary intentions about the chaos that went down.

Three: What about the hugest chunk of the picture we received from that night? The connection Foley and I made while poring through security camera footage after Faline and her minions kidnapped Emma and Lydia—when we discovered the tattoo behind Faline's ear marking her as a member of the Scorpio crime cartel?

Yeah. What about *that*?

The answers haven't come as quickly as I'd hoped, especially because our team has had to carefully cover our steps in every inroad to the Scorpios. The cartel hasn't become one of the world's most powerful criminal organizations by turning a blind eye to its intruders, even the mildly curious—and our interest is far more than "curiosity." And while the men standing with me are among the best in the world at subtlety and subterfuge, there still can't be any room for error.

In short, "creeping and careful" has damn near become our team's motto. Yeah, even now and even here, where most of the crowd seems fixated on getting in selfies with the celebrities in attendance. Even in those circles, there's a hierarchy. The C list wants to be seen with the B list, and *that* list is on the hunt for the A-listers who have already arrived and retreated. I've spotted several of them heading toward the parking lot already, hiding out near the Charlie Turner trailhead until their assistants' phone calls will summon them back to the party for the main ceremonies of the night. Though Foley already looks like he wants to join them, and I'm sorely tempted to, it's bad form for the honoree of the evening to be sweaty after a jog in from the parking lot, even in La-La Land.

Foley tosses a shrewd side-eye at Mitch before addressing the guy's comment in a low mumble. "I mix business and pleasure as little as possible, dude."

"Which makes my point a problem...how?" Mitch counters. "Because your woman looks like pleasure on a platter tonight, *dude*." He jerks his look to me next. "Yours too, boss."

"Thank you," I reply. "But I had very little to do with it, other than suggesting a few good stylists. She picked someone named...Fabergé, I think."

"He *thinks*." The giant standing close to Mitch grunts and tugs at his tie. Since his neck is the width of a subway tube, it surprises no one that Kane Alighieri looks like a chained tiger in the thing. "A name like that, and he *thinks*."

"They *all* have names like that," I volley. "The whole is-she-a-person-or-a-perfume thing." Then include Mitch in my regard. "Why *is* that a thing now?"

Mitch's lips twist. "We're gay recon specialists, not fashion designers. I barely found a matching tie for this getup."

As Mitch gestures at his suit, Kane mutters, "And you don't want to know what state I found it in on Monday, on the *floor* of the closet."

Mitch huffs. "That's what dry cleaners are for."

Kane growls. "Honey, that's what *hangers* are for."

"And now that we've settled *that* first-world problem..." Alex, who could've been a circus master in another life with his sunny showmanship, sweeps a hand my way. "We hear you're making good progress on the Team Bolt hermit cave."

At first, everyone rewards his comment with affable

chuckles but finishes with gawks that look like a crowd of fanboys awaiting first edition *Star Wars* figurines. But I can guarantee our cave will have *a lot* more bells, whistles, twinkling lights, and gadgets than Han Solo ever dreamed for the Millennium Falcon.

But they know that too—which is why they'll clearly wait as long as it takes for my answer. Probably why I choose to fuck with them for a second, rubbing my chin and murmuring, "Shit. I guess they didn't tell you about the cave-in, then?"

"The fuck?" Kane recovers his voice first.

"The *fucking* fuck?" Foley grits out next.

"So how much longer does that mean we're pretending to be 'scientists' at the downtown building?" Alex finally growls.

Mitch, looking like the guy who missed the preorder cutoff on the figurines, pulls at his hair until his dark-brown roots are exposed past the purple. "At least I finally found a great udon place over on Grand."

"Oh, yeah." Kane nods. "That place *is* good..."

"Well, don't get too used to it." I rock back on my heels with a shit-eating smirk. "Though I'll be sure to tell Anya that udon's a necessity for the team's menu once a week." Then tap one finger at the edge of that smirk. "And considering that you'll all be setting up in the new digs in just a couple of months..."

Foley, the closest to me, jabs an elbow as proxy for everyone else. "Ass bucket." He throws in a good-natured shoulder bump. I grab him by the forearm to return the favor with double the intensity.

"Oooooh," Alex teases. "Catfight."

"Hmmmph." Foley shrugs to reseat his dress jacket on his shoulders and then fishes his ponytail out from the collar. "You're just jealous, sweetheart."

"Fuck you," Alex chuckles back.

"Awww, come here, sugar." I approach Alex, arms wide. "There's enough love here for you too."

"And fuck you too." Alex adapts a boxer's pose, dancing on his toes in similar fashion.

I laugh louder, warming up to the reverie. It feels good to have brothers again. The last time Chase or Tyce messed around with me like this, I wasn't yet ten. As soon as they hit puberty, our boyhood disappeared behind their prep schoolwork and sports—and in Chase's case, girls. And Tyce? Oh, he enjoyed girls too—the same way he enjoyed fast food. Down in three bites, finished with a lot of sugar, and then crumbs tossed into the waste can on his way out the door.

And sometimes the timing of my mind is eerily in tune to the convergences of my life.

This time, pretty damn literally.

Approaching us from one side of the lawn, her sparkling gold gown surpassed only by her glowing gorgeousness, is the woman I'll worship for the rest of my life. From the other side, my father is strolling over, accompanied by Mom and a man I don't know at all—and then two more I know all too well. By first sight, at least. Beyond that, I don't hold out much hope—to the point that their presence here has me beyond baffled. Still, I battle past the bewilderment to at least growl, "What the...fucking..."

"Dude," Foley prods. "What the hell? You bracing for a First Order star destroyer to jump out of light speed?"

"No." I shake my head. "This is probably worse."

"Huh?" Foley insists. "Why? And who the hell are those guys with your dad?"

I inhale deeply. "Don't know the one in the gigolo suit."

Yeah, colored suits are on-trend for men this season, but there's orange and then there's *orange*. The stranger next to Dad, with his swarthy looks and equally dark glare, is turning the outfit into a bad Halloween costume or the next fashion "thing." Clearly, he's banking on the latter.

"And the other two? The normal ones?"

Hard snort out before I can help it. Not that I want to. "The one in gray, who looks like he's on his period? That's Chase. The dude in the bespoke charcoal, who looks like he just screwed a waitress in the catering truck? That's Tyce. They're my brothers."

"Seriously?" There's genuine surprise in Foley's voice. "Well, that's cool—unless it's not."

"I'm not sure what it is."

"So you need a wingman?"

I toss him a fast but grateful glance. The guy may have a few strange skeletons hanging out under all that surfer-god hair, but he never fails to shove them aside in the name of standing with me.

I take my hands out of my pockets. "Thanks, schnookums, but I'd better brave this party alone."

"Yeah." In one grunt, Foley conveys a thousand versions of empathy, helping me at least shore up my posture and step clear of our bromance huddle. For reasons I can't explain other than bone-deep instinct, the less my family knows about Team Bolt, the better. I even wish I could extend the same protection to Emma, but since she's going to be a Richards— just the thought of sealing that deal injects me with even more courage—I suppose this part of the game had to happen sooner or later. Besides, I meant every word of what I told her last night. I'm trying to bleed more often for her, no matter how uncomfortable the ordeal.

Or how much introducing her to my brothers is going to feel like feeding her to the wolves.

CHAPTER FOUR

EMMA

"Emmalina! What a happy coincidence."

I'm still too far away to see whether the forced pleasantry in Trixie's voice extends all the way to her eyes, but I'm sure I'm about to find out—just as I'm certain the cause of her unease is due to the men who accompany her. Okay, not *all* the men. Lawson's holding her hand with comfortable affection, as always, and the older, distinguished guy on her other side seems to be a friend dressed as the love child of Annoying Orange and *The Mask*. But as I continue down the path, every step bringing me closer to meeting their progress, neither Lawson nor his buddy are the source of my fixation.

It's reserved for the pair behind them.

Whom I already recognize, courtesy of the few photos I've managed to yank up on the internet.

Whom I already feel weird about, courtesy of all Trixie's revelations from yesterday—and the subsequent follow-up of a meltdown from the man I love.

Whom I regard now with even more suspicion, courtesy of this not-so-tiny bombshell in the evening. During an event that's supposed to be about Reece's victories as a new man, not the downfalls of his youth.

"Happy is what we're all here for, right?" I finish the

response with a listen-up-you-two look at Chase and Tyce Richards. Might as well put my figurative foot down, along with the stiletto heel in which it stands, right now. *Cause my man any distress, and both of you will learn what a Louboutin in the lungs feels like.*

"Perfectly put, as always," Lawson praises as we all stop at the crux of my path and theirs. He waits for Trixie to step over and air buss me on both cheeks before doing the same. "And in stunning togs tonight too."

"You took the words out of my mouth, darling." Trixie slides a hand down into mine, using our clasp to "swish" me back and forth. The folds of my gold satin sweep train flair out a little, colliding softly with her fuller skirt, fashioned with forest-green taffeta. "Few but you could pull off a full crew neckline, Emmalina."

"Why, thank you, ma'am." I joke with a bad Southern belle accent in the hopes of lightening the mood before Reece gets over here. My periphery is tracking every one of his wide, determined steps, though every pore of my being has been ignited from the second I first set eyes on him. Holy shit. He's the hottest man in this whole damn park tonight, even though he looks like a matador ready to take down a bull—or five— and he's completely, thoroughly mine. "I'm...sorry?" I finally manage to stammer to Trixie, not hearing a word of whatever she's just asked me.

Fortunately, the woman observes that I'm off track due to ogling her youngest, which intensifies the twinkles in her eyes as she repeats, "I was asking where you got this creation. I may need to make the shop a stop before we depart back home."

"I have no idea." I shrug and then laugh. "A stylist brought it on a rack with six others. The beadwork called to me."

"Excellent call." The woman's friendly tone washes over me now, providing assurance I hardly knew I was craving. The gown is modest for this jaded crowd, with its fitted, cap-sleeved bodice decorated with subtle silver-beaded lightning bolts surrounded by swirling "clouds" in gold beads, but in the end, how does supporting my man via fashion differ much from tattooing his name on my boob or wearing his flower in my hair?

Trixie's subtle approval gives me permission to sneak in a relaxed breath before steeling myself for the night's strangest plot twist. It's beyond my fathoming—and clearly Reece's too—why Lawson and Trixie have suddenly expanded their annual West Coast visit to include their two eldest sons. Like Reece, both men are employed by arms of the Richards family empire—though they head much more significant aspects of the business than Reece, who technically is still in some probationary phase of his reentry into the family's good graces.

While he's been out saving lives on the side.

Which only now hits me hard as the major suckage that it really is.

Which brings an equally rough chaser of self-rebuke. *Why* have I never been more pissed-off about this? The answer is as easy as taking in the noble, beautiful profile of my man—who becomes my hero in so many more ways by showing what *he's* doing about the disparity. Thriving in spite of it. Moving on and living past it.

Because of what he confronted last night about it?

I'm not sure of that answer—nor does it matter in the scope of how proud I am of him right now, standing here with such undaunted strength and unblinking aim. No longer is he the lost man who bared himself to me yesterday in the cave, but in so many ways, he's never been more that person. He used that agony to push harder past his walls and then through his emotional valley. And sometimes, fighting through the valley is the only way up the mountain.

And right now, this Reece—*my* Reece—is on top of his mountain.

I see that acknowledgment already from Lawson, who nods in deference before striding over with one hand extended. After their palms meet with a loud smack, he meets Reece's stare with a smile that consumes his face. "Good to see you, son."

"Thanks," Reece murmurs, albeit with hedged caution. "You too."

"You're looking well, Reece." The comment is issued by Chase, who favors his father in the looks department. With his toffee-colored hair in a shorter version of Lawson's Billy Idol spikes, his Lego block jaw is emphasized to its fullest. He smiles with apparent sincerity in response to Reece's self-deprecating chuckle.

"Uhhhh, thanks man," Reece replies around that mirth. "I see Joany talked *you* into a shower and shave tonight too."

"*Pfffft.*" The interjection comes from Tyce, who finger-scrapes the near-black waves off his forehead. He's more like Reece in the looks department, with swarthy coloring and gray eyes, though the angles of his face are more elegantly carved, lending him the air of a dark angel. "Of course he looks 'well.' He's able to laser out his own crow's feet now."

Everyone's gaze drops to the grass—except mine, which remains on Reece, and Trixie's, which slices over to her eldest. "*Tyce,*" she hisses.

"Joke?" the guy snaps back. "It was a *joke*, people.

Remember those?"

Chase shakes his head as if the guy just pulled out a Bolt Pez dispenser and downed every pellet in the tube at once. "Jokes are about timing as much as content, man."

"And people unclenching their assholes," Tyce retaliates.

"Don't be a dick."

"*Gentlemen.*" At last, Mystery Man speaks. There's an accent to his baritone, but I'm unable to peg it from just three syllables.

"Maybe we should just skip the opening act." Reece's intercession comes with a look that, in one fell swoop, ages him well past his siblings. It shatters my heart to register that, but then I take every one of my broken shards and fuse them with his. Together, our union will get us through this—whatever *this* is—a truth I silently send when he darts a fast glance my way.

Though he responds with a single, subtle nod, it's all I need to understand him in return. He gets it. He gets *me*. He knows that I'm with him, sharing so much of what he's feeling about his family's strange ambush—commiseration that increases from my end as soon as Lydia appears, walking to Sawyer with his whiskey neat in one hand and her club soda in the other. I love my sister without measure. I always will. But even she can't undo the margin into which I got scrawled as soon as her star began rising on the tennis circuit. I was an early teenager when it all started to go out of whack, probably close to the same age as Reece when he started oiling skateboard ramps and learning his breathtaking beauty went a long way in the game of girls.

So he'd scribbled outside his margin by breaking curfew, flunking tests, and likely trying every page of the *Kama Sutra* before his eighteenth birthday.

I'd colored outside mine by eating real beef cheeseburgers, going to arthouse films with the geek kids, and learning how to live in a city without a car.

This city.

In which Reece has damn near been a new precinct of the police department by himself. In which he's served tirelessly as a businessman *and* a superhero, leading to him being honored by its leaders tonight—at the party he should be enjoying right now instead of dealing with whatever twist Lawson and Trixie have brought to his doorstep.

Damn it.

So far, it's been pretty cool to have begun sunny, smooth sailing with both my future in-laws—with Lawson, in his assistance and advice in getting Richards Reaches Out up and running, and then with the heartfelt words exchanged yesterday with Trixie—but if the two of them are here now to bring family drama into *his* special night, they're both beneath Square One with me.

"Reece is right." Tyce's statement is suddenly—and shockingly—sincere, prompting my subtle double-take. According to the media, Tyce is the asshole in the middle of Chase's white knight and Reece's prodigal bad boy. "The gang's all here." He turns his focus to Reece. "And we've come because of you."

Whoa. More meaningful candor, prompting Trixie to visibly fight back tears. None of it is lost on Reece either, who jumps his dazed scowl between his brothers. "Me? Why?"

Chase swaggers forward and wraps a hand around his mother's shoulder. "A little birdie told us you're being honored by the city brass tonight. Something about a key to the city and all?"

Trixie, basking in the affection of her eldest, flushes with happy warmth down to her gown's shawl collar, which is accented with strips of layered gold satin. Her eyes shimmer as brightly as her emerald earrings as she chimes, "Chirp chirp."

But Reece still isn't ready for the family group hug. Not yet. I don't blame him, especially when he states, "I'm sure the same 'bird' informs you when I'm in New York, which is a hell of a lot easier commute for you guys. So what makes all this different, other than the chance to fondle my prop key and ogle some movie stars?"

I'm surprised the universe doesn't cue cricket sounds to fill his family's palpable stillness of a reply. The whole scene is saved from going full-tilt awkward by a low chortle from the sophisticated stranger. "Well, well, well." He strokes his chin with the curve of his knuckle. "The Bolt has, how do you say, bent you over the barrel?"

Aha. The man's full sentence makes his accent an easy call now. He's French and proud of it. And now that I know *that*, clearer assumptions start to form about this not-so-random Richards family reunion. Another quick look at Reece, and I'm certain he's collecting the same data—especially because Lawson has sent him at least an email each week about the progress on the Virage, the new Richards Resorts flagship hotel that's opening in Paris's most luxurious arrondissement. Six months ago, before everything turned upside down at the RRO's fundraiser gala, Lawson had openly and avidly asked Reece to be the family emissary for overseeing the property's grand opening.

But that was before the world changed again. For all of us.

Most of all, for Reece—who now cocks up one side of his mouth, along with one cynical brow, at the little man with the slicked hair and cunning smirk. "Wouldn't that barrel be better used elsewhere, monsieur? Perhaps creating a fine wine or riding down Niagara Falls?"

The man's eyes bug—right before he spurts a hearty snicker. "Oh, I *like* you," he proclaims. "I like him," he emphasizes to Lawson. "*Oui, oui.* This is going to be a huge success."

"*What's* going to be a huge success?" Technically, I'm not interrupting, but I'm also not a real part of the conversation—an aspect Reece looks determined to change as he grabs my hand and then yanks me to his side. For a second, I give in to smelling him and damning him at once. He knows what it does to me when he wears the newest Tom Ford cologne. And damn it, we're still at least a couple of hours away from the nearest possibility of getting naked again...

Reece tugs me closer still, emitting a growling grunt I've never heard from him before. "Apparently, it's about what they've all come across the country to talk to me about, Velvet. And in Monsieur Guerrin's instance, an *ocean* and a country."

The Frenchman's eyebrows turn into jumping slashes—for two seconds. Urbanity intact again, he drawls, "Reasoned that all out, hmmm?"

"Your pocket square is embroidered with the Guerrin Motors logo." Reece nods at the artfully arranged silk in the man's dress jacket. "Figured I had a better than decent chance that you're Paul Guerrin, the maestro who's been helping my father negotiate the maze of the French government in order to build a sixty-story, all-glass designer hotel in the middle of a luxury neighborhood known for buildings that go back centuries. And also, last I checked, you're considering becoming a partner in said venture—on top of the alternative fuel company and movie studio you've just acquired as well."

"Ah!" The man brings his hands together with a giant *whop*. "*Magnifique!* If my own advisors even knew as much by half..."

"I really *am* more than a pretty face and a fast backup generator, Monsieur Guerrin."

"Exactly what I am counting on, Monsieur Richards."

"What we're *all* counting on." But Tyce's new attempt at brotherly bonding hits the air with all the discomfort that backed it. I really think the guy is trying, but diplomacy isn't called an art for nothing. Though I try to send the guy an at-least-you-tried smile, the glare I get for my trouble has me burrowing tighter against Reece.

"Well, that's hunky-dory to hear," Reece rejoins. "Except that I'm still stumbling in the dark here, and I'm the one with flashlights for fingers." He swivels his stare back to Lawson. "So this *is* about the Virage? Your last email stated the property's still six months away from an opening date."

"Yes, well..." Lawson pops a wider gaze back over to Guerrin before circling around to his sons again. "That plan has changed."

Reece scowls. "Since when?"

"Since they just announced that for the first time in over a decade, the *Grand Départ* for the Tour de France is being moved to Paris."

"Typically, the race only concludes in the capital," Guerrin fills in. "And cities from Europe submit special proposals to be considered as the departure location. But a week ago, this year's chosen departure city suffered a terrible explosion due to a faulty natural gas line. The main road was demolished, as well as many sewage pipes and electrical lines. The city is simply unfit to accommodate the fans, media, athletes, and support vehicles for our country's largest sporting event."

"And this year's Tour will be bigger than ever." Reece is so grave about adding a nod to it, I almost giggle. "That hotshot sprinter from Indiana has pulled back a lot of American attention to the sport."

I'm damn glad for the last-minute hesitation on the laugh. *Hell.* He's serious. My Dodgers, Rams, Chargers, Lakers, and Kings-loving fiancé is also a bicycle-racing fan. It's kind of dorky. It's super cute. It also has me wondering if I'll ever get to see him in a pair of those skintight cycling shorts.

Muses the girl with a fiancé who wears custom-tailored suits for his day job and fitted leathers to his night gig? Poor, poor missy. Women across the globe are sobbing for you. In the fictional world you just created.

"You are correct again, monsieur." Guerrin strokes his chin from the other direction. "Because of the extra interest in the 'hotshot,' there will be extra press and spectators traveling to Paris for the race this summer..."

"And clamoring for high-end American-brand hotels to stay in." I finish the thought for him as the comprehension slams me as well. "So you're going to push up the Virage's opening." I step away from Reece by a couple of inches while taking in that truth now writing itself across all their faces. "By a lot."

"By *a lot.*"

Chase is the first one to dare the new emphasis, though Tyce is quick to move up next to his brother and add, "Which means we can't do it alone."

Lawson shifts to stand in front of them both. "Which means I need you now more than ever, Reece."

"And not just for your pretty face." Chase smirks.

"But we *might* have considered your hot bod," Tyce deadpans. "Come *on*—the marketing possibilities. We can jack the door charge on the pool bar if it's leaked that Bolt Boy and his wonder whang will be there, clad only in a Speedo..."

"*No*," Reece spits.

I spear him with a glare.

He winks and then backhands Chase's chest. "How was *that* for timing?"

"Keep trying, dick face," Reece growls.

"He's just jealous." Chase imitates the expression.

"Screw you," Tyce sneers.

"*Boys*," Trixie censures—but the happiness behind her eyes is unmistakable. "Have you all reverted back into ruffians?"

Chase drops a tender gaze to her. "Would it be so awful if we did?"

Unsurprisingly, nobody in the group challenges him.

Reece is merciful about not letting the sentimental silence linger for too long. "Well, at least this A-Team turnout has now been explained," he states—and while he's pragmatic about the reasoning, it's clear he's still affected by the attention...that for the first time in a long time, he hasn't had to break a limb, a law, or a heart to earn. When his visual sweep around the circle ends with Lawson, he ventures to his dad, "I assume you need an answer about this as of...oh..."

"Yesterday." Guerrin, again proving his thorough French-ness, is accomplished at the teasing-not-teasing tone.

"Yeah." Reece firms his jaw. "That's what I thought."

"That still doesn't mean right this minute." Trixie steps over to smooth invisible lint off her son's lapel. "Not in the

middle of your special night, dear—with your very special lady."
She tilts her head and winks my way. "You two will need to talk
this through privately, of course—but Emmalina, if everything
works out, don't you worry about needing to get back to the
States from Paris at any time, should RRO business require
you here."

"Hold up." The interjection belongs to a clearly confused
Tyce. "Emma would...go *with* Reece?"

"Yes." Reece and I blurt it together.

Tyce rocks back with his hands up. "Can't blame a brother
for voicing the obvious."

"The obvious...what?" I ask.

"No." Reece's resigned murmur is definitely not my
answer. Nor is his renewed handclasp, a move elegant as a
prince claiming his princess, before he finishes, "I can't and
don't blame you, man."

But the fraternal bonding is hacked in the form of a wide-
eyed woman from the Observatory's special events team.
The name tag on her staff lanyard dangling over the plunging
neckline of her black wrap cocktail dress may as well say Team
Bolt Fangirl Leader instead of Greta, especially as she beams
at Reece like he just zapped the moon out of the sky for her.

"Mr. Richards? We're getting ready to begin the main
presentation on the West Observation Terrace."

Reece gives her his formal but friendly smile. "Thank you.
Miss Crist and I will be right there."

"Of course." Her blush nearly blends her into the sunset.
"Take all the time you need."

But he doesn't need much, and I'm glad. After ensuring
his family and Monsieur Guerrin that he'll have an answer for
them soon, the two of us get a stolen moment of "solitude" in

the form of our walk to the terrace—and I'm determined to take full advantage of it.

"All right, mister." Since our hands are still clasped, I add a slight squeeze to my prompt. "Either you or Tyce still owes me an answer."

Low growl. "Well, you're *not* getting it from Tyce."

"Okay..." I extend it, implying the question mark, but when he doesn't reply, I prompt anyway, "Why?"

"Because he'll embellish."

"On the 'obvious'?" I lean over, ensuring my air quotes are seen. "Is that possible?"

"With Tyce?" A pulse jumps in his jaw, though humor glimmers in his gaze. "Likely."

And what does *that* mean?

But I stick to silence on that one, a choice for which I thank myself as soon as we take two more steps, onto the observation terrace, and find *ourselves* being the observed— and photographed, flattered, and fawned over—as soon as the crowd realizes that their guest of honor has appeared for the festivities.

Just like that, Reece switches himself into public-persona mode, becoming every woman's Prince Charming and every man's admired peer, as I simply struggle to keep my balance beneath the barrage of camera flashes and excited shouts. Through it all, he continues to be my anchor, never relenting his hold as we wind our way toward the risers that have been scooted together into a small stage for the evening's ceremony.

With a protective hand at the base of my back, he guides me up the two shallow steps and parks me safely on one of the chairs lined up behind the podium, an imposing thing with the city seal carved into the front. He releases me, but only after leaning over and lifting a hand to my cheek so he can coax my lips to his cherishing brush of a kiss. In his eyes, the iridescence of every light in LA seems to shine and pulse especially for me.

"I love you," he murmurs for my ears alone.

"As I love you," I answer in a matching whisper.

"I wouldn't be here tonight without you."

"Yeah, you would." I gently thumb away the lipstick that's smudged on the corner of his lush mouth. "But I'm glad you're not."

He rolls his eyes before turning and making his way on stage. I watch him go with my usual appreciation—and adoration—of his long, masterful stride and his high, firm ass.

I settle back in, rearranging my skirts before lifting my head again. In the seat next to me, there's a gorgeous woman I feel I should recognize, with her dark hair piled into a purposely undone up-do, with tendrils that brush her high, defined cheekbones. She turns and smiles, showing off a glittering gaze that's offset by flawless smoky makeup.

"Hi." A wider grin, making her even more glamorous. "Emmalina, right?"

"Ummm. Yes. I mean...errr...right. That's me." *Right there. The top search result for "dorks who don't know their own name."*

"Hi. I'm Gabriella." She offers a hand, though she handles mine more like we're at a girlfriend meet-up instead of stranger-on-stranger. "That's my man up there with yours." As she gazes up at the mayor, I'm shocked not to see little hearts and birds twittering around her head. "Can you *even* believe this is our life? And I thought getting to be in movies together was unreal. But there's Troy, mayor of our city, getting ready to hand off his first key to your superhero boyfriend."

I feel a smile coming on. A *real* one. If a celebrity like her can openly claim her stupefaction, then so can I. "Unreal is a good way to say it," I laugh out. "Though if my brain's in an alternate reality, why can't my feet go there too?"

"Right?" Gabriella hides a giggle behind her free hand. "This thing was bumped up a month because of the lunar eclipse, right? Which means nighttime. Which means pajamas. Which means *slippers*, gang, not stilettos."

I shake my head. "The theme was definitely decided by men."

"Word."

But the next giggle we share is cut short by the start of the ceremony. Though both our guys keep their speeches mercifully short, the president of the Observatory's board cancels out their benevolence by giving a detailed history of the social, fictional, and historical significance of lunar eclipses. Though Gabriella and I attempt to pass the long minutes with meaningful stares that pass for everything from *Save me now* to *Christopher Columbus sounds like an asshole* to *Help, I have to pee*, there's nothing much we can do between those diversions except amuse ourselves with crowd watching—except in the odd cases where we discover the crowd actually perusing us in return.

Like when my stare lands on Tyce Richards.

But I wouldn't exactly label his look a pondering perusal. Or even a mildly curious gander. To get technical and uncomfortable, the man's not even returning my stare. He's weirdly fixated, to the point that I wonder if I'm just paranoid, courtesy of his abnormal intensity about everything coupled with his genuine shock about me accompanying Reece to Paris. I wasn't blind to the flash of disappointment beneath his reaction. Maybe he'd been entertaining fantasies of Paris as a dazzling single man's buffet to be enjoyed in full with his wild little brother at his side.

Tyce will embellish...

And a few overblown expectations in his head.

A psych major I never was, but a general emotional landscape of Tyce Richards begins to form, aided by the continuation of his hangdog stare. The middle son of a goal-driven father, sandwiched between the golden boy and the royal screw-up. Able to skate through high school and college on his looks and sports ability but rudderless since then. While his place in the family company is secure, he's still not sure about his place in the world as a whole and has compensated by jumping in and out of relationships that don't last once he's asked to commit—and came tonight thinking he would seal the deal and enlist Reece as his wingman for Paris. He just didn't anticipate the advent of *me*.

The certainty of all that is solidified with all my new glances at the guy—who gets creepier by the second. Though I'm positive some of this has to be my mind playing tricks on me, I'm still elated when the Observatory guy finally stops droning and the mayor can give his blissfully brief closing remarks.

"Come on." Gabriella seizes my hand, steering me down the opposite side of the risers from where all the men exit. "They'll be out on the Promenade with the press and vid media for at least fifteen minutes. Once we get to the bathroom, that gives us ten minutes of peace."

I give her fingers a fast squeeze. "Not even my favorite Harry Potter spell sounds that magical."

The dramatic lighting, tiled floors, and elegant exhibits in the Hall of the Sky are such a change from the noise and lights outside, I almost halt as soon as we're inside the door. Goal achieved—who the hell needs the bathroom? But poor Gabriella and her I-gotta-pee-*now* imploration keep me clattering in her wake until we reach the ladies room at the juncture between the Hall and the Central Rotunda.

As I gratefully collapse onto one of the settees in the powder room—why don't they make public restrooms like this anymore?—Gabriella does her business with a long, blissful sigh.

"Holy crap," she yells from the stall. "I can finally think clearly again."

I chuckle while yanking out my cell to check messages. "Been there, done that," I call back as a new text beams across my screen from Lydia.

Where did you go?

I frown as a new line immediately follows—filled with three urgent-face emojis and an exploding volcano. I blink, wondering which of my reactions is stronger: bewilderment about her message or shock that there's actually an exploding volcano emoji.

Either way, she's clearly not settling for *just a minute* as an answer.

"Hey," I call to Gabriella. "Do you mind if my sister joins us?"

"More the merrier!"

I laugh while texting 'Dia back, along with explicit instructions that no boys are allowed to have the secret rendezvous intel. Her responding message lends a little insight about her urgency to find me.

All the boys can kiss my tight
sweet ass right now.

Since I don't have any idea how to answer that, I don't. Instead, after Gabriella washes up, reapplies her lipstick, and plops down on the settee beside me, I make her watch my measured breath in and then out before I state, "A disclaimer— and possibly an apology. My sister might be in quite a state."

She pulls in a sharp hiss, letting her teeth show a little. "Ooooh. Boy trouble, huh? Or maybe...girl trouble?"

I'm unable to get in an answer due to Lydia barging in with the grandeur of a female Liberace. Yes, down to the hair she flings like a stage cape and the wounded animal sigh she emits while sinking into the chair that faces the settee. "Men. Fucking. *Suck.*" She swings a wincing glance toward Gabriella. "Gawd. I'm sorry you had to hear that, Madame Mayor. Errrm...Madame Mayoral Wife? Mrs. Mayor?"

"Gabriella is fine. Or Gabi, if you prefer." The woman crosses one gorgeous leg over the other, with her dancer-tight calf escaping from the side slit of her red sheath gown. "Because right now, I'm just another girl in the bathroom who needs to hear you spill it, girl. What asshole has made you feel this way?"

"Ding ding ding." I raise a finger. "I got this one covered... *if* his name is Sawyer Foley."

"Sawyer Fo—" Gabriella's eyes widen. "Hold up. Wasn't I just introduced to a guy named Sawyer right before the ceremony? Face like Beckham and Hunnam had a love child? Surfer-god hair and bod?"

"Ooohhhh." Lydia slumps deeper into the chair. "*Don't* remind me."

"Why?" Gabriella and I ask together.

"Because all that beauty is what keeps bringing me *down* with that fucker."

"Hold up the tamale cart." I hitch up my skirt and shoot to my feet, despite how they only just started speaking to me again in these strappy Louboutins. But right now, I need the extra few feet of leverage over my sister. "For months, the only place you wanted to *be* with Sawyer Foley was down, down, down—as in on your back with him, doing the nasty in every position with him, drowning in sweat and all the other bodily fluids..."

"All right, *all right.*" Lydia flings up a hand, flushing furiously. "Nobody needs the graphic optics!"

Gabriella rocks her head from side to side. "Speak for yourself, honey."

I spread my arms. "But for the sake of argument—and because we really don't have all night, apparently like Sawyer's sex drive does—"

"*Emma.*"

I chuckle but swiftly sober. "So the sex is good?"

Lydia squirms. "Fine. For the sake of argument, *yes*, the sex is good."

Gabriella leans forward as 'Dia buries her face in her hands. "But...you want more than the sex now?"

A new groan unfurls from my sister. "Oh, gawd. Yes. *Yes.* That *is* what I want." She drags her hands back, threatening to destroy her fancy up-do with a crazy clutch at her hairline. "I'm a bad, *bad* person, aren't I?"

As if we've choreographed it, Gabriella and I fall to our knees together in front of Lydia's chair. "How the hell does that make you bad?" Gabriella beats me to the demand by two seconds. "For wanting a deeper emotional connection with the guy you've already got awesome sexual chemistry with?"

"'Dia." My soft chide comes with a grab at one of her wrists. Seriously, she's about to turn her hair into a wild mess. "That *doesn't* make you bad. That makes you human."

As she returns my gaze, the angles of her face soften—for two seconds. All too quickly, she's back to being a full emo rock video queen, anguish carving her features. "Not in Sawyer Foley's world," she rasps.

"How the hell do you know that?" I return.

"I just do." Her expression loses its petulance. Only the determination remains, stamped into the firm line of her lips and the crystal surety of her gaze. "It's his unspoken line in the sand—and it's drawn in really dark ink."

Gabriella settles back on her ankles. Nods knowingly. "A darkness that attracted you to him in the first place."

Lydia snaps her stare over. At first, she looks bewildered, as if wondering how the woman figured that out, before a shrug of acceptance takes over her lithe frame. "There are a lot of layers beneath all that golden-boy gorgeousness," she asserts.

"And you think that a relationship beyond sex will make him hide those layers," I say with big sister sagacity.

"I don't think it," Lydia whispers. "I know it."

I push out a heavy huff. "But you're doing the exact same thing to *him*, honey—right now, by hiding *this* truth." The glower she shoots up at me only shores up my scowl. "No relationship, of *any* kind, is good when secrets are involved." As soon as she drops her other hand, I wrap it into my insistent grip. "You know that as well as I do, 'Dia. Secrets are just a fancy way of lying. We learned that by watching it firsthand, didn't we?"

Pain creases the edges of her eyes—and soon, the breadth of her forehead. She doesn't try to battle her hands free from mine. Maybe she knows she'll lose—just like she knows I'm right.

"Sawyer and I are nothing like Mother and Father."

"No?" I hate piercing her whisper with my brutal tone, but isn't painful honesty what sisters are built for? "You're not racing off to the lido deck for a nooner with the club's towel boy, but you're hiding something just as vital from him. Your truth. And believe me, sister, that's just as unfair."

So much for being unconcerned she'll break free. As 'Dia does just that, all but catapulting herself out of the chair, she lashes, "We're *not* married!"

"So because he's your lover and not your husband, you don't owe him the truth?"

"Do *you* tell Reece everything?"

"Yes." I use the chair to push up, ignoring the shrieks from my toes this time. "And believe me, it's not easy. But nor was it a picnic to learn how a relationship can be poisoned by secrets—even 'little white ones.'"

My sister slumps her shoulders. Refuses to turn my way. But when she dares a glance at Gabriella, the woman turns up both palms, her brows slanting ruefully. "Sorry, girlfriend. I'm in the Team Emma jersey for this one." When the latest hip-hop hit blares from her purse, she rolls gracefully to her own feet but doesn't answer it. "Annnnd I take that back. Team Chan calls again." She checks her phone, confirming with a nod. "Back to the grip-and-grin, kids. But rest assured"—she steps over, hauling Lydia in for a bone-crushing hug—"you're going to figure this out. I have complete faith!"

As soon as Gabriella's out the door, my sister's Debbie

Downer face sets in again. "Well, *she* might have faith..."

"She's not the only one." I tug on 'Dia's shoulder and rock her in a tight sibling hug. "You're not just a badass on the tennis court, Dee Dee. You're a strong, amazing woman—in your heart and in your character—and you really do deserve more from a man than his cock."

Her long sigh primes me for the sappy mush with which she's about to retaliate. And sure enough, with tear-swollen eyes, she steps back and—

"But gawd, what a *cock*."

"Gaaahhh." I laugh-choke it, giving her a grimace usually reserved for her worst farts, before stumbling back to retrieve the phone going off in my own purse. As the grinding rhythm of Imagine Dragons' "Warriors" shakes the table, I smile. "And with perfect timing, Team Reece calls me back to the fray as well."

"Not before Team Lydia gives you one last hug." Her embrace is fierce and tight, matching the smack she gives my cheek. "And all the thanks in her heart and soul for being the best sister she could ever ask for."

I laugh again, shaking my head. "Save it for after you've talked to Sawyer."

"Deal." She flashes her bright winner's grin, but it quickly dissipates into a wince. "And...errr...sorry about my lipstick making out with your cheek."

"No worries. I have to fix my face and take care of the bladder before facing the world again anyway. Now shoo. Go find your man and pull him off to a dark corner for that 'chat.' Those shouldn't be too hard to find once the eclipse starts."

By the time I reach the stall to take care of the white wine and water practically making my eyeballs float, her footsteps have died off—or so I think. Right before I flush, the restroom door creaks open again.

"Okay, dork-a-'Dia," I call while leaving the stall, double-checking to ensure I haven't accidentally tucked my gown into my underwear. "What'd you forget this..."

My voice gives out.

My knees nearly do the same.

Just as every thought in my head turns into a cold, cosmic-level void—

Except one.

It was more than paranoia.

"Tyce." I blurt it out but wonder how I did. My brain is still struggling to comprehend its other truth.

It was more than paranoia.

"Emmalina. Hi there. Glad I could...catch you."

It was more than paranoia.

Every passing second of his quiet, eerie regard is a new confirmation of it. A fresh window into the disgusting truth of it.

"In the *ladies'* restroom?" By some miracle, I'm able to issue it all without hitches, though I can't say the same for masking the agitation in my gaze or the tremble of my stance. I battle to tell myself that this is stupid and that I'm overreacting to nothing but a friendly gesture from a guy who's going to be my brother-in-law someday. Okay, so he's intense. And a little too fond of emo-punk video style stares. And not afraid to march into a women's restroom to...

Do what?

What the hell is *he here for?*

For now, he seems fond of just peering around—though not avidly enough to sacrifice his stance, with hands braced on both sides of the doorway back to the powder room. Which contains my purse, still on the settee. And my phone lying next to it. And, for that matter, the exit door...

"Well, it's a nice restroom," he murmurs. "As restrooms go." Then drops his stare, calmer than the scrutiny he unleashed during the show but still daunting in its proximity, back to my face. "And it's a chance to be alone." His subtle smile sneaks up as his perusal slides lower. "Which is always a good perk."

Before the snakes of apprehension turn into wraiths of panic, I pivot and turn on the water, scrubbing my hands for the full Alphabet Song count. "Well, speaking as a girl who's worked hotels for a few years, perks are overrated."

"Speaking as someone who's done a lot of fucking around in them, I'd agree." The guy says it at normal level over the roar of the air dryer, meaning he's leaned in close enough for me to hear. But when the air shuts off, Tyce doesn't back away—and even moves in by another step, forcing me to back up against the partition between two of the stalls. "But sometimes, an opportunity is just an opportunity, and those of us without a lot of options have to jump at the perks."

Somehow, there's still a few extra inches of space for me to rear back more, allowing my drill of a glare back at him. "What the hell are you talking—"

Whether it's his gouge of a grab at my waist or the aggressive hiss from his lips, my harsh gulp sends my voice into tight silence—with which the bastard seems fine. "Regrettably, talking can't be on the agenda for this little meeting, sister."

"I'm *not* your sister." I claw my fingernails into his hand. He doesn't move an inch.

"Well, that's not far off, is it? But there are some things that need to be settled first, right?"

His voice, slipping into a husk, sprays an array of strange sensations through every pore of my body. It's damn clear what this is all about—what this asshole wants from me. *Or is it?* I've been pinned like this before by a man. By a group of them. I knew exactly what every one of them wanted from me.

But this doesn't feel the same. At all.

What. The. Hell?

I spit all three words at him, in exactly the same cadence, only to be cut off by a hiss five times fiercer than his first. "Be *quiet*, Emmalina. We don't have much more—"

"Quiet? Are you *freaking* kidding me? And *you*, asshole, do *not* have the right to call me Emmal—"

"I said be quiet!"

"Go to hell!"

"I'm not going to hurt you."

"Oh, so it'll feel good? Best I've ever had? Is that your angle?"

"Oh, for fuck's—"

He's cut *himself* off this time, groaning as if I really did deliver the gut punch and the ball jab that have been tempting my instincts. But that's not the end of the sound. His outburst is infused with something else. An undertone I know all too well because I've heard it vibrate through Reece so much.

Pain.

Deep, unstoppable, physical pain.

He slackens his hold. Drops his shoulders as if the whole planetarium has fallen on top of them, and lets his head plummet the same direction.

But not before I get several seconds' worth of the new grimace on his face.

His face?

No.

A gargoyle. A burn victim. Maybe even a heroin addict gone so far off the rails, he's turned into another person. But in the space of three seconds? With flesh that suddenly looks like a preschooler's tried to fashion a face out of Playdoh?

The transformation is so sudden and the sight so unexpected, I can't help my visceral reaction.

I scream.

Loudly.

Apparently, for a while—because the reverberations from it are still making the whole room ring as Tyce seizes me again and jerks me next to him with feral force.

Then whispers words into my ear that render me silent again. And slack-jawed. And bug-eyed. And helpless to do anything for a long second except watch as an insane electrical pulse blows the locked restroom door right off its hinges.

Followed by a beastly bellow that makes my screams sound like kitten mewls.

Followed by the sight of my towering, wrath-filled man, his beautiful suit frying away from his leathers, the force of his rage *whomp*ing the air like an EMP explosion.

"R-Reece!"

At least I *think* I've stuttered it. The force of his entrance is still ringing in my ears, and raw shock still paralyzes a majority of my body—though I'm not one drop of stunned when Tyce wheels and falters as if he's just chugged a whole bottle of Patrón. As soon as the dickhead grins with equally trashed whimsy, I wonder if his common sense is just as thoroughly sauced. And does it even matter? The rage on Reece's face, contorting his features as if the eclipse is really turning him into a werewolf, conveys everything I need to know about how this is going to go down.

Correction.

How Tyce is going to go down.

Shit. Shit. Shit.

I'm galvanized—and in spite of how my limbs are still the consistency of pudding, I force them to move with the same speed at which Reece does. By the time I peel off my Louboutins, toss them into Lydia's moping chair, and get to Reece's side, he's already hoisting Tyce up by the back of the collar and flinging him into the rotunda like a rat into the rain. The fierce worry in his eyes is my only clue about why he spins back, clutching me by both shoulders. In return, I curl my hands into the thick collar of his leathers and yank. Hard.

"Reece—"

"Are you all right?"

Shit. His growl really does border on werewolf octaves. I roll through a semblance of a nod.

"Yeah. I'm fine. *I'm fine*, honestly. But he wasn't—"

"Good." His face hardens as he starts to pull away, but I refuse to let go of his collar.

"Reece. You're getting this—"

"Damn right I am."

"*Reece!*"

I won't *be fine if you murder your brother and spend the rest of your life in jail, damn it.*

He pries my fingers loose. Quickly lifts them to his lips. "Stay here."

I jerk my brows to my hairline. "Excuse *me*?"

"Fine. Then stay out of the way."

Oh, God.

"Reece!"

He stops but only jerks his head back around, though

that's enough for me to glimpse the electrons now firing in his glare. "What?"

"Felons don't get to be superheroes."

As he whips his head forward again, there's no missing the new ropes of tension beneath his shoulders, spiraling down his arms...into the brilliant blue glow of the fingers he curls into matching fists.

"And sometimes, heroes need to forget about being super—and only worry about what's right."

CHAPTER FIVE

REECE

The Observatory is either going to love me or hate me for this.

In the "love" column? Nothing's broken except—likely—my brother's arrogant nose. And now, the articles about the event won't be just front page of the society section. If I take another swing at Tyce—and holy *fuck* is that a better idea by the second—the Observatory's rotunda will be more recognizable than the Capital Hill dome by tomorrow.

But now for the "hate" column. Tyce is bleeding all over their vintage floor. And a superhero with boiling blood and glowing fists is stealing all the thunder from their silent-auction tables.

Maybe more than thunder.

The crowd presses in around me, their confused and scandalized whispers careening off the high dome of the rotunda. There's more volume from the equally weirded-out murmurs of the media reporters, stammering to improvise commentary for a Los Angeles society event that's taken a sharp turn into what-the-fuck territory.

I'm beyond caring.

The only thing I focus on is the strange expression of the man at my feet now sitting in a puddle of his own blood. Eerily, Tyce is...grinning. Not a lot but enough, his perfect white teeth outlined in blood as he wipes the back of a hand across his fractured nose. The knowing, cocky air continues up to his gaze, glittering back at me with a mixture of pain and—

What?

Is he mocking me? Admiring me? What the living fuck?

Unbelievable. My brother has bested himself at the art of being a true bastard.

With a snarl I don't bother to hide, documented by flashing cameras and live video feeds, I turn to the woman who's just watched me drag Tyce across the rotunda with electric ropes, only to deactivate the bonds and lay into him with my bare fists. Because sometimes, flesh-to-flesh is the perfect emissary for the message—especially when it comes to beating the crap out of the brother who locked himself into a restroom with my screaming fiancée.

And not wanting to stop until the fucker is dead.

But I force myself to do so when the woman of my dreams begs me not to make her the girlfriend of a felon.

Because in true Tyce Aaron Richards style, the bastard beneath me has managed to pull off a victory of true asshole artistry: doing the crime but damn near ensuring I'll do the time, if the faces of the throng's newest arrivals can be interpreted correctly. Mom and Dad, having clearly sprinted their way over here, have just as obviously hit the brakes on their Reece bandwagon. So much for the road Emma worked to smooth over for their ride.

So much for thinking *anything* has changed about the Richards family dynamics of the last twenty years.

Yeah, I got in the first punch. And the last. And the six between them.

But I'm still the loser.

That cold reality brings strange comfort. At least the ice in my heart helps freeze-dry the goddamned tears.

"Reece. *Reece?*" As Emma approaches me on wobbly steps, turquoise-colored drops track down her cheeks. "Come away," she urges. *"Now.* He's... It's... This just isn't what it seems, okay?"

"It's only okay if *you're* okay." I tug her close but look her over. Instinct says I got to the bathroom before Tyce let the dick between his legs speak for the one inside his head, but I need to hear it straight from Emma. Nothing will calm me down before getting it directly from her.

"Yes. Of course. Just listen to me, okay? I want to go home. With you. Right now. Please. Can't we..."

"For fuck's sake." Tyce, with a drawl in his voice but challenge in his eyes, pushes up onto an elbow. "Would you listen to her, brother? This isn't worth it."

I shove a hand down, palm out and fingers curled, modifying a martial arts move for the Bolt playbook. In two seconds, the electric pulse I've joined to the move has him flattened again. "Little piece of advice, *brother*. In my world, this woman is *always* worth it."

"Noted," he returns. "But there's a larger picture to focus on here." There's a discernible falter in his grin—and a heightened glint in his eyes. "You *know* this."

"I 'know' this?" So much for tiptoeing at the line between composure and rage. As the force of it thickens at the edges of my vision, I bare my gritted teeth at the asshole who's sneering at me like I'm ten years old and all he's done is walk through my corner of the playground. "You know what I know now, asshole? That I'm not your scrawny disciple anymore. That you don't get to walk away from the mess you've made this time."

"All right. Fine. Whatever you say." His hands are up before I can aim the pulse for a solid throat punch. Of course. Diplomacy is a cinch when a guy has Mom and Dad Richards at his back. "Just chill *out*, Reece," he grits. "Take a breath. Talk to Emma. I was just messing around."

"Just messing around." My echo is edged with disbelief—and fury that makes Emma cry out, too late, as I haul Tyce up by the knot of his designer necktie. "Let me make something clear, shithead. Emmalina Crist *is* the larger picture for me. That means she'll *never* be yours to just mess around with again. *Ever*. Are we clear?"

"Yes. *Christ*." Tyce twists, trying to break away, until I swing down my other hand, pushing him from beneath with a concentrated burst of electrified air. "For the love of *fuck*, Reece."

"Are. We. Clear?"

He looks left and right with a bugged-out gaze, no doubt accessing what damage I'll really attempt in front of a crowd including the mayor of LA, half of Hollywood's elite, and a hell of a lot of press. His theory is right. Sort of. I can't deck him again, a rule that'd apply even if I hadn't just received the key to the city and made a speech about the essence of a superhero lying in their character choices and not their fight choreography—but I can deliver an equally horrific fate in the form of the energy jolt against his ass. With a slight tweak to the beam's girth and angle, he should start feeling some "unique" sensations down there...right about now...

"What. The. Fuck?"

"Something wrong, bro?" I dip my head so he alone can hear my murmur. "You look...uncomfortable. Like maybe you're about to have the shit squeezed out of you in front of all these nice people." A knowing grin. "But don't think anything of it, Ty. I'm just messing around, all right?"

"Damn it," he grates. "Reece—"

"Not the words I need, sweetheart." I rotate my hand, ensuring he feels his electric enema in a few new spots of his sphincter. "Just answer me one question and we can be done."

Another rotation, resulting in his clenched grimace and my grim smirk. I know it's not really a moment for smiling, but we Richards boys have always had bizarre senses of humor. A twisted code, cultivated by Dad's "eat or be eaten" version of tough love, demanding unquestioning loyalty and hefty sacrifices. In the name of "manning up" to earn that love, I'd allowed Tyce and Chase to raid everything from my toys and clothes to my mind and self-worth. Because real men helped their brothers cheat on math tests, right? And real men let their brothers win at *Call of Duty* so they'd impress the hot girls who'd come over to study for that math test. Real men also took the blame for spilling printer ink on Mom's Aubusson rug so the brothers wouldn't miss getting to go on a hot date with the smitten girls.

I've resigned myself to a lot of that bullshit now. The past is the past. But my future? My Emmalina? She will never be included in their twisted game. *Ever.*

Which is why I smile, this time without a shred of shame, as Tyce finally snarls, "We're clear."

And why I drop him and then turn, this time without acknowledging Dad, Mom, or Chase, and leave the building completely.

And why I squeeze, this time without hesitation, as Emma slips her hand into mine during our trek to the limousine holding area. And why I sigh, with more than a little irony, as she asks, "You okay?"

"Velvet." I cup a hand to the back of her neck. "Shouldn't *I* be asking *you* that?"

She purses her lips. The bottommost of those plush pillows is jutted into a gorgeous pout. "Oh, I'm just dandy—aside from being the reason my fiancé just punched the crap out of his brother, likely burning every stick of the bridges he's built back to his family."

"You mean the bridges *you* helped to build?"

I don't know how to interpret her answering look. It's more than an eye roll but not a full glower. "Bylines aren't important right now. What *is* important—"

"Is the fact that he deserved it?"

She stops short. Pulls her hand free. "I was going to say getting the whole story, but you're clearly not concerned about being fair here, are you?"

I widen my stance. Return the new force of her glare by refusing to blink mine. "You were *screaming*, Emmalina. How do you want me to fill out the rest of my view from there?"

She huffs through bared teeth—but as Zalkon spots us and drives the black L7 stretch up to the curb, her next breath is instead a wistful sigh. "Shit," she whispers as we climb into the back and instantly wrap ourselves in each other's arms. "Maybe..."

"Maybe what?" I prompt, stroking her temple as she breathes soft warmth across my chest.

"Maybe...you're right," she confesses. "Maybe we're just asking fate for too much." With quiet tenderness, she rubs her fingertips over the space atop my heart. "Maybe smooth sailing with our families is just never going to be part of the course she's charted for us. And maybe she just figures we need a few interesting storms."

I grunt into the citrus softness of her hair. "Because we've had such balmy weather already?"

"Technically?" she ripostes. "Yes. We've got a couple of great places to live, with a custom house on the way. We're in jobs we love and have friends who kick ass. And oh yeah, there's the whole superpowers thing..." Her voice softens into a cute-as-fuck purr as she roams those entrancing fingers down and spreads them over my stomach. "And we can't discount abs like *this*..."

I layer my chuckle to her hum as she loosens a couple of my shirt buttons—but my mirth is slain by a strangled choke when she keeps going, sneaking a hand across my navel before venturing lower. "I had no idea that abs counted in the cosmic weather report."

She stills her hand. Lifts a gorgeous, wide stare. "Where else are they supposed to count?"

As she renews her little caressing circles, I buck my hips. "Guess you'd better batten down the hatches."

"And put myself on storm watch?"

"If that'll help wash away the crap we just had to wade through..." I pull her in a little closer, nuzzling my mouth down to the edge of her jaw. "Then fuck, *yes*."

A giggle escapes her as perfect as the spatters of a surprise summer shower. Goddamn. I'm seriously the world's luckiest fucker. Without trying, the woman is always the sun beneath my darkest clouds, the laughter in my most dismal moments.

And as much as I want to be the same for her in return, especially as she starts a playful hum of "Singin' in the Rain," it's my place to be Mr. Realism here. It has to be. So with resigned firmness, I form my hand over hers and murmur, "Velvet?"

"Hmmm?"

"You know there *will* be more storms now. My Tarzan act on Tyce has likely made me the Richards problem child once again."

The *likely* is for her benefit only. I already know the truth, having caught a good look at my parents' faces before I let Emma pull me out of the Observatory. It was déjà vu to the days when my school absences outnumbered my attendances, yet I was nailing every test and exam, as well as half their bridge club's daughters.

Simply put, they still don't know what to do with me.

And yet, they don't know what *not* to do with me.

But as soon as they figure it all out, I'm damn sure I'll know.

Along with the fact that said plan will be a punishment, not a promotion.

Just to confirm that tidbit, I'm sure my old friend shame will be here any second, ready to start his preparations for the funeral of my self-esteem. I brace myself, getting ready for the fucker to start pounding away...

Only he's not anywhere to be found.

Maybe he's having trouble sneaking past Emma's lingering touch, with her fingers now swirling closer to my waistband. Or maybe he never made it past the force field of her spirit, still filling the inside of the limo with her happy hums. Which leads me to think that maybe *she* didn't hear *me*...

"Emmalina?"

She switches off the soft song. "Hmmmm?"

"Did you hear me?"

"Mmmmhmmm." Then turns her humming back on. "You're Tarzan the problem child. And that means we've probably got storms coming."

"Which means..."

"I need to get a cuter raincoat."

I drop a cement block of a huff. "That wasn't what I meant."

"I know what you meant." She pulls away until she's upright and able to look me in the eyes. "But what good is all that angst going to do us right now?" She props her elbow to the back of the seat and brings her head to her knuckles. "Your parents are going to do what they're going to do—but somehow we'll handle it." With her free hand, she strokes the edge of my jaw. "As long as we're together, we can handle anything."

I turn my face toward her palm, filling its center with the pressure of my lips before lifting a hand to lace my fingers through hers. I keep our grip locked as I murmur, "Yeah. You're right."

"Damn right, I'm right."

But while her words are assuring, they're accompanied by the skitter of her gaze. Suddenly, she's too damn fascinated with the passing scenery, even as the shadowed greenery of Griffith Park gives way to the urban landscape of Los Feliz. Yeah, even after I tug her face around again, kissing her reverently in the glow of passing streetlights, the haze in her eyes looks like it belongs to another time, another space.

I pull her closer and wrap her elbow around my neck, but her body doesn't soften by one inch. Even with the blares, blasts, noise, and insanity of an LA night, there's a growing tumor of silence weighing the air between us.

I circle my hold tighter around her—sensing the matching tension growing thicker by the second inside her. "What is it, Velvet?"

"Nothing."

"Bullshit."

"Oh, *crap.*" She pushes back, worrying her lip as convincingly as a B-movie actress playing off a green screen. "*Lydia.*" She plunges a hand into her clutch and pulls her phone back out. "We left so fast, I couldn't make arrangements for her ride home..."

"Which I'm sure Sawyer will be happy to handle." With a smooth sweep, I've got the phone out of her grip and her arm back around my neck. "Nice try, beautiful."

Her lips compress. "At what?"

"Why don't *you* tell *me*?"

She races her gaze away again—and swallows hard.

Fresh fury chomps the pit of my gut. "Christ."

"Okay, *stop.* Slow your roll, okay?"

"Slow my fucking roll? Are you kidding?"

"*Breathe,* damn it."

I comply only because it's her behind the order. Even so, I dig my hands in against her waist. "Tyce really did try some fuckery, didn't he?"

"Reece—"

"Tell me."

"*Reece!*"

"*Goddamnit,* Emma!"

"Oh, for the love of—" She finishes for herself with a shove so virulent, I wonder if her finale will be leaving the car completely. We're stopped at the corner of Western and Hollywood, and thanks to her, I know there's a metro stop on the other side of the intersection—a station she won't think twice about marching for to get on a train back to the Brocade, despite how I once saved her ass from a bunch of thugs in a station similar to it. Yeah, I already see that resolution in her eyes. That undaunted threat.

That complete lack of fear...

Which makes no sense, if she's really a woman who just got jumped and pawed by her future brother-in-law.

Which means...

I have to tell the rage to go gnaw on somebody else for a while.

Because now *I'm* the one tucking in for the big meal. Staring down at my huge plate of crow.

"Stay." It bursts from me as a command, made all the worse as I pry her fingers off the door handle, for which I apologize by bowing my head into her lap. "*Please.*" I drag back and straighten, refusing to let her hand go. "Tell me, Emma," I entreat, coating it in more contrition. "The truth this time. I promise I'll listen."

She gulps again. *Not good.*

Then spurts out pieces of a giggle. *Good?*

Then looks out again at the intersection, with its array of Hollywood Boulevard crazies, like all of them are still a better choice than confronting me.

Fuck. Not *good.*

Then turns fully back, working her grip tighter into mine. So...*good?*

Crap on a platter. I'm completely lost, unsure how to decipher what my instinct—or whatever the hell this creature now feasting on my guts is—is telling me. Emma's mien, with her hard and full breathing and deep V between her eyebrows, doesn't give me any further clues.

After pulling in a breath that's even deeper than her others, she finally lifts her head and states, "Your brother did seek me out in the bathroom tonight—but not for what you've assumed."

I wait a significant second, wanting to let her know I've heard despite my reply. "As you both told me. Repeatedly."

She pinches her lips. "Are you ready to hear why, or am I going to get out at Sunset and hoof it to the train station from there?"

Well, shit. "I'm zipped," I growl.

"Good." But her composure glitches the next second, turning her exhalation into a weird stutter before she mutters, "Th-That's damn good."

"Is it?" And again, I'm not at all certain of the answer myself. "Jesus Christ in guacamole, Em. What the hell is it?" While we've tossed out the garbage of suspecting Tyce of trying to get between her legs, whatever happened in that restroom is still clearly haunting her mind—perhaps even worse than a flirtation gone wrong.

She bends over to press fervent kisses to my knuckles. I gape at the top of her head in bewilderment. She's *leaned down* to bestow the kisses...not brought my hands up so she can meet my eyes at the same time, like she normally does.

Just as strangely, she's flipping her head back up, shaking her head as if ordering herself not to cry in a sappy movie— which she always does anyway. For which I adore her, anyway.

"God," she finally utters. "I'm sorry. I'm probably overreacting..."

"To *what*?" I'm growling now. "Velvet, you're leading me through the dark, but I'm not sure *you* have a flashlight. What the hell are—"

"Tyce told me that he found me and cornered me because he needed to get a message to you. That he needed me to listen carefully and relay exactly what he told me."

"Okay." I barely resist extending the syllables and turning

it into a question. There's no need for it, though, since I follow up with, "So why didn't he just pull me aside sometime during the party?"

"Exactly what I thought," she fills in. "But he emphasized the same thing. The message had to go straight to you."

"But why? Did he explain that?" Once more, her averted gaze supplies the answer. I can't believe that the unlimited seafood buffet we're passing is *that* fascinating. "What was it?"

She pulls her gaze away from the All-You-Can-Eat Shrimp banner but reaffixes it on the clasp of our hands. "He said there was no way in hell you should go to the Richards Clan *Kumbaya* in the City of Light."

"*What?* Not go to Paris?" I let my fingers go slack as confusion makes everything but her go fuzzy. "I don't understand. He can't be that big of a prick, can he?"

"Baby." She reaches for me, her expression softening. "He looked like anything but a prick, okay? Even when he—"

"Even when he what?" I demand it from gritted teeth when she stops, again clearly torn about going on. "Damn it, Emma. When he *what?*"

"Nothing," she rushes out. "It— It was nothing."

"And I'm the fucking King of Persia."

She jerks up her head. Squares her shoulders. "Just...the way he looked...right before..."

"Right before *what?*"

"He told me he owed it to Alpha Three."

My lungs stop.

My vision clouds.

My head spins. And gongs. And pounds. And screams.

"Did... Did he say anything else?" My blurt is muffled by the chaos that continues in my senses.

She pulls in another shaky inhalation and follows it with an equally uneasy exhalation. "No."

"Then why did you scream? *Emma?*" I don't mess around with the dictate, palming the back of her neck when she falls into palpable silence. She responds then, but only to shake her head and slam her eyes shut, as if struggling not to relive a bad memory.

"It was just...the way Tyce looked—"

As she interrupts herself with a strangled sound, I peer at her harder. Normally, just having this direct contact is all the access my instinct needs to know her thoughts. But right now, she's nothing but a muddle to me, and I struggle against the fear that brings.

"The way he looked...how?"

She opens her eyes, but that gives me no clarity. They're the color and texture of storm clouds at midnight—backlit by a moon of anxiety. "I don't know how to describe it. He...well, he changed. Almost as if he became another person." Her features twist, and she chokes out a tiny sob. "And it was shocking. And so I screamed. But now, I don't even know if it was real. He switched back to normal as soon as you came in."

"While coming to the worst conclusion I could."

The din in my mind finally subsides. A little. I send a hard swallow down my throat. "Well, the assmunch got his way. Dad won't be sending over a plane ticket to Paris."

"Not that you're going to let that stop you." Despite how far away her voice sounds compared to the ruthless buzzing in my ears, I'm aware of every bittersweet note in her voice. How her pride in me has declared war on her fear for me. How she knows, once she spoke those two words, there'll be nothing stopping me from trying to get to my brother—or Paris—now.

Alpha Three.

Holy. Shit.

What's Tyce's tie to him? Is the Consortium simply using him as a messenger? If so, why would Tyce say he "owes" the guy? Does that mean Tyce is part of the Consortium too? And if Tyce is involved with the bastards, is Dad as well? Is Chase?

But if that's the case, why is Tyce trying to get me alone? And more than that, why did he feel the need to send the message through *Emma*, going through the trouble and effort of cornering her in the bathroom to do it? Why did he not even trust that message with an email or a phone call?

A thousand more questions pile in, encasing the lightning in my blood in icebergs. On top of those floes, my thoughts careen like penguins in ballet shoes, the riot stopped only when my phone starts buzzing. The screen is filled with an avatar of a coconut with gummy bears for eyes. Sawyer. *Thank fuck.*

"Hey. *Hey.* Dude...you there?"

His voice sounds like a dream too. *A dream.* Yeah. That has to be it. I've fallen asleep in the limo, and Foley's somehow in it too, and I'll wake up any second and not have to deal with...

The insanity that crashes in on me all over again.

Alpha Three.

Words out of my darkest nightmares. My deepest hell. My hottest crucible.

Spoken to my secret fiancée—by the brother who's apparently hiding as many mysteries as I am.

"Reece?" Emma's query, matching Foley's for confused concern, makes me realize I've said the words aloud. "Baby? You okay?"

I shake my head like one of those flopping balloon creatures outside strip malls. "I don't know." When a disembodied voice answers me instead of her, I realize my phone has slipped from my hand and Foley is shouting at me from the limo's floor. But once I scoop the thing up again, it's backward. I fumble to press the thing correctly to my ear while a stream of confused profanity pours from the thing.

"*Foley*," I stab into his tirade with my gritted command. As soon as he falls into stunned silence, I order, "Gather the team. Meet me at the Research building downtown."

That handles the *who* and *where* of things. The question it doesn't answer, tumbling out of him next, is the one I'm not prepared to answer at all.

"Why?" Foley demands. "What's up, man?"

Not prepared at all.

Because what we learn after this will change everything.

It'll turn my brother—and possibly my father—into my closest compatriots or my darkest enemies.

And damn it, how I hate the answer my gut has already sided with.

And the boulders that tumble and settle there, just to ensure I don't forget.

⚡

Hours later, those rocks have fused and become a cement block in my stomach. The burden weighs every step I pace across the lab's polished floor. My agitation is likely giving Foley eye twitches, though he hides them well behind a focused scowl while keying and clicking at his computer as fast as he can.

Outside, downtown LA starts to stir in the early morning hours of a brisk spring day. Even the building around us begins to bustle, with elevators whirring, coffee machines chugging, and delivery men whistling. The distinctive rush of freeway traffic begins to flow through the city like melted snow into a mountain river bed, quickening everyone's pace—even Foley's.

But he's still not fast enough. Not for yielding the information we need. The information *I* need. More accurately, the information I don't need. The dead-ends I all but order the guy to keep arriving at—at the ends of informational paths I've also authorized him to keep following.

No matter how painful the process gets. No matter how deep we have to go.

I need to know.

I need to be positive.

I need to make sure, no matter how huge or small the bread crumbs are, that Foley follows every last, crazy path that might link Tyce, Chase, or Dad back to the Scorpios or the Consortium. That the cryptic message Tyce relayed through Emma was a bizarre fluke, and that in my brother's world, *Alpha Three* doesn't come close to what it means in mine.

Are the tests on Alpha Two almost done?

Affirmative. Took two doses of the depressant to tame him this time, but he's finally finished.

Good. Alpha Three's still being prepped in his cell, but he'll be ready for transport in five.

I'll need about that long to take the rest of the needles out of Two. I have about ten more to go...

"Air." I blurt the word on a shudder as my arms and legs turn into a thousand pinpricks. I even look down, stunned not to find those extremities looking like neon porcupines.

"Huh?" Foley barely pauses his frantic typing. "What is it?"

"I need air." And am reassured he'll understand. He's had similar episodes in front of me before, and I've simply nodded without any more questions. For all the public rhetoric about PTSD, sometimes the best "therapy" is being near someone who gets it.

Or in this case, getting away from them.

The verb fits. As soon as I get downstairs and reach the atrium between the Richards Research building and the Brocade, I force my lungs to grab every oxygen molecule they can and then greedily suck down even more. *Do it, guys. Keep me sane.* Right now, I don't even care how the effort makes my equilibrium swim. For now, I'm just fine with doing the balance backstroke for a bunch of minutes. It's yet another appropriate metaphor, matching the direction I've been propelled over the last two days and nights.

And it all began with an innocent girls' lunch.

Mom's visit to the new house, which entailed her heart-to-heart with Emma—and then my own journey to the dust of the past, in the mud of my soul-changing passion with my amazing woman. Then a bigger mud bath from the past, in several different ways during the Observatory's event. What's the best way to top a key to the city from the mayor himself? Try a massive information bombshell, courtesy of one's own brother.

And father?

Fuck. Me.

I can't believe I'm even considering this possibility. Its very reality. *Is* it reality? What the hell is real anymore? Up or down? Left or right? Friend or enemy?

Family...or betrayer?

Goddamnit.

I have no idea I've spat it aloud until a movement in my periphery prompts me to swivel my sights—and be confronted by a pair of awestruck stares. But there's a new element in the way Fershan Bennett and Wade Tavish gawk at me now, their hero worship mellowed by genuine curiosity. An inquisitiveness for which I find myself oddly thankful...

"Mr. Richards?" Wade queries, shaking ginger curls out of his eyes. "Errmm...Bolt?" he revises, moving close enough to see I'm really in head-to-toe leathers. "We were just taking a break and noticed you over here, and...well, what I mean is... are you all right?"

"What he *means* is"—Fershan throws a fast but frustrated side-eye—"we *know* you are all right, but perhaps...well...do you need any help?"

As he issues that, my phone vibrates. It's a text from Foley.

Gone as far as I can, but some of the
Scorpio's firewalls can't be breached.
Out of ideas. Sorry, dude.

I look up from the screen.

At the two eager faces, still expectant and ready, in front of me.

"Either of you ever seen *The Matrix*?" I realize it's practically a rhetorical question, but better to be safe than sorry.

"Seen it?" Fershan is the first off the block with a reply. "I've *memorized* it."

Wade snorts. "Yeah, whatever. You still don't have the collectible sixth-scale Neo figure with all the guns, a removable cape, and four pairs of interchangeable hands, *still* in the box."

Fershan rolls his eyes. "What is the point of four pairs of hands if you never take it out of the box?"

Same question on *my* mind, though Wade's muttered profanity makes me glad Bennett got it out of the way. Besides, I have more pressing things to ask.

One more pressing thing.

"All right. What if I asked you to finish your break and then meet me in that building"—I nod toward the glass doors into the Richards Research lobby—"instead of that one." Then roll my head the direction of the hotel. "And what if, once you were inside, I offered you a blue pill or a red pill?"

Both their jaws drop open. I hold up a hand, already owning the kick-ass Zen of my inner Morpheus. "Don't answer now—because you need to think about this. There's no action figure that goes with this one. No flashy premiere. No taking off the cosplay when your boots get too tight. This is the red pill for real, gentlemen. If you swallow it, your life—and everything you know about it—is part of a new reality." I harden my stare. "Mine."

For the better part of another minute, I remain that way—until the phone in my hand buzzes again. It's a text. The sender? *Sally.*

Without another word to the pair now standing in the atrium with sweating soda cans in their grips, I pivot and walk back inside, quickly tapping back a message to Foley during the trip.

Hold current position.
Will advise action ASAP.

The lobby of Richards Research is still fairly quiet, even

with the guy at the newsstand puttering around, making it all too easy to hear the footsteps besides my own on the polished marble floors. But the cadence isn't coming from the direction of the atrium. A smile grows on my face as recognition sets in. The noise is emanating from the door of the secret subterranean tunnel between the two buildings.

Resulting in my personal version of a perfect daybreak.

One involving sunshine-colored hair, turquoise-sky eyes, and a smile that could turn even London fog into a Malibu dawn. As she strides closer on wedge heels, now out of her party dress and into capri pants and a pink spring sweater, a good chunk of the darkness in my heart lifts, despite the urgency of the task still at hand. But that's what Emmalina Crist does to my life. With her near, the load is just easier. The path is a little brighter. My world is simply...*better*.

"Hey." Her forehead pinches with concern as she stands on tiptoe to softly kiss me. "Did you get any sleep yet?"

"Did you?" I press on both words, making it clear whose question is more important here. Yeah, I'm pulling rank. And no, her rebellious pout doesn't concern me. Much.

"A little," she finally admits. "But the bed's empty without you."

She strokes her fingertips through my stubble, letting her gaze convey her next question—probably because she already senses how I'll answer. But I still owe her the words, so I draw in a deep breath and get them out.

"Foley's found nothing."

She dips a thoughtful nod. "But that's a good thing, right? If there's nothing there, then there's probably nothing there. Maybe Tyce was just being epic asshole Tyce and taunting us with something he randomly overheard—"

"From where?" I grate. "From who?"

She purses her lips, falling into silence. I let the same cloud engulf me, since there's zero we can do to clear out the fog after Tyce's figurative bomb. I want to believe her newest theory, but how realistic is that? What Tyce told her last night isn't exactly the kind of shit a guy "pops" into a conversation— if that's even what their encounter can be labeled as.

"I want to believe these are seeds I've grown into a tree of crazy by myself, Bunny." I tuck her close, dipping my head to inhale the sweet tropical goodness of her hair. "I really do."

"But?" She offers up the word at which my tone already leads.

"But Foley's search isn't complete." I set her free so as to brace my stance and fold my arms. "He's hit some firewalls."

"That even *he* can't crack?" As she processes that stunner with a whoosh of frustrated breath, the door from the atrium reopens. She pays the sound no mind, continuing to mull over what I've conveyed. "So what do we do now?"

I square my shoulders. Regard her as evenly as I can, even as the two figures rush at us from across the lobby. "What any wise superhero support team would do."

She lifts her head, gaze already narrowed. "Which is...?"

"Add new characters."

"New characters?" Her frown tightens. "Like who?"

"Mr. Richards!" The interruption comes in stereo, precluding Wade and Fershan's final approach. But the airport analogy is appropriate, since they skid in like a pair of planes slamming down the landing gear before crashing into the terminal.

Except that Emma now gapes like a passenger stuck in that terminal.

After bouncing her bugged gaze from me to them and back again, she finally utters, "Are you freaking kidding me?"

Fershan moves in before I can conceive one word of an explanation. "We want the red pill!"

⚡

"This is one freaky-as-hell red pill."

Wade's amendment, tumbling out half an hour later, finally gives Emma a reason to let go of her thunderhead expression—but only as long as it takes for her vindicating "ha!" to pop out. Clearly, there'll be more words from my woman to come about how she feels about the two newest members of Team Bolt, though at this moment those recruits look ready for the challenge Foley's asked of them. Yeah, even after the backstory Sawyer and I just laid on them. And yeah, even after the illegal acts we've asked them to perform because of it. Granted, even if they leave behind enough electronic "fingerprints" for the Scorpios to follow, the IP addresses will lead those bastards back here, not to Wade or Fershan personally—but being the guy who actually pushes the buttons always implies a certain risk. Foley's had a lot of years and a bunch of training to get used to that risk. Tavish and Bennett have been briefed for ten minutes.

Looking at the men's faces brings that certainty head-on—though I still have to zip up my composure to keep from talking them into the fun of this game. The truth is, there isn't a lot of fun. The red pill only looks that way in the movies.

At last, Fershan quietly pushes off his bar stool and turns to take one more chug from the can of energy soda he's asked for as a beverage—and even chuckles at the colorful images on the container that are from some fantasy video game he and Wade have likely beaten a dozen times by now. His action sparks a similar action from Wade, who drains his can and then smashes it into an inch-thick disk.

Together, they walk over to the computer command station at which Foley still sits, look down at him, and intone one word. "*Move.*"

Fershan takes the chair in Foley's stead, while Wade remains standing but hovering. One types as the other clicks. Neither stops muttering, as if they're finishing each other's sentences only to start newer thoughts. It's a fast-moving code with which I'm thoroughly fascinated, but it doesn't seem to jolt Emma or Foley at all.

"I've seen them on their breaks before," Em explains.

"I've seen lots like them on their breaks before," Foley adds.

"And just *how* fast can we get them added to the payroll?" I volley, though am already set for Emma's renewed fume.

"You mean suck them further down the damn rabbit hole?" Her fury is sincere but adorable, enticing me closer until I'm wrapped around her from behind.

"As I recall, you begged to jump down the rabbit hole."

The edge of her jaw clenches beneath my caressing lips. "I'm a grown woman," she defends. "And I'm also in love with the captain of the rabbit hole. Wade and Fershan are—"

"Grown *men.*" Wade doesn't veer his fixation from the images through which Fershan now scrolls on the largest of the four workstation screens. While yanking out a pair of eyeglasses with wide red frames, he states, "We're grown *men*, Emma, who can hear and process every word you're saying, on top of the eight *other* things we're doing at once."

"Including making up our own minds about being on the Team Bolt payroll," Fershan interjects.

"Thumbs up on that from this grown man," Wade mutters.

"My thumbs are occupied at the moment," Fershan comments. "But nonetheless, they are also up and— *Whoa*."

His bellowed exclamation is a team effort, courtesy of Wade lurching forward at the same time. Their excitement spurs the rest of us over, though I'm not sure the radioactive globs in my chest would qualify as "excitement." Not when Wade takes Fershan's place in the seat and starts enhancing the grainy image they've blown up on the main screen. Not when parts of that picture start to look familiar.

Horrifyingly familiar.

Wade clicks and taps and clicks some more, his actions starting to sound like a hunter prepping his rifle in morning mist. The sounds are dull but deafening. Swallowed by silence but enhanced by violence.

And the prey in his crosshairs?

Goddamnit.

"The fuck?" Foley yanks the shock right out of my head with his gritted blurt.

"Oh, my God," Emma mutters, stepping over and pressing against my side. "Am— Am I really seeing this? Is that..."

"Faline." I say it for her because I have to say it for myself too. Because I have to hear it out loud in order to confirm my eyes aren't deceiving me. Because every cell of my blood and every beat of my heart yearns for Sawyer or Emma to turn and tell me I've gone batshit crazy. That it's Beyonce, Oprah, Minnie Mouse, *any* of the Kardashians, the fucking Queen of England—anyone, *anyone* other than *that* bitch posing for *that* picture, laughing in the sun at a picnic table full of people...

With her head nestled against my father's shoulder.

"Who is she?" Fershan queries.

"Besides the goddess of everything gorgeous?" Wade mumbles.

"And a succubus with a chainsaw for a heart?" Foley counters.

Wade groans. "God*damn*it. Real life's supposed to be different than video games."

"This isn't real life, dude." Foley *tsk*s. "Remember?"

Emma pivots forward to get a better look at the screen though drops her hand to keep our fingers entwined. "Who are all these other people? What event is this photo from?"

Wade leans back in the chair. Pushes away from the desk and circles to face her. "Well, that's the interesting twist," he declares.

Fershan nods. "We were trying to jump over Scorpio cartel firewalls, looking for a loophole or a back door. But many times, the best back door is the front door."

"Huh?" Emma frowns.

"They're right." Foley all but growls it. "I've been thinking so hard about all of this, I *over*thought it." The growl finally erupts as he palms the center of his forehead. "The easiest entrance. The softest sites to hit. Social-media pages, photo collection or video scrapbook web pages..."

"Easily located by searching for hashtags with the Scorpios' shell companies," Fershan finishes.

"Only reason this one took so long for us to find was because it was taken three and a half years ago," Wade adds. "It's from a Flickr page. Says it was taken at the Consorcio Sciences board retreat...in Barcelona, Spain."

Emma starts to tremble. The trembles become shivers.

The shivers become sobs.

"*Consorcio.*" Foley sounds like he's ready to hurl. I don't know whether I'm more tempted to join him or Emma in her rising tears. In the end, my rage eclipses both—especially as Wade voices the fact that drives this shocking dagger in deeper.

"Consorcio. That's Spanish for...what? Consortium?"

Foley snarls softly. Emma snuffles harder. And all the glowing crap inside my chest and gut now congeal into a payload of nuclear-grade explosives ready to be cut loose and detonated over one prime target.

The man looking like a goddamned Valentine's Day card with Faline in that picture.

Surrounded by a bunch of people who, like that bitch, are marked with the same scorpion tattoo on their necks.

Who have been working with the Consortium. Who have been financing their "fringe science" experiments. On non-voluntary human beings.

Like me.

"Fuck."

It falls out of me as I wheel away from them all, hands dragging through my hair, dread weighing my steps. Just one word on my lips but representing so many more, all burning and terrible. The nuke in my heart has turned into a vat of lethal, searing liquid.

What was Dad's relationship with Faline? Were they lovers? Just "close chums"? Did he know about the real organization all his fellow "board members" represented? Was Consorcio Sciences the genesis for the Consortium—and how far they chose to take torture in the name of advancing "science"? And did he know *that* too?

And if he did...

"*Fuck.*"

I can barely stand to summon the thought to my brain. To even form the words, though silent, in my psyche.

But I have to.

As much as gouging out one of my own eyes seems like a less painful alternative, this is where the fucking rabbit hole has burrowed to.

If my father knew about the Consortium and their plans, did he betray me into their captivity? Did he offer me for their lunatic experiments?

On the other side of posing the question, I'm confronted by an even more relentless pain.

That of not having an answer.

And the compulsion, a unique torment all on *its* own, of needing to find out.

Only when I'm glaring at the cuts across my fist, and the blood turning purple because of the throbbing blue light beneath it, do I realize I've marched across the room and tried taking out my fury on a framed pop art poster. Not able to meet anyone's gaze, I duck my head, hunch my shoulders, and head for the bathroom to clean up.

As I expect, Foley follows me in.

As I also expect, so does Emma.

After dunking my hand beneath the faucet, I let the mirror convey the violent tempest still ruling my senses. My irises have gone silver, and the white orbs around them have filled with spikes of furious lightning. Neither of them flinches, thank fuck. Emma, with her pumping chest and tear-tracked cheeks, humbles and moves me more than ever. Even now, in the middle of this insanity, my soul connects to hers in a new, raw reality of utter honesty. For my heart to belong any more to her, I'd have to carve the thing out of my chest and lay it in her hands.

Foley, thank fuck, is a lot less emotionally invested. Oh, he's pissed to be sure but is clearly capable of thinking beyond the blast zone of this new revelation. I bore my gaze directly into his, hoping like hell I'm correctly interpreting his scrutiny.

"Hit me with it." I add a determined nod now. "What's your plan?"

For the first time, Emma rips her gaze away from me. "You have a plan?" she demands at him.

Sawyer twists his lips. "I wouldn't call it a *plan*."

I succumb to a grimace. "So you *are* thinking the same thing I am." My voice is dismal. "*Fuck*."

"Which is what?" Emma ping-pongs her stare between the two of us, obviously barraged by the same questions in the wake of that photo—which is corroborated by more shots of Dad and Faline from other events, judging by Wade's and Fershan's outcries from the next room.

Foley jams his hands into his pockets. Squares his shoulders. "In order for you to get those answers about your dad, you've got to get close to your dad."

I coil one hand into a fist against the counter. "And that means getting back on the Virage project."

"And that means cleaning yourself up and issuing a public apology to the city and your family," he confirms.

But simply hearing the words detonates the explosives inside my chest all over again. Having to get on camera and appear contrite is on par with a colonoscopy. The end is worthy; the means is a goddamn mess.

Then I'll just have to focus on the goal. Wiping the slate with the mayor. Smoothing the path back to Dad. Clearing the air with Tyce—and hoping he'll recognize the gesture, despite its impersonal delivery method, to try to reach back out to Emma or me once more.

I snarl again, harder and deeper.

Focus on the goal.

Do what's right.

No matter how hard it sucks.

I lean over the counter, wondering how many punches it would take to break open the marble slab beneath my palms.

"Do it."

I snap my head up at the pair of words that break the silence—coming from the woman who now steps back next to me. Emma palms the side of my face while pressing tight against me. The electric rage in my eyes now reflects in hers, but against her turquoise depths, the light turns into glimmers like a vast fairy tale lake. Because that's what this woman does to my life. In her view, my ugliness is turned to beauty, my darkness becomes light.

"Do it, Reece," she repeats in a whisper. "Do it, and know I'll be at your side through every step of the journey and every second of the storm...no matter what."

For a long moment, all I can do is stare. My mind bursts with amazement; my soul implodes with love. How have I come to deserve this woman? What did I do to earn her belief in me and this insane existence, in which she's ordering me to apologize to the world in order to determine how far the monster factor really runs in my family?

I have to shut my eyes as those questions take a terrifying turn.

When will I have to make an equally tormenting sacrifice for her?

When do I decide that the storm is too dangerous—and it's time to let her go?

I pull her tighter against me, mashing the beats of our hearts against each other, and pray like hell it's the one question I'll never have to answer.

After several long minutes, I reluctantly release her. We leave the bathroom hand in hand. Back out in the office, I scoop up my phone and punch in the autodial for my office at the Brocade. "Joanne," I utter after my assistant gives her cheery greeting. "I need you to call the media reps at Richards corporate. Tell them I need to call an emergency press conference for today at noon Pacific. They'll already know what it's about."

Because the storm's already started.

PULSE

PART 8

CHAPTER ONE

E M M A

"Kneel before Zod, my ass."

The tight grumble, belonging to my sexy-as-hell but secret-as-purgatory fiancé, is practically muted by the chaos of camera shutters and reporters' shouts that accompany his exit from the Hotel Brocade's ballroom. Reece's tone matches his look, as somber as his three-piece gray suit and as stiff as the quart of hair product taming his tumbling chestnut waves.

"Reece! Reece! Just one more question! Just one more, man!" But they're already contradicting themselves, because at least five of them bellow the same damn thing at once, making that five questions and counting. His straight, strong jaw hardens into a rigid line, clarifying he's come to the same conclusion, as he grabs me by one hand and starts tugging me across the foyer—not that the mob lets us get more than three more steps. They're back, forming a human barricade between us and the door Sawyer Foley is holding open, leading to the freight elevator that's waiting and ready to transport us to the ground floor and out of here.

Away, at last, from their gauntlet. And the hundred ways they've made Reece run it for the last damn hour. And now, their blatant desire to double that number in a fraction of the time.

"So why, exactly, was your brother in the Griffith Observatory's ladies room with Emmalina last night? Did he ever *really* tell you?"

"If it was all a big misunderstanding, why did you insist on dragging him out and beating him up anyway?"

"Do you consider yourself mostly a hero, a vigilante, or a terrorist?"

"Did you use the Bolt Jolt to break any of Tyce's bones?"

"...fry any of his nerves?"

"...damage any other key body parts?"

"Why did you wait until now to issue an apology about it?"

"Why were your parents included in the apology too?"

"Have you spoken to your family since last night?"

"What did you do after leaving the gala?"

"Do you and Emma watch late-night TV?"

"Who makes the best Bolt jokes? Kimmel or Fallon?"

"Do you two have snacks in front of the TV?"

"Do you two sleep naked?"

I pull in a long breath in place of dropping my jaw, mostly because I don't know if it'd be to laugh or snarl at the bunch. Every one of these has already been asked and answered— yes, even twelve different versions of the naked activities— by the man at my side, enduring how they pummel him like a criminal less than twenty-four hours after extolling him as LA's guardian angel.

Surprise, surprise—one of the anchors who led the bunch last night shoves to their forefront now, his model-perfect facade from last night replaced by stubble, a wrinkled suit, and an expression aimed at grizzled and tough. Add a fedora, and he'll have the others calling him Perry White in no time. He obviously agrees, clearing his throat in order to bark, "I have it on good authority that the Griffith Observatory is pushing for a lawsuit now. The place is an historic treasure to the city, after all."

"All right," I mutter. "That's it." I stomp forward, narrowing a glare at the pompous douche. "So you're saying that an architectural 'treasure' is more important than a human one? That the hundreds of occasions in which Bolt has laid his life on the line for the betterment of this city, including its Observatory, don't matter?"

"Velvet." Reece's growl, close to my ear, is filled equally with soft pride and commanding caution. "No poking the lions unless they're me."

I step back with pursed lips, visually daring the munchkin to ask his question again, but his retreat only makes way for a curvy brunette who clearly fancies herself as the next Katie Couric. "But what about the reports that your brother, Tyce, was seen after the altercation with bruises so bad, he looked deformed, even burned?" she fires, rendering me without a comeback now—because there's a chance she's right. All too vividly, I recall Tyce's face just before Reece found him in the Observatory's bathroom with me, appearing as if to be pushing himself on me. That hadn't been the case, but Reece had reacted to his first impression, leading to the scene that's become the latest viral video and—obviously—the new object of the media's obsession. But one memory from last night sticks the hardest with me: the bizarre transformation to Tyce's face in those split seconds Reece's rage had fully ramped up. I'd honestly thought I'd been served a spiked drink. "Burned" or "disfigured" were perfect descriptions of that change.

I'm yanked from the memory by the Couric wannabe.

"And is it also true he was admitted to Cedars-Sinai under an alias, to undergo emergency surgical procedures for the damage you inflicted?" she lobs, adding a well-rehearsed stare of "journalistic" intensity.

Reece *tsk*s at her. "Who'd you pay for that little tidbit, Renee? Because I'd be asking for a full refund if I were you."

"So you're denying it?" pipes a guy standing next to her who looks eerily familiar, with the exception of the twirly tipped mustache taking center stage on his face.

"Yes," Reece utters at once.

As he cocks his head, his man bun gives him away. It's the asshat hipster from the press throng that invaded the lobby last year, having switched out his purple-rimmed glasses for the impressive 'stache. "So if we call Cedars now, asking for a 'Richard Dangler,' they'd tell us there's nobody admitted by that name?"

Even with the tension barnacled over every inch of his frame, Reece joins a few of Snidely Whiplash's peers in visibly tamping down a smirk. "Oh, Pete. I'd give Tyce more credit than that, wouldn't you?"

Now the guy looks ready to actually twirl his mustache. "Why, Mr. Richards. That sounds like full-on brotherly love, right there."

"Which shouldn't come as a surprise to you, Pete. Or were you so busy trying to get a lollipop boost on your phone that you missed the full apology I just gave to my brother, my family, the mayor, and the city?"

Pete isn't fazed. "So you're saying that all is well in the land of the Richards empire? That they've already *accepted* your apology?"

And crazily, Snidely himself has just set up Reece for the

sole thing he needs to say the most this morning. "I'm saying they have no reason not to."

In the space of those five seconds, I watch an entire layer of tension leave his body. Doesn't mean the seven beneath it are going anywhere, but it's a better start than I expected. Reece actually smiles at the mob now, beaming the panty-slayer grin that has landed him on the cover of more magazines than I can remember or track, and states, "Now folks, you're *really* going to need to let us go." He releases my hand to tuck me fully against his side, curling a possessive hand around my shoulder. "My girl's stood by me through a lot of hell the last few days, and now I intend to thank her with a bit of pampering."

As if he's Moses and the words are a magical rod, the mass parts down the middle like the Red Sea—including several faces, of both genders, turning into gawking, envious fish as we walk by. I don't waste time stopping to point out they all wanted Reece's head on a platter an hour ago. As life has been teaching me in epic object lessons, the media is a fickle trade wind. Wait five minutes and the direction will favor another direction.

And right now, I'm only focused on one main direction.

The same one Reece reiterates as soon as we reach the portal where Sawyer is standing.

"Get us the fuck out of here, Foley."

Reece's growl doesn't stop Sawyer Foley from chuckling as the three of us hurry down the hotel's service hallway. Despite our near sprint of a pace, I dart a reproving scowl at the guy—though not fast enough for my all-observing man, even in his purposely powered-down state.

"It's all right, Velvet." Reece slides his hand back down, once more fitting it solidly against mine. "If that press conference wasn't one of the shittiest things I've ever had to do, I'd be laughing too."

Sawyer and I trade a fresh glance. In the guy's seafoam-green eyes, I discern the same recognition that's just hit my head and heart. Reece Richards's list of "shittiest things I've ever had to do" is a lot different than anyone else's, with things like "escaping from mad scientists" and "thwarting a bitch from killing his woman in an airplane turbine" topping the bunch. But I also have to remember that Sawyer was at Reece's side for that second adventure and that it wasn't the only occasion the man was *my* man's solid Sundance Kid. In the seven months since Reece first hired him to help out with intel and tracking duties on the Consortium, Sawyer's been a wingman beyond compare.

So I take a deep breath and let the chortle pass—especially when Sawyer follows it up by encouraging, "Well, Zod got his ass handed to him in the end, so buck up, Clark Kent." He reaches over to push Reece's glasses up his nose, earning him an instant slap-down, which results in his snarky sing-song, "Have fun on Krypton."

"Excuse me?" I charge, wheeling on Reece like a lawyer with a murder suspect. "Have fun *where*?"

But my demand is drowned by Sawyer's slam of the lift's roll-top door. While rising, he tacks on a subtle chuckle. Damn if the guy isn't the epitome of *adorkable* right now, still dressed in his suit from last night's event—which looks shockingly great, considering the evening wound up with Reece managing to spatter Tyce's blood everywhere but the historic building's walls. That was a good thing, since that was where fate chose to splatter its writing for us.

We hadn't wasted time reading the message twice. And

got the hell out of there while we could.

But that had only handled the physical shambles of the night. The emotional loose ends are a new tangle—a mess that would make even LA's best shrink ponder early retirement. Setting aside the weirdness of Reece's dad having invited Reece's estranged brothers, Chase and Tyce, as last-minute party guests, we're trying to sort out why Tyce was willing to let Reece think he'd made naughty moves on me, just for the chance to relay a message through me. Then there's the crazier twist: the message contained the words *Alpha Three*, possibly linking Tyce to Reece's imprisonment with the Consortium. And yes, the most bizarre dig for last: we discovered an obscure online image connecting Lawson Richards to the Scorpio crime cartel, who are likely priming the Consortium's pumps from a financial angle.

But now I'm really standing here, just as obsessed with yet another plot twist to all these "fun" events, courtesy of the intimation my fiancé's smirking friend has casually plunked into the conversation. Not that Reece's responding scowl is going to get him an inch of mercy from me.

"Hey." I backhand his shoulder, trying not to linger my touch on the luxurious feel of *his* suit. I swear to God, nobody fills out D&G as perfectly as this man. "Question: me. Answer: you."

He captures my hand, flattens it to his chest, and shoots me a look that infuses me with the scared-meets-aroused mix that only he can bring. My heart gallops faster as he adds a cocked brow and murmurs, "Sorry, lady. All out of answers. Gave all my verifiable statements back in the war zone."

Without a single argument against *that* truth, I have to settle for a resigned fume as we ride the rest of the way down.

But as soon as the elevator bumps at ground level, I take advantage of having to grip his lapel in order to keep upright in my new Balmain boots. With my chest pressed to his, I reinforce the enticement of my pout. "You're seriously not going to fill me in?" Okay, so at this point, I'm not past going for feminine wiles, as well as celebrating what they do to the heat in his gaze and the jerk of his hips. Serves the man right, since I've spent the last hour being dazzled by *him*, marveling at his sorcery over the press corps even after they ambushed us in the foyer. His sincerity and wit—and *that grin*—had every one of them chopped into bite-size pieces all over again, perfect for the palm of his hand.

Which is where I long to be right now, as well.

Resting in the center of his touch.

Moaning from the sizzle of his fingertips.

Bowing to the Zod of his magnificence...

Silver shards ignite in the depths of his eyes, telling me he's read every one of those thoughts straight from my brain. Damn the man. How does he do that? And why do I love *and* hate him for the ability?

"Let's just say we're not really going to Krypton," he finally offers, quirking one side of his mouth.

I answer with my own version of the look as we stride off the lift. "*Very* good news," I murmur, sidling back against him with a sultry upsweep of my gaze. "Because I think there are a couple of pillows in a bed upstairs that miss our heads—and a few other body parts."

He tugs me a little closer, his irises turning the shade of gleaming pewter. "Well..." And just as everything between my thighs starts to pulse because of it... "They'll have to wait."

I almost jerk to a stop—until he pulls me through the

double doors leading to the hotel's VIP porte cochere, where Zalkon, in all his grinning Armenian glory, waits with the back door open to the black BMW L7 Reece prefers for weaving through the crush of LA traffic. In most cases, Reece prefers being the guy behind the wheel himself, but he's obviously, and wisely, determined that being awake for thirty hours straight doesn't make him a responsible driver right now.

I let a wider smile take over my lips before stepping through the doors. "I think they'll be just fine with waiting."

"Meh." Sawyer's snide interjection stops us both beneath the awning, and we turn just in time for his next smirk. "Those pillows won't even know you're gone."

"Huh?" I dart a confused glance between him and Reece, especially when realizing my man takes the pronouncement in complete stride. "Sawyer, what're you..."

But I toss aside the rest of my demand when a new arrival steps onto the gold entry carpet. With fresh curls in her blond waves and an impish glint in her bright-blue gaze, it's clear my sister is in on the guys' shenanigans—whatever they are.

"Yeah, don't worry about the pillows, Em. Chainsaw and I will make sure they don't go lonely."

While watching her step over and shoulder bump Sawyer, I'm not sure whether to join her in the giggle or gulp in abject fear. Her physical security isn't my worry. I've seen Sawyer stand his ground even when Reece goes all glowy-showy meanie on him—but I also know Lydia well enough to detect when she likes a guy and when she *likes* him. I'm getting neither of those impressions now—which means she's way further over the cliff about Sawyer than she's admitted to me. Or likely admitted to *herself*.

"*Chainsaw?*" Reece drawls, meaning I only have to tilt my

head to add my own emphasis. Yep, there are a lot of advantages to having one's man on the same mental wavelength.

"Yeah, well." Sawyer gives a head shrug. "Representin' with the performance review. What can I say?"

'Dia grins. "Emphasis on *performance*."

"Ew." I grimace.

"Jealous, sistah?" She slides over with shoulder bump love for me this time. "Or do you just want to compare notes on grind speed and intensity levels?"

"Okay, you are *done* with the oversharing." I toss her a glare while wrestling my hand free from Reece, joining it to the other in a dual slam over my ears.

"Why, whatever do you mean, baby girl?" she teases back. "You testy because that roomful of reporters wanted to know about your midnight snack choices and what color underwear you sleep in? And what *was* that other one? The real doozy?"

"Stop," I growl.

"Ohhhhh, yeah. Your *safe word*."

"Stooooop."

She stops snickering long enough to sneer, "*Now* you're paid back for spilling about Princess Purple Pants."

"Which means the pillows in the suite had better be in pristine condition when we get back tomorrow."

'Dia widens her shrewd smirk. "Tomorrow, hmmm?" Before I can start to unravel *that* meaning, she waves a hand toward Reece. "Take her away and make sure she's Bolted, Mr. Richards. *A Lot*. She needs it."

Sawyer chuffs. "*He* needs it."

"Amen and a half," Reece murmurs—and while I don't doubt what all their surface meanings imply, I can't escape the instinct that's settled on my senses since the freight elevator ride, rising to my lips as soon as he and I climb into the car.

"Reece." I curl my fingers around his before he's done pulling out the seat belt and securing it into the slot near my hip. "Where *are* we going?"

For a long moment, he's still. I'm certainly not complaining. With his gaze fixed on my hand and his presence leaned over so close, it feels good to rewrap ourselves in a bubble that's all our own, in a stolen drop where only we exist. I almost wince when he pops the seal by lifting his head, despite keeping his face close enough to nearly go nose-to-nose.

"Trust me?"

His rasp curls through me with sweet roughness. The vocal brown sugar finally coats every inch of me, resulting in my slow, full smile. Once upon a time—okay, only six months ago, but it feels like a lifetime—I'd issued the same words to him, tugging him into a golf course sand trap so we could escape the crowds and cameras in another magical bubble of our own creation. And damn, had that been a really incredible bubble...

So maybe I'll let the froth gods lead yet again...

"Yes." I affirm it to him by stroking my hand up and over his arm until wrapping my fingers across the broad plateau of his shoulder. I slide my other hand around his opposite triceps, stopping there for two reasons. One, getting to feel the coil and release of his muscles is a sublime sorcery of its own. Two, if I copy the grip of my other hand, the temptation will be too great to keep going. To circle my arms all the way around his neck. To use that grip and welcome him all the way atop me, then to position him between my open legs, and...

God.

So much for resisting temptation. My imagination's

already gone there and then some. Will I *ever* be able to be near him and not fantasize about fucking his gorgeous guts out? And do I ever really want to know that answer?

"Yes." I underlined it by dragging my lips from his chin to his Adam's apple. "I trust you." Then speaking that oath against the corded ridge in his neck, savoring how it bobs beneath my nipping lips and tongue.

After he follows the gulp with a dark panther's rumble, he dips his mouth into my hair. Another growl later, he dictates, "Say it again."

His tone, quiet yet commanding, curls into me at once. Reaches to a part of me that opens for him alone. That succumbs solely to him. From the depths of that spiritual space, I utter, "I trust you, Reece. Completely. With my own life, if that's what you need."

"Damn." His hot breath flows through my hair. "How I love those words on your lips, Miss Emmalina Crist."

I suckle higher up his neck. "How I love *you*, Mr. Reece Richards."

No more growls from him now. Instead, he vibrates with a fierce, feral groan as he twists his head in and down, clearly bound for one destination. When he reaches my mouth, he captures my lips with a single, brutal sweep. I'm conquered and subjugated and opened, left with no choice but to spread for his thorough, perfect invasion. For that minute and at least the twenty after that, I'm lost to his devouring heat, his passionate mastery, his thorough desire, his urgent caresses—until the car rolls to a stop once more.

And the divider to the front seat slides down.

Reece chuckles as I push him away, catching a fast glimpse in the descending glass of my kiss-stung lips, mussed hair, and wide eyes. In short, I look exactly like a girl caught sucking face with her boyfriend in the back seat of a limo.

As we pull up to the curb in front of the VIP terminal at LAX.

"Oh, my God," I mumble.

"You rang?"

I shove him harder as he caps the crack with an extended snicker. "Don't push it, buddy." I fumble for a frown, but the task is impossible in the wake of my mounting excitement—and damn it, how the man can already feel it. How he's probably predicted that as soon as I caught sight of the tarmac and inhaled a good long breath of my insatiable wanderlust, I'd be up for any adventure he has in mind for us today. And after all the wrenching twists of our *yester*day, maybe this is exactly what we need.

The door swings open, revealing Z's dark fingers on the handle of my rolling overnight bag. After a second, his cheesy grin pops into view as well. "Ready to go, Jackie O?" he quips while Reece completes the trip around to this side of the car.

I refine my responding giggle, paying homage to the icon Z has just invoked. "Why yahss, my dee-ah friend," I answer, butchering the elegant accent but at least getting things right with how I slide on my sunglasses. "Let us go and go propahly."

The snorts we share are abbreviated as Reece helps me out of the car with princely regality. At once, Z is all professionalism again too. Not that the guy is ever a slovenly jerk, but there's something nice about having him around as a fellow LA native to help with funny things like making sense of a New York country club accent.

"The flight is running on time, sir," he ensures Reece. "So you'll have an hour to relax here before they drive you across to the tarmac."

"Thanks, Z." He pivots to me and kisses my knuckles, a chunk of his dark hair finally breaking free from the pomade and tumbling into his eyes. "I couldn't book us a private charter on such short notice," he murmurs with apology in his voice. "So we'll have to settle for first class."

I'm not sure whether to swoon or laugh again, so I try to funnel both into the smile I beam up at him before popping onto my tiptoes, circling my arms around his neck, and laying one hell of a lingering kiss on his full, strong lips. "I think I can deal with first class."

Only once we've been driven out to and boarded the plane—a giant jet plastered with the familiar logo of a larger world airline brand—does my comprehension get blown to pieces.

In the middle of the aisle, I whirl back toward Reece and blurt slowly, "First...class."

"Yyyessss..." His reply is drawn out with curiosity. He glances from bulkhead to bulkhead. "Are you disappointed?"

"Disappointed?" My stare is bugged out.

"What's wrong?" His is narrow and dark as asphalt.

"This is *first class*." I spin around.

"I think we've established that part, baby."

"This is *all* of first class."

He tilts his head. More hair gets loose, colliding with his jaw. "So...you're not disappointed?"

"Oh, my God." I smack a palm into my face, remove it, and flip it around to tap at his. "I'm *not* disappointed." Then I grab him by the neck and slobber a bunch of kisses across my impact area. "I'm just..."

The worshipful wonder in his eyes contrasting with the masculinity of his stubble and ruggedness of his cheeks sucks the words out of my throat. Probably a good thing, since a flight attendant looking like a hummingbird with feet appears, giving us a warm but impatient smile.

"Monsieur Richards, Mademoiselle Crist. *Bonjour* and welcome to the flight. My name is Cosette, and I will be your in-flight assistant to Paris today. Can we ask you to take a seat, *s'il vous plaît*? Truly, *any* seat is fine."

And *that's* the moment my words are truly, officially, gone.

REECE

"Velvet?"

It's the third time I've repeated her name, and we've only just turned onto the runway to get airborne. Now I'm vacillating between pressing her for a fourth time or just demanding that the plane be turned around so I can seek some medical attention for her.

"*Emma*. Talk to me, damn it."

More dumbfounded blinks from her side of the second-row seats we've finally decided to occupy. But nothing else. Not a sound. Not a gasp.

"All right, that's it. Cosette?"

"*Oui*, monsieur?" The diminutive blonde appears like our own genie in a flying bottle.

"Can you please inform the pilot that we need—"

"A couple of glasses of champagne." Emma's interruption is like a game show contestant getting an answer in under the buzzer. She underlines the comparison by reaching her arm across me to pound a hand on the elbow rest. All she needs now is a TV studio buzzer. "Yes. Champagne," she repeats. "If you please, Cosette."

"But of course." The attendant beams. "*Un moment.*"

As Cosette walks away toward the galley, I take instant notice of the slender arm still draped over my midsection. Now *here's* an opportunity I'm not going to fuck around with...

And at once, prove as much to the creature to whom the gorgeous appendage belongs. With a wolfish hum, I trail my fingertips up and down the area between her wrist and elbow, repeating the circuit several times over. At the same time, I allow myself a long, rapt stare at the fine blond hairs along her skin, turned into white gold in the light from the overhead lamps. So many times, touching her is like unwrapping a piece of gold filigree. I'm afraid to open it but unable to stop myself.

Finally I venture, "Well."

Emma moves her hand up to the middle of my chest. Flows her fingers down the back seam of my tie. "Well."

I feel my smile warm, though I keep my voice formal. "Miss Crist."

"Mr. Richards." An equally professional line, though her tug at my tie turns playful.

"Does this mean you're okay with my version of Krypton?"

Her face is overcome by a wave of emotion I'm not sure how to interpret. It seems part confusion, part adoration, but completely Emma. I focus on the latter as she pulls her thoughts together and declares, "I'm not sure if 'okay' scrapes the surface of my reaction. But hold on, Sparky." She turns her hand over, thumping the middle of my chest. "Before you turn that into scissors and run with it, let me clarify. That's a *good* okay, even if I'm a little weirded out by it."

"Weirded out?" I let my scowl add the *why?* onto it.

"Because I've always known you had a damn good strategic mind." She shakes her head and furrows her brow as if being asked to spell "appoggiatura" in the final round of a spelling bee. "I just didn't know *how* good."

"Thanks." I don't try to put away the frown yet. "I...think."

"I mean, I see it all now," she goes on. "The urgency of the press conference, though purposely not inviting any of your family—because now it's *their* turn to respond to *you*. And if they're going to respond, why not make it in the city where you need to reestablish that common ground with them? Now, you're the one setting the stage—and controlling the curtain, the lights, and the sound at the same time."

I press a hand atop hers and use my other one to cup the side of her face. Her incredible aqua eyes are sparkling. "And the woman calls *me* brilliant," I utter before leaning over to take her lips, using the kiss to convey my awestruck tenderness.

When we drag apart, her gaze is glimmering with deeper shades of blue. Her soft smile adds new angles to her stunning beauty. "I'm just grateful to be along for the adventure."

"To a point," I clarify. "Because adventures are for fiction, baby—and when this one turns into danger, you can't just be along for the ride." I push my forehead against hers. "If anything ever happened to you because of some bullshit Bolt has to walk into..."

"I know." She slides her hand up to my neck. Squeezes hard at my nape. "*I know*, mister. And I promise I won't be stupid about things."

I pull away. Only a little. "Says the girl who just ordered champagne when we've got all of first class to ourselves?"

"What's *that* supposed to mean?"

I'm waylaid from answering her by Cosette's return with our flutes of French bubbly. "*Merci*," I murmur, smiling when Emma says the same with an impressive accent.

"*De rien*," the attendant replies. "I must prepare for the takeoff now, but is there anything I can get for you once we are airborne?"

Emma's features brighten. "Do you have any macarons?" she queries. To Cosette's soft oui, she responds, "And how much extra do you charge for pink ones?"

I can't help my chest-deep laughter. Cosette, with bewilderment stamped across her face, flings a stare between us as if Emma just asked what the airline charges for toilet paper. Deciding to put both women out of their distress, I offer, "My love, they'll get you pink macarons even if they have to bake them exclusively for you. And they're *not* extra."

"But of course." Cosette's concurrence comes along with her pleased smile. Nothing makes the French more amenable than the promise of witnessing true love at work, whether it's theirs to experience or not. Sometimes I wish the whole world were more like France.

For now, I'm dedicated to enjoying my own version of those rose-colored glasses instead of dancing at the end of everyone else's marionette strings. My strings are my own again, and for the moment, I want them occupied with a very short list of tasks.

Enjoying this champagne.

Reveling in having my woman to myself.

Hoarding her goddess perfection of a face. Her blinding glory of a smile. Her temptress's perfection of a body...

And maybe, if the champagne does its job well enough, doing a little more than just gazing.

⚡

It's been an hour, but now that the possibility has entered my head, every electron in the rest of my system won't let it go.

We're above the clouds now, with a second round of champagne *and* macarons before us, officially laughing about shit that has nothing to do with the world that's now tens of thousands of feet below us. On the in-flight entertainment system, she's managed to find episodes of a show called *Reign*, which is supposedly about Mary Queen of Scots, though beyond the names of the key players and the basic events, I'm having trouble believing anything I see. Then again, I'm a guy once known to the world as the Heir with the Hair who still hasn't fully explained to the masses why my fingers sometimes turn into lightsabers and my "hangover eyes" resemble Miami hurricane skies.

"Okay, you have to watch this part." She points at the screen, half-filled glass in one hand and a macaron with a bite mark in the other.

"Watching." And completely lying. Her profile is ten times better than the girl on the screen, who's wearing what looks like a complicated prom dress, resulting in my happiness that Emma's in nothing but an A-line skirt and matching sweater set. And her legs... Holy *shit*, her legs. They're bare and sheathed to the knee in high-heeled boots, which of course means I've had nonstop thoughts of jumping her since the second I saw them this morning...

This morning.

A lifetime ago.

A world away.

Thank fuck.

"You are *not* watching." She swipes at my jaw, trying to redirect my gaze. "And it's getting to the good part."

I chuckle and swing my head back down. Before she can react, I capture one of her fingers between my teeth and get in a teasing bite. "But what if I'm already at the good part?"

No. Better than good. Watching her is more exhilarating than the surge of the plane as the pilot guns the engines. More uplifting than our new rise in elevation. And much, *much* more amazing than visiting any of the world's wonders. This woman is my personal Taj Mahal, Machu Picchu, and El Caracol. She's my Victoria Falls, Mount Everest, and Northern Lights. She's a revelation at every second, an astonishment with every new glance. And yes, she's all that even when nibbling on a little pink cookie.

Especially then.

Fuck, how she enchants me.

Entrances me.

Makes me so damn hungry for all kinds of sweet pink things...

"Ohhhhh!" Her sigh modulates between octaves, adding to the perfection of my view because of the pink crumbs along her lips' surfaces. "Look. Oh, my God. Bas loves her *so much.* Look, Reece!"

"I am."

"You're *not.*" Finally, she averts her gaze from the screen to me—and that's it. The cocoon that's all *us* is all *ours* again. Her adorable little gulp is more than enough confirmation for me. It's followed by the hooded meaning beneath her gaze, now dripping down to take in my lips.

Almost unconsciously, she finally licks the pink crumbs free from the succulent curves of her mouth.

I growl low.

She releases a shallow breath. "Reece?"

"Hmmm?"

"You're...ummm..."

"What?" I press a thousand sensual "crumbs" of my own into the tone—mixing in a gaze through which I flow every drop of my complete carnal focus.

"You're letting me hog the macarons." As soon as it's emitted, she returns to cleaning up the cookie mess with her tongue.

I turn my hum into a low growl while roaming my stare across her face. Let her shiver a little beneath my adoring scrutiny, lingering on every graceful angle and satin-soft curve, before centering my attention once more on the sweet dessert of her lips. "That I am."

Without veering my attention, I join my fingers with hers on the crescent of cookie she's still holding. I rearrange it so one end points to her and the other to me. I lift the cookie, prodding it at her lips so she opens for a bite—at the same time I lean over, biting into my half.

At once, our mouths meet. Lips and sugar and need are a warm, soft, enticing mix between us, mashing as we chew and then swallow, not waiting to devour each other as soon as the food is gone. *Jesus,* she tastes amazing—and it doesn't have a damn thing to do with the cookie. It's her, all woman and passion and freedom. It's the person she turns me into—a man helplessly, giddily in love for the first time in my life.

And the last.

There will never be another woman like this for me. She's it—for always. For forever.

With that vow my new sugar rush, I lap her up without

restraint or reserve. I suck all the remains of the frosting still on her tongue and then move outward to keep her chin encased in my grip as I lick the fresh array of sugary crumbs away from her parted, sighing lips.

When I finally pull back, it's only by an inch. "Delicious," I grate, celebrating how her eyelashes stutter along her cheeks and her breaths pump in aroused rhythms in her chest.

"Yesssss." As she whispers back, she pulls my hair with one hand and the knot of my tie with the other.

Letting her keep those possessive holds, I tell her softly, "I want to watch you enjoy your dessert more, Velvet. In better ways..."

As the sibilance of my offer winds through the air between us, Emma's gaze jerks back open. She crisscrosses the look over my face, emitting another gasp when I've apparently answered her wordless wondering.

"Now?" she rasps. "*Here?*"

I make her gape flare wider as I twitch my lips like the Big Bad Wolf. "Well, now that you mention it..."

"*Reece.*"

"Hmmm?"

"Oh, dear God."

Her words are tiny squeaks as I push Cosette's call button. With her predictable agility, the attendant appears. The attentive service isn't a shock, since I've likely given Cosette the easiest money she's ever made over the Atlantic Ocean. Inside the next hour, I'm going to make that paycheck even easier.

"Yes, monsieur?" she murmurs.

"Mademoiselle Crist and I have some complicated contracts to go over in the next hour. We'd prefer to be completely undisturbed."

"Oh, my God." It's just a whisper from Emma now.

"Of course, monsieur." If Cosette has put together an inkling of what I'm about, nothing about her demeanor betrays it. But this is definitely not the first time she's seen a couple sprint for the mile-high club in her first-class cabin.

Though never again will she witness it done by a couple deeper in love.

That, I completely promise.

CHAPTER TWO

EMMA

"Holy shit."

At least it's not *oh, my God* again—not that it means anything different. Not that I'm taking in Reece's face, so beautiful that even Cosette does a double-take at him before she disappears, as if she can hardly believe the hot, heavy need across his stark features is just for me.

Hell. I can hardly believe it myself—even while beaming a bashful grin and demure blush up at her, communicating two messages at the same time. *Yeah, he really means all of that* and *yeah, he's really all mine, so don't even think about secretly passing your digits, lady.*

Reece, catching the tail end of my move, kicks up a smirk. So the alpha likes his bunny morphing into she-wolf mode, hmmm?

But before I can redress him about any further lupine grandeur, he's already surging over and damn near atop me. Pushing in so that he's fully kissing me. Plunging down to consume me, tongue and lips mashing and claiming me, until all I can taste is him again. Every breath I take is filled with his smoke and spice masculinity. Every thought I can generate is dominated by his energy, his force, his passion...his drive, his desire, his near-violent need...

So good.

Dear God, it's always *so* damn good with him.

And we're only getting started...

And just like that, I couldn't care less if we were in a puddle jumper over the Amazon forest. But we're not, thank God, and Reece is shoving the armrest back between our seats and sliding closer until he's angled all the way over me, raking his hand up beneath my skirt, seeking my throbbing, excited core. I moan as he finds me, sending the sound into his mouth as he rubs his powerful thumb across the triangle of my panties, at once taking me to a realm that feels like we've catapulted out of the plane and into the clouds.

Shit, shit, shit!

He doesn't relent, even now, and I gnash my teeth into my lower lip to abstain from crying out as he rolls my clit beneath his thumb until I'm trembling and undulating underneath him. "Ohhhhh!"

"Yeah," he snarls, his primal rumble vibrating against the base of my neck. "Yeah, sweetheart. That's it. *Exactly.*"

My lips fall open, though my teeth are locked and my breaths are brutal rasps. I dig my fingers into his flexing biceps and meet his silver-fire gaze with what must be a conflagration in my own.

"I'm close." Holy *hell*, I can hardly believe the revelation is here already. "I'm so close."

But I instantly regret my loose lips—as soon as the formidable hills of his take on the angles of wolfish cliffs.

"Oh, Bunny," he snarls softly. "You're just getting started."

Shit, shit, triple *shit.*

Sure enough, as I'm on the brink of crashing into my cataclysm, he backs off on the heavenly massage at my core.

As he pulls away more, he hooks a couple of fingers around my panties, gliding them all the way down my legs and over my boots. With the garment free from my body, he raises the bunch of satin to his face. As he breathes in, his eyes grow heavy. As I gawk at him, mine do too.

"Fuck." The word is drenched in so much of his lust that it comes out more like a German version. *Fukkkhhh.* "Perfect, Velvet." He pries his gaze open to watch my reaction, savoring my whole face. "You're fucking perfect."

"Merci." I attempt to be coquettish, but the intent of his stare, now darkened to the shade of shadows, sends me into silence again. Heart-halting, breath-stealing silence.

He angles himself deeper toward me again. In a tone originating from the center of his chest, he corrects, "Merci... Mr. Richards."

Dutifully, almost as if a shy wallflower has taken over my being, I whisper, "Merci, Mr. Richards."

His growl, curling from the same place at his center, stirs inexplicable sensations through more than just my shivering pussy. I'm affected so much deeper, awash in emotion and warmth despite him borrowing a page from some *Doc Savage* novel. Perhaps, I even feel this way *because* of that. I'm admired. Coveted. *Craved...*

"Very nice." He intensifies the praise by inhaling the crotch of my panties again. The sight of the pale-pink fabric against his burnished, taut skin is so hot, I gush from the inside out again. Every inch of my sex is soaked. Both of my breasts are hard and pointed. All my extremities are tingling and alive. And why that torment is worsened as I watch him reach for the plate of my uneaten macarons, I have no damn idea...

Until he growls at me again.

"Say it again, just like that, and you can have more dessert."

Air stutters in and out of my chest. Without even stopping to think, I rush out, "*Merci*, Mr. Richards."

His eyes turn the color of diamonds.

"Good girl."

My sex turns the texture of magma.

"Now...dessert."

And heats up, even as he divides the halves of his murmur by lifting the hem of my skirt.

My breath hitches with harder force. I'm bare and exposed, my skirt in puddles at the outsides of my thighs, yet all I think or care about is what the sight of my exposed crotch does to the depths of his gaze. I feel like that necklace the old lady tossed overboard at the end of *Titanic*, with my modern-day Moses who's parted the sea to find me.

"Reece." Still, a girl's got to make at least a bid for modesty, right? "Is this...I mean we're..."

"Ssshhh." He imposes it while taking the cookie in his fingers—and sliding it directly through the wettest part of my panties. "And enjoy your dessert."

"But—*ohhhh*." If Cosette's listening now, I barely care. He lowers the cookie now, teasing its sugary curve against the lips of my entrance before rolling the thing up and over my slick folds.

"Ohhhh...*gaaahhh*..."

"Sssshhh." His order is just that now—a full, guttural mandate—as he continues to work the cookie through my pulsing petals. "No words, my Emmalina. Just enjoy. And let me watch it all. Let me *see* it all."

We both start breathing hard. Then harder. With every new inhalation, I can smell the tang of my arousal with the warmth of fresh sugar. I clench my teeth, holding back moan after moan, but as soon as Reece slides the treat over my clit, the silence turns into anguish.

"Good girl," he praises.

I nod frantically, though surrender to a long hiss. In desperation, I clamp a hand around the armrest he hasn't lifted yet. With my other hand, I secure purchase around his neck, quivering in anticipation of how he'll redefine "dessert" next.

Our stares lock and tangle. The center of his eyes are liquid steel, reflecting the brilliant blue at the tips of the two fingers he extends, letting me watch as he grazes the edge of the cookie, softening the creamy middle into an erotic pink puddle.

"Spread for me." His voice, now rough and aroused, is a direct contrast to the cream he drips over me, coating my intimate flesh with liquid sugar. Every squeeze he gives the macaron gushes more of the frosting over me. It's sticky and hot and decadent and nasty, equating to what is undoubtedly the wildest sexual adventure of my life. For him. *Because* of him.

God, how I love him.

He doesn't stop. The glaze teases at every sensitive inch of me. Some of it even escapes and trickles between my legs, sliding sugary drops across the quivering rim of my back hole.

"Holy...*shit*."

"No, baby." He pries my fingers off the handrest, moving them down to the candied eddies between my thighs. "Just dessert." He rolls my fingers over everything, stopping only when I cry out again. Dear *God*, that icing feels incredible on my cookie. "Make it the best one I've ever had."

If his words don't get across his full command, the focus

of his gaze does. He's riveted on my pussy, and all the swirls of my fingers through it, during every second he takes to unhook and unzip his placket. After shifting around so both his hips are free, he jerks down the wool far enough that his cock can spring free, long and erect and offering beautiful beads of white frosting in his own right. Now, I'm just as transfixed with the sight of him. I lick my lips, yearning to feel his silken arousal on the tip of my tongue...

And for once, I'm damn glad the man can read my mind.

With an efficient swipe at the tip of his purple bulb—I swear, the man's fingers atop his penis should be a vision for one of those office motivational posters—he's got a sizable jewel of his precome captured.

Without hesitation, he extends the digit to me.

Without shame, I bite my lip as that hot bead approaches.

Without another thought, I open my mouth and extend my tongue.

Just an inch out, Reece holds his hand still. A rogue's chuckle escapes him in answer to my needy growl. "You want this?" he taunts.

"Yesssss." My hiss is threaded half with lust and half with frustration. Damn the man when he wants play time!

But there are shadows in his gaze, *lots* of them, that don't play at all. That darkness informs the tone of his reply. "Then say that you do." Once more a growl that's all command—to which I'm all too happy to be his wanton, compliant slave.

"I...I want it." I huff when confronted by his disapproving scowl. "I want it, *sir.*"

More dark nuances to his gaze. "Give me all the words, Velvet."

I give him a rougher sigh. Parts of me declare open war

on each other. I'm not the dungeon dolly type and he knows it, but sections of my heart and soul adore his authoritative side, especially tonight. After all the insane, incredible, nearly unbelievable events that have led us to this moment. Since October, so many people have barged in on my life to take control of it—the thugs in the metro station, Angelique La Salle in her bad girl bitch phase, and just about every member of the entertainment press corps. All of it has led to a different Emma Crist, one not so willing to hand over control, even when the situation calls for it. I'm grateful that most people in my immediate world—the management team at Richards Reaches Out, my sister, my friends—not only see it but understand it. But that still doesn't make it okay or even healthy.

But right here, right now, it feels healthy.

It feels right.

It feels natural and real and perfectly, wonderfully good.

"I...I want your come." With a hasty smirk, I add, "On my tongue. In my mouth."

Reece's features harden. His beautiful lips part. But he doesn't lower his finger. "Tasting me?"

"Yes. *Yes*, sir. Tasting you."

"Sucking all of me in?"

"Sucking all of you in."

A ruthless grunt unfurls from him. Angels singing couldn't improve the sound. At the same time, another milky pearl appears in the slit atop his cock. I lick my lips while watching him wick it off. The man's penis is such a work of art, I'm shocked they're not selling replicas of it next to space blankets and Bolt blue nail polish in the airline's sky market magazine.

"Then take it."

And finally, *finally*, he's slipping that finger past my lips, wiping the silky essence along the length of my tongue...

"And take me."

He thrusts his perfect cock through the sugar and cream coating my pussy, penetrating all the way into my body.

"Mmmmmm..." My moan is long and anguished and pleasured and stunned. Another spills out right after it as Reece pulls out nearly all the way, rolling just his cockhead in the mix of frosting and juices near my entrance, until pushing all the way back. The air between us fills with an erotic slick of sounds as he refills the emptiness in my core again and again. I close my eyes and drown in the wonder of his breaths, the rhythm of his passion, the very beats of his heart. I'm lost in him. In us. In the charge that binds us beyond electricity and sexuality. It's the fusion of our souls. The perfection of our love.

After plunking the used macaron back to the tray, he twists back around to position himself between my legs. As my gaze stays fixed on him, he hooks two fingers from his free hand into my mouth.

Oh...*wow*.

"Spread wider for me." Though his voice is a sensual command, his face is a visage of stark lust. What he's ordering me to do for him with my body, he's giving back to me a hundredfold with his undaunted desire. "Take me deeper, Emma. In your creamy cunt. In your gorgeous mouth." He fucks into both orifices more forcefully, and my sex shudders as my throat gags. "God*damn*." The ferocity on his face is blurry now as my eyes water. "You like deep throating me, don't you, beautiful?"

"Mmmmmm." I try communicating the feelings with my tone, but the groan isn't doing much good. I hope he can see the real feedback in my eyes, with the tears running from the corners as he adds yet another finger from each hand, shoving them even deeper as his cock pulses and expands inside me. With the angle of our bodies in the seats, his abdomen strokes my most sensitive nub with each lunge too. I'm close to imploding, and I try telling him so with frantic licks of my tongue between his fingers.

"*No.*" He emphasizes by jabbing his thumbs into the hollow beneath my chin. "No playing with my fingers when they fuck you. Take them in your mouth like your pussy takes my dick. Damn. *Damn.* Yes, Emma. Fuck, *yes!*" He jams his fingers harder, likely cutting himself on my lower teeth as he stretches my lips, ramming into my mouth. "So pretty, letting me invade you everywhere. Letting me fill you up..."

I respond with sounds but am past making sense of them. They're primal whimpers and harsh little chokes, the verbalizations of a woman gone to another plane...of surrender, of sensuality, of utter abandon and perfect affirmation. I'm so gone. So lost.

And now so consumed, as I'm gripped with total, carnal, white-hot ecstasy.

"*Ooonnngggg!*" I let my moan take over as the first zap of my orgasm hits, with my mouth clamping over his fingers as my pussy milks every lurching inch of his stalk. He's right. I *am* filled. With his exquisite, kinglike fingers. With his long scepter of a cock. With his demanding dictator's orders, still pushing into my ear as he charges toward his own awesome completion.

"Stay here. Right here, Emma. Jesus *God*, your cunt. And your mouth. They're mine. All mine." He plunges all six of his fingers deeper inside me, fucking my mouth at the same cadence his cock takes my tunnel. His movements get harder, faster, more demanding. I moan, feeling the fuse burning closer to the dynamite of his control.

"Close, baby," he rasps, his lips hot and harsh against my ear. "I'm so close. I'm going to come inside your tight channel, and you're going to take it."

Yes. Yes. Yes!

And suddenly, he's flooding my womb with his essence. Filling me up with his passion. And yanking everything free from my mouth to replace it with his tongue. As he trades the lunges of his fingers with the stabs and slides of his mouth, I finally cut loose with a full scream into him, hitting my second orgasm as strongly as my first.

His electric semen soaks me, taking hold of every erotic particle of me from the inside out. I'm fire and fury. Light and glory. A thousand stars of ultimate surrender, giving him everything I've ever been and am, taking him deeper and farther and higher and hotter than I ever have before. On the outside, we may be in a tin can flying through the sky, but on the inside, I *am* the sky, spreading out and around and against the perfect billowing gray thunder of him...and the blinding consummation of his silver lightning.

We're locked against each other like that for long minutes. Hours? I'm beyond caring—and *far* beyond thinking. And why start now on that one? If logic was really a requirement for being with this man, my application would've been rejected a long time ago. Sometimes, even now, it's a struggle to wrap my mind around how we're here...how *I'm* here, wrapped in the glory of him. Loving the whole of him. A part of his incredible world.

And sometimes, when he cants his head and wallops me with this exact gaze, feeling like his whole world.

Gulp. Big-time.

Which, of course, he notices at once. "Hey. What is it?" And demands with just as much a take-no-prisoners growl in his voice. As if I'd even think about turning him down anyway. As if I'd want to. Sometimes the only way to survive lightning isn't to hide from it. The lightning himself has taught me that in the easiest *and* hardest ways.

"This," I murmur at last. "Us." I let him see all the creases that creep across my brow. "Sometimes it just feels like..."

"A lot." He brushes his lips from one end of those furrows to the other. "I know. *I know*. Me too, baby."

I nod but still push out a soft huff. "I...I think you're trying to. But do you? And *don't* start with the chest thumping, Kong. I just mean..."

"What?"

"You *are* chest thumping."

"You see my hands anywhere near my fucking chest?"

Deep breath in and then out—serving as a reminder of how deep his sex is still embedded in mine. "Maybe we need to continue this without being glued together with macaron cream."

With a roll of his eyes, he separates himself from me. With gentle swipes of the cloth napkins that accompanied the cookies, we clean ourselves up as best as possible. As I scooch back into my panties and straighten my skirt, he takes care of dumping the excess cookie mess at the galley.

By the time he returns, I've got my skirt sorted out and tidied my hair a little, securing it into a bun at my nape. With at least an outward appearance of professionalism, I find the subject at hand a little easier to approach—despite him continuing his Kong-worthy glower.

Another full inhalation as I face him, folding one of his hands between both of mine. "Let's just look at the situation with open eyes, okay?" When I get his tight but acquiescing nod, I go on. "How many visits to Paris will this be for you?"

Beneath my touch, his hand stiffens. His whole stature follows. "I don't see how this—"

"How many times?" I insist.

His shoulders jerk, edging at a shrug. "I...don't know. A dozen, I guess."

"And with just as many women, right?"

"*Emmalina.*"

"I'm not trying to rub your face in it. I'm just stating facts for what they are. You're three years older than me but have seen thirty times as much of life."

His whole body turns the texture of an I-beam. "Because I've gotten on some planes and gone places?"

"That's part of it, yeah."

"So, essentially, my giant rubber band ball has more layers on it than yours." He arches a brow, though his gaze is still nothing but steel and stone, so I still can't tell if the line is an open attempt at levity or not. "Is that it?"

"To be blunt?" I volley. "Yeah. And like I said before, it's not a sulk or a complaint. Your life has been what it is, and mine—"

My glib line is decimated into a conflicted groan from the moment he crashes his mouth on mine and then breaches me with his tongue. His possession is brutal and angry and invasive, and damn it, I love every moment—to the point that by the end, I've released his hand to grab on to his forearms, then his elbows, and then his massive shoulders. As he stays poised, persisting with the lock of his stare from less than an inch away, I remain a panting, needy mess.

At last, he yanks at my waist—not to pull me closer but as some kind of reprimand. "You don't get it, do you?" he rasps.

"Get wh-what?"

"You snapped the rubber bands, Emmalina." His grip turns painful. His eyes become the texture of thunderheads. He dips back in to bite-kiss me. "Every single one of them." As he starts rubbing his hands up my sides, over my hips and waist, he professes, "You disintegrated them all. Turned me into a pile of rubber shards. Something new. A person I've never been, trying to reformulate into a man who can be worthy of you. Who can know you and meet you on the same level to which you've elevated me."

With his hands sprawled over the sides of my rib cage, he aligns his gaze to mine. Our noses collide and our heartbeats thud against each other. "My angle's the same as it ever was, woman. You're not just my *more*. You're my *life*. You're my *new*. And that counts for everything, damn it. Every day, in every way. From waking up with you to kissing you good night in my arms...life isn't just something I get through anymore. It's something to be lived, to be fought for, to be strived for in all its best ways."

As he grips me with more insistence, I close my hands in from his shoulders, grabbing hold of the thick, messy, dark-brown strands that play at the edges of his collar. "And you're succeeding," I tell him. "You're giving life your best, and it shows. And I feel it."

A substantial breath moves through him. "If you do, then you already know, deep in your heart...you're all my rubber bands, Emma. The rest are nothing but shreds at my feet—and now I'm laying them at yours." His face is steel and solidity; his energy is commitment and intensity. "You're my everything, Velvet. You're my love."

I let him kiss me again. No. He takes over me. Rakes his marauding tongue and hot lips through me and across me until every breath I take is full of him, smoke and steel and strength, a consummation as searing and meaningful as what he's just done to my body.

And I'm toast.

Burned toast.

Charred beyond viability and blackened to the point where even butter isn't going to work on livening me up. I'm probably a damn good core for a few rubber bands right now, but I can barely comprehend adding those to my charcoal brick of a psyche.

And it doesn't matter.

Because joy is a long-burning heat.

And this joy is the only force in the world I want or need right now.

Here, in the clouds, it's the sky in which I choose to fly. The firmament that welcomes me into one of the deepest sleeps I'll ever enjoy.

Because why think of dreaming when a girl is already living in a dream? Why fight the call of slumber when what's waiting on the other side is just as perfect? Why be afraid of surrendering to the dark when complete safety is ensured by the arms of the man who's just told you about being his life?

Answer?

You don't.

Thank God.

REECE

No more than a few minutes after she falls asleep, I pass out too. We sleep like hibernating bears for the rest of the flight, cocooned beneath a few blankets Cosette has undoubtedly brought as soon as my snores started filling the cabin. But I can only guess it went down like that. I've been told, by a good many of the traveling partners to whom Em alluded, that booze on plane rides morphs me into Yogi Bear when it comes to snoring. Of course, I never polished off two glasses of champagne and then got any of them off using my laser fingers and a macaron before.

Since that's exactly the memory inundating my mind as Cosette wakes us up for the descent into Paris, I'm not shocked that I've got morning wood, the airline-ride version. Not that it diminishes my shit-eating grin by one millimeter. Without a doubt, this is the best transatlantic flight I've ever been on.

The landing path for this flight takes us close to the heart of Paris, living up to its name in every dazzling way. The City of Light seems to have gotten the memo that Emma Crist is headed for town and has cranked its illumination settings to eleven on the one-to-ten scale just for her. Against a sparkling crisscross of gold and violet, all the cultural icons of the city are brightly lit, making them look like rare pieces of jewelry inside a vast treasure chest. Emma gasps every time she identifies a new one.

"That's the Pantheon, right? And Sacré-Coeur? And is that the Louvre Pyramid?"

"Oui." Even Cosette is enchanted by my woman's excitement—though secretly, I'm sure even the native Frenchwoman doesn't tire of this panorama. I notice as much while extending a small envelope her way.

"*Merci beaucoup*," I murmur, securing the gratuity against her palm. "For the service *and* the discretion."

The tiny blonde *finally* gives in to an authentic smile. "It is always a pleasure to help the cause of true love, monsieur."

I acknowledge her praise with a quick wink. "Even when it's followed by close to eight hours of snoring?"

Her forehead furrows. "But...there was no snoring, monsieur."

"None?"

"Both of you seemed...well needing of the rest, *n'est-ce pas*?"

I chuckle. "Yes. Of course."

At the window, Emma suddenly bounces again. "There it is!" she exclaims. "It's sparkling. It's sparkling!"

In response to my curious glance, Cosette explains, "The Tour d'Eiffel. They shut off all the main lights at midnight, but the 'sparkle' comes on one more time, at one o'clock a.m."

"I want to see it all." Emma clasps my hand as I lean over and rest my chin against her shoulder, looking out over the sights with her.

"And you shall." I kiss her ear with the promise. "Perhaps we'll walk some of it tonight since we can't get into our place until around seven."

She swivels her head, blasting into me with a gaze threatening to out-sparkle even the lightshow below. "Our *place*?"

"I didn't want to check right into the Virage," I explain. "My parents don't appreciate being taken by their jugular. While my on-camera apology was a ball bounced the right direction, the play is now in their court—and they won't want to be forced into making that move." I stroke back and forth between her shoulder blades. "On top of that, I feel better knowing we have a fallback location—just in case what we learn about Tyce and Dad is the worst-case scenario."

"Sure. I get it."

And clearly, she does—only that doesn't mean she's pleased about it.

"Games, games, games. Why doesn't everyone just say what they mean and get the bullshit out of the way?"

I slide my hand up, squeezing the back of her neck. "Well, we still have at least a day until the games begin again, so let's enjoy the time."

The light on her face looks like it got another socket's worth of boost. "Perfect plan, Kong. I'm not even tired."

"That's why they call me King of the Jungle."

"Errrmmm...that's Tarzan."

"Potayyyto, Potahhhto." I weather her light smack at my cheek with another soft chortle until I'm snagged by the fresh crinkle of her nose and distress in her eyes.

"Crap," she mumbles. "Am I dressed all right?"

"For now, yes," I reply. "Though I'd suggest replacing the boots with some leggings and flats." Though I can't believe I'm saying that. Leggings mean tougher navigation to her lovely pussy, which I plan on giving the full assortment of French experiences as much as the rest of her. "Though part of today's plans will have to include some shopping. I tossed in a little of everything into your overnight bag, but it won't go far, and I'm not sure how long we'll be here."

A happy little hum flows off of her lips. "Well, damn," she mutters. "Twist my arm, mister."

I nuzzle into her neck. "With pleasure."

To that, I add a wide smile against her skin. She's happy again, and that eases my nerves about all the unknowns about to come. But thanks to the sleep she's gotten, along with the magic of the city below, she seems to have tucked away her rising insecurities from before, thank fuck. I won't delude myself into thinking that my declarations made a lot of difference in her resolve. If I were Emma, I wouldn't take credence in what I said either.

You're my everything. You're all my rubber bands.

Jesus.

It's so corny, I'm ready to mash it all up and roll hot dogs in it. And yeah, that might be the largest spoke in keeping my integrity wagon rolling here. Because, sure, I've followed the boyfriend handbook and been as honest as I can about everything she's asked, including the painful truth about the faceless dozens who have been in her position before—on an airplane, descending into Paris with my lips at the back of their neck—though absolutely none of them got what she and I shared eight hours ago, in the aftermath of frosting and fucking. Or anything of the eight hours before that, preparing for a trip to hell, press conference style. Or the eight before *that*, in which I nearly turned my brother into a permanent part of the Griffith Observatory architecture for cornering her in the bathroom there.

None of them have gotten even a fraction of what this woman has awakened in me, with or without the supercharge of my blood along to help, since the first night she came into my life—and changed my world.

But she still doesn't believe it. Not really.

The only way to prove it to her is the same way we made it to *this* moment. With more time. With more magic. With more communication. With more connection. With more trust. With more proof.

Which all sounds so easy—in my head. At several thousand feet over the earth. Without reality, in all its fucked-up glory, to interfere.

But even if she won't believe me directly, Emma believes in our love. I know it. I *feel* it. And now, I'm banking on it.

Okay, not right now.

But in about five hours it may be my only salvation.

CHAPTER THREE

EMMA

Even in the very early hours of the morning—perhaps because of them—this city is everything I've dreamed of and more.

Around every romantic curve in each street, in the carved stone alcoves and the wrought-iron filigrees, in the pristine black stanchions and the crisp striped awnings, are all the tiny touches that differentiate this place from any other on earth. In so many ways, I'm grateful for the chance to see it all like this, still and quiet, as if getting to watch a rare rose at the brink of blooming for the sun. The city, dating back to the Romans, is filled with so much beauty, I don't want to miss any of it in the name of dodging cars and scooters and people.

The visual ambiance is just the beginning of the Parisian spell. As Reece and I roam the cobblestoned streets, using only the river and the landmarks as our compass, we're happy with the world and each other. Well, that's how I choose to approach it. Though Reece has never been a Chatty Cathy for the sake of hearing himself talk, I force myself to recognize the unnatural length of his silences since we got here. And while I'm tempted to pry at what cat snagged his tongue, I also remember that a little over twelve hours ago, he was facing the media during the wildest "chat" of his life. Having to apologize to his father and brother, both of whom might be mixed up with the Consortium, had to be right up there with a rectal exam in his book—and that probably wasn't the toughest part of this journey for him yet.

Now, we're waiting.

And hoping.

And banking on the success of his lies.

All right, so they were white ones—but even back in LA, during the drive between the Brocade and the airport, I could tell that swallowing crow for the sake of mending fences with Lawson and Tyce wasn't in his natural wheelhouse of topics to be dishing with the press—especially because he still feels justified in going caveman on Tyce. In his shoes, in those circumstances, I'm not sure I would have refrained from the same stunt.

Water way under the bridge.

These moments are for us.

For walking and savoring and soaking everything up in the moment. For getting lost in the best city in the world to do that in. For watching the glow from streetlamps tango slowly through the trees, dancing to distant accordion and harmonica tunes from players down in Métro stations. For listening to *bateaus* call to each other on the Seine, their proprietors preparing for a busy day on the water. For watching the sky become an enchanting ombre because of the rising dawn, its peach and pink hues contrasting with the cobalt shadows still ruling over the streets and alleys. One by one, flares of neon flicker to life against the darkness, announcing another patisserie or café owner has arrived for their work day.

In front of one of those shops, on the quai across from the Île de la Cité, Reece tugs me to an abrupt stop. I peer at him curiously—and to be honest, a bit impatiently. Just a block up the way is the famous Shakespeare & Company bookstore, akin to a Mecca pilgrimage for booklovers. Though the little shop is still hours away from opening, I'm looking forward to having him take my picture, nonexistent makeup and all, in front of the iconic green storefront with its mustard-yellow sign. But the aromas wafting out of the bakery are worthy of their own holy worship—though we're shit out of luck on getting to do that too.

Or *are* we?

I stare harder at Reece as he cocks his head, perusing the inside of the bakery. No, a person *inside* the bakery—a man I'd mistake as his brother had I not already met Chase and Tyce in LA two nights ago. God, it feels like two *months* ago...

"You fucker!" The man throws open the front door, ringing an obnoxious bell over the jamb, before lunging at Reece and bro-hugging him like they're a couple of linebackers who just won the Super Bowl. "Couldn't believe it when I got your text."

"Yeah, well." Reece shrugs, his face taken over by a grin I've never witnessed before. It's the smile of a boy long since gone in chronological years but lurking deep down inside of the man all the same. And unbelievably, it adds a sexier new element to his rugged handsomeness. "Sneaked into town this time."

"No shit." While the guy mutters it with his mouth, he travels his curious gaze over to me. "And I'd say the reason is well worth it."

"Hey." Reece draws it out with long, semi-pissed emphasis. "Watch that shit, Connie."

A gasp escapes me as the man decks Reece in the arm—I mean, *hard*—on his way to taking up the space in front of me. He flashes a rogue's grin that really could make him the long-lost Richards brother, highlighted even more by the contrast of his thick, dark stubble. His apron, smattered with flour, sugar, and an array of fruit jellies, is ineffective for hiding the strain of his biceps at the confines of his gray T-shirt. His timber-log thighs are matching strains beneath his white baker's pants.

"Hi," he quips, waggling his brows. "Connor Barque. Reece the Piece and I went to prep school together. Or should I say, made the rounds of every prep school in New York together. But you probably know that, because I'm sure Mr. Richards has told you all about me by now. *Enchanté*, mademoiselle."

But the guy's only halfway down to kissing the back of my hand when he's hauled back by his collar, recalcitrant puppy style, by my growling fiancé. "Not in a thousand years, you don't," he orders.

"Holy fuck." But Connor's already laughing again.

"I told you she's different."

"And, evidently, meant it this time."

This time. I'm not expecting the remark, so it's damn near impossible to prevent my reacting wince from showing through—but Reece ropes his other arm around my waist, refusing to let me wallow in my insecurity. Or anything other than the kiss he works over my mouth and between my lips, completely ignoring his friend's approving applause.

"Well done, Monsieur Richards." Connor's shout attracts the attention of some passing cyclists, who add their assorted whoops and whistles. None of it deters the attention of my breathtaking man, who pulls away from me with shiny, swollen lips and a tender, adoring gaze.

"Well, fuck," he finally murmurs. His expression is tight with bemusement.

"What?" I prompt, palming one side of his face. "What is it, gorgeous?"

"I got it all wrong."

"Wh-What all wrong?" I keep my hand where it is, though tense up just in case the reunion with his fellow hellraiser has made him realize the settled-down, secret engagement life really isn't for him after all.

He precludes his answer by jogging a glance at Connor. "I told you the wrong thing, man." Swings his gaze, now reflecting the gilded parts of the sunrise, back down to me. "She's not just different. She's *the* difference."

Well...*hell.*

Screw getting to *watch* the sunrise. Now *I'm* that collection of brilliant colors and beaming sunshine. I'm the sparkling river beneath that perfect light, a rose-gold glow coursing through a metropolis of my awakened fibers and marrow, stirring and reaching for the stratosphere of him. *My* difference.

My love.

I repeat it to him with the force of my gaze as I pop on tiptoe, grabbing him to drag him into another wild, needy tangle of a kiss. While more cheering cyclists are joined by hollering guys on scooters, it's Connor Barque who eventually breaks us apart, bellowing so everyone within a mile can hear, "One more minute of this shit and I'm going to start charging admission for the show, you two."

But no more than five minutes later, the guy has mellowed and has insisted on serving us hot caffeine and fresh carbs. By the time he's set up a little quayside table and topped it with steaming cafés au lait and hot apple croissants, I've long since forgiven him for announcing to half of Paris that I was just welcoming the new day by sucking face with his adolescent chum. My stomach turns into a lion as we sit, but my throat supersedes even that growl, erupting with a sound of animalistic pleasure from my first bite into the confection of buttery dough and tart apple filling.

As a chuckling "Connie" appears in the doorway, I swallow enough down to ensure him, "This is the best damn thing I've ever put in my mouth."

"*Second* best." Reece mutters it so smoothly, circling the rim of his coffee cup the whole time, that Connor's and my laughter is delayed by a good couple of seconds.

"Excellent point, Mr. Richards." And since the table is draped in a long linen and I'm wearing just my flats, I let one of them fall to the ground while extending a leg up—straight into his crotch.

Reece chokes on his next sip of coffee.

Connor bursts into an even harder laugh. "Oh, I like her," he drawls, folding arms across his meaty chest. But as Reece trumps my move by drawing a line of apple filling into my cleavage and then licking it up with his tongue, the guy's chortle gives way to a groan. "I'm not sure whether to be fascinated or nauseated by you two."

"Neither." Reece pulls back from me with a self-satisfied smirk, his gaze locked on the points of my nipples now visible even through my sweater set. "But if you must pick..."

"*Pfffft*," the guy retorts. "Where's Rianda when you need to be set flat on your ass?"

Still no waver of Reece's focus, even when another woman's name is brought into the exchange—which I'm stupidly relieved about. "Now that you mention it, where the hell *is* she, really?"

"Who's Rianda?" I query.

"The one who became *his* difference," Reece replies.

"And, subsequently, kept him here—for which I'm grateful every time I eat one of these." He finishes by chomping into his pastry.

"Yeah, well. Your asshole maw aside, she's the best thing that's ever happened to me." There's an interesting tenderness in the guy's voice now, backed up by his bashful smile as he adds, "Which is why I finally decided to lock that shit down."

"Fucker!" With a joyful laugh, Reece springs to his feet and rushes to his friend, bro-hugging him with twice the force of their first clinch. "A ring and everything?"

Connor nods and rolls his eyes. "Even took her to the Pont des Arts to pop the question. We couldn't put the lock on the bridge, so I gave her a diamond one on her neck...and then one on her finger."

"Shit." I get up too, bringing my napkin with me. "Now *I'm* going to lose it."

Connor smirks. "Well, fortunately she did too. Errr, not the ring," he qualifies. "Just her shit. Which was kind of the point, seeing as I refuse to let my kid grow up without a proper family name."

"Your—" Reece cuts himself short to let his jaw plummet all the way. He recovers quickly, once more decking his friend in the arm. "Fucker! You held out the best part for last!"

I throw aside my napkin for the privilege of moving in to hug Connor for myself. "I promise mine doesn't come with a punch." With arms around his NFL shoulders—seriously, the guy wouldn't even need pads on these things—I add, "Just lots of happiness for you and your bride. Congrats."

"I'm psyched for you both." Reece's encouragement is genuine. "And *that* explains why you've got the early shift instead of her now."

"I've got the *only* shift." Though the guy sounds tired, he looks invigorated. With a personality as outgoing as Connor's, running his own shop along the Seine is probably a dream come true. "Ri's in La Rochelle, seeing her parents," he explains. "She'll be bummed she missed getting to see the badass Bolt man."

"Yeah, well." Reece shrugs, using his backward grip on the back of his chair for more leverage. "Badass Bolt man is the real loser here." He lifts his sights back to his friend, his smile turning wistful. "She's a good woman, Con. And the two of you are going to have a good life together."

Connor rocks back on his heels with his hands now parked in the deep pockets of his apron. Almost as if time folds on itself, I have a vision of him cocking the same pose, looking just as handsome, thirty or forty or fifty years from now. "That's the plan, man."

"Yeah." Reece's hearty laugh alerts me that this isn't the first time they've bantered around that expression. "That's the plan, man."

The words serve as closure on that chapter of the conversation. Though we hang out with Connor for another half hour or so, never again do the men come back around to subjects like their shared bad boy days or how Reece's continued pursuit of that life might have contributed to him becoming Bolt. Oddly, Bolt is never brought up again either, even when a bawdy comment from Connor makes Reece gaze toward me with such lust, his fingers turn into an *E.T.* army. If Connor notices, he doesn't let on at all. Without faltering, he just moves on to mentioning that the best part of a visit to Notre-Dame—its iconic towers now defined by the morning's salmon sky—is by touring the archaeological crypts underneath the front square.

From that point, even during the men's final embraces, I sense the strange stillness wrapping around Reece once again—meaning I'm not shocked when we return to a comfortable-but-not-comfortable silence while walking along the quai, the shimmering river to our right and the stirring city at our left.

At last, I venture, "Everything all right, Mr. Richards?"

He loops an elbow around my neck, nestling me closer. "Couldn't be better, Miss Crist."

I watch some birds similar to seagulls from back home take flight off the water before I respond softly, "Why don't I believe you?"

He stops for a second. I peer up, struck by how his profile is so similar to the architectural glory we've seen for the last few hours. Dark beauty even in dawn's gold. Austere strength framed with such romantic touches. The way the wind plays with his hair, and the light of the day in his serious gray eyes...

"I'm grateful for my life," he finally says into our tentative silence. "And since you came along, there's not a day that goes by that I don't remember how lucky I am to be here, instead of in some cell inside the Source..."

Comprehension rolls over me as I catch his glance back along the river, toward Connor's shop. I push in a little closer, rubbing a hand over the center of his chest. "But there's part of you that just wants to bake bread in the morning and watch the world go by each day."

He kisses the top of my hairline. "And fuck my gorgeous wife every night."

Light chuckle. "Well, there's that too."

He pauses before swallowing with solemn weight. "And watch her grow with our child."

And just like that, I've joined him in the snowball-of-emotion club. Rammed with the enormity of what he's just confessed. Moved to the core of my womanhood by the need he's just exposed. Rocked by the strange loss I now feel along with him...mixed with a bizarre new joy.

"You...want to be a parent with me?"

His kiss is more reverent now. "More than anything."

Ding ding ding. Correct answer, mister. I show him so by intensifying my cuddle, pretty sure he can also feel the joyous bells of my heart, endorsed by the resonant peals from the towers of Notre-Dame itself. "Well, then let's be parents," I declare. "I mean, not right *now* or anytime soon..."

"Or even if they're not our biological children."

Everything inside me goes silent again. Yet at the same time, no thoughts have ever blared with louder clarity. "Is that what this is all about?" I finally prompt. "And Reece, how can you be sure—"

"Because I'm *sure*, baby." He scoots me away and then tilts his head over, making sure our gazes are reconnected for this now. "I've been all over you like a rutting bull since the night we first met, and you've still been as regular as software updates on your cycle."

"But that's because—"

"You're on the pill?" He dips his head and furrows his brow, going all-in on the Lenny Bruce for cynicism. "Sure. And you've kept that up religiously, despite learning your boyfriend's a mutant, moving out of your apartment, shuttling between a couple of homes, starting a nonprofit from ground zero, getting kidnapped by a bitch on wheels..."

I halt him with a couple of fingers across his firm lips. "Point made," I insist before replacing my fingers with an adamant smack of my lips. "But it doesn't matter." I add a brace of my fingers, rubbing through the bristles of scruff that I adore so much. "*Reece.*" Then kiss him again, with more fervent feeling. "It *really* doesn't matter. We'll find a bunch of epic kids to call ours and give them our name and our home and all of our hearts. Love is love is love, Mr. Richards—and we have more than enough of it to spread around."

As I make my ready-for-Broadway stance, Reece's eyes have come alive at last. He streaks an ardent gaze across my face, sulfur fire and silver speed igniting so many deep parts of me, before he dips back in to lock his forehead against mine. "You're right," he rasps, softly forming his lips over mine again. "And you're also amazing. Beyond what I've dreamed or deserve." Another kiss, twirling tingles down to my toes, as he wraps his arms back around me and meshes our bodies as well as our mouths. Oh, dear *hell*, how this man can kiss. And oh, dear *God*, how I want to let him, here and now, in the land so fond of the act, they named a whole kissing style after it.

Yes. *Yes.*

Oui, oui...

When he finally drags back from me, his heavy gaze still riveted on my swollen lips, my head is spinning and my senses are racing. For a resplendent moment, I forget about all the subterfuge and insanity that were our impetus for having to come here. Right now, I'm just a joyous girl in love with a breathtaking boy who's just kissed her senseless on the banks of the Seine—a moment I'm wanting to stick so hard into the spiritual scrapbook, I almost don't want to ask my next question. But time can't be folded back on itself, and every subject must be changed at some point, especially when it's one that can't be altered for the moment at hand. I stow away my fantasies of Daddy Reece, refocus on Parisian hunk Reece, and get the damn words out.

"So, Mr. Richards...where to next?"

I'm not surprised when his mood takes another stony turn—and not out of affectionate fun for the figures on the Pont Neuf, now stretching across the river in front of us. "To take care of our lodging."

And yes, it's the answer I halfway expected too—though I still lean my roller against the balustrade and fully fold my arms, forcing out my truth in response. "And I'm feeling weird about that answer...why?"

Reece's shoulders visibly tense. He uses the glimmering waters below us as a focal point for his averted gaze. "Because you might not be so enamored with the accommodations I've secured."

I crunch a tighter scowl. "Oh, come on. I'm sure the Mutant Turtle Lair is going to be *trés* awesome."

He chuckles, though the expression never makes it to his eyes. "The Lair, eh?"

"The *Mutant Turtle* Lair," I insist. "And I'm sure it's going to be fine." It's one nuance away from being an admonishment, but I'm not going to elaborate. Clearly, the man has already forgotten about my living conditions in LA before my life was permanently Bolted—and reminding him isn't an option. My apartment wasn't fancy, but it was *mine*, the first real time I could ever say that in my life. A few months ago, when he finally convinced me I'd be safer by giving it up, my heart had chafed at the choice, despite what my head had dictated. And that was after the man bought a full valley and hilltop in the open space north of LA for me.

"The Mutant Turtle Lair." He punctuates it with a gruff smirk, giving me hope that my loving shout-out to his childhood obsession has assuaged the weirdness about me not being enamored with his selection. "All right, Velvet. If you insist."

I pull his face down to mine for a quick but tongue-tangling kiss. "We could call it *Le Petite Shithole* and I'll be happy, okay? Haven't you figured out by now that anywhere I'm with you is my idea of heaven?" I stop to circle my gaze around. "Much less in the heart of Paris freaking France?"

With his head still lowered, he strokes a hand along my cheek. Pushes out a long breath from his nostrils. "Emmalina Crist," he utters so close that even the bellow of a river bateau doesn't drown the sexy timbre of his tone. "I may have lightning in my veins, but you're the fucking fire in my heart."

Thank God I already see the new kiss he's planning, shooting like plasma balls in the depths of his eyes. Even so, this collision is like standing my ground against a jolt from the skies, power pouring through my body as he fully and forcefully claims my mouth.

By the time he's done, I'm standing on tingling toes, fighting not to grind my body along his, and order him to just take me on top of the little wall where my bag sits as a lonely sentinel. "Holy *shit*," I somehow find the energy to gasp.

He curls a grin that's part horny wolf and part self-sure ninja turtle. "Stole the thought right out of my head, woman."

I almost gloat—but decide better of it. There are too many *other* things I'm way more in the mood to do right now. Most of all: him.

"Mr. Richards, this lair better be damn close."

His smile is the embodiment of sinful seduction. "Your wish is my command, baby."

He keeps true to the promise. Just a block and a half

later, we're entering a charming stone building and walking up polished wood steps to an apartment that faces an interior courtyard with quaint iron chairs and tables surrounded by greenery and flowers. The door to the apartment itself is ornate and beautiful, the wood carved with a fancy art deco pattern. I almost feel like I've walked into a French valentine that was crafted a whole century ago.

Until Reece's soft knock on the door is answered by the last woman on earth I want to see right now.

REECE

"Bienvenue."

It's not the first time I've heard Angelique murmur the word, but never have I gotten the chance to enjoy it without the addition of her subtle little sneer. When the woman isn't trying to impress anyone, her voice is actually a lovely sound—and the recognition is such a surprise, I smile.

Wrong, wrong, wrong *move.*

Which now, I almost want to laugh at myself for. After all the *other* wrong moves I'd stressed about making with this one—asking for Angelique's help in the first place, accepting her offer of this apartment as the "Ninja Lair," agreeing she should stay in Paris in case we needed someone with strong local connections to assist with any fuckery that got thrown at us—a simple, instinctual smile wasn't anywhere on the list.

But here I am, wishing like fuck for the chance to backtrack time by thirty seconds. No, by five minutes. Back to the moment on the sidewalk next to the Pont Neuf, when I should have extracted my brain out of my dick and prepared Emma for this instead of composing a fucking sonnet about lightning bolt blood and hearts catching fire.

A lot of good that mush is doing me now.

As if Emma cares about a syllable of it anymore.

As if she *remembers* it anymore.

But of course she does—I practically watch it all replaying in her head as she scans my face—and arrives at the same conclusion I've just ramrodded into myself as well.

"Bienvenue." Her reiteration is closer to retaliation but hints enough at a sob that I instantly realize how much my paranoia for security has led to my stomp into a Clifford the Dog-sized shitpile.

At once, every cell in my blood bellows with remorse. Too damn little, too fucking late. Still, I turn and attempt to utter, "Emma—"

"*Bienvenue.* Isn't *that* swell?" She bites it out this time, and there's no concluding sob. There's action. She sets her roller bag free with a brutal shove, letting it collide with a little table in the hallway adorned with a single daisy in a bud vase. Shockingly, the vase and flower jiggle but don't fall or shatter. I take that as a good omen—and yeah, right now I'm desperate enough to grab at stupid symbolism like that. At every damn reinforcement I can get.

"Emma." Including the dictator's growl in my own voice. "This isn't—"

"What it looks like?" Her retort cranks her bitterness nozzle higher, which reopens the spigot for my frustration too. "Hate to say this, buddy, but you've exhausted the quota on that one."

At first, I don't say or do a thing. After a few seconds of steadily studying her, I retrieve her bag from under the table. My attention doesn't veer from her by an inch. "I was going to say this isn't my first choice of a solution either. But Angelique has earned her place on Team Bolt, and if even I can see that, you owe it to me to do the same."

I stop and wait again. I know my conclusion must feel like a kick in the gut for her, especially after subjecting her to a figurative version of brass knuckles to her heart.

You owe it to me because you already promised you'd try.

And though the curved angles of her face waver, declaring how she remembers uttering that oath to me, her stance stays as rigid as the iron legs beneath the hallway table. Her gulp is resigned, thudding down her tight throat.

Well, what the fuck now?

For a second, I toy with the idea of just checking us into a hotel anyway. If we stay away from the Virage, maybe the media won't get wind of us being in the city. The Vernet and the Georges V are both discreet, but there's still the chance of a greedy busboy or valet willing to sell tips to the highest bidder. Still not a travesty—until we really do need to disappear.

My second option is feeling better by the second. I'm about to put it into motion, gauging exactly where I need to plow my shoulder against Emma's midsection to land her safely over my shoulder, when Angelique herself presents a third option.

"Please, Emmalina. Just come inside for five minutes. If you are still distressed after that, I shall call for a car to take you back to the airport."

Well, who knew?

Sometimes, common sense from one female to another really *does* work.

At least that's what I'm hoping, as Emma lurches the roller's handle out of my grip, barely breaking her stride, to follow Angelique inside the apartment.

The place is exactly how Angelique described it over the phone. The décor is a little faded but comfortable, mismatched traditional pieces in tones of dark blue and cream, with big throw pillows that add to the overall comfort factor. In the living room, there are built-in bookcases stocked with classics in French and English. In the kitchen, modern granite surfaces are mixed in with the art deco cabinetry. There's a gas stove, a microwave, and a large refrigerator. The floor plan is reminiscent of the place I rented with Foley in New York six months back, with opposing sides of the main room branching off into large bedrooms.

We walk in, and Emma all but flops onto the couch. I join her there, able to see her renewed conflict right away. Her mind doesn't want to rejoice in the fact that she's finally getting to rest after walking half of Paris, but her body is clearly on board with the plan. Though I sense that Angelique knows this too, the woman keeps her observations closeted. On the outside, she's almost as composed as a psychologist who's about to launch us into couples' therapy—and on the inside, I'm sure she might be wondering if that's scarily close to the truth. *I'm* sure as hell on the brink of thinking it.

"Emma." She takes a seat as well, crossing her long legs and leaning on the arm of the Queen Anne chair. She's dressed in faded blue jeans and a baggy sweater, though her makeup is still piled on like she's about to change into a sequined dress and club heels. Her blond curls are piled on top of her head. "I know how you must be feeling."

Her empathetic tone inspires me to reach for Emma's knee, but she jerks away before spitting, "You don't know a thing about me, Angelique, and I'm too tired to pretend otherwise."

Angelique raises her own hand, manicured nails catching the sun streaming through the arched windows. "Of course. I meant no offense. And please be assured that I do not mean to stay, either."

The statement works at least one magic trick. Emma finally slackens, at least by a little. When I cover her knee once more, she no longer looks ready to bite it off finger by finger. "But...isn't this your place?" she asks, peering around again.

"Yes and no," Angelique answers. "I am renting it through an alias identity. It..." She cuts in on herself with a choked sputter but recovers with a petite cough. "It is where..." She pushes to her feet and spins from us. "Dario and I used to meet here." With one hand, she swipes beneath both eyes. "When... when we could. When the Consortium was not watching so intently." Her shoulders visibly tauten, even beneath the thick sweater. "It was only possible for a few times, but we were so happy. There was never a need to go out, to go anywhere. All of Paris just floated by on the river, outside the bedroom windows. As for getting to see the rest of the world...I only had to look into his eyes."

As soon as she whispers it, I rivet my gaze back to Emma. And watch the conflict race across her twisting profile. And see every thought that races across her mind, as plain as every new angle that takes over her graceful features. At first, she looks ready to give in to another sob. She's hit by Angelique's heartache like it's ridden another sunbeam down to the couch. But all too quickly, she hardens her jaw, clearly fighting the empathy she feels for the woman who delivered me to the Source and into the hands of Faline and her flunkies. Not to be ignored is the final monster who invades her countenance—the not-so-little green monster that reminds her exactly how the woman led me to my damnation. By my cock.

A truth that Angelique unknowingly rubs in while stepping back around, her posture elegant and her long legs eating up the room's floor space despite the sorrow still brimming in her huge green eyes. "*Je désolée.* I wanted to stay and show you where everything is, but...I just cannot..."

"It's all right, Angie." I rise, compelled by the anguish in her eyes, yanking her into a hug. "I'm sure we'll figure it all out."

She doesn't return the embrace. Her form is as stiff as wood, and her reply is like a puppet carved from the stuff. "Ummm...all right."

And only then, like the idiot I really am, do I realize I've just doubled the size of the big dog shitpile and have rolled every inch of myself in the damn stuff.

Angie.

Fuck.

Angie.

Then this hug.

Especially this hug.

"Goddamnit." I'm saved from having to hurl Angelique away by her own determined jolt back—but by the time I whirl to try to save my own bacon with the only woman in the room who really matters, I'm gaping at an empty couch. "God*damn*it!"

And because the universe really wants to put a cherry on the fuck-up sundae, my final syllable is overshot by the slam of the bedroom door across the living room.

Angelique clears her throat with delicate care. The sound is comforting, and I'm beyond grateful she has the tact not to back it up with any more physical moves—unlike the dumbass with whom she's standing.

"I suppose I shall leave now," she murmurs. "If you have any questions about the apartment, you have my new cell, *mon ami*—but please remember, if she is holding a knife and you are holding your penis, the emergency line in France is one-one-two."

"Thanks." My mutter coincides with the slam of the door, leaving me to slide into a chair for a few minutes to weigh out my goddamned options.

The problem is, I'm not clear about what those are.

I'm not usually the one in this fucking position.

Okay, revision...

I've probably been the one in this position plenty of times but have simply chosen not to be anymore. In my life, the exit door has always been clearly marked, well-oiled, and happily used.

The exit door is *not* a fucking option here.

Which means...plan two.

Fighting for the right to stay.

Fighting...for us.

There's just one little hitch to that particular plan.

I don't have a clue how to start. And something—like, ohhhh, the voice of goddamned reason?—tells me that a Google search isn't the key for quality content there either.

I'm going to have to do exactly what I promised Emma I would.

Come clean.

Expose all that's really *me*.

And holy fuck...I hope like hell it's enough.

CHAPTER FOUR

E M M A

I drift in the Neverland between sleep and consciousness, not wanting to leave—especially because my first rational thought has consisted of nothing but *uck*.

I know, I know—not the most mature way of describing the situation, though probably the most accurate. And regrettably, because most of that shit is aimed right back at myself.

Uck.

Because I was dumb enough to start thinking that maybe, just for a little while longer, Reece and I could continue playing the Paris honeymoon ruse. That we'd come to this beautiful place just to get more of each other, thinking of nothing but drinking great wine, eating a thousand kinds of cheese, and madly fucking each other's brains out.

Uck.

Because I also lost my respect for the real reason we came. Reece's anticipation of getting back on good footing with his family again so we can get to the truth behind the bizarre evidence linking both Tyce and Lawson back to the Consortium.

Uck.

Because even after promising Reece that I'd work on being more benevolent to Angelique, I shut down the very second I laid eyes on her. No. That wasn't just shutting down. It was freaking out, ramping up, and checking all the way out.

Leading to the last and most awful *uck*.

Her heartfelt confession. Her heartbreaking tears. Her heartrending goodbye—all the way up to the point that Reece felt like giving her "heart" some extra attention of his own.

And the way *my* heart had instantly reacted.

Not seeing a woman who was hurting or the generosity of the man needing to comfort her.

Only feeling like the dorky girl from the OC who didn't belong in the same room with "the worldly ones." The woman who couldn't show him half the moves in *Angie's* sexual repertoire. The one who'd always be less sophisticated, less knowledgeable, less elegant, less connected...

Just *less than*.

"Uck." The need to acknowledge it with volume overrides the yearning to stay hidden in the bedroom—where I've been avoiding the confrontation he and I will eventually have to face. Though I've heard him come and go a few times, he's never stayed, for which I've been both grateful and regretful. While the man is being respectful of my need for "rest," I also know he won't let this tension fester. I've known this about him ever since learning he's the man in the Bolt leathers. In many ways, watching the man zero in on criminals is a lesson about how he deals with relationship issues. Direct attention. Complete demand. Laser focus on identifying and then destroying the core of the problem.

Even if that core is just going to regrow itself.

Because I can't seem to figure out how to make my mental weed killer work.

Seven months into this superhero girlfriend gig, and I'm

still sprouting a garden of insecurity—sprinkled with a *lot* of I-don't-belong-here dandelions.

Especially when I watch him with perfect roses like Angelique La Salle.

"*Uck.*"

Although I mutter it into the pillows this time, the bedroom's door creaks open. And before he even angles his head in behind the panel, I feel his complete focus on me. How he just seems to know the expression I crave on his face, intense but tender, seeking but not pushing...

Damn it. Don't just know *this, Reece. Don't just know* me. *Please. Please...*

But he enters anyway, virile and breathtaking in the track pants and T-shirt into which he's changed. His feet are bare and his hair is mussed, an electrifying god despite the fact that no part of him is silver or blue right now.

Shit.

It just can't be right that he's so damn gorgeous all the freaking time.

His face changes as if I've let *that* slip out too but babbled it in Klingon instead of English. Or maybe he just likes tormenting me with his mussed-and-perplexed look, which he's rocking the crap out of right now.

"Hey."

I scoot over a little, anticipating he'll want to sit. He usually does when it's time to laser torpedo into the truth between us. "Hey."

Bizarrely, he stays on his feet. Still, he leans over and squeezes my foot through the crimson throw blanket under which I'm still nestled. I have no idea where the covering came from, having stormed in here without anything but my hissy rage and my prideful confusion, too embarrassed to emerge even after I heard Angelique take off as she'd promised. It hadn't taken long for exhaustion to set in, and then...

"What time is it?" My eyes are grainy and my muscles stiff, so it feels like I've been sleeping for a few hours.

"Almost four in the afternoon."

Okay, more than a few.

"Shit." I shoot upright, stabbing a hand through my hair. "I've been out for most of the day?" That's way more than a few hours. Essential sightseeing hours. "Damn!"

"Because you needed the sleep." He grips my foot again, as if ordering me to believe it.

"I slept on the plane, Reece."

"On the *plane*, Emma," he counters. "Which only took care of the fact that you'd been up a lot of the night before that."

"You mean the night *you* didn't sleep at all?" I hit him with a charged-by-eight-hours-of-sleep glower.

He sucks in a full breath. Releases it. I'm not going to get pushback on my argument, for which I should be chalking up mental *atta-girl* points—but instinct holds me back on the celebration. An awareness I can't attribute to any outward observations of him but know with the same certainty. There's a difference in him now. A new cadence to his vibrations on the air. A new smell of his skin in my nostrils. A vast difference in how he holds himself, although his muscles are all still in the same place. It's as if he's peeled off the old containment system and replaced it with...

What?

"I didn't come in here to argue sleep tables, Velvet."

I sit up straighter. "I know." I don't hide the dread from my tone. Wonky changes or not, I don't expect his MO to be *that* different. The man is here to clear the air; that much is evident in the set of his jaw and the steely focus in his gaze. "Okay." I pull the blanket up around my waist, uncaring that it's wrinkling my skirt even more. After two eight-hour naps, the thing is beyond ready for the cleaners. "Park it, mister. Let's do this now, because my day of touristy goodness is wrecked."

Yeah, it's a little bossy, probably because I know it's my last chance for guiding any part of this for a while. But damn it if Monsieur Richards doesn't even let me have that concession. With that peculiar energy still changing his aura, he moves from the foot of the bed to a spot where he can extend his hand, palm up, looking for all the world like a beautiful knight asking his lady to dance with him at court. Yeah, even in his track pants and T-shirt. And yeah, even with me in all my rumples and tangles.

"Will you come with me?"

And yeah, flipping my heart just like that nervous medieval maiden.

"Where are we going?" I rush it out even as I slide my fingers against his. But his only answer is to walk me out of the bedroom with slow, careful steps. His pace doesn't change as we traverse through the living room and then into the kitchen— where one of the chairs from the dining nook has been yanked over and positioned in the middle of the floor. When he circles me around, positioning me in front of the thing, I finally grab him by the forearms. "Reece? What's going on? Why—"

"Will you sit here for me?"

I oblige because I'm a little scared not to. Maybe more than a little. Though his voice is far from a monotone, I can't help but feel like he's in some automaton mode. What the hell happened to him while I was playing Sleeping Beauty in the bedroom? I heard Angelique leave, so I know she didn't have anything to do with it. So did he hear back from his father? From Tyce? Or did Wade and Fershan uncover more shit about either of them off the deep web?

From there, my mind takes off in crazier directions. Why am I on a chair in the middle of the *kitchen*? Did our wild episode during the flight inspire him to think up some new kinky stuff? Just because I don't see any rope and handcuffs doesn't mean the man hasn't had the chance to order something up and have it delivered—and that I might be just a little tingly about it. Does stockroom.com deliver in Paris? Not that I've ever looked at anything on the site except out of curiosity. Yeah, *curiosity*...

Which the man himself takes to DEFCON status the next moment.

By falling to his knees in front of me.

"R-R-Reece?" I'm unable to control the stutter. It's not just the action of his body. It's the totality with which he's committed to it. The desperation in every inch of his limbs. The burden across his shoulders. The torment transforming his face into a sight worthy of some tortured angel in a painting down the road in the Louvre. "Hey." I cup both sides of his face, curling my fingertips into his thick hair. "What's going on?"

But he drops his head anyway, continuing the plummet until he's laid his face in my lap, hunching his shoulders over my knees. "*Emma.*"

Hard swallow. I'm not sure what to do with this strange voice from him, his thick emotion mashing into a growl and a groan at the same time.

"Reece?" I manage to rasp.

"You're the one person on this planet I can't bear to think

of hurting," he finally utters. "Yet that's all I seem to keep doing to you. And putting you through. And every time, I swear it's going to be the last damn time you're ever in pain because of me, but then..."

As he falters into silence, I curl a hand back into his hair. Stroke my fingertips through, gifting him with the silence, knowing it's what he needs right now. Knowing he has to claim it as the apology he's unable to form into words.

Just knowing.

As only I can know about him.

The same way he knows so many of those crazy, secret nuances about me.

Because that's what people in love do. What they have. What they understand, above and beyond anyone else on this earth, about each other.

And I realize, just now, that the silence is just as much for me as for him.

A silence I want to go on forever...but realize that *he* needs *me* to end, with whispered words only I can give him.

"I know."

Words of absolution.

"I know. And I'm sorry too."

Words of reciprocation.

"We're both trying. And then we're both going to mess shit up. And then we'll both just try again."

Words of affirmation.

As I slip my hand down, out of his hair and along the top of his back, I feel the sorrow dissipate from his shoulders. I welcome the weight of him against my thighs, the warmth of him against my body, the completion of him in my arms.

But I'm still bewildered as hell as to why we're doing this

in the middle of the damn kitchen.

Until he raises his face again, meeting my gaze once more.

And not a shred of the desolation has drained from those dark-gray depths.

He's not done yet. There's a further plan for his contrition. Some extra proof he needs to give, as if his agonized voice and humble crouch aren't nearly enough. Doesn't he know that they *are*? That I love him with everything I am and everything I will be, and that even the pain is part of that love, meaning I won't trade any of it, no matter what has happened or how many mistakes are made or how we both have to keep fucking up...

Because when we get it right, the pain is nothing but a blip.

And getting it right is better than a thousand Paris sunrises.

But I don't tell him that right now. He won't listen anyway. I'm already as sure of that as my own heartbeat and every breath that it gives me. Not that it matters. The same way he gives me everything I need, I need to be here to provide everything he needs. And right now, whatever the hell this is, he *needs it*.

So all I do is nod. And watch him rise. And wait for him as he walks behind me, making his way to the area between the refrigerator and the sink. And order myself not to turn around to watch. Wholly trusting him, though trying to decipher the sounds I hear. The water running into some kind of a container. The clank of that container, probably against the sides of the sink.

What the freaking...

When he steps back around in front of me, he's holding what looks like a roasting pan—filled two-thirds of the way with clear water. There's a big fluffy towel over one of his shoulders, with a smaller washcloth layered atop that. I take it all in with a stare that must stretch as wide as the Pont Neuf by now, but for the first time since I woke up, Reece's face is washed in complete serenity.

No. Solemnity.

And something even more.

A minute ago, I compared him to an angel—but now I'm close to convinced that's the spectrum to which he's committed himself, lowering the pan in front of my feet with the reverence of someone wrapped in utter worship and selfless humility.

"Oh." I practically breathe it out as he lays both towels across my lap and strips the shirt away from his torso. When he kneels again, straddling the basin with the inside edges of his knees, I can't help but flutter a hand across his back, wondering if I'm really checking for the nubs of wings beside his shoulder blades. "Oh, Reece."

Gently, he removes my hand from his back. Tenderly, he rolls his face around to press his lips into the center of my palm. Strangely, I grow all too aware of his energy field on the air, a phenomenon I've grown so used to that it rarely affects me much anymore. But here and now, the force of his feelings strings through the air around us...swirling around him and then me...binding us and completing us...

Before striking me motionless.

The rod for his lightning. The object of his adoration. The center of his worship.

The woman who loves him beyond her own soul's bounds.

"Reece..."

"Ssshhh."

He says nothing else while wrapping his long, strong

fingers around the back of my ankles, pulling my feet forward. And then lifting them into the water.

He still doesn't say a thing as he settles them against the bottom of the pan, ensuring they're submerged in the perfect warmth. And holy shit, do I mean *perfect*. After all our walking last night even in my flats, every square inch of my feet has proclaimed itself a new definition of pain, now guided to heaven via this soothing, softening bath, given with his silent, absolute adoration. The attention affects me like a drop of sun on the eddies of the Seine, spreading and growing through my entire body now slackening in the chair. The only thing keeping me from totally slipping off is my conscious effort to grip the edges of the seat, clinging all my fingers around with blissful anticipation. My lips part on a high sigh, a visceral interpretation of a desperate prayer for more.

More...

Heard and hearkened by the angel at my feet.

He lowers the washcloth in, joining its soft swath with his magical fingers to wash me, caress me, revere me, adore me.

And more.

Yes.

More.

He's always, *always*, my more.

Especially now.

Even more so now...as I crack my eyes open and take in the three-quarter profile of his face, still absorbed with attending to me. He's so beautiful, tiny tears burn the backs of my eyes while soaking in his dark, rugged intensity...his crucial, remarkable beauty. He almost shatters the confines of this pristine white space with the potency of his presence—but at the same time, twisting his features as if he knows that and hates it. As if all his moves, so gentle and careful, are those of a fallen angel returned to paradise for the sole purpose of begging for readmission.

I feel it too. I feel *him* too. Every cell in my being craves to scream to the universe in advocacy for him. Longs to reach out and wrap him in my arms exactly how he's drenching me in his comfort.

Listen to him.

See him.

Know him.

He doesn't know how to say all of this, but you need to see. To hear. To accept.

And because the pleas of my soul evidently aren't enough, soft strains of music echo across the inner courtyard of the building, sifting in through the kitchen windows facing that way. A male voice singing in French but carrying the tune of a song that was originally recorded in English by Elton John. A song of being struck by lightning but realizing it too late. Of sadness and absurdity and the hardest words to say...

He's sorry.

Let him back in.

Because if not, I'll fall to be with him.

Falling...

Yes.

Ohhhh, yes.

The sensation takes over more and more of me as Reece works the washcloth up over my shins and calves, but as he arrives at my knees, he leans over to add another element to his special bath.

His mouth.

Oh, my dear hell. Or, as the case may be, heaven.

As he nips and laves me with his lips and tongue, I have no choice but to watch...and to marvel. And to thank the Almighty, in all His grace and glory, for this perfect prism of a moment. The sight of this massive man bent over me like this, his umber waves tumbling as he licks every crevice and curve of my knees, fills me with a heady rush of emotion...

And, in a rush I can't control, a surge of flawless arousal. *Ohhhh, God.*

Not here. Not now.

But why not? *Ohhhh, why the hell not?*

There's a tiny angel on one of my shoulders. But the devil on the other? She's already hopped down to my right knee. Then my left. Then back over to my right, depending on which side Reece chooses to focus on with the passing moments.

I guess I really am falling. All the way to hell.

But what an awesome ride.

As the plaintive music echoes through the building, almost as accusing as a choir singing Bach, I struggle to keep my head in the same pure space as Reece's. But damn it, he had to go and add his mouth to the whole process.

Oh, *God.* His *mouth*...

Never mind that the thing is already the cause of many— *many*—a wicked tremble for me merely when I *look* at him. Now he has to intensify the torment by subjecting my skin to all that sensuality? And *I'm* the one contemplating a tumble to the depths of hell?

But maybe I can still stop the slide into Hades. If he doesn't go any higher than my knees...

Just don't go...

Any...

"Reece!"

"Ssshhh."

And I'm unable to do anything but comply. To let him become my guiding demon, spreading me wider as he turns his licks into kisses, forming a trail along the most sensitive path between my knee and my core. Along the inside of the other thigh, he traces the same route with the tip of a finger, sending tremors up and down my flexing, convulsing leg—

Which he hikes up and over his shoulder—just before he moves closer in. Sloshing one of his knees into the pan. Drenching my pussy with the fan of his breath.

I'm hot. Helpless. Plunging into hell with him. *For* him. Giving over to him...

"Ahhhhh!"

He doesn't silence me this time, thank God. The groan he returns instead is a perfect gift of permission, allowing me to move my grip from the chair to his scalp, twisting his thick, dark strands between my fingers as he brushes his masterpiece lips over the triangle of fabric guarding my quivering center. His hands skate up my thighs, pushing back the folds of my skirt, turning the drops he's already splashed up on me into arcs of moisture that shiver from the new kiss of cool air.

And still, all he does with his mouth is tease. And breathe. And slide. And promise...

"Mmmmm!" It vibrates the seam of my lips as he digs his fingers in at both sides of my other set. The lips now trembling and tantalized...needing and pulsing...

He exhales against me there but holds his breath on the inhale.

For one second.

Two. Three.

And I'm suspended there with him. Afraid to breathe. To move.

Four. Five. Six.

"May I, Emmalina?" His breath is now a prayer, vibrating my pussy like confessions on candles. But his fingertips are demons, razing my skin as they seek a way inside my panties. With one of them, he finally burns through the lace atop my hip. He leaves the other side intact, poised and waiting, as if anticipating I truly might say no. His fingertip traces the thin threads, but he doesn't go any further even while repeating in a thicker rasp, "May...I?"

I claw my fingers at his scalp. Dig my raised heel into his back. "Yes. Dear *fuck*. Yes!"

My words have hardly hit the air when he turns his fingertip into a hot knife, releasing my panties—and baring my mound. As the French Elton John continues to croon around us, the afternoon wind soughs through the apartment with more insistence. It smells like daffodils and lavender and bread and wine, braided atop a breeze of distant traffic and laughing tourists. The textures of vibrancy and life, so perfect for backing the soft hum of his magical fingers against my skin...

As he rolls and works my labia...

As he caresses and opens my entrance...

As he flicks aside the hood over my hottest button...

"*Reece!*"

As he replaces his fingers with his breath.

"May I, Emmalina?"

"*Yes.*" I barely remember blurting it. Begging it? "Please. *Please.* Yes!"

And then he's there. At first just with the tip of his tongue but soon flattening his wet, full flow of worship until I'm on the brink of complete carnal fulfillment...

And then...

Directly licking my illicit button...

Sending me to ecstasy.

My throat becomes a scream. My body lifts and bursts and transforms, becoming a soaring, sensual seraph bursting into a heaven of nothing but light and freedom and wonder. And I'm flown there by the dark angel himself, who's scooped me away from the choirs and the harps and the clouds, showing me the true magnificence of paradise. The sun itself.

But the splendor doesn't stop there. When my pleasure wanes enough for me to reopen my eyes, I smile with the comprehension that the angel is still here—and is even more beautiful than before. Sometime in the midst of my explosion, Reece freed up a hand to shove his pants down to his thighs. His most glorious part juts proudly in front of him, a stalk of taut purple crowned by a throbbing red crown. But the most stunning sight comes from the cobalt pulses of his veins, glowing and swelling and gorgeous. There is literally no other penis like his on earth, and I make it a point to silently thank the Divine Power who gave him to me.

Only to me.

I know that now simply by lifting my head and taking in the silver force of his gaze. By welcoming every drop of love he silently offers...but most of all, giving him my love and adoration in return. And yes, my forgiveness—but only because I know that right now, he needs to see it. To accept it back for himself. To see, across every inch of my face, that he never really needed to ask.

But I yearn to show that too.

And I do.

By reaching for him. By taking his length in my hand and then stroking down to the throbbing balls inside his bulging sack. By bringing my fingers back, savoring the pattern of his veins against his stiff skin. By pressing my thumb into the slit at the top and rejoicing in the milky drop that soaks me in return.

Then I coax him closer, continuing to marvel at the flawless stalk in my hand that reacts to every one of my touches and squeezes. Still mesmerized by the determined clench of his body, obviously holding back for me...waiting for me to tell him the dark angel can fly free again.

Even as I pull him closer. Tighter. Raising my leg, still curled atop his shoulder, nearly to my ear. Throwing my other leg over the side of the chair. Aligning my hips to ensure the trajectory of his cock is poised to penetrate the core of my sex. Just one inch farther, and he'll be stretching every illicit inch of me.

"Emma." He's quivering so hard, it's nearly one husky syllable. His chest knocks at my sweater because of his labored heaves. With one hand, he grips the back of the chair to keep us both from falling over.

"Yeah?" I'm panting too, every breath filled with heat and lust and need.

"May I?"

A part of me—a *huge* part—wants to give him hell by just rolling my eyes and guiding him into me, but there's a huge glitch to that plan. Our eyes are still locked with each other. In that bond is a rare gift from the man. A tunnel down into his thoughts, without the barriers of lightning or lust. Somehow, in some bizarre way, he's kept all that out of his eyes—allowing me to see the one thing he still needs here.

The last act of penance he needs to perform for me.

And damn it, just the comprehension of it makes me three times wetter.

Holy shit, this is going to be good.

I take a longer breath, steeling myself. I prepare *him* by delving my hands back into his hair and tearing at the sweaty strands until he hisses from the pain. Despite that, the need in his gaze goes on.

Yeah. He's ready too.

So I jab my chin up at him and order in a low snarl, "Say it again."

He gulps hard. His jaw turns to a brutal slash of flesh against bone. From gritted teeth, he answers, "May...I?"

I give him a sultry smirk. "May you do what?"

"May I...fuck you?"

"And how will you do that?"

His lips part on harsh huffs. A new bead of precome teeters at the end of his crown. "With...with this."

"With what? The *words*, Reece." I yank at his hair again. Smile a little wider. Turning the sexual tables on him is a better rush than I anticipated. "Give me the words. All together."

"May I...fuck your cunt...with my cock, Emmalina?"

He's shaking like an addict in detox now. And as weird as it sounds, I'm savoring the hell out of every moment. I'd hate myself for the twisted sadism, except that I know with every fiber of my being that he's basking in the switch as thoroughly as I am. Maybe even more.

With that recognition in my arsenal, I brace my hands at the sides of his fierce, sculpted face. Burrow my nails into the perspiration at his hairline. Use that leverage to haul his mouth down to mine, where I punish it with a brutal, biting, ravenous kiss. I don't stop until he moans from the pain and a bead of bright red blooms on his bottom lip.

As the drop of pure white falls from his cock.

And now, heaven and hell can merge.

"Give it to me," I order him in an urgent rasp. "Fuck me with it. Hard. Until we both— *Ahhhhh!*"

As he thrusts his lightning cock into me, he pushes his mouth back onto mine. Taking over both my holes at once with the brutal beauty only he can bring to me. In my pussy, I'm stretched and pounded and claimed. In my mouth, I'm ravaged until I taste the tang of his blood and feel the start of his orgasmic moan. I breathe hard and deep, my lungs filled with lavender and spring, attempting to borrow their essence to soften my body and welcome him deeper. It's no use. He's going to take the space, whether I give it or not. He fills me, invades me, dominates me, drenches me. The symbolism is right there on the floor, as the water from the pan splashes out farther with every one of his bestial drives.

His face, still framed by my hands, turns savage and stark. His stare flares as he licks and sucks along both my lips, until his passion clearly takes over and he slams a hard, ferocious kiss on me...into me.

"Give it to me, Emma. All of it." He rears up over me, impaling me with the blistering blue force of his mesmerizing, miraculous gaze. "Tell me you will. All the fucking words."

And just like that, the world is right again. *We're* all right again. The joy of it detonates through me, supplying everything he demands from the willing reaches of my heart. "I will. You'll have it all," I rasp. "I'll come for you, Reece. My pussy *needs* to come for you. Oh...God. I'm close. *I'm close...*"

"Me too. Oh, my little fucking Velvet..."

"I'm...I'm going to..."

"Wait for me, baby."

"I can't!"

"You can. You *will*." He secures the leg he didn't dip into the pail, the one now powering most of his thrusts. "*Fuck*, Emma! So good! So...*fucking*..."

"Reece!"

"Now!" He bellows it while screwing into me so hard, I swear I feel it in my eyes. Once he's in, he stays, pushing at the walls of my sex as his cock bursts and floods me with streams of heat and electricity and energy. The fireworks double the slam of my climax. It's beyond intense. Beyond reality. Beyond any pleasure I've ever known possible. I'm lost to a long scream as Reece utters from between his bared teeth, "Emma. *Emmalina*. Holy *God*. You're tearing me apart. Don't stop. *Don't stop*."

He's completely serious.

He really doesn't want me to stop.

And, insanely, makes good on his promise by riding me through a third and then fourth climax, each implosion even better than the last. *Holy hot pursuit, Bolt Man.* In this case, I can't even laugh to myself about it, because it's the truth. As much of a turn-on that it can be to watch the man go after criminal assholes, there are no graphic novel adventures that can take the place of a front-row seat for the guy's pursuit of giving pleasure...over and over *and over* again.

The Carnal Crusader has triumphed yet again.

Up, up, and *holy fuck* me away.

When I'm finally nothing but a ball of satiated mush, he stands—a miracle in itself because I'm not sure *I'll* ever be able to do so again—and kicks his pants off the rest of the way before lifting me out of the chair and carrying me into the living room. There's another big throw blanket draped on the back of the couch, which he pulls free and uses to wrap around us both.

For long minutes, we both are simply still, catching our

breaths and regathering our thoughts, as the Paris afternoon gives way to a warm spring night. Outside, the buzz of traffic becomes a calmer hum. The lavender and daffodils on the air give way to night jasmine, along with the aromas of more savory foods—resulting in a lion suddenly making itself known in my stomach. Then again.

After the second growl incites Reece to a long chuckle, I press my flushing face into one of his pecs.

"Oh, dear. I'm so sorry."

"For what?" He pushes his lips to my temple. "In the last twenty-four hours, you've had a few cups of coffee, one apple croissant, and two-point-five pink macarons."

I giggle. "Yeah, but what macarons."

"Now my favorite cookies." He nestles me a little closer and starts to scrape the hair off my face. Dear God of all that's good in this world. What's the next entry in the postcoital guidebook after *hot mess*? I'm sure the French have some eloquent phrase for it, and I'm glad they're all out shouting and honking at each other on the street instead of up here to see my rat's nest hair and fucked-twice clothes.

Then again, maybe they'd all just be jealous.

Not that I want to dwell on that useless emotion ever again.

Not that I'm promising myself that I won't. But right here and now, I'm just promising myself that I'll try.

"Hey." His murmur vibrates into my hair, already sizzling because of the lasers he's just pried into my mind. Damn the man and his crazy ESP, which always seems tuned to the frequency of me. "What's going on up here?"

Okay, so the sex fuzzed him out a little too. His lasers aren't fully back online, since he actually had to ask. And it's not that I don't want to spill to him, but I'm enjoying the small respite from our deep and intense mode, especially after he turned the apartment's kitchen into a temporary chapel. Which still has me wondering if we should prioritize Notre-Dame on the sightseeing list for tomorrow...

"Emmalina?"

I sigh. So much for pretending I didn't hear him this time. "Yes, sir? How can I be of service to you this fine evening?"

"Hmmmm." He props his head a little higher against the couch. "For starters, how is it possible that you're still wearing every stitch of clothing you got here in?"

I quirk up a brow. Glance over my shoulder toward the kitchen floor, where my seared-apart panties rest in a puddle of sloshed foot bath water. "Not *every* stitch."

He chuckles. "Good point."

In the ensuing stillness, I violate my own mandate to keep this break light and frothy. But he did ask about the grease in my mental gears, and he has a right to know. About *all* of them.

"You know, mister..." I push up a little, propping my chin on my curled hand. "That was pretty astounding."

There's a new tightness at the corners of his eyes, and his lips form a firm line in the middle of his stubble forest. "For me too." He circles his fingertips along my cheek, my chin, my neck. His gaze is steady, silver, and unblinking. Next to my elbow, his ribs expand and fall from his fuller breaths. "Thank you, my beauty."

"For what?" I'm truly perplexed.

"For hearing what I couldn't say." The tension closes in over his brow now, setting furrows into it. "For just...being open."

I extend a few fingers up, smoothing the tips along both

thick arches of his eyebrows. "I'll always be open," I whisper. "If you find a way to talk to me, I'll always be here to listen. You and me...we don't always need words." I flow my hand back down and rest it on the middle of his chest now. "We just need these."

He slides his hand down and rests it against the middle of my sternum. "I'll always hear you too." A leaden gulp thuds down his throat. "Christ, Emma. I can't imagine *not* hearing you. Not listening for you..."

As he cuts in on himself with his own frustrated grunt, I lean up to capture his lips once more with my own. "I know," I tell him once we've dragged apart. "I *know*." Then I kiss him again, knowing he needs that too—especially because of where I'm about to go with our subject matter. "For the record, not all of the drama here was *your* doing, either."

Reece shakes his head. A bunch of his hair flops into his fresh scowl, but I steel myself against pushing it out of the way. Lydia's right about that stuff. It needs its own Instagram page, especially so *I'm* not so tempted to indulge myself in times like this.

"Let's not go there." He throws up one hand. "I know, I *know*. You feel like you overreacted and then ran away before we could talk it out. Both valid, both true—but both wouldn't have been necessary had I trusted your input about this part of the game. Last-minute necessity or not, I was still approaching all this like the sole guy in charge of the mission instead of the guy with a partner at his side." He glares up at the ceiling and shoves a hand through his hair. "It wasn't until I ran the plan by Foley and he asked me if you'd been briefed about everything that I even comprehended the misstep." His mouth thins. "He was the one who laid the proverbial cards on the table for me—

though we happened to be standing in the john at the Brocade, right before you and I left for the airport, when he did."

A laugh tumbles out of me—spurred significantly by the first half of his confession. *A man with a partner by his side.* Holy hell, that feels nice.

"Well, maybe it was *your* turn for the crazy public restroom confrontation of the week."

He chuffs. "Except that Foley's message wasn't so crazy."

"And maybe Tyce's wasn't either." I hate putting a figurative sledgehammer to our exchange, but as long as we're revisiting reality, I take the chance to plunge in and go there. "Speaking of which...did you hear from either him or your dad during my *petit somme*?"

His hair falls back into his face as he gives me the physical negative on that. "To be honest, I'm not expecting anything this soon." He lowers his hand, scrubbing it down his face. "Dad and his squad are likely regrouping. Floating all the test scenarios and hypotheticals, weighing whether it's better or worse to give the prodigal Bolt Boy another chance."

I press my hand to the middle of his chest again, scraping my fingertips in the dip between his muscled slabs. "I know this can't be easy, baby." I don't hold back on the empathy, as much for me as for him.

He curls his other hand around to brush my ribcage through my sweater. "It's all right," he affirms. "I mean, Chase is probably having the time of his life with the graphs and readouts. And it's not like you and I are sitting around twiddling our thumbs."

I reward him for the optimism with a tinkling laugh. "Oh, yeah. Paris has been a *blast* so far."

Though he gets the humor and even joins in the chuckling,

I'm all too aware that the sentiment doesn't reach all the way to his eyes—even as he suddenly rolls up, springing off the couch as lithely as a panther hopping off a tree. "Up," he commands after whirling back around, offering his hand. "You've got me on a mission now."

On my feet now, and with every one of his tall, naked muscles at my thorough disposal, I slip my arms around his waist before forming my hands to the perfect spheres of his ass. "Ohhhhh," I hum. "Am I part of that mission?"

He dips his head, taking my lips in a slow, thorough, mushy mauling. And the best part? He does nothing to dislodge my caresses from his backside. "Mon petit," he growls lowly. "You *are* the mission."

"This is sounding better by the second." I quip it as he yanks me toward the bedroom, though my pout comes out as he keeps going, landing us both in the bathroom. "Hey. I think you missed a turn back there..."

"Nope." He's all rogue panther mystery, even while cranking the shower on and tucking in his hand to check the water temperature. "We're getting cleaned up, and then we're going out. The museums and cathedrals may have to wait, but your 'Paris blast' starts tonight with dinner at Lasserre and that shopping you really need."

Okay, so now I'm squirming. And maybe jumping. A little. But honestly, I'm not certain what has inspired this excitement more—the treat of a date night ahead or the way in which he's promised it. No. *Commanded it.*

As they say in this land, *mon* freaking *Dieu.* The man has taken my breath away from the very start of our relationship, but instead of slowing down on the sigh factor, he just keeps cranking shit up. Higher and higher...and *higher.* Especially now. *Especially* today. From being the wicked beast who obeyed all my erotic commands to being the worldly wolf who now strips me and then steps into the shower with me, he's taking me back to the clouds again—then even higher than that as soon as we're beneath the spray together. With wordless authority, he twirls a finger, silently commanding me to pivot so my back is to him and the hot water cascades over my front. It feels *amazing*, but that's just the prelude. I release a long, nearly orgasmic moan the moment he squirts some shampoo into my hair and begins to lather me up with smooth, sure strokes.

"Ohhhhhh..." I tilt my head back so he can have better access. The motion also serves to pelt more of my body with the perfect hot spray...especially my taut breasts and tingling mons. "*C'est divin.* Merci beaucoup, monsieur."

"*Trés bien.*" Reece utters it with the same mesmeric mood that his massages dictate, his baritone flowing into my ear with sophistication. Paired with his expert touch, it's not long before he has me mixing sighs with the steam, reveling in how pampered and treasured I feel.

And utterly, divinely French.

And along with that, perhaps a little bold.

Perhaps a lot bold.

"Reece?"

"Hmmmm?"

"Teach me some more French."

For a second, his hands halt against my scalp. The man knows me, especially when my voice alters into another vocal range. The tones I usually save for the bedroom. Or, in the case of getting to hide out with him in a little apartment along the Seine, the kitchen.

"All right." The rumble is *his* naughty kitchen voice too—and again, it's a perfect accompaniment to how he touches me. And strokes me. And glides his soapy hands down, down, down, until he's reaching slick fingers around to find the wettest, neediest part of me. "What would you like to know?"

He circles a fingertip at the top of my cleft, putting secondary pressure on my slit, until I let out a high gasp. At the same time, he slides his other hand between my ass cheeks, quickly locating my tight rosette.

"Oh." It rides atop another sharp breath, coinciding with the slap of my hand against the shower wall. "Oh, my *God.*" And then the other hand.

"I thought you knew that one already." His own voice is so damn calm, it's infuriating. I *do* get it. He can't cut loose in here or the water will turn to lightning and neither of us will get to have a mouth orgasm from Lasserre's spiced duck and pear soufflé tonight. But holy *shit*, that doesn't make this power imbalance any easier. "So...how about 'may I have another glass of wine, please' or 'my, how lovely the Arc is at night.' Or maybe 'which way to the ladies' room?'"

I lock my teeth. Let out a growling, furious moan. "How about, 'Monsieur Richards, if you don't get your cock inside me now, I'll scream the whole building down'?"

His chuckle is nasty and low against my neck—as his fingers work more leftover lather into my pussy and ass. "I have a better one. *Je préfère regarder mes doigts dans votre minou.*"

I snarl at him again. There's enough there that I don't need the translation. "No. *Please*, Reece. Inside me. Get *inside* me."

He pushes tighter against me. His nipples are erect points on my back, and his cock starts swelling against my spine. "You mean *baise-moi*, s'il vous plaît?"

"Yes!" I spread my stance and rock my ass back toward him, going half on instinct and half on calculated risk. Seven months with a man, and a girl begins to know at least a few things—like how the sight of her ass drives him wild. "Baise-moi, Monsieur Richards. *Entendre et maintenant.*" I rise up to tiptoes, rolling the top of my back crack against the sack at his base. "Here. Now," I reiterate. "Please, Reece. S'il vous plaît. S'il vous— Ohhhhhh!"

I've been so preoccupied with entreating him to take my pussy, I've completely missed how he's moved back—and repositioned his cock at the ring to my ass.

"Even here?" His demand is the texture of a lightning strike, sizzling and frightening but electric and beautiful. I watch, temporarily speechless, as he grabs a bottle from the little ledge next to my right hand. Lube. *Of course.* In the *shower.* How had I forgotten this place used to be Angelique and Dario's love nest?

A thought that should be squicking me out—but oddly doesn't. Maybe it's the memory of how she spoke of this place being filled with love and passion. More obviously, it's probably because of Reece's demonstration of devotion out in the kitchen.

More immediately, it's because of the spell the man's weaving over me now. Slicking the warm fluid into me. Relaxing my muscles by massaging my ass cheeks and then spreading them out in preparation for how he's going to fill me there.

Dear God, yes.

I need him. His large, rigid body behind me. His long, perfect penis inside me. Invading me until I can't think of anything but the sun he's flying me to, even if that means christening our Paris shower like this.

Yes. Yes. Yesssss...

"You haven't answered me, Velvet." Though the bastard's voice and the throbbing pressure of his cockhead are already hedging his victory with wicked intent.

"Yes," I growl out. "Yes, even back there."

He works his cock in a little deeper. Shudders with pleasure as he rolls his hips in time to his fervent fingers against my clit. "Now...*en francais,*" he orders. "*Baise-moi dans ma derrière.*"

"Oui." I stammer it readily, for at that moment, he pushes aside the covering of my most sensitive place and claims my center with intent that can't be mistaken—nor denied. Just as he was my toy back in the kitchen, I'm now his...and it's beyond amazing. "Oui, monsieur. S'il vous plaît, baise-moi dans ma derrière."

And perhaps...beyond even the sun.

"*Parfait.*" His praise is a rough, dirty contrast to the fragrant steam and liquid heat surrounding us, which only notches my arousal a level higher. And then, with the soap and the lube assisting him, he fills nearly all of my back tunnel in one gliding, hurting, stretching lunge. The second his balls knock against my perineum, his cock throbs and spurts generous precome inside me—adding to the blinding, dizzying force of my climax. I wail from the delicious, consuming pain, working my pussy back and forth along his tapered, godlike fingers—rejoicing, at last, as the man's groans climb to the frantic pace of mine.

"My gorgeous, perfect Velvet." He issues the words between my shoulder blades, swiveling his head to deliver feral bites to both those mounds of bone, as he starts a relentless, ramming pace inside my quivering ass. "Something tells me we're going to be very, *very* late to dinner."

Worth it.

This man is always, *always* worth it.

CHAPTER FIVE

REECE

Somebody's singing Elton John again.

Only this time, it's not the French guy on the stereo downstairs.

I can understand the words now. And it's a woman softly crooning the tune. And she's singing about feeling the love tonight, only it's not night. *Definitely* not night. The crazy-bright sunlight through the curtains tells me that much, along with the bustle of the city in full weekday mode.

I roll over in bed, wrapping the sheets around my naked hips as a full smile takes over my lips. I remember now. It's Wednesday, and I'm not waking up in some swanky hotel suite, fighting to recall even the first name of the woman in the next room. I'm in a secret apartment tucked along the Seine, and the female here with me has a fully memorable first name, middle name, and last name.

Emmalina Paisley Crist.

The love of my life.

The woman who, crazily enough, loves me in return. Maybe to the same depths that I love her.

A truth I wouldn't have believed possible until yesterday—but a truth I went ahead and tested, with my soul bared and my heart open and my fears unsheathed, knowing what I had to show her wasn't a let's-wait-until-the-new-crisis-has-blown-over kind of thing. If what we're dealing with here is even a crisis anymore...

Holy fuck, let this all just be a tempest in a teapot.

A quick check of my phone doesn't reveal any new messages from Wade and Fershan, who have stayed back in LA to keep taking punches at the dark web for any more shit linking—or, please God, delinking—my father's apparent contact with the Consortium and the Scorpio cartel. Nor is there any kind of contact from Tyce, though that's a hell of a lot less surprising. He cornered Emma in that restroom, risking that I'd jump to the conclusion that I did and try to rearrange his face in front of the mayor and most of Los Angeles's upper crust, just to get an off-grid message to me. A message he never had the chance to relay—but bearing a preface containing two words that I must give him credence for. Two words I can't forget. Will never forget.

Alpha Three.

But now isn't the time for that black, *black* rabbit hole.

Right now, I take a second to tap back a message replying to the only text that really matters right now—from Foley, who notified me the second before he was airborne out of LAX and on his way here. That was four hours ago, so I know he won't see my reply until he hits the ground at Charles de Gaulle, having informed me he was going to catch some z's during the flight in anticipation of whatever storm we're waiting to get struck by here.

Which, at this moment, still doesn't seem to be manifesting. At all.

But rather than debate whether that fact is troubling or heartening, I bound out of bed with the sole certainty I *do* have. There's not a damn thing I can do about it right now.

There is, however, something I *can* do in this moment.

Quick smirk.

Okay...some*body* I can do.

Who can really hum a mean Elton John but sounds much better husking French profanities to me from the depths of her gorgeous, creamy neck. And then screaming my name as her sweet cunt vibrates around my plunging cock...

Surprise, surprise—and oh, how conveniently—that's the very same body part taking the lead for my strides now, guiding me out to the dining nook like a heat-seeking missile on a no-abort call.

My brain tosses back an enthusiastic *roger that* as soon as I lay eyes on Emma. She's already up and dressed, looking like a perfect Parisian beauty in one of the outfits I bought for her last night, when several of the stores in the Galeries Lafayette reopened for us. Normally I'm not a fan of the tourist-magnet mega mall, but it was the fastest way to ensure Emma got everything she needed for a while.

A while.

And exactly how long is that to be defined?

More uncertainty. More of this damn waiting on Lawson Richards, every second making me feel like a damn mutt in the rain, wondering if my humans are going to ever let me back inside near the fire...

Get over it.

And focus on the things you can *control.*

Like exactly how beautiful this woman's new "song" is going to sound when she's orgasming for the fifth time for you an hour from now.

Oh, yes. I'm going to settle for no less than five. That's so doable. We got to four yesterday, and I barely fired up any of the fingertips for the cause.

She's all mine. Right now.

No less than five...

Every goal-oriented cell in my body fires to life. Okay, the lazy ones roar to life too—propelling me in all my naked glory to the space right behind her chair and then in to swoop my mouth down on her neck in a take-no-prisoners snarl. She drops Elton at once in favor of a blissful squeal, which turns into a thready gasp as I slide a hand under her striped shirt and tweak fingers around her plump nipple. *Fuck*, that's nice. As much as I adore her breasts when she's aroused and erect, there's something organic and fun about fondling a woman when she's at full rest. Any lover can inspire a nipple to look like it's ready for a porn short. A *partner* is the one who gets to touch it the rest of the time.

Of course, my metaphysical musings now make me want to see both those tips looking like red gumdrops—and at least a dozen other sexual similes. That's just the tip of the erotic iceberg for the places I want to take her pussy...and her mouth... and maybe even her ass again...

"Well, oh *my*, Mr. Richards." She jumps to her feet a second after I circle in to plant my mouth on hers, resulting in the collision of my erection against her shoulder and then her stomach. "Someone's already having an awesome morning."

"Damn straight, my hot little *lapin*."

An enchanting blush flows over her face, as she clearly remembers how I started using the French version of *Bunny* after taking her to bed when we got home last night. We'd screwed with long, slow intensity, leaving the drapes open so the moonlight could reflect off the Seine and through the bedroom sheers. It was damn sweet and damn good. Maybe I'll love her the exact same way right now. At least until she has her *first* orgasm...

"Guess it's a good thing I told Angelique I'd meet her at the café down the block."

Or...maybe not.

Emma cups a hand over her mouth, obviously battling back giggles in response to my what-the-hell gape. Not that the disappointment is helping to dampen the morning wood, merci fucking beaucoup.

"Angelique?" I finally fire. "What the living hell?"

Emma lets her hand fall. Her new expression is more sober—though I don't miss the wistful glance she affords my dick before she turns to face the window next to the nook. "I was up early," she murmurs, "and came out here to read a little. And to think...a lot. As I watched dawn come over the garden, it just hit me all at once..."

"What did?" I fill in her silence with the new gravity in my heart too. I don't just believe every word she's uttering because of how they paint her face into loveliness I can hardly comprehend let alone accept as reality. It's what I feel from her heart. The special recognition she's come to, inundating the air with its incredible magic...making me speechless with gratitude.

"That when Angelique and Dario were here together, they probably thought they had dozens more times to treasure together. In a second, that all changed." She drags in a ragged breath, also recognizing the substance of what she's just uttered. With the light from the atrium limning her from behind, she circles back toward me, her arms crossed. "Life can't be thrown away like you have more of it tomorrow." She slowly shakes her head. "I've somehow always known that when it comes to you and me—but taking that truth and applying it to other people in my life...and yes, even to Angelique..."

As she goes into a verbal void, clearly grappling for the right words, I step over and pull her in with a tight, comforting clasp. "It's okay," I assure, breathing the words into her hair. "It's really okay. And even a little awesome."

"Yeah?" She snuggles her head against my chest, pushing out an emotional little sound—which, damn it, sends a new comet of heat straight down the middle of my body. Back to morning wood. A fucking Sequoia tree full of it.

"Christ," I mutter.

"Oh, my," she snickers.

"This is your fault, you sexy-as-fuck woman." With a determined growl, I spin her away from me—another backfire, since her ass is outlined into a perfect little heart by the formfitting navy capris that go with the top. "Just get the hell out of here before I make you text Angelique that you'll be an hour late."

She flips a gawk over her shoulder. "An *hour*?"

"By the time you get back, it might be two."

"By the time I get back, it'd *better* be two."

I grin. Hard. "Deal."

"Will you be okay in the meantime?" she queries while grabbing her purse. "You want me to bring you back something?"

"Just a coffee." While she's checking to make sure she has everything, I fish my laptop out of my shoulder satchel. "I'll find something to munch on while catching up on emails. We're pretty well stocked for food."

"And drinks and booze," she adds. "I notice how Angie

took care of all that too."

Surprise, surprise, the sequel. Factoid of the day: pure shock is fantastic for whittling morning wood. *"Angie?"* I challenge with one cocked brow.

She answers me with a smile as brilliant and breathtaking as the sunshine now seeming to pour in through every window. Appropriate, since that's how she drenches every inch of my heart in this ineffable moment.

"It's a new day, Reece Richards."

I smirk with deeper determination. It's either that or sprint across the room, lay her out on the couch, and tackle her for a quickie for the road. But goddamnit, when has it *ever* been a quickie with her?

"Yes, it is, Miss Crist."

After giving me one more lingering look, making me weigh the decision to really make her push off with Angelique, she's out the door and down the stairs. Of course, I rush back into the bedroom to get in one more eyeful of her, though I'm respectful enough to the neighborhood to throw on a pair of sweats first. Sort of. "Thrown on" is an upgrade from how I position them just to the point of covering what's necessary for common decency, ensuring the woman sees exactly what will be awaiting her attention when she returns. The torso. The V. The trail of dark hair thickening and then disappearing beneath the gray flannel...

She stops to sigh. Then again. Then, with a soft laugh, turns and heads for the quaint café a short block away.

I'm tempted to stand at the window and watch her until she disappears in the crowds on the sidewalk, but it's obvious the wuss bug has already crawled in and claimed too much of my blood. I push away from the window, yanking my pants up to a decent level this time, and add a navy short-sleeved Henley on top in honor of the predominant color of Emma's outfit.

Wuss Man, hear me roar.

The tiny trumpets accompanying the rally are enough to get my ass plunked at the dining nook to attack my mounting emails with vigor. Summer will be officially starting in Southern California in a few weeks when the Memorial Day holiday hits. At the Brocade, we're rolling out a new water park area to entice more families to visit the hotel, but I'm still in a semi-playful sparring match with Neeta and the management team about giving the theme. They've all proposed to call it *Bolt Bay*. I wonder why in hell that's even an option when we have two dozen world-famous beaches down the road as inspiration.

I groan as Neeta pings back my IM, citing the market research and focus group feedback numbers indicating how much more revenue we'll make from fucking *Bolt Bay*.

And all I have to sacrifice for that is my goddamned dignity.

"Says the guy who dressed matchy-matchy with his woman today?"

I'm saved from my neurotic grumble by a firm knock at the apartment door.

After messaging Neeta that I'll be right back, I jump up and hurry across the living room, checking my watch as I go. An hour has flown by, meaning the *two* hours I've promised Emma are closer at hand. She's obviously aware of that too, meaning her time with Angie must've been fun but brief. Thank fuck.

"Hey. Welcome back." I throw the deadbolt free and twist the knob but take just one extra second to lower my sweats until I'm nearly showing butt crack goodness again. "I thought you checked for your key when you were..."

My voice trails off.

Correction. My choke ushers it into silence.

As I blink at who's really standing in the hallway, a subtle smirk spreads across his broad mouth. A mouth still marred from the trio of damn fine punches I landed to it three nights and five thousand miles ago.

"Hey, dickwad."

Outwardly, Tyce is still the epitome of trendy cool and male model chic, but just as blatant as his black tailored ensemble, his ten-thousand-dollar smart watch, and the entire salon full of product atop his black waves, there's a strange glint in his cobalt eyes, reminding me of the darkest parts of the forest when we went to camp as kids. A darkness none of us ever wanted to be lost in.

It's almost enough to sway me. Almost the visceral detail that pushes me over into believing he's friend not foe and that the cryptic connection he forged to Emma back in LA was worth a trusting step back now, really believing he's representing Alpha Three in some strange way.

But the thing is...he's here.

Here.

At a location nobody else is supposed to know about. A location, Angelique assured me, that even the Consortium never learned about.

Have they now?

"What the fuck are you doing here?"

He blinks for a couple of seconds, looking like I've actually decked him again, before unleashing the old Tyce snark as he leans against the doorframe. "Well, you see, it's cookie season, and if my troop sells just fifty more boxes of the caramel chocolate ones, we'll get to take a trip to the zoo. And oh yeah, ice cream afterward."

"Are you kidding me?" I'm planted to the spot, unable to move forward or backward. I'm furious, but I'm cognizant enough to realize it's anger because of fear. *A lot* of fear. And right now, not even for myself. If Tyce has been putting us all on, perhaps even acting in collusion with Dad, then the Consortium's in on this shit and we've been made. I'll be dead inside ten minutes—which doesn't stress me out as thoroughly as fast-forwarding my mind to Emma's eventual arrival and realizing she'll be next on the asshole's list.

But if I can get to my phone still lying on the dining nook table next to my laptop...

Yes.

There's still hope—slim but better than standing here with my dick in my hand—of notifying her to stay away. To get her ass into a car and over to the airport, where Sawyer will be arriving in a few hours.

My thoughts clear because of the strategy, and I jerk my head at Tyce. "Get your ass in here."

I wait, letting him stroll—*stroll*—past me into the living room. "I know this is kind of crazy."

"Yeah. Fifty boxes? Don't those caramel things move the fastest?" I keep it to a drawl, matching his for sarcasm, though the tone is deceptive. There's nothing relaxed or mirthful about me right now. I rake him over with a watchful gaze, checking in all the normal places for all the normal things. Bulge of a gun, outline of a boot sheath, even the line of a wire...but my Spidey senses are completely fried. Though his clothes fit his form like a well-made glove, they're completely black and very thick. About as close to leathers as cotton-blend shit can get.

"Usually they do." Weirdly, Tyce's steps have stiffened since he entered. Eventually, he comes to a complete stop, his back still facing me. "But this might be giving some of my customers second thoughts."

I have only a second to process how his voice has gotten weird, along with his stance. No longer is his wisecrack delivered with his worldly whisky murmur. It's dry and labored, like a corn husk put to vocal cords...

The same way one entire side of his face looks as he turns back around toward me.

"Holy *fuck*!" But even his marred features aren't the instigation behind my stupefied gasp. That honor goes to the fact that even the smooth side of his visage *isn't his*. There's something familiar about the male model perfection there, but I can't even stop for that dig right now. I can't comprehend or care about anything at the moment except for one glaring, horrifying fact.

My brother is gone.

"Reece. It's all right."

Only...he's not.

The voice is still there. Tyce's voice. Kind of. Buried beneath the three-packs-a-day rasp is the buttery assurance of the man I know.

The brother...I trust.

"Reece."

"I...I don't understand." I have to clench my teeth to stay the heat behind my eyes. Jesus, if this is freaky for me, I can only imagine what he's going through.

Hold the fuck up.

I *can* imagine what he's going through.

"Holy. *Shit*." I pace across to him, hating how I lean over as I go as if I'm approaching a damn rabid dog. "This is what *they* did to you...isn't it?" I reach out, cupping his shoulder, shaking as hard as he does at the contact. "You're not doing this *for* Alpha Three, are you, Tyce? You...you *are* Alpha Three."

The stranger-brother in my grip shudders again. The motion takes over him, rushing down to his feet and then back up again, consuming both sides of his face in a terrible grimace. A stare of pure pain, loneliness, anger, and bitterness.

"*Jesus*," I choke. "Tyce."

We fall against each other, clutching hard and holding on, struggling to comprehend the enormity that a horror now binds us thicker than blood—a nightmare that isn't even over.

Perhaps it's barely begun.

And because of that, my mind all but detonates with a tumble of new questions. When was he taken? *How* was he taken? Are his abilities the same as mine? How did he escape the Consortium? And most pressing, how the hell did he know about this place?

I'm on the brink of demanding his response to that one when a key rattles in the apartment's door, accompanied by the music of two women joined in laughter. Sure enough, before I can think of what to say or even how to hide Tyce, Emma bursts in with Angelique at her side—though they both stop cold as soon as their gazes land on Tyce.

There are a thousand questions in Emma's eyes.

There are a thousand tears in Angelique's.

Only then do I realize that the most bizarre twist of the day hasn't even happened yet. That comes as soon as Angelique finally finds her voice and stammers out one word in a querulous question.

"Dario?"

PULSE

PART 9

CHAPTER ONE

E M M A

Some sights in life are truly unforgettable.

And while I hope I live a long, long life after this point, I'm pretty certain this moment will be one of the few I still recall when I'm a half-loony ninety-year-old telling people about the craziest moments of my existence.

Because this is crazy, right?

Point one: I'm walking into the Paris hideout I've been sharing with my sort-of-fugitive superhero fiancé, arm-in arm with his ex-girlfriend, the woman I'd once written off as the bitch nemesis of my existence.

Point two: discovering that the hideout isn't as covert after all—because now there's a stranger in here—who doesn't seem to be a stranger at all, if everything I'm reading and feeling from Reece's posture and demeanor are accurate.

Point three: the former bitch on high? She's now launching herself at the stranger-who-isn't, raining sobs and kisses on him with such frantic passion, I wonder who hardwired the guy's pheromones into her central nervous system.

One glance at Reece, who's looking more flummoxed than fugitive, and I see I'm not alone in my massive clump of dazed. Thank God for him—and his brilliant mind that's never too far from my wavelength.

"Dario. Dario. *Dario.*"

As Angelique croons it nonstop, Reece and I exchange new gapes of *what the hell?* Why is the woman calling this stranger the name of her supposedly dead lover, though interjecting her cries with mewls so plaintive, I wonder whether to go looking for cat treats or condoms.

I peer even harder at Reece, grateful for the strength and sanity that are mainstays on the face of my superhero hunk. Clearly, he has a few more pieces of this puzzle than me—but only a few. And now maybe a few less, as his jaw drops and his eyes bulge.

"Dario." He stresses the name with different awe than Angelique. "Of course. The photo...back in LA...that's where I've seen you bef—" Unbelievably, his features expand with more astonishment. "Wait. *What?* Tyce, what the fuck?"

"Tyce?" Now I dive into the astonishment. "Baby, what the hell are you— *Whoa.*" I choke it out as the stranger brings his head back up—now with Tyce Richards's features in place. Talk about a dog paddle into the deep end of shocked.

"*Mon Dieu.*" Angelique's cry is garbled, as if pushed out through bomb fallout—probably the most apt comparison for what this guy has just *kaboom*ed on us. Less than a week ago, I was squaring off against Tyce Richards in the ladies' room at the Griffith Observatory. Everything in front of me now fits the paradigm of that chiseled stud. The "Richards plateaus" of his shoulders. The deceptively lean arms. The hewn torso tapering into his fit waist. The long runner's legs. Tyce had crowded all of that iconic glory right into my personal space but then insisted he hadn't come to assault me—and had proven good on that promise, though he'd brought a fun parlor trick that made me scream for my life anyhow.

For a couple of insane seconds, he hadn't been Tyce anymore.

Now it's happening again.

His face...changes. Becomes a mess of mottled flesh on one side, a scowling prince on the other—a prince who *isn't* Tyce, at least on the outside. Neither was a real reason for me to scream at first, but together like that? So suddenly like that? And where the hell has *Tyce* gone?

Before I can even contemplate the answer, Tyce returns as if we all have just fallen into a fugue state and hallucinated the half ogre.

Oh, my God.

I get it now. Holy shit, do I get it.

The ogre *is* real. And somehow, he's Tyce. Or...Tyce is him. *If* this is even Tyce...

But if it *is* Tyce, then where the hell is Dario?

And how am I *even* taking these questions seriously?

But I am. Holy shit, I really am. Another look at Reece yields the confirmation, albeit in a darker and fiercer way, that he's still on the same holy-crap-I'm-really-thinking-this bandwagon.

Tyce—or whoever the hell this is—sets Angelique back by a step, though he's clearly reluctant about it. He underlines his contrition by pressing a lingering kiss to her lips. "*Mi amore,*" he murmurs, accenting the words like he's just stepped off the plane from an Italian island. "It *is* me, Angelique. Please, my love. No more tears. You're tearing me apart."

While Angelique dutifully nods and sniffs—slamming me with another tidal wave of surreal shock—Reece starts tipping the scales at the other end of the reaction scale. "So what the hell have you done with my brother?"

"I'm right here too, Cheesy Reecy."

After eight months of being with Reece Richards nearly every day, I've never watched him pale this much or this fast. "Shit," he sputters. "It *is* you."

Tyce slides out a lopsided smirk. "Now that we've got *that* cleared up..."

And this time, the three of us get front-row seats for the Tyce Face Flip show—resulting in three jaws hitting the floorboards in unison. "Oh, my God." I finally get the chance to unload it aloud—though I'm still having trouble reconciling what I *see* to what I believe. No, I really haven't leapt out of *The Matrix* or jumped off Platform Nine and Three-Quarters. I'm truly looking on as Tyce's striking handsomeness fades from the center out, as if curtains are being opened on a museum's rare new painting. The portrait revealed beneath is that bizarre double visage again: on one side, the features so classic they could grace a Roman coin, but on the other, a mottled collection of flesh that looks like an artist globbed pigment onto a canvas and then decided to do some finger painting.

As the transformation completes, Angelique follows my soft exclamation with a soul-wracked moan. "Dario." She closes the gap back to him, lifting her palms to the sides of his face. "My love. *My love.*"

He spreads his hands up, meshing his fingers between hers. "*Mio Angelina.* Look at you. Still so beautiful." He dashes his head down again. "But now I'm nothing but a monster."

"You are *alive.*" She rages the words, giving way to more sobs while yanking up his face again. "You *survived*, Dario. You have brought the sun back to my existence, the breath back to my lungs. You have just given me the best gift of my life. Do you think I care what paper it's wrapped in?"

A massive lump clogs my throat as he strokes her cheek with a shaking thumb, now soaked with her coursing tears. I pull in a rickety breath. Another. It's no use. The heat behind my gaze goes to liquid as well. Reece gathers me close, his embrace engulfing and comforting. While I use his Henley as my handkerchief, I can feel the stiffness still dominating his stance, the tension in every breath he takes. Though he strokes my back in motions meant to soothe and protect, his fingers are as rigid as the pylons of all the bridges across the river outside. It comes as no surprise when he clears his throat with an equally strained sound.

"Tyce," he grates. "What the hell is going on? And before you begin, are we going to need alcohol?"

I nestle my forehead between his pecs, kissing the spot over his heart. "I think that's a question of *when*, not *if*, baby."

"Wine and ale are in the refrigerator," Angelique supplies. "A bottle of decent Pinot Gris and some Duvel Citra."

The normal side of Tyce's face bursts into a delighted grin. "Duvel Citra? Seriously?" He directs it to Angelique like a kid with the Willie Wonka golden ticket.

"But of course." Her fairylike laugh is stopped short by his fierce, appreciative kiss. Again, I observe their exchange like a dumbstruck voyeur, unable to help myself. Angelique is a brand-new person to me right now. A woman transformed by love. But my most astonishing realization? If Tyce had returned to her looking like Homer Simpson, she'd still be this overjoyed. And yeah, that means a new conundrum. It's damn hard to keep thinking of her simply as the temptress who guided Reece to his ruin. Like him, maybe she really was a cog wooed to the Consortium's machine by promises of heaven, only to be rewarded by tragedy.

I refocus on the couple as they end their kiss with a giddy smack. "You've really kept it stocked?" Tyce murmurs to Angelique.

Her eyes brim once more. "Always."

He grasps her by the back of her neck. "Because you never gave up."

"Never."

Just as her tearful whisper is going to make me lose my emotional shit again, Reece comes to everyone's rescue by swooping in, clapping his brother on the back, and booming, "I think those ales are screaming our names louder by the second, asshole."

While looping one arm around Angelique's waist, Tyce swings a hard punch at Reece's arm. "Who you calling *asshole*, asshole?"

Reece cocks his head, sending a chunk of thick strands into his eyes. "Call me anything you want as long as it's not *Easy Reecey*."

"Well, hell," I grumble. "Because inquiring minds *do* want to know..."

Reece glowers toward the kitchen. "No, they don't."

Tyce tosses me a wink from his good side. "Catch me later, Emma. I owe you for that scare in the bathroom at Griffith."

Reece groans and rolls his eyes before leading the way into the kitchen with the stride of a king leading his courtiers to the war room. I gladly follow, sneaking in a gawk at his ass in those sweats while trying to wrap my mind around the bizarre turn of the last fifteen minutes.

Fifteen minutes.

Have I really just come from being in the cute café down the street with Angelique, sharing laughs over croissants and coffee and thinking designer dog sweaters would be the craziest sight of my day? Do I really have to rethink what I shared with Angie back then—that my fiancé's electric blood would go down as the most bizarre sight of my life?

"*Merci*," I murmur to Angelique as she sets a glass filled with liquid the shade of pale lemons in front of me. Before she can pull away, I grab her hand for a quick squeeze and eagerly accept her returning pressure. A lot of people would call our truce complete lunacy, but after everything that's happened over the last hour, especially watching the woman fall to her knees in thanks for her beloved's return from the dead, I'd be seriously tempted to give all of them a nice view of both my middle fingers.

After entwining his fingers with Angelique's once more, Tyce sets his jaw, straightens his shoulders, and draws in a formidable breath. He sets his determined gaze back to Reece. "Where do you want me to start?"

For a second, my man becomes a visible chunk of discomfort. No eight-point-five on the expectations Richter scale. After everything Trixie Richards disclosed to me about the dynamic—or lack of one—that her sons have, Tyce's sudden openness is a logical stunner for Reece. I'm not surprised that Reece gets over it with the focus worthy of the lightning in his blood, by propping his elbows on the table and lasering Tyce with his stare. "In this case, I think the brutal beginning is best," he states before riffing off of Tyce and also hauling in two full lungs of air. "Yes or no—*you* were Alpha Three? And are you still?"

"Yes." Tyce lifts his ale and takes a long swig from the frosty bottle. "And no."

A pulse ticks in Reece's jaw. "And did you know I was Alpha Two?"

Tyce knocks back a longer drink. "I had a damn strong hunch."

I grip the side of the table and lurch forward. "And you didn't do a damn thing to try to help him?"

Reece curls a hand around my shoulder with misleading calm. "He couldn't, Velvet. No more than I could help him. And believe me, though I had no idea who he was, I wanted to." His words are crunchy with emotion.

Tyce not only hears it all but wears an answering wave of emotion across both sides of his face. Yeah, even the mottled putty of his bad side is twisted with the stuff. "Of course you wanted to—because that's the kind of person you are."

Reece's gaze bugs. "Oh? That so?"

Tyce shakes his head. "And there you go again, trying to cover it up."

"Says the guy capable of changing from my brother into other people at will?"

"Just my face," Tyce counters.

"Great. Thanks for *that* clarification." Reece's grimace betrays his mix of confusion, frustration, and straight-up fear. "Do we get the behind-the-scenes on *your* cover-up now too? Or morphing. Or holographing. Or CGI shit. Whatever. Different definitions, same cover-up job, right?"

As his rant ramps higher, I wrap one of his hands in both of mine. It'll likely do little to help him calm down, but I have to at least try.

"Listen to what he's saying, baby," I urge. "Please."

But Reece's features are already in granite-cliff mode, fortifying his ramparts before Tyce or anyone else can nick them. Throwing up the ramparts is as easy as breathing for him, since he's been doing it his whole life—a truth I likely knew somewhere deep inside even before Trixie Richards verified it during our lunch last week. The woman simply provided the details to back my intuition. This man was once a boy who desperately wanted to matter to his family; he then grew into a teen who acted out so he would; and then he became the young man who turned that act into an art form. And he would've spent his whole life perfecting that masterpiece if not for the six months that altered the portrait forever.

That mashed up the paint...

A situation his brother gets now more than ever.

But my surety of it goes beyond the literal symbolism of Tyce's twisted-paint flesh. The same instincts that haunted me for so long about Reece have returned as emotional wraiths on behalf of his brother too—shades that fly tighter and closer with every passing minute we're spending with the guy. By now, they're starting to help me snap logistical beads together about all this...

Connections that hold tight, despite Reece's sneering retort to my appeal. "Listen to him?" he snaps, adding a rough chuff. "And you'd be referring to...what, exactly, sweetheart? An account of how he's seen the light about the integrity of my soul? About how the hell of the Source opened up some heaven of cosmic collectiveness for him, and now he wants to be buddies? Bond over 'the good ol' days' under the Consortium's thumb?" He see-saws his head, aiming his ears for opposite shoulders. "And electrodes. And probes. And needles..."

"He was there." Angelique stuns the rest of us with her vicious spew. "He was *there*, you bastard—and paid just as high a price for it as you."

My jaw falls an inch more when she all but filets Reece with the jade glass of her glare. In that look, the subtext of her statement is clear. By *just as high a price*, she really means that Tyce's final ticket was much higher than Reece's.

"*Angelina*," he murmurs, kissing her knuckles. "Hell doesn't pick favorites. None of us was unchanged by that hive of horror."

And there's my opportunity to speak up. None will be better. During the three seconds Angelique takes to answer him with a quiet fume, I lean forward to examine Tyce at much closer proximity. Searching for the truth that has to be gnawing at him from inside—the part of the confession he's debating about how to express.

"Only there's one huge difference to your experience," I issue. "Isn't there, Tyce?" I slide my hand free from Reece's, needing the added authority of the pose. "You volunteered to go into that hive of horror, didn't you?"

REECE

I'm waiting.

Still waiting.

Any second now, Tyce is going to capitulate to a tell. He has at least twenty, and I know them all. When we were younger, I actually studied them and learned every one of their meanings. When I grew up, I tried emulating them—and even succeeded. A finger to his lips? He's still figuring out the most smartass way to trump someone. Subtle scrunches at the corners of his eyes? He's already tossed out his respect for the guy. Small jut of his jaw? He's in a corner and he's going to come out swinging. Hard.

But my brother has answered Emma's allegation with nothing but stillness. Openness. A calm that has me wondering why someone isn't barging into the room to proclaim him the next Dalai Lama.

What. The. Living. Fuck?

My lips part, and I'm tempted to blurt exactly that. I'm not sure how, because there's no room inside me for a goddamned *thought* around the edges of my astonishment, but somehow I choke down a breath. But as soon as I inhale, the accusing words threaten again. Not that I can form them—any more than I can believe what I'm seeing. Across *both* sides of this fucker's face.

"Tyce?" My utterance is ragged on the air, blending with the soft music filtering from down below. It's French Elton John again, only today he's singing "Daniel." As the crooner starts in about his brother heading for Spain, my chest tightens like miles of knotted, wet rope. I know that Tyce gets it after one second's worth of his sad half smile. "*Tyce.*" I can't help growling it. "Goddamn—"

He ropes me back by lifting one finger. Then, as he lowers it, exhaling like a man three times his age. "First, for the record"— he arcs an eyebrow at Emma, irking me and encouraging me at once—"I didn't volunteer for a fucking thing." He swings his stare all the way back around, now revealing the subtle glow behind his eyes. His color is different than mine, luxurious pewter and chrome instead of a dying sparkler, which actually gives me a second of electricity envy before he continues. "And second, I'm only telling you the whole story because it's vital that you know all this now, *not* because I need a fucking Teddy Ruxpin. So keep it parked over there, shit sprocket."

I touch two fingers to my temple. "Yes sir, Ricey Tycey." Then smirk because I can, having dealt a blow on behalf of little brothers across the globe. It's the last chance I'll get for a while. I resecure my hold on Emma with hardly a conscious thought. I need the knowledge of her there. The life in her pulse. The comfort of her grasp. The core courage to which she's inspired me just by asking the toughest question of this exchange.

How the hell did Tyce wind up in the Consortium's grip?

Across the table, my brother nearly drains his bottle. "So once upon a time, there was this dude, Reece Richards, who disappeared off the face of the planet..."

"And his brother was the only one who noticed?" I return.

"Ding, ding, ding." Tyce rings an imaginary bell.

"How'd you know?" I ask. "Because those assholes were damn good at covering every angle of the illusion."

Angelique's face pinches as if she's been stabbed. "Using me as the girl with the mirror and the drape, for which I will never be able to apologize to you enough, Reece."

"Water under the bridge," I murmur—despite the fact that I'll never be able to forget falling from that bridge. Writhing on a lab table as the faceless monsters in the lab brought in a monitor so I could watch myself attending some fashion show in New York with a model I'd never met, an orchestrated stunt for the paparazzi performed by a putz who looked like me. The same night, I was apparently at a Broadway sneak preview, dining with *another* model, and hitting the hottest night club in town—different venues and different putzes—for the very reason Tyce explains now.

"That was just the problem," he states. "An illusion is only as good as its distractions, and distractions have to be believable." With the tip of a finger, he traces the condensation left behind by his bottle. "And *none* of that bullshit was believable, even for a hardcore stud like you." The undamaged side of his mouth quirks. "Thing is, it takes another stud to know that."

I groan. Emma and Angelique giggle.

"So you started to suspect something was hinky?" I interject.

He narrows his eyes. "Did you really just say 'hinky'?"

Emma tucks her knee under her backside. "He picked it up from me."

"Well, in that case, it's cute."

I yank a daisy out of the vase on the sideboard and lob it at him. "Brooding Phantom thing or not, I'm not above breaking your knees."

"I believe that is your cue to continue, *ma panthère*." Angelique purrs into his ear.

My brother turns his head and leans toward her with every focus of his being, as if the only place he can fathom "continuing" is in the bedroom. I feel my gaze narrowing. Their affection is kind of gross yet really cool. And my gut has never been weirded out more.

But after a second, Tyce is back with all of us and cocking both elbows to the table. Thank fuck. With his fingertips, he twirls the flower I've just tossed. His expression seeps again with that contemplative sadness, as if the flower fascinates and infuriates him at once. I know what he's feeling. I've been there. Holy fuck, have I been there. Asking so many questions, only to learn they circle back to just two key queries.

Why did I survive?

And why are there so many moments when I wish I hadn't?

"So, yeah," he begins again, his murmur as quiet and careful as before. "I noticed something was...hinky." He winks at Emma. "And the more I started really looking at everything, the crazier it all got. I mean, beyond crazy. Did you know that one night, 'you' were actually in Ibiza and Milan at once?"

I snort, attempting to infuse it with a laugh. "Christ. They'd really have to crown me the world's party god then, yeah?"

Angelique joins my chuckle, but I can see Emma isn't amused—and, I sense, not for the obvious reasons. The way she bites her lower lip and drums a couple of fingers against the table conveys a violence that's not normal for her.

I don't waste any time angling my head and penetrating her with a silent message. *What is it, Velvet?*

There have been rare occasions when she's grateful I've read her mind. Thank fuck this is one of them. After a short but meaningful huff, she discloses, "I'm finding it hard to believe that a group of genius-level criminals were that stupid."

Angelique shrugs. "Einstein loved to sail but did not know how to swim," she offers. "And Michelangelo never bathed."

Emma grimaces. "Ew."

"You ever study Tesla?" Tyce's question earns him a new smirk and kiss from Angelique. Again, I'm not sure whether to laugh or glower for myself. Are my brother and Angie, who in another life would be invited to every red carpet on earth for their combined sophistication factor, really trading factoids about dead geniuses?

"But this was just standard logic," Emma insists. "Granted, a lot of people wouldn't notice just because they didn't follow the celebrity gossip mill, but there are a lot of *other* people who do keep up with that stuff. I have to believe that someone, somewhere—"

"Yeah," Tyce cuts in. "And that someone was me."

I redirect my gaze over to him again, ensuring he sees

the gratitude in my eyes. What I don't show him, or anyone else here, is the doubling of my confusion. For close to twenty years now, I've thought my brothers only tolerated me. Forget about whether they'd notice if I'd been gone for several years, let alone months. But I can't say that my behavior earned their regard, either. After high school, I gave up trying. To know Tyce *was* paying attention, even if it was just by a few glances, cranks the winches holding the ropes across my chest.

"And after you started looking at all the hinky pieces"—I quirk an edge of my mouth—"what did you do with them?"

My brother's growl drops between his ribs. "What I probably shouldn't have done."

And in the middle of my own torso, a thrum of dread gains a lot of volume. "You went to Mom and Dad."

He grows very still.

Then ominously quiet, even while tossing back one last sip of his ale—before returning the bottle to the table with a violent slam, which makes both women recoil.

I don't join them in the flinch. I expected the outburst. "It's all right, T." I murmur it despite knowing it won't lighten his bitterness by any degree. "I would've done the same thing."

He truly seems to absorb my words. Not the comfort I send with them, but at least the truth of what I'm saying. "They told me I was being a drama queen," he confesses. "Those were Dad's words, at least."

I swallow. It burns. "And what were Mom's?"

"Not the same, of course. More to the effect that we all had to accept that your oats were wilder than Chase's or mine, and we had to be patient and wait for you to work it out of your system."

I clench my jaw. That hurts too. "All out of my system," I

grate. "So...even when I didn't call or get in touch..."

"She was still getting texts from your number, man. We all were."

I whoosh out a harsh breath. "Of course."

"And of course, the week I took all my hunches to Mom and Dad—"

"You mean your hinky hunches?"

He twists his lips. "Now who's begging for a knee breaking?"

"Move along, move along." I flick the tips of my fingers against the air, savoring the chance to toss shade only a brother could get away with. And damn, do I mean savoring. Never have I dared to believe that I'd be able to mess around with either him or Chase this way. The bonds have always seemed permanently severed. Yeah, the three of us were always linked by the threads all siblings share, woven into the fabric of our lives by the commonality of a shared childhood—but that childhood was a long damn time ago, and sometimes "water under the bridge" just means the riverbed has gone dry. But my river is filling up again, flowing as sweetly as the music from downstairs that talks about brotherhood and scars and seeing things beyond the face of the stars...

"Anyhow," Tyce goes on, adding his mushed-skin version of an irked brow, "that was the week when some man-bun choad from the press decided to float the theory that it wasn't really you next to that catwalk in New York." He shakes his head while returning a finger to the bottle condensation race. "*Pffft.* What a tool."

I laugh without humor. "I think I know the one."

"The only person on the planet who believed him was Mom, who thought it was cute that Reece look-a-likes were springing up everywhere."

I grunt softly. "That's not surprising."

"You have a point."

"Now let me guess Dad's reaction."

"Why?" Tyce retorts. "You *that* much into pain?" Again with his funny mottled-brow lift. "You been giving me *hinky* all this time when you really mean *kinky*?"

"Move *along*." I jab up a middle finger as embellishment.

"Ah, well. Since the spoilers have already been given, I'll move quickly past Dad's part—except to say that he dismissed you with impressive speed as a waste of humanity."

"*Impressive*, huh?"

Tyce is waiting with a *down boy* hand in response to my obvious seethe. "Cut the updraft, lightning boy. I meant impressive in that he left an *impression*—and it wasn't exactly the stuff I'd write a Father's Day card about." As he lowers his hand, he huffs tightly. "I was so grinded about it, I even went back the next day and called him on it."

My bark is all acid. "Bet *that* went over well." Translation? I'm beginning to get a picture of how my beautiful but ruthless brother began the transformation into this marred creature who is, for all intents and purposes, the only person I can call a comrade from the hive.

"Well, it didn't go over at all," Tyce replies.

"What do you mean?"

"Just that." Both sides of his face convey perplexity. "I asked him why, even after I presented clear evidence that things were off when booting up the Reece Richards hashtag, and didn't get one shred of a replay from the night before. Not a single wounded papa bear call-out. Not half a growl about you pissing on the Richards legacy. Not even a self-righteous Billy Idol sneer."

Next to me, Emma makes a fast-fisted upswing. "I *knew* it." Then makes a *duh* face at me. "Idol? Your dad? Hello?"

Jesus God, she's enchanting.

As I take a second to press a smitten kiss to her lips, Tyce focuses out the window, as if attempting to memorize the trees in the garden. But I already know his mind's eye has flown all the way back to New York, reliving a memorably strange meeting with our father. After hearing his admission, I'm damn sure I'd choose the same option.

"I've never seen Dad look that way," he utters. "Like he had some kind of crystal ball into a truth no one could see. He was...quiet. Distant. Barely there with me."

The bands across my chest constrict again. I breathe in and out, seeking the place inside where I can stow away enough emotion so I don't turn into a glowing isotope right now. "Did he say anything?"

Tyce wheels his posture back around and looks up—but he's only looking, not seeing. Inside, he's still at Richards Hall, probably in the library or Dad's study, with the gardeners buzzing outside and weirdness cascading inside.

"He said that you weren't my worry," he utters. "That you were doing just fine, that all would be 'sorted out' in a while, and that I needed to just get back to my life and stop fixating on yours." After two ponderous blinks, he's back in the here and now, though he's brought something back from the memories. Casually put—because this moment needs that shit—he's got the feels. A lot of them. Emotions, I'd always assumed, that he literally didn't have the DNA for.

But wasn't that what the world once thought about me too?

I'm blown back by the recognition to the point that Emma

notices and takes over things. Thank God. "What did you do then?" she asks.

"What could I do?" Tyce returns. "Staying for a leisurely lunch and a round on the putting green wasn't an option, especially because I knew I had some work cut out for me. As soon as I got back to my place in Manhattan, I dove in. I started backtracking to the dates when your feeds stopped making sense."

Emma squeezes my hand tighter. She's starting to realize what I do. This is going to be the difficult part to hear. Angie's composure changes in the same way. She presses her lips into a terse line.

Still, Emma gets out, "How far back did you have to go?"

At once, I long to kiss her again. It's the same question searing my mind, though I acknowledge the answer won't mean anything. Inside the Source, every day was an eternity. After I escaped and went into hiding, it was strange to learn only six months of my life had been stolen from me.

"A little under six weeks," Tyce answers her. "But as soon as I made the conclusive call, the rest fell easily into place." Both his temples tighten. "Almost too easily, I suppose—which should have thrown up a red flag for me. But maybe the flag *was* there, and I refused to see it."

"Which means what?" Again, the question comes from Emma.

"That as soon as I spotted and identified the last woman Reece had been spending real time with"—he caresses Angelique's hand from wrist to light-pink nails—"I pretty much wanted her for myself."

During his declaration, my regard switches to Angelique, where I see composure settings that the woman never dialed into with me. She's trés gaga over my brother, proven all too clearly as she murmurs to Tyce, "And began to chase relentlessly."

Tyce kicks up half a smile. "Well, it made things a hell of a lot easier..." His voice dips at the end, turning into a rough breath as he meshes gazes with Angelique. They're like that for a long pause, completely tied into each other, until he snaps away with a self-conscious head shake. "Sorry, man," he mumbles. "Not trying to make this weird for you."

I chuff out a laugh before purposely landing my gaze back on my gorgeous woman. "We've all been through hell, brother. Sadly, there's nothing like that to make a man see his true heaven—and appreciate it."

I speak the last words right to her. *Into* her. Emma absorbs them with such a powerful potency, I swear *she's* about to glow. But the woman has been that way since the moment I met her, with those wide turquoise eyes reigning over soft, flowing features so full of passion and life. I'll never see a sunrise or sunset that captivates me more. The only feeling more addicting for me is knowing I do the same for her—confirmed the moment she leans over in a sighing rush, forming her lips to mine. Within seconds, we're a tangle of tongues and moans, with me hauling her into my lap just so I can have more of her near me, wrapped around me, pressed against me.

"Love of God." Tyce's growl punches the air, confirming there's still a healthy chunk of his sardonic bastard side left. "You two want to get a damn room?"

"Have one," I rumble while parting from Emma and sending a derisive side-eye across the table. "Ten feet away. So let's do the rest of this, okay?"

My dictate is met by more trademark Tyce in the form

of his arrogant smirk—which comes as a welcome sight right now. The fucktards in the hive didn't strip him of everything, though I sense we're all about to find out how deep the rest of his damage goes.

After he copies my move, tugging Angelique until she's cuddled in his chair with him, he states, "So I'll skip over all the parts where I chased this luminous creature around half of France and Spain with a perpetual boner..."

"Yeah, please do." Though my sarcasm fades the next second, as everything about my brother turns to unmistakable tension.

"The fuckers grabbed me just after midnight, outside a bar in Madrid. Funny thing was, Angelique was there as bait for them to catch someone else, and she never knew what a prize they'd really gotten that night. To this day, I'm not sure how I was discovered or recognized. It had been about ten days, and I had a good beard grown in." He snorts. "I even dressed like a tourist and wore retail cologne."

"Not *that*."

He starts a snigger but plugs it short. To the outside world, my levity might be disrespect. To the two of us, it's a toehold on sanity. "Anyhow, they knocked me out damn fast. When I woke up, I was strapped down to a steel slab. They never told me how long I'd been out, and I knew better than to ask where I was."

He stops to get in a long breath. I take one with him, sharing our survivors' version of a stiff shot. Inside the Source, there was no Señor Patrón or Madame Absolut to help with the hundred or so "rough spots" in each day. There was only the hope of another heartbeat. The solace of more air. The grit to hold on and reach through the pain. To get to the next breath.

Another inhalation.

Another long agony of letting it back out—because I know that pulling it back in will bring on more memories.

And it does.

And from the middle of those shadows, I finally reply to him, "Would it have mattered if you *did* know?"

Tyce sits and listens to several lines of the song that echoes across the courtyard. As French Elton sings about clouds in eyes, several gray and white billows scud by overhead, temporarily turning the morning to twilight.

Into that stolen moment of gloaming, my brother releases his bleak whisper.

"No." He slides one hand atop the table again. Palm down, fingers flat, tips pressing until they're white. "It wouldn't have mattered at all."

The clouds move on.

The sun sends a new glow back into the room.

But the tips of Tyce's fingertips glow even brighter.

Brighter still.

And *now* I reach out to him.

With a forceful slide, I bring my hand up beneath his, locking our thumbs and then our palms. As I wrap my fingers against the back of his hand, their glow emanates all the way up his arm.

We're silent, doing more of those deep-breath shots for another minute. The song from downstairs finally ends, thank fuck, and French Elton moves on to a new track: "Don't Let the Sun Go Down on Me." Well, at least it's not "The Last Song."

Maudlin tunes or not, my brother and I lock stares once again—in the mutual agreement that a crucial moment between us is finally here. It sucks, because we've both been in denial about having to face it until this moment—but now that it's here, we both understand we can't run from it any more than our own destinies.

"Tell me." I say it softly but command it with authority, recognizing it's likely the only motivation he'll be able to use for speaking the rest of this truth.

His truth.

Probably saying it aloud for the very first time.

So after directing him, I brace myself—knowing this is liable to get fucking messy. Knowing I'll likely have to tell him, more than once, what Emma was there to tell me when I finally trusted my story to spoken words. And unguarded confusion. And unhindered shame. And unbridled guilt.

You didn't ask for this.

You didn't deserve this.

The pain is in your body, but it doesn't have to be in your soul.

And yeah, even the last one, which I'm still not sure I believe—but it's become the reason I keep putting one heavy foot in front of the other, each and every day.

It's going to be okay.

Eventually.

CHAPTER TWO

EMMA

It's another one of those surreal but all-too-real moments, stamping itself with darker ink onto the fabric of my existence. As these once-estranged brothers clasp hands, I share a look with the woman I once considered my bitter enemy—and the two of *us* share a new bond too. A moment of brand-new understanding, empathy, connection...forgiveness.

Two brothers. The two women who love them. Four hearts suspending their beats, giving bitter respect for the truth they're about to endure.

"Tyce." Reece has steel armor on his voice now, ready to face off against the obvious growth of his brother's remorse. "It's all right, man. None of it was your fault."

Tyce caves his shoulders. Hangs his head. "Don't you think I fucking know that?"

Reece grinds the back ends of his jaw. I feel the *no* already fulminating in his chest, but he swallows it down and growls, "Then you know none of this crap was your fault. That the Consortium is a nest of messed-up maniacs with overblown god complexes and tiny dicks."

Tyce lifts one side of his head. Eyeballs his brother from the midst of Silly Putty flesh that's now spidered with glowing cobalt veins. "And Faline?"

Reece grunts. "She has a tiny dick too."

I swing a curious stare at Tyce. "So you know who Faline is?"

"Oh, yeah. I know who Faline is." The verbal dungeon of his voice is all the incentive I need not to ask how or why. I have a horrific feeling we're about to find out anyway.

"So she supervised your...experiments...too." The pauses Reece stabs into it aren't surprising. Beneath my fingers, the taut cords of his neck and shoulder still belie the noun he really wants to say.

Torture.

"Oh, I was one of her favorites," Tyce relays. "But only because of you, man. I was like the B side of the Reece Richards chart-topping hit. She liked calling us her 'exclusive Richards collection.'"

"Cute." Reece sets his brother free in order to sweep up his ale and knock back an angry gulp. "But if she was going for a matched set, she only snagged two out of three."

Tyce pulls all the way up. His face—*both* sides—is stony. "I'm getting to that part."

Reece slams his bottle down. His profile turns feral. "*What?*"

"Breathe." After waiting through the full minute it takes Reece to recompose himself, Tyce goes on. "Like I said, we were the exclusives. The elite. Whatever the Consortium wasn't finding in the other Alphas, they'd found in our Richards DNA."

As I swivel to face the table more fully, my hand slides to the middle of Reece's chest and lands right over his thundering heart. "Faline told you this?"

"Not in so many words," Tyce answers. "But yes."

The throb of Reece's heartbeat becomes the snarl beneath his voice. "She never told me any of that."

"And disclose to *you* that they'd nailed *me* too? And that would have benefited her...how?" Weirdly, Tyce finishes it with a smirk. "You were the one that bitch was always the most paranoid about, Reece. The star she freaked the hardest about keeping roped down."

I squirm against Reece despite how he tries to comfort me—but despite my overwhelming urge to puke, I force myself to assert, "Because he scared her the most."

I don't bother checking for anyone's affirmation. I'm already sure of it as absolute truth. I might have only spent six hours beneath Faline's thumb, but after just six *minutes*, I knew the enormity of the woman's obsession for my man.

But Reece's baffled scowl also confirms more of what I already know as fact. This is total news to him. *Well, peachy.* Guys really *can* be that dense sometimes.

"*I* scared *her*?" He snorts. "In what world is that logical, considering she had needles in my balls?"

"The needles were *because* of her fear." Tyce matches my certainty. "Obviously, the bastards were getting different outcomes with every new subject they experimented on. With me, they got an electronic shapeshifter able to bring them one of three new faces at will. One day, I heard them talking about one of the Omegas being able to jump sixty stories in a single bound. Another can stretch her arms by ten feet apiece. As they've played with voltage and treatment duration, each guinea pig has returned a different result."

Reece's lips twist. "Even death."

"Oh, especially that," Tyce asserts. "At least a couple of dozen before we came along, according to Faline."

"If she can be believed," I mutter.

Tyce tilts his head. "Even if she's right by half, that makes the Consortium a posse of scary fuckers."

Angelique, who's been carefully quiet through the exchange, releases a watery sigh. "They believe in their cause the same way religious zealots do. Even Faline, in her strange way. They view the dead as martyrs for the greater cause of mankind."

"And the escapees as traitors." Tyce's edict corresponds with a new song on the air from French Elton John. More specifically, "The Last Song." I glare out into the courtyard, silently wondering if the downstairs DJ needs a hug or two hundred. As I pull my focus back inside, Reece curls his extended hand into a taut fist against the table. The stench of fried electricity invades the air as silver and blue sparks pop free from the gaps in his fingers. The tiny explosions hop a few times along the table before fizzling out. Thank God for protective shellac.

"So," Reece finally ventures. "You found a way out too?"

Tyce's nostrils flare as he pulls in a deep breath. Then another, twice as deep. "Not exactly."

Reece's inhalation is equally ominous. "So you're still on their goddamned radar?"

I lurch off his lap, already knowing he's going to follow me. Pacing is the only way he'll be able to burn off his fury. Some of it, at least.

Dear God, I hope.

That outcome depends a lot on what Tyce has to say. The bouncing ball of logic isn't landing him in the home court of believability anymore.

"Not...exactly."

And so not the words to help cool the nuclear reactor of Reece's wrath. "Okay, brother," he spits. "So, *what* exactly, then?" He's already covered the length of the kitchen in three furious bounds and whips back around in the archway to the living room, hands laced at the back of his head. "You here as their fetch dog, like she was back in LA?" He jerks his chin at Angelique. "At least she brought gifts. Or are you hiding the cufflinks in your back pocket?"

Angelique surges to her feet. "*Fils de pute.*" Her gaze is green flames. She rolls her shoulders like an Amazonian on a mission. "Do you *see* what those *connards* did to him?" Her voice pitches higher. "I thought he was *dead!*"

"I almost wished I was," Tyce mutters, reaching over for her before he's done. "I'm sorry, Angelique, but I did. I was certain I had nothing left to live for. That they'd dealt the same treatment to you, only worse." He clutches her against him with a big hand at the back of her head. "They hinted at it in all their taunts. Told me how they'd violated you, burning your face off as they did, until you begged for your life. They used it to make my tears come, so the salt would run into the flesh they were rearranging." He yanks her closer before croaking, "Dario's flesh."

"*Putain!*"

As hoarse and hurting as Angelique's grief is, I'm glad for it. While I knew none of this would be easy to hear, the pit of my stomach rolls over on itself, and I clutch hard at the pain. When Reece rushes over and pulls me close, I twist my free hand into the front of his Henley. "Dario's flesh," I echo in a rasp. "The face he was wearing when she first met him, inside the hive. The face she first fell in love with."

For several long minutes, we're no longer four people in

one room. We're two completions of souls, unities of spirits, and symbioses of love. Needing each other. Healing each other. Though our men give us shelter in their arms, Angelique and I are the quarries from which they gather their strength and rebuild their ramparts. Neither can exist or edify without the other.

As "The Last Song" ends—thank God—and gives way to "Goodbye Yellow Brick Road," Angelique relents her hold on Tyce by enough to tell him, "They did none of those things, *mon amour*. This I give you as truth. They likely thought me sufficiently broken by the news of your death, since I pleaded so convincingly for them to keep me in the fold."

"Which was a brilliant move." Tyce adds to the praise with a fervent kiss to her forehead. "Brilliant but fucking dangerous."

"Said the bull fighter to the sky diver?" Reece charges.

Tyce swoops a glare over. "You talking to me, Monsieur Bolt? After spending months facing off with the finest asswads of LA's underworld?"

"Not a time clock I'm punching anymore, man."

Tyce's response to that is strange. Resignation grabs at his shoulders but intensity claims his stare, as if his will alone can change what Reece just said. "Not regularly," he echoes. "But still often enough, right?"

Reece scowls. "Meaning what?"

"That you're still retaining the badass moves? And you still know what you're doing around thugs and henchmen?"

"Yeah, maybe." The furrows deepen between his eyebrows. "Okay, probably. But why?"

"Because they might be needed."

"For what?" I add one hell of a forward stomp at the end

of my demand. Something tells me I'll need the extra steel in my stance—and not in a bring-on-your-shit-I'm-Wonder-Woman-and-can-take-it kind of way.

That dread in my instinct is only confirmed by the harsh lift of Tyce's chest as he squares his own posture, which jams his gaze to the same latitude as Reece's.

"Because Dad is in collusion with the Consortium."

And then drops that fun tidbit on the air.

And, if the warring blue lights in his eyes can be believed, isn't even done yet.

"They're going to use the dinner party for the Virage opening team as a cover for their trap."

Reece's gaze fires like a Tesla coil. "Their trap for what?"

"Not *what*," Tyce returns. "*Who*." He swallows hard. "It's been their plan all along—to get the three of us in one place at one time. They knew neither you nor Chase would be able to resist the invitation. For you, it was a matter of shedding your black sheep wool once and for all. Luring Chase simply meant making the deal interesting—and lucrative."

"And what about you?"

Reece asks it in a growl of tight wrath.

Tyce answers in a growl of tight grief.

"If I ensure you and Chase are both at this thing, they'll perform the reconstructive surgery on this." He gestures toward his deformity with fingers curled like claws. "I told them if I have to live the rest of my life as a caged beast, I refuse to fucking look like it."

"Caged beast?" My echo is as taut as his declaration. "Tyce?" I demand. "What the hell are you saying?"

He drops his hand while circling a new look at the three of us. An expression filling him with such despair, the normal side of his face closes in on matching the marred side. "Faline wants her matched set of Richards brothers, and our father's going to help her get it."

Nope. He's definitely not done.

Not by a horrific long shot.

REECE

Eight hours later, I'm enjoying the serene beauty of Paris at twilight on the outside but still dealing with the nuclear fallout of my spirit on the inside.

Emma walks along the Seine with me, beyond beautiful in another one of the ensembles from last night's shopping spree. The dress is a little trendier than what she'd normally pick, but I'm glad I talked her into the ice-blue creation, with its one-shoulder bodice and fringe-enhanced hem, paired with high-heeled shoes that look as if a knot-tying certification would be needed before wearing them properly. I'm damn glad she went through the trouble, though. The intricate laces, crisscrossed up her elegant legs, make me fantasize about doing the same to her sometime using silk rope. Or whipped cream. Or streams of my come...

And now, no matter how halcyon this whole scene is, I'm officially in agony. Nothing says *oo la la, Paris* better than a raging erection in the middle of the Parc Rives de Seine, right?

And because it always wants the last laugh, my cock jerks even more when Emma pauses and leans over to pet a couple of fluffy pups being walked by a handsome woman on the arm of her guy. Like me, the man is dressed but not too dressed, in light wool straight-legs and a fitted blazer with a bright pocket square over a white dress shirt. Yep, that's us. Just a couple of gents walking our ladies in another one of those French sunset dreams that have been nearly canonized in poems, songs, photos, and films throughout the ages. And why not? Nowhere else on earth is *romance* a more revered word. Nowhere else on earth is passion considered a celebration, audaciously carved into the buildings and grown into the flowers and reflected in the people.

And in the midst of all of it, all I can think about is wanting to kill my father.

She knows that too. My beautiful, near empath of a woman, who rises from the gawks of the dogs only to be confronted by all the commotion in *my* gaze, which hasn't changed since Tyce dropped that warhead in the apartment this morning. And the bomb after that. And the one after *that*.

But Emma, who already knows that, returns to my side with the grace of a queen and the eyes of a healer. She reaches for my hand, hers possessing the strength she's offered to me all day. Strength that asks for nothing but demands everything— because it has to. Because she needs to keep showing me that even if I fling my ugliest thoughts at her, there's no way she's going away. That's a damn good thing, because I'm not sure the monster in me is bugging out anytime soon.

A monster who's the son of a monster.

Another thought to which I give her full, hideous access.

Another blow she endures with just another heavy gulp, though she adds a tentative chew on the inside of her lip before tugging me along again.

To our left, more dogs chase each other across a lush lawn. To our right, lovers lounge on the grass adjacent to the water, many with picnic blankets and wine, though they're all much more interested in each other than what's in their bottles. One couple is even writhing and kissing with such gusto, they've knocked their wine over, sending russet-colored rivers through the bright-green grass.

And *there's* the sight that finally nicks Emma's composure. Not much, but enough that I see beneath her "amused" laugh to the aching female beneath. The woman wondering what it must feel like to maul her lover along the Seine during a candlelight-colored sunset, uncaring about spilled wine and barking dogs and mad scientist sadists who want to put her fiancé in a mutant trophy case along with his two brothers...

But I see it. I see *her*. I may be enraged and contemplating murder, but I'm not blind. Not when it comes to her. Please God, *never* when it comes to her.

Only now that I *have* seen, I feel like the heel on every loaf of bread within sight. We're in fucking Paris, and I'm still brooding like I'm stuck in an Adele video. And I didn't learn my lesson from trying to borrow from the woman last fall? And it's not like Tyce's announcement came as a strike out of the blue. Three nights ago, after seeing that incriminating photo of Dad and Faline at a Consorcio Sciences staff retreat, I was prepared for damn near anything.

Or so I'd thought.

"Wow."

Emma's sighing exclamation at last breaks into my brain. While my gut may still be contemplating murder ideas, I follow the trajectory of her gaze to where the dipping sun beams across the statues bracketing the Pont Alexandre III. The gold-winged horses, atop their high pedestals, look ignited and ready to fly over the waters that now swirl with reflected golds, blues, pinks, and purples.

"It's...beyond beautiful." After whispering it, she

visibly holds her breath—as if she can freeze the moment by suspending her every motion.

"It is," I murmur back, yearning for the exact same thing. The catch in my voice throws her off for a second, and she gives a little *piff* while lightly smacking my arm. "Ooohhh. You meant the *river*?" I use the absent wave of my hand as an excuse to catch hers, playfully kissing the center of her palm.

By now, we're near the middle of the bridge, looking out toward the Eiffel Tower. The elegant icon is etched against the brilliant yellow sky—but now Emma's the one not paying attention to the view. Her gaze is filled with as many shades as the waters below us as she intensely studies my face.

"Reece." Her rasp is practically a plea, and I frown with curiosity until she says, "It's all right. You don't have to pretend, okay?" She rotates so we're facing each other and fits her forearms atop mine. As she scrapes her fingertips against my biceps, she emphasizes, "This isn't date night, and that's all right. You don't have to be Mr. Witty, Mr. Romantic, or even Mr. Richards. I don't care. I just want *you*—and to just be here with you."

For long seconds, I'm completely still. And stunned. No. More than that. Have I been thrown off the bridge, dunked in, and then yanked back up here to stand in just as equal a shock? The declaration is the last thing I've expected—even from a person this extraordinary. A woman from whom I've learned to expect the unexpected. "And if I *want* to be any or all of those?" My sardonicism is a small step back toward a mutual comfort zone. We're dressed up. We're out. Sometimes—many times—acting the illusion is easier than being the truth. For good measure, I slide out half a smirk and add, "Or maybe someone else? Like Mr. Wicked-on-the-Pont-Alexandre-the-Third?"

But as soon as I dip my head and tug on the backs of her elbows, she defies my pull. "Not even those," she states firmly. "Don't insult me, damn it."

I'm stopped in place again—and don't hold back my vexation. "Insult you? What the—"

"I'm your fiancée, Reece, not some mindless dance floor dolly you picked up in the Oberkampf—so please, *please* don't start with the player-hunk charm as your smoke screen." Her nostrils flare. "I said it's all right not to pretend, and I meant it."

I start in on an incensed glower, but fuck that shit and all she's expecting from it. Instead, I give in to the half grin I really want, ruthlessly taking advantage of the tiny huffs from her pursed lips, timed with her anxious foot shifts. Clearly, she's already debating her own damn words, and I couldn't be fucking happier.

As seconds pass, she keeps exposing more of her truth. Damn it, she wants to take this shit to a hot and heavy kiss as urgently as I do—but for some reason, she needs the justification of a verbal skirmish to get there. Maybe it's because of all the insanity that's gone down today. Maybe she really does need the outlet of the rage first. Well, fine. If she needs to play it that way, I'll be anyone she wants me to be—even the "player hunk" she professes to diss but now reacts to with a pair of cute, hard nipples defying her dress's lined bodice.

"Hmmm. Sorry." But as I brush back an errant strand of hair from her collarbone, I let my fingertips ignite with faint blue glows against the creamy expanse. "But maybe...not sorry."

She sucks in a breath. It's wobbly, even a little woozy—and it's my dream high. Knowing what I do to her...that the electricity in my touch does this to her... It's a heaven I never imagined my mutant beast would ever know, and it heats even more as she breathlessly pleads, "*Reece...*"

"Christ, baby." I lift my other hand, gliding my soft glow along her opposite shoulder. "You're beyond stunning."

"St-Stop." Lamely, she tries to smack my hand down. "I mean it, okay? You don't...you don't have to..."

"What?" I dip my gaze to watch frissons of arousal tumble down her sexy frame. *Jesus.* I wasn't lying, not by one syllable. She's the most exquisite thing I've ever seen, with the twilight in her hair, the city lights in her eyes, and the desire coursing through her body. For me. *All for me.* "What don't I *have* to do, my little Parisian Bunny?"

She tries to step back, but every movement is a jerky stumble. "For God's sake, Reece. Your brother didn't just pull off his own mask, as it was, this morning." As she starts pacing in a wide circle, her grimace is a contrast to the ornate joy of the bridge's embellished lamps and springing cherubs. "If *I'm* still reeling over what he revealed about your dad..." She slams a hand to her forehead. "Holy *shit.* How could Lawson let himself owe so much juice to the Scorpios that he's willing to let them take all three of his sons for the Consortium? What kind of a man does that? What kind of a *person—*"

She cuts herself off with a sob but muffles it by sliding her hand over her mouth.

Well, shit.

I rush back to her side, already hurling player-hunk Reece into the river in my mind, but it's too damn little and too damn late. I wheel her around and clutch her close, roping an arm around her waist and securing another against her head. And though I squeeze my eyes shut, willing her to feel my acknowledgment of her misery, she's already stiffer than any of the poles holding up the bridge's lights.

"Obviously, he's not a person," I finally utter. "Not anymore, at least."

And as soon as the words are out, I swallow against another urge to throw myself into the river—along with five gallons of disinfectant. Looks like it's my turn to become a light pole, but as soon as she wraps her arms around my neck, suffusing my system in the warmth of her comfort, I can at least breathe again.

I can do this.

I can face anything—shit, even the insanity of what I've learned about Dad—as long as my Emmalina is in my arms, by my side, consuming my heart.

"How come you sound so calm about it?"

Her query, mumbled into my chest, makes me hold her a little tighter. I rub my lips in her hair, wordlessly comforting her, just needing to be her strength for a little while. Maybe longer. She's spent so much time today helping me wrestle with this hell that she hasn't had her own chance to go a few rounds with it.

"It's kind of simple." My pragmatic tone sounds strange and distant, though it's reverberating in my own skull. But as she softens against me, I'm reassured she's accepting it as truth now. "I've been sailing the rocky seas of Lawson Richards since I was a kid. While this is the largest tidal wave the motherfucker has ever thrown at my boat, it's not the first."

She turns her head, flattening her cheek against my chest, and adds a curious compilation of a sob and a growl. "The fact that you can say that so easily makes me hate him more." But then the sob gains traction. "I'm sorry," she mutters into my shoulder. "I'm so sorry, but—"

I stop her with a hand in her hair and the plummet of my mouth over hers. Not half a heartbeat goes by before she's letting me part her lips and plunge in with command, both seeking and giving the electric connection that's ours alone. *Christ, yes.* The last time I kissed her like this was this morning when she left for coffee with Angelique. Too damn long ago. *Forever.*

When I pull back up, I refuse to set her gaze free. While massaging my fingers against her scalp, I'm still sovereign with my hold. Another heartbeat of losing myself in her turquoise depths, and then I compel words back to my lips before I can give in to driving my tongue down her throat again.

At last, I command quietly, "Say it again."

I don't have to be more explicit. The understanding across her face is my complete confirmation. "I...I hate him."

"Again. Only without any remorse. *Do it.*"

She jerks her chin up by a decided degree. The sheen in her eyes vanishes. "I hate him, Reece."

I nod by the same measure before bringing my other hand up to frame her head. "Now tell me you love me."

Not a dictate this time.

A supplication.

Met by her instant, unhindered adoration.

"I do love you. Oh, God...with everything I am, Reece. With every shred of my heart and corner of my soul."

"No matter what?"

"No matter what."

At first, I give her my thanks with a long, determined breath. Then with a longer mash of a kiss. Then with a new lock of my stare as I testify, "Good. Now you'll understand when I have to kill him."

EMMA

I yank my head free from his hold. I'm tempted to add the rest of me to the retreat too, but I decide to give him time for a retraction. A wink or a snicker to tell me he's not done with player-hunk Reece yet, and this is his way of letting the guy have just a little more fun...

At the expense of my Zen setting.

Okay, that's a stretch. Nothing's been Zen about any of my "settings" since the moment this man barged in on his brother and me in the bathroom at Griffith Observatory—but right now, he's slicing apart what threads of the stuff I've managed to stitch back together in the last seventy-two hours. With *big* damn scissors. And a steady, stern stare that flutters my pussy and challenges my sanity in the same freakish swoop.

He's got to be kidding.

I rock back an inch more, giving him ten more seconds to come clean about it.

Fine, then. I'll lead the damn beast to water myself. "You're kidding."

"*You* tell *me*. Am I kidding?"

And then there's dealing with an ox who believes he's a camel. With two full humps.

"Okay." *Stay calm. Stay reasonable. Maybe he'll explain how this new life goal happens without him ending up in the hands of the Paris police or the Consortium.* "And when, exactly, are you planning to make this happen?"

I'm not concerned with how; nor do I want to know. One check of his jaw's harsh slashes, and I know he's already fantasized a dozen ways to rain silver fire and blue brimstone down on Lawson.

"During the Virage dinner party, of course."

Did I just compare him to an ox? And I gave him that compliment...why?

Because right now, I'm gaping at a man who's traded places with an ostrich. And left his brain clearly jammed three feet below ground somewhere between the apartment and here.

He even lets me shove free from him as if the muscles between his shoulders and hands have turned to feathers, though I suspect I caught a strange break. Nothing has relented about the grip of his gaze, which the moonlight is rapidly turning into daggers, matching the harsh blades of bone his jawline has become as well.

Fine by me. If he wants to go hardcore avenging angel and earn wings out of his ass—with the ostrich stance, he's already halfway there—then I'll be happy to give him some walls to crash through on his way. And hope to freaking God they'll bash some sense into him instead.

"Okay, so indulge me one more teeny question here." As demure as I'd like to be about it, I can't stop my hands from bracing to my hips. Considering the thigh-high shoelaces and their platform bases sufficing as my "shoes" tonight, I need all the help I can get. "What part of jacked-up-beyond-all-definable-logic do you *not* understand about this new mission?"

One corner of his mouth ticks for a second. Not a smirk... more like a notation. "Hmmm," he grunts. "That's more colorful than I'd anticipated. I'm impressed, Bunny."

I laugh. All right, it's more like the bark that belongs to the moment when the Camp Crystal Lake counselor goes into the woods with Jason. "Bunny isn't here right now, *Ox*."

A higher lift of his lips. "Ox, eh?"

"Wasn't my first choice." Every syllable is a defined bite. "But I'm being kind because I love you." *God help me.* "Your turn for shelling out the grace now. No, wait." I throw up a hand, one finger pointed. "Screw the grace. You owe me this. Why the *hell* is this remotely *close* to a viable plan?"

"Emmalina." *Crap.* It's not the good kind of *Emmalina*, either. It's the kind I'd expect from my father about to tell me a Justin Timberlake concert isn't happening on a school night. "This is the *only* plan."

I repeat the Crystal Lake bark. "And now you're really joking."

A deeper tilt of his head. Hair falling into his face, *not* helping me set aside the stark beauty of his face in the golden glow thrown down by the lamps. "Jokes aren't usually the best call for a subject like this."

"Really?" The bark becomes a snarl, and I welcome it. "Because you could've fooled me, mister—and your own life is the damn punchline here."

He jerks himself back up to full posture. "Do you think I haven't run this on any other scenario? On a *thousand* others? Taking him out on the street isn't an option unless the likelihood of civilian casualties isn't a problem for anyone— and it's a fucking problem for *me*. Sneaking into his suite at the hotel seemed a better concept, until I had Wade and Fershan attempt to dig into the Virage's system for blueprints and security systems covering the hotel's top floor."

I narrow my eyes. "*Attempt* to?"

His nod is terse. "They came back with nothing. Those plans only exist in physical form and are likely locked in the vault in the hotel's security center—which makes Fort Knox look like a sorority house."

"Which Sawyer and a good security team could crack."
I refuse to accept his finality about this, especially because
Sawyer's flight touched down hours ago. The man is one of the
best there is, a fact Reece doesn't even try to negate despite the
continuation of his grim expression.

"Of course they could," he affirms to my assertion. "Given
a couple of solid weeks, at the least."

"Two weeks?" I clarify it, incredulous tone and all, just to
be sure *he's* sure. When Reece doesn't move a muscle toward
retraction, I lock fingers in the space over my churning belly
and start to pace. I mean, *pace*. As in holy-crap-he's-really-
thought-this-out pacing. As in holy-crap-he's-really-going-to-
attempt-to-kill-his-dad pacing.

"Two weeks," he states again, "that we don't have."
He jams his hands into his front pockets, and I know why.
The intensity of my emotions isn't easily bouncing off him
anymore. I envision his fingers, long and elegant and aglow,
curled against each other inside those recesses. Just like that,
my imagination fills with how they look wrapped around that
body part at his center...and I have to stop, clenching my thighs
to stop the fantasy from making all of me quiver.

What the hell were we talking about again?

Oh, God. I remember.

And just like *that*, the epiphany of his penis is gone.

And I only see the only possible outcome of his insane
idea to take his father down at the Virage team dinner.

In my mind, he's beautiful and blue again.

But this time because he's dead.

I wrap my arms all the way around my middle now. My
strangled sob spills out anyway. Then words I can't control, no
matter how deep the cracks they spread across my heart.

"I...I can't do this."

And I'm twisting away, banishing his magnificence from my view. Tearing myself out of his incredible energy bubble. Unable to accept his magic anymore, if all I have to do is give it up once he returns to Lawson's inner sanctum again. Because he'll refuse to let the Consortium take him alive...

"Emma. *Emma.*"

As soon as his footsteps quicken and harden behind me, I hasten my pace. But damn it, I'm no match for him in these flimsy shoes. At least I anticipate his hard clap over my bare shoulder and am ready to rip free—and actually succeed at it—for a couple of exonerating seconds.

"Let me go. *Damn* you, Reece, just let me—" My damn body betrays me, heaving lungs not letting me have the rest of the words. Hell, they barely allow me breath. They've been kidnapped by a bastard named heartache and his sidekick despair. "Let...me...*go*," I seethe out between the wretched rasps, despite how he turns me and tries pulling me close again. *Tries.* I'm a ragdoll now, praying for limp nothingness. Being numb means I don't have to picture him dead anymore.

"The fuck I will."

Damn him, squared. And his tormenting, bone-melting grip. And his *whomp* of ferocious force on the air, all but puddling my knees. And the carved perfection of his face calling to every pore of my body and craving of my soul, even in the midst of his fury. God help me, especially now. He's so dark and noble and beautiful and—

"I *can't!*" My heart swells and bursts with it this time, and I writhe in his grip from the emotional shrapnel. I'm bleeding out from desolation, but the man won't let me get away to mourn him alone.

To mourn him...

Period.

"Talk to me, Emmalina."

"No!"

He clamps both hands to my shoulders. Then again, as if to drive home his point. He's not letting me go. Not that it'll show him what he wants. A grief I can't confront. A loss I have no control over.

A choice that's already been made for me.

With the blast of that thought, something must finally flare enough in my eyes to make him back off. By a little. Not nearly enough.

I'm not above pushing again for the full retreat, though. "I'm not doing this," I level at him from tight lips. "Not right here, not right now."

His mouth goes rigid too. And screw my life if the look doesn't turn him into five times more of a burnished, beautiful badass. "The hell you aren't."

"The hell I— *Gaaaahhh!*"

If I felt like a gawky gull on stilts before, my stunned screech seals that deal—as the man dips down, reaches over, and throws me over his shoulder like a fisherman taking a trout home for dinner. The world is flipped and upended, sky, then buildings, and then grass whirring by before being consumed by a view of his ass I'd normally be enjoying the hell out of. But right now, I'm not focused on joy. *At all.* I'm still screaming and grabbing on to his belt for dear life. While his arm feels like a human binder clip around my thighs, I'm not taking any chances. His pace is fired by too much fury, and the concrete still looks too damn close.

"Reece! What the *hell*—"

"Hush."

"Are you kidding me? And for God's sake, my *skirt*. Would you get my damn sk— *Aahhh!*"

He's spanking me.

Even more than once.

I'm so astounded, especially when he gets in a second smack even through all the fringe on my hem, that my shriek turns into a squack.

"I said *hush*."

Holy.

Shit.

Is there a word that exists to describe this level of utter asshole?

Is there another word that exists for *my* level of stunned stupidity? And completely turned-on compliance?

What the *hell* is wrong with me? *Why* the hell am I not wrestling him with more than a few pointless moves, which succeed more in grinding my crotch into his shoulder, my face against his back, and my glare closer to the perfect spheres that work with caveman rigor to carry me off the bridge, down some stone steps, past a dark archway seemingly leading to under-the-bridge dungeons—*oh, dear hell, no*—and along a concrete walkway next to the water? What the freaking *crap* is going on? And why, why, *why* is my heart racing with a hundred kinds of rage but a hundred *more* kinds of arousal?

I should *not* be hot and mushy for him right now. I should be riled and raging. And not just because of this, whatever the hell *this* is.

Once again, the image of his lifeless form floats on the rushing blood in my brain, reminding me exactly what that reason is. But the second I let out a protesting groan and consider kidney-punching him as retaliation, he's walked out onto a narrow gangway. The concrete I was just wary of has become water.

Shit, shit, shit.

"*Bon soir*, monsieur." The greeting is deep and jovial, reminding me at once of Lumière from *Beauty and the Beast*.

"Bon soir," Reece responds. "*Parlez-vous anglais?*"

"*Oui.*"

"Excellent. Are you available tonight?"

"For the *entire* night, monsieur?"

"Yes."

"Oh, my God," I grumble into the middle of Reece's spine. "Damn it, Reece. What the hell— *Ow!*"

Another spanking. Just one *thwack* this time, but it's double the intensity of his others. "What the *living* hell?" I shriek.

"Ssshhh." Reece's rebuke is quiet, but he cups my backside so solidly, it's a full promise of another spank if I don't chill out. For a second, giving in to the luscious mix of fear and anger he's stirred into my arousal, I think about really challenging him. But just for a second. I'm much more interested about how the man defines "reward" than "punishment."

"Oui, monsieur." There's a hint of humor in Lumière's tone now. For that I write a mental note to give him nothing but glares once I'm on my feet again.

"Fan-fucking-tastic." There's not a shred of mirth in Reece's voice—surprise of surprises—as he stomps forward again, eliciting my exaggerated *oof* the moment he stops and then takes a definite downward plunk. I'm just as amazed-not-amazed to observe he's toted me aboard one of the fancier river limos, with an interior cabin that has an L-shaped leather couch, a side bar with a champagne bottle on ice, and a platter of assorted macarons.

Macarons. Oh, hell.

But Reece deposits me in an unceremonious heap on the couch, as far away from the delectable cookies as I can be. Just in case that hasn't communicated his message already, he looms over, digs a forefinger and a thumb into the sides of my chin, and yanks my face up until our glowers are openly fighting each other.

"Stay," he snarls, ripping his hand away. "And *don't* touch the macarons."

"Or else what?" It spews out before I can stop it, earning me a sharp tick of one dark Reece Richards brow. And damn it if I don't automatically sit up straighter and consciously compress my lips just in case any other random thoughts decide to get me in trouble.

Trouble.

And *me.*

In the same sentence?

What the hell *is* going on here?

I'm not opposed to trouble. It's just that I like it more when I know it's okay to cause. So technically, that doesn't make it trouble anymore. I'm good at pretending.

Only this isn't pretend anymore.

Which is also not the only crazy thing about this.

Not only am I not pretending...but Reece isn't glowing.

I mean, as in *nowhere.* Not his eyes, not his fingertips, not even in the veins popping against his arm muscles as he shucks his coat and rolls up his shirt sleeves, causing me to shift in place to ease the pulsing tension between my thighs. Which, of course, doesn't work. I'm left to fume with my lust, now layered on top of my confusion and anger, which can be totally blamed on his marauding George of the Jungle act.

But oh God, what an act.

I watch as he converses with Lumière the skipper, though they're speaking too low for me to hear. After Reece lets the guy run his credit card for payment, they start pointing up and down the river as if mapping out a course for our "cruise," though I have a feeling I won't be getting a dreamy romantic float-by of all the city's sights tonight.

As Reece pivots back around, pinning me all over again with his multi-daggered stare, I toggle that feeling into the category of certainty.

And as he whirls and swings back into the cabin, all with the grace of a guy just switching out one jungle vine for the next, I battle the urge to welcome him back in with open arms and open lips.

Though I'm not sure I have any choice about that either.

CHAPTER THREE

REECE

As the boat's motors power to life beneath us, I slam the cabin's little door shut behind me.

I clear the three steps to where Emma is still braced in the curve of the couch and extend both arms, dragging the window curtains with me, sealing out the rest of the world.

When I get to her, I bring my hands in again—and reach for her with all their cupped, taut need.

Now, it's only us.

Now, she's only mine.

Including every damn detail of her truth.

A moan rolls out of her as I curl my fingers in, filling my grip with the stunning sweeps of her jaw. Then the high apples of her cheeks. Then the soft planes of her temples. When my touch finally coaxes out her tender shudder and soft sigh, I jam my hands back into her hair and yank hard enough to turn her breath into a pained cry.

Fuck. *Fuck.* That sound...what it does to me. I'm not out to hurt her. I only want to wake her up.

I barely clench back from groaning myself, funneling the energy I'd have used for it back into keeping the lightning at bay from my fingers and my gaze. Emma's noticed my abstinence. I see the bewilderment in the backs of her eyes—but my purpose now is to banish even that. I'm going to make her mindless. I'm going to strip away all the fences my bunny tried to escape through back on the bridge. In the middle of the Seine, there are no fucking fences.

I thread my hands through her hair until my fingers meet at the back of her neck. I scratch them into that silken column until she winces another time, and my cock threatens never to let my temper do the talking for my body again. Because of my wild-hair idea to make the woman wait for her infusion of lightning love, nothing she can see betrays the blue energy now. Sexually, I'm taking us back to the night we first met—because emotionally, I have to take her so much further.

"Stand up." It's not a pretty request, and nor do I mean it to be. Though Emma's not happy about complying, since she has to lean on me or fall right back over in those crazy shoes, she obeys nonetheless.

As soon as the boat rocks once, she's grabbing my biceps for balance. I smirk. She glares. Then almost topples backward anyway.

"Shit," she spits, her lips twisting as soon as I flash a new grin. "You're loving the hell out of this, aren't you?"

I let the crack fly by despite wanting to tell her how gorgeous she is, even with clumsy land legs on a river that's no more than ten meters deep at this point. But that's not relevant to the purpose right now. *Our* purpose right now.

"Doesn't feel good, does it?" I state instead. "Being caught off guard. Not knowing what's coming next. Thinking you're going to have support for your steps but not getting it."

Her gaze flares with blue fury. "That's low, Mr. Richards— even for the ass-clot you *used* to be."

I restrain my flinch. Barely. The bald truth is, she's

probably right. All of this is painted in shades of old-school Reece, except that dick would've likely princess-carried her down to the boat so he could fuck her like anything but a princess. Now, I've handled the most important woman of my existence like a sack of potatoes in order to properly worship her and reset the sanctity of *us*. So yeah, if that means being an ass-clot again, so be it. No matter how thoroughly I hate the bastard.

During my rumination, she's clearly done some processing of her own, but the results aren't auspicious. "Damn it, Reece," she grates with the same acute hurt crunching her beautiful face. "I support you. Damn it, I *love* you. Don't you know that by now?"

The deck surges from a larger swell, meaning we must be cruising in the middle of the river now. I grip tighter into the curve of her waist, wishing I could be as clear about a course as Tristan, the vessel's captain, but right now I'm in the middle of a goddamned ocean without a compass or sextant. These waters are dark and strange. Ass-clots never have to worry about shit like emotional transparency and truthful communication.

So yeah, perhaps I *have* relied on some of my old tricks.

And maybe, if my smoldering cock and thundering senses can be believed, I'm not done with the loan. Right now, I'm not above it. A little direction goes a long way in a dark sea.

"Of course I do, baby." As I respond to her, I lower my forehead against hers. "And every morning, I thank the fuck out of God for your love. For your passion. For your trust." I angle my head so my lips can roam across the perfect curves of her face. The graceful sweeps of her eyebrows, the soft slope of her nose, even the feisty jut of her chin. "But I also need your honesty. *All* of it."

As I rise up, going for direct contact with her mouth, she yanks away—just as the boat hits a bigger swell, giving her the perfect opportunity to twist around. With her balance off, she grapples at the bar for purchase. Fine by me. Even better, in fact. At once, I'm pressed up against her, barely stifling a moan as the bulge of my cock mashes the firm curve of her ass.

"Damn it." She attempts the spitfire angle again, but the oath is caught short by her gasp as the boat sways again. I prevent her from face-planting in the champagne bucket by hooking an arm around her waist and planting my free hand against the bulkhead. "*Damn it.* Reece—"

"Hmmm?" It emerges from low in my throat, matching all the fresh wickedness in my senses—inspired just from the sight of her one exposed shoulder. But now, planning how I'm going to get the other one bare, as well as the things I'm going to do to her after that, brings Bad Boy Richards roaring back with a vengeance. If the woman wants him gone, she'll have to stop trembling so perfectly when he slides his mouth down the slope of her shoulder. And then rocking against him as he rolls his hips forward, pinning the apex of her body between his crotch and the bar. And then emitting a gorgeous little keen when he grazes back up to her nape, biting into the flesh there like a starving man.

"Oh...*God.*"

"What a coincidence. I was just thanking him again." Though it's a certainty I'm going to hell, mentioning the Almighty with my mind consumed by such filthy intent for this woman and her irresistible curves. Maybe the big guy upstairs will be more lenient when observing I've seen the light in at least one way. If this is the way to navigate the waters to open, honest communication, who am I to slash the sails? "Damn, Emma. *Damn,* you taste so good."

Her breaths come on fast, sexy little pants as I stroke the spot I just bit with the flat of my tongue. I linger there, inhaling deep, savoring this new version of her scent in every pore of my being. Paris and this woman are a fucking intoxicating mix. There's the familiar essence of her citrus shampoo, though it's now tinged with cherry blossoms, old books, fresh crepes, even a little smoke. And fuck...the musk of her lust now too...

Fuuuuuck.

"Reece." More of her sweet, shallow gasps. "*Reece.*"

"Hmmmm?"

"You...you can't keep doing...I-I mean, if you want to..."

"Oh, I want to." Since the waters have calmed, I remove my hand from the bulkhead and use my fingertips to trace the inner curve of her bared shoulder blade. As her skin pebbles for me, I utter, "And I'm pretty damn sure you want to."

"I meant *talking.*" She bucks against me, but it's a feeble effort. With a growl, I trap her tighter.

"Oh, we're going to talk as well."

"As...as well?" She ends it on a gasp, which extends into a sigh as I glide my fingers down to tug at the dress's zipper. As soon as her bodice is loosened enough, I push down the dress from the shoulder she still has covered, exposing that creamy curve to my questing lips.

"I like talking this way." I stare from over her shoulder as the blue material slides down farther, including the built-in pads over her breasts. Oh *Christ*, yes. Swells of silken flesh. A hint of strawberry gumdrop tips. "Don't you?"

But just when her chest is about to spill free, she catches the bodice with one hand and clutches it to her sternum. Crazily, I'm just as mesmerized by that mash of fingers and fabric, billowing up and down from the air rushing in and out of her lungs, as I would be from her exposed flesh. Now there's a phenomenon the ass-clot could've never claimed. But who am I kidding? This has nothing to do with the new Reece and everything to do with the woman who can captivate his cock—and the rest of him—just by breathing.

"N-Not when you avoid the damn s-s-subject." She twists the dress tighter. I'm not concerned. Her desperate fist even intensifies my pleasure, reminding me of how wound up my dick already is for her.

I hum into her hair while pulling the zipper down another inch and then drawing little circles on the shivering skin beneath. Her breath snags. Her fist loosens. My libido soars. This is like winning the World Series—maybe even more incredible—knowing nothing but the certainty of my fingers and the pace of my tease are the fuckers responsible for the obvious unraveling of her composure.

"And what subject, exactly, would that be?"

She pushes out a strangled laugh. Reins it back before snapping, "You're kidding. Wait, no. You're probably not."

I draw the zipper to the bottom of the track. Straddle her spine with the splay of my hand, my lungs working harder for air as I palm her flawless flesh. God*damn*, she's beautiful.

"Indulge me."

And Holy God, do I mean that in more ways than one. I've dipped my sights, drinking in the naked nip of her waist and the dimples just above the waistband of her panties—if the damn undergarment can be called that. Because of the dress's tailored fit, the woman in the shop actually suggested Emma go commando underneath. My girl, blushing to the roots of her hair, had asked for something to keep her stylish but decent.

But there's not a decent thing I want to do to her right now.

"You. Your father." Not a snag or a laugh or a gasp in *that* one. Suddenly, she's so all-business, I wonder if a spreadsheet is about to materialize in her grip instead of the dress top. Not that I'd complain, even if she *has* switched trajectory for my jugular now. "And the fact that you've already made up your damn mind about walking into his pooch screw of a trap."

I've already lowered my other hand, slipping it beneath her thong next to the other, but now I abruptly halt the descent. "*Pooch screw?*"

"You heard me." She's still in the groove with the boardroom girl growl, but her body betrays her mind's intent, every muscle beneath my hands clenching as she fights her climbing arousal. "And you know exactly what I mean."

I exhale hard. "Damn it, Emma. Do you think I have a choice about this?"

She doesn't tremble anymore. Or clench. Or gasp. As soon as she uses the leverage of the bar to shove away, she's nothing but a solid glare—and makes damn sure I get the brunt of it as she starts backstepping toward the couch. "You have a huge damn choice, Reece—and the answer for it is called *just say no.*"

For a second, I forget she's standing there with her dress in just one hand and her heart brimming in her eyes—or maybe the sight is exactly *why* I growl. "Sure. I'll get *right* on that, baby—as soon as I forget that this little soirée of my father's might be one of the best things to happen for us."

"*Best things?* For *us*?" Her gaze flares and then narrows. "No, wait. You mean you and Foley."

"I mean *you* and me—and the life we'll be able to have once these fuckers are taken *down*." I lean forward, stretching my arms out again. If I could reach out through the windows and scoop up every drop of water in this tributary to prove how adamant I am, I'd do it this second. "Don't you see, Velvet? We've been looking for these bastards, without *any* viable hits, for *months*. Now, a whole load of those cockroaches are going to come crawling out of their sewer in one place and on one night—"

"Because they're lying in wait for *you!*"

In seven words, she pitches from a furious snarl to a full yell, with her stab of a finger as punctuation. It's not the hand gripping the dress, but she's shaking so hard that the garment falls anyhow. At once, its leather fringe catches at the strings of her shoes, messing with her balance all over again. She stumbles backward onto the couch in a heap of blue fabric, a lot of huffy profanity...and breaths that are weighted by barely restrained tears.

Fuck.

She claps her hands over her face—which gives me one of the most stunning views of her breasts that I ever remember. And damn it, I remember all of them.

And, until now, have savored every single one.

This is *not* a moment for savoring.

"Fuck." Even muttering it aloud doesn't give me a kickback of grim satisfaction. I'm left with a hollow gut and an unhindered, unnerving twist of self-doubt. Out of all the feelings I've processed through this insane day, that definitely hasn't been one of them. But it's determined to have its say now.

Was this the wrong move? Pulling back on Bolt and unleashing Tarzan in the name of ripping her truth out the old-fashioned way? All right, so it was the Reece Richards version of old-fashioned, translating into getting her out here alone, with no more emotional hideouts or hindrances, and then screwing it out of her—but *that* plan was as winning a plan as the pullout method for birth control. Now she's destroyed and defeated, and I'm hard-up and pissed-off—and ready to clock the dickwad who glowers back at me from the round mirror beneath the champagne bucket.

I bring my head back up when she starts kicking so hard, the dress becomes a blue dervish on the air. By the time she frees it from both her ankles, it's got enough thrust to fly across the cabin. In the same motion, I catch it and discard it behind me as I step forward, hell-bent on getting to her as fast as possible. As drawn to her as the first night we met, when everyone in the office at the Brocade recoiled from my damn mutant force field but her. Now, *her* agony and fury are the storm dominating the air, and I'm standing here like a ridiculous Frankenstein, looming and moping, when she clearly needs me.

Me.

Not Tarzan with the you-Jane head games.

Not player-hunk Richards with the seduction setup.

The man she loves as desperately and wholly as he loves *her*. Apparently, a concept that he overlooked in making this whole lame move...

"*Don't*." Her charge scythes the air as soon as I breach the area near the couch. I'm still a good four feet away from her. "Damn it, Reece. No more. Just. *Don't!*"

I nod slowly, letting her know she's been heard and acknowledged—just not believed. She's yelling *stay away* with her words but begging *don't leave* with the aqua storms in her eyes and the tormented twists of her lips. My system answers with a matching conflict, the heat in my crotch warring with the ice storm of my remorse.

What the hell was I thinking?

Wearily, I slump into one of the two leather bucket chairs facing the couch. One knee I keep bent while sprawling the other out in a straight line. My foot hits the front of the couch directly beneath where she's sitting. No flinch from her this time. I don't know whether that's a good or bad thing.

But I do know—*know*—she doesn't want me to go keep Tristan company up on the deck. As bent as she is with me for the dirty tactics, she still doesn't mind me taking up a bunch of air and space over here on my side of the imaginary boundary line.

Though, as I look over, I wonder if she's even keeping track anymore.

Because over on her side, a lot of boundaries are clearly coming down.

What. The. Hell?

I try not to stare but can't help doing just that. Then confirming exactly what evidence I'm observing in so many beautiful ways.

Her eyes are exhausted but clear. The plush bow of her mouth is firm with concentration. Her hands, with knuckles curled against each other between her raised knees, aren't tense or trembling anymore. Her cleavage, now shielded by her knees, rises and falls with a focused thrum instead of staccato panic.

Yes.

This.

Right here.

It was the point all along.

I was just trying too hard. Navigating the straits in a zigzag instead of letting her hoist the sails herself.

Chalk another fucked-up voyage up to the ass-clot.

Several minutes pass filled with nothing but the engine's drone and our mutual silence. Hands down, they're the best moments of my day. I even beg fate to add a few hundred more to the collection and do it with confidence. I've paid Tristan to cruise the sightseeing loop all night, and right now, with this creature before me in all her tousled, half-naked truth, I can't think of a better value for my money.

But amazing moments are called that because they're *moments*—and this one gets its inevitable end in the form of Emma's determined head jerk, exposing every opalescent light in her gorgeous blues and every strong angle of her raised hand, which she scrapes back through her hair. As she grabs at the strands, lifting them into a white-gold burst at her crown, similar light explodes through my chest. She's never been more fucking beautiful. I've never been so fucking smitten.

In the next moment, her gaze finds mine again. She sends a heavy swallow down the creamy column of her throat. "I see it now," she rasps. "Why you've done this."

Correction. *Now* I've never been so smitten.

"Back out there"—she waves her other hand toward the aft of the boat—"I *would* have walked away from you again." Her forehead crunches. "I hate having to admit that—but I also hate having to say that getting angry was a much better alternative than facing my fear." She uncurls her hand from her hair and slides it until her fist is supporting her forehead. Her eyes are squeezing with shimmering tears. "And damn it, I *am* afraid."

I ball up my own hands. It's the only way to keep them positioned atop my thighs instead of lunging out, extended and open, to reach for her. Jesus, how I ache to hold her. To cradle her. To kiss every one of those damn tears into nonexistence. "It's okay to be afraid," I grate.

"No," she rebuts. "It's *not*." With a peeved snap, she straightens her head and swipes at her tears. "Not like this!"

"Oh, yeah." I nearly growl it. "Like *this*." And dare to push forward again, punching my fists together while ramming my elbows atop my knees. "Exactly like this, Emma. Each and every day." And I square my jaw, conveying to her how thoroughly I mean it—inciting her into a clear-cut case of *what the hell now?*

"When I accepted your ring," she rasps, "there were stars in the sky but none in my eyes, okay? I knew—I've *always* known—what this life with you would hold." She unfurls the fist in order to angle the tanzanite stone on her finger more fully into the light. As soon as that happens, the bright-blue reflections shoot across her face like the thousand stars from which she's just fought to distance herself. "I knew what this meant, Reece—and what it still means. Loving you brings a breathtaking view, but that means we have to walk at the edge of the cliff with no safety ropes." She inhales with ragged stutters. "It also means that at any moment, you might get pulled all the way off. And that I'll have to watch it happen."

Well...fuck.

"Emma." It spills from between my teeth, as much a plea as a reaction—with a heaping side dish of atonement. This was supposed to be about her facing the truth so she could get braver about it, not taking on the beast, restyling its fur, and then hurling it back to bite me in, apparently, my very exposed emotional ass. "Holy shit..."

"It's all right." She lowers her hand. Wraps it around the other and then rests her chin atop their prayerful hold, over her closed knees again. Despite the clamshell pose, her stare sends nothing but the clarity of love my way. "It *is*, Reece. It has to be. I see how deluded I've been, thinking that the command center would somehow supply you with enough intel and firepower to take down the Consortium. But wars still aren't won just with drones and guided missiles, are they? It requires boots on the ground. In this case, *your* boots."

She ends it with a hitching sigh—which is, in a heartbeat, the snapped lock on my self-restraint. I'm not a goddamned Jedi, though she sure as hell is my guiding Force, and right now, I'm the lightsaber compelled to her side in a growling, glowing rush. I crumble to my knees next to her, inundated with the yearning to strengthen her, to serve her, to even destruct armies for her. As I push my head onto her lap, barely seeing her bare breasts in my face now, the curl of her body makes me moan with raw gratitude, pledging my fealty to her all over again.

"My beautiful Velvet." I breathe it into her navel with as much admonishment as comfort and as much command as succor.

"My beautiful storm." And unsurprisingly, her tone contains all the same elements.

"I'm not falling over the cliff."

She pushes a kiss into my hair. "I didn't say you'd fall."

"I know what you said." I shift away and then up, though latch my grip around her hands as I do so she has to swing her knees over, abutting them to my chest. "Look at me, Emma." As soon as she drags her lashes up, giving me even a peek at the turquoise splendor of her irises, I repeat, "I *know* what you said."

She thrusts out her chin. "So how can you say you won't—"

"Because I won't be doing any of this alone."

"Damn right you won't be."

Her insistence isn't unexpected, but seeing it in living, breathing color, enhanced by her spirit and beauty, is another advent altogether. My answering surge of protectiveness has nothing to do with craving a reboot on caveman Reece, either—and everything to do with fear. Lots of the shit. The exact same terror she's so bravely unveiled for me but to which I now cling as if I'm standing here on the edge of an Andes cliff instead of the middle of the Seine.

Fucking. Pussy.

I can be fine with that. Extra fear means extra adrenaline. And extra adrenaline means more awareness of any fucker at that party who decides to pull a Faline, attempting to get at me through her. I will *not* be merciful meting the hellfire for it this time.

Trouble is, Emma's not in the mood for mercy either—and makes no secret of it as I mutter, "I was referring to the tactical team Foley's already starting to gather, but—"

"But what?" Nope. No mercy. Definitely not. The unwavering angles of her face are proof enough, but when she slides her hands up and clamps her fingers around my wrists, I already know any argument is a lost cause. "You had to know this would be my contract addendum, mister." She pulls hard, urging my hands closer to her thighs and then her hips. Air leaves me in a massive rush. I spread my fingers along her exquisite curves, drawing ten distinct circles into her warm, wonderful softness. "And it's not negotiable. I'm on the team."

Lost. Cause.

I know it as soon as my caresses leave light-blue tracers down her thighs. They're faint enough to appear like jet trails but dark enough to be something kinkier—a musing that ensures I'm not about to find my way back to composure now.

But perhaps Emma doesn't want to be findable either. As I send soft sizzles into the flesh between the band of her panties and the curve of her knees, she skates her touch back up to my shoulders. Her breath comes faster. Her chest heaves harder. The tips of her perfect tits aren't so easily disregarded now, with their peachy areolas puckering around nipples the color and texture of their fruity pits. So dark. So hard. So perfect.

And I'm officially lost. Deliriously, gloriously *lost*.

"Addendum accepted." I rumble it out, delighting at once in her responsive little squirm. She joins another to it, with a little more adorable need, as soon as I go on, "But I have some clauses of my own as well." With wider fans of my fingers, I roll across the tops of her thighs toward the seam where they're still tightly pressed together. "Equally nonnegotiable terms."

"T-Terms?" It tumbles from her in breathy stammers as I tease my touch along the satin triangle covering her center, with its delectable damp patch at the middle. I know she's wet, and getting wetter, as soon as she parts from the steady, sure command of my thumbs against her inner thighs.

"Nonnegotiable," I confirm, spreading her even wider. The muscles beneath my hands flex and constrict, pulsing in time to the throbbing blue lights beneath my fingertips. *Jesus.* Her hesitation has all but disappeared. She's a writhing, shaking picture of need, her desire palpable as I lean in, my lips inches above hers, and murmur, "Fixed...and binding."

At once, the dark spot in her panties widens.

As the most succulent scent in the world fills the air.

Her.

That pussy. That arousal. That magic.

"*Jesus*," I grit out. "Yessssss, Bunny." When she only emits a long, high hum in return, I tuck my head down and inhale long and lustily. "All right. Term number one." I curl my index fingers up and under the waistband riding against her hipbones, slicing clean through the satin on both sides. "This is now my official good luck charm for the mission."

As I draw out the ruined garment, she's consumed by another shiver, though it concludes in a tense little laugh. "You know, you could just ask for a hankie."

Her mirth is mesmerizing. I don't stop staring at her even while lifting the succulent satin to my nose and inhaling long and deep. "Keep the hankie for cleaning up after I'm done with you."

The mirth drains as fast as it came. Now, her eyes blaze at me with the intensity of one need alone, feeding every corresponding desire that pounds back with equal ferocity from my blood. As she slides her hands in, dipping beneath my collar to pull at the ends of my hair, she squeaks out, "Wh-What's term number two?"

After stuffing the panties into my pocket, I secure my hold on her thighs, though this time, it's at the spot halfway to her knees, where I finger the tidy double bows into which she's tied the leather cords of her insanely sexy shoes. My fiddling isn't playful, an intention she picks up on at once. As I jerk one cord free, the air in her throat snags sharply. As the laces loosen and tumble down her leg, that sound becomes a tight choke.

I skate my hand down to the puddle of leather near her ankle. As I start winding the cords around four fingers, I plunge my stare into hers. I soak up every glittering, gorgeous depth I see, certain that her eyes rival the gem on her finger for crystalline brilliance.

I need to add even more to their fire.

I need to give her pure electricity.

Dear fuck, I can't wait.

I twist the ties even tighter. With my other hand, I dig harder into her other leg. Emma's eyes and nostrils flare, but she says nothing. My breathtaking warrior bunny is hell-bent on proving she's ready for this. That she's ready for anything.

In another world, she'd be such a kick-ass superhero.

But not in this one.

Never in this one.

Not as long as I'm still alive—and goddamnit, I plan on that being a long, *long* time.

The closest she ever gets to the shit in *this* life is attending this crazy soirée with my monster of a father, and only because it can't be helped. Asking her to kiss me goodbye when I'm off to take care of misdemeanor thugs is one thing; ordering her to stay and "watch the cave" when it's Godzilla I'll be facing is another. If the proverbial shoe were on the other foot, I'd already be throwing the damn thing through the window before we even left the apartment tonight.

So, fair is fair.

And for now, she's on the team.

But there *will* be terms.

And she *will* abide by them.

Just to make sure I drive in that point with precise clarity, I rise up to a full kneel and crowd deeper into her personal space—including the open V between her thighs. She reacts in kind, angling back until her head bonks against the curtain-covered window and she's wetting her lips, clearly expecting that I won't stop...

But I do.

Several inches over her face, where I can still absorb what my nearness is doing to her—*really* doing to her—now. Where I can watch what happens as I unspool the leather shoe tie, slowly and deliberately, into tight spirals up her leg. Where I can gauge if she likes it when I repeat in a smoldering snarl, "Nonnegotiable." As soon as she nods, I demand, "*Say it*, Emma."

One hard gulp. Then that Imperator Furiosa uptilt of her chin, determined to meet me move for move on this, even if she's got to do it with one arm. "Nonnegotiable," she calmly states.

I draw in a deep breath. Then issue with matching certainty, "You're on the mission for the whole night—as long as you stay by my side the whole night. If *anything* goes sideways about this thing, and I don't care if it's a speck of pepper on the linen or one off-timed moment about the service, you agree to leave the event on my first command."

At first, she really looks ready to give her Furiosa fuller rein. Her gaze narrows; the cords in her neck go taut. But suddenly—and, I admit, eerily—she's all peaceful waters and spa candles again, to the point of slipping her hands free from my neck and lolling them against the top of the couch's cushion on either side of her head. Naturally, the little minx is aware of what that does to my view of her chest, so I don't hide the obvious evidence either. With lust-thickened eyes, I drink in the perfect landscape of her firm, flawless hills, jutting straight at me with their shiny red crowns. At the same time, I advance deeper into her most intimate zone, tapping at the mound between her legs with the zipper throbbing between mine.

She rewets her lips.

I slam mental duct tape over my groan.

"But what if I have to go to the restroom?"

Christ. Now she's tugging those sweet pink pillows beneath her teeth. "Then you wait for Foley or me to take you. Period."

"Will I need a hall pass too?"

And now, damn it, giving Furiosa a dose of naughty schoolgirl. *Fuck me.*

"You'll need Foley or myself." I'd like to say my tight-teethed Mad Max is an indication everything under my hood is hunky-dory, but it'd be a lie. I'm desperate to know how far toward cheeky she really wants to push here. I'm burning to know how far she'll let *me* push. "Is *that* understood?"

She twirls her hair with a finger. "If you take me, do you get to come in with me?" A smirk plays with one edge of her mouth. "You *are* a lot of fun in bathrooms, Mr. Richards."

"And you're a lot of sass on boats, Miss Crist."

I underline it with just enough resolve that she curiously eyes me for a second, but then she's back to twisting that hand through her mussed strands, too pleased with herself to realize that once I push up, using the ball of my shoulder in the crook of her knee, her hand and mine are inches apart. And still twined in my fingers? The leather laces, now in a perfect position for—

"Whaaaa?"

Her shriek, though a surprise when it doesn't shatter the champagne glasses, is one of the sexiest sounds I've ever heard the woman gush. When her stunned chokes follow, I'm glad my head is already dipped to supervise getting the ties looped all the way around her knee and wrist together before twisting them a few times and separating them for another pass underneath. I cinch the bond with a simple knot, guaranteeing I can set her free with one yank, though it's impossible for her to reach the ties at all.

I swivel and then dig my other shoulder into her corresponding knee, though now I throw more might into the effort. I've lost the element of surprise and anticipate her initial struggle.

"R-Reece!"

"Emma?" I thread it with a little pleasure, easily subduing her feisty kick—which barely qualifies as a struggle at all. Maybe she already knows her gig is up now that I have a full view of her open core—and every dazzling drop of nectar with which it's already seeping for me.

Does Furiosa the schoolgirl like a little detention?

Then call me Professor Richards.

"Wh-What the hell are you doing?"

I lift my head—but only to give her a second's worth of my determined smirk before smashing her with a conquering kiss. When she mewls around my tongue, I snarl around hers, rolling my head to taste her even deeper, even harder. Jesus *God*, she tastes so good. A little bit of French wine. A little bit more of French night. A whole lot of passionate American woman.

The better part of a minute later, I finally lift from her lips but stay hovered over her face. With my hands freed again, I emulate the liquid swells beneath us with the rhythm of my strokes. Up and down her graceful curves I go, reveling in every texture from the glide of her neck to the fullness of her breasts to the dip of her navel...and then lower.

"I'm making sure you understand the contract, baby."

Her eyes widen. "Like *this*?"

"It's a valid business practice, Miss Crist." I lean down, kissing the pebble at the tip of her left breast. Her right. "Come on. You haven't been out of hotel management *that* long. It's called managing the client."

She wriggles, her lips parting, only to give me a great view of her locked teeth. "I don't think this is in any approved management manual."

"Maybe it should be." I roam my lips higher, across her chin and bottom lip, while sending my fingers lower...starting to explore much different lips. "Especially when they're being nervy about the most important contract terms." Though dear God, with a pussy as soft and soaked as this, no wonder the woman thought she could get away with her sarcasm...

"Nervy?" she huffs. "What the hell? I was just having a little— *Ohhhh!*"

As she groans and writhes, I grin and suckle—before twisting my hand to penetrate her deeper with two of my fingers. "That's what I said, my wicked little one." I savor her next moan even more, flattening my tongue along her neck as its vibrations take over her throat. "Dear fuck, *yes*. So wicked. So illicit. So open for me. And you fucking love it."

"Ohhhh." It reverberates up from her chest this time, halting as her throat clenches up—at the same moment I add a third finger to my carnal invasion. At once, she's drenching me all over again. And writhing harder. And trembling deeper. "God. *Yes*." Her syllables are more croaks than words, forced from a mouth that's gone dry from gasping and screaming for me.

But I want more.

All the air in her lungs.

All the honey in her pussy.

All the submission in her body.

All the surrender in her soul.

I rear up again, watching waves of heat and awakening chase each other across her face despite how she's let her head fall back and her mouth gape open. "Emma," I bark, relishing how her eyes obediently pop open. "Lift your head. Look at me." But as soon as she complies, I damn near regret the call. One look into the thick glaze of her brilliant blues, and my cock nearly loses its load in my pants. "Oh *fuck*, beauty." My wry laugh is my rescue, helping to stay the embarrassing burst. As I pull my hand out from her channel, needing every finger I can get to help with grappling at my belt and fly, I chuckle out from my own parched throat, "I've corrupted the hell out of you, haven't I?"

She tilts her head. Licks her lips. A hint of humor swirls into the dazzling oceans of her eyes. "Said the spider to the fly?"

"No." It's such a virulent grind from my lips, matching the angry red length of my dick, that it almost breaks off into two syllables. Appropriate, since this fucker is throbbing so painfully, I wonder if it *will* break off before reaching the salvation of her body. "Not the fly." I wrap my hands around her thighs and pull her closer. I kiss her tenderly and then forcefully. Then, with our lips still pressed and her breasts pillowed against my chest, dictate to her, "My *butter*fly."

She curls her lips upward. "Who's still in your corruptible trap."

A shudder racks my whole body. It's not just her teasing words. It's her gorgeous, sultry tone. And her bound, spread body. And her eager, high sighs. And the gleaming, wet slit of her tight, intimate entrance...waiting for me...*waiting*...

With a feral snarl, I grip her by the waist. With a crushing roar, I yank her in.

Ramming her all the way down onto my cock.

"Shit!" Emma screams.

"Fuck!" I bellow at the same perfect second.

"Oh...my God," she rasps during the excruciating moments I take to pull out and hiss in approval as my cock flares and gleams, coated from crown to balls with the gleaming evidence of her arousal. "You *are* corrupting me."

I wait for her gaze to drag open and find my face before shaking my head, once more copying the motion of the ageless river beneath us. "No, baby. This part is called *teaching* you."

Though I long to kiss her again, especially as she parts her lips as if to prep a perfect zinger of sass, I do one better. While pulling her back onto my length, I join in with a vicious lunge forward, ensuring my cockhead has now said hello to her eye sockets. She starts a scream, but now I give in to the lust for a kiss, filling her mouth with the ferocious domination of my tongue and lips and teeth.

"Now," I grate, despite the huge heaves of my billowing lungs, "we're going to review the contract clause you seem to be having a few problems with."

"I—" she gasps out. "I...I don't h-have any prob—*Ahhhhh!*"

I can't help tossing a wolfish smile as I watch the effects of my actions across her squirming form. She strains her hands at the ties, rolling her wrists and curling her fingers. She's tossed her head back again, exposing the cords of her neck for the possession of my bites. Her stomach and abdomen are clenched, indicating how tightly she's constricting her pelvic muscles to milk every inch of my surging, sizzling dick.

My gorgeous, sweet girl.

Her open, hot obedience.

My wrecked, obliterated heart.

Now who's in submission to whom?

The answer is clear as I work harder to bring her the

best fulfillment she's ever had. With full rolls of my hips and targeted drives of my cock, my world becomes focused on *her* world. On searing every corner of her, from the inside out, with the fire of my body, the devotion of my soul, and the commitment of my command. And as a result, the freedom she can claim...the pleasure she can now fly to...

"We're going to review anyway, Bunny." I secure her attention again by easing out until only my tip is still encased in her body. With defined undulations, I circle my stalk around and around, slicking every sensitive surface of her gorgeous, glistening opening. "You have to be clear about all this." I latch her gaze with the intensity of mine. "I swear to God, Emma, I *will* keep you safe when we go do this fucking thing."

Just when I thought the woman couldn't bemuse me anymore, her little half smile proves me wrong. "Aren't we doing this 'fucking thing' already?"

A burst of a chuckle—again, beyond my expectations or control. But I get even by feeding her another inch of my erection, savoring the loud groan from her lips and the wet grab from her pussy. "Oh, baby," I drawl. "This is just the starter course."

Her moan turns into a needy hum. "Th-The...oh, *God.*"

I notch a small shrug. My shirt goes nowhere, sticking to my skin, but I don't give a crap. If anything, my lust spikes higher from the reminder that I'm still mostly clothed while my precious fuck bunny is completely naked. She's my priceless treasure to protect. My unique gem to guard. "I've got no problem with God," I quip. "Invite him in—if he'll help you remember our terms better."

"Damn it," she fires back. "I already remember, okay? I"— she interrupts herself with a gasp as I slide another inch into her—"I *remember!*"

"Good." And another inch. I'm nearly all the way back in, and my leisurely pace is turning her into a writhing, mindless mess. *Exactly* how I want her. "Then you'll have no trouble reciting it all back for me."

"Reciting...it..." Her comeback is broken up as she thrashes her head left and right. With each sweep, her tunnel pulls harder at my cock. As I swell and jerk, I'm unable to hold back my precome any longer. As those first drops spread through her womb, she cries out in desperate agony. "Oh...oh, God!"

Low growl. "He's not doing a good job of helping you remember, Velvet."

"I *remember*!" she yells.

"Then fucking tell me!" I bellow back.

"I...I can't *think*—"

"Yes, you can. And you will." I scrape my hands down her thighs and hook my fingers beneath the leather ties to use the bonds as brutal leverage for my quickening thrusts. "You'll give me the words, Emma. All of them. And don't you dare come yet."

She whips her head back to center. Drives the gleaming blue blades of her glare into me. "Or. What?"

I almost laugh. Oh, fucking *hell*, this woman and her constant, vibrant fire. And I thought I'd never meet a female who could handle my mutant passion, let alone eclipse it.

Channeling my mirth into a buzz saw of a snarl, I loom inches over her face before ordering, "Do. Not. Come." Making good on the threat in my words, I withdraw until all she's getting is the bulb at my tip again. "Not before you give me the words."

She gasps. Shakes. Incinerates even more of my being with the smoky side of her fire and brimstone. Holy fuck. She

ANGEL PAYNE

doesn't have to summon God. She *is* my god, and now she's going to rain her beautiful, blazing destruction on every last corner of me. Perhaps she already has.

"I...I won't wander off," she breathlessly rasps. "I won't leave your side for a damn moment, Reece. I promise. *I promise.*"

Her plaintive oath is still a ribbon of sweet smoke through my system, though now I wonder what she's laced the vapors with. Does it really matter? I only know I'm so fucking high on her submission. Utterly wasted from her compliance.

"R-Reece?"

I slide my cock all the way back inside her. Groan hard as her walls close over me, dragging a few more drops of precome from my lurching length. I do it one more time, a hard slam and then a pulsing throb, before dictating to her, "Say it again. Tell me you promise, Emma."

"I promise," she declares at once, lifting her face to be closer to me. "I promise, I *promise.* I won't even use the damn bathroom without you. I promise!"

Her words are starting to spew more as gasps than volume. As those breaths race faster and faster, her chest pumps urgently at mine, and I can feel her erect nipples even through the cotton blend of my shirt.

I grip her bonds tighter. Drive into her pussy harder.

"You mean it, don't you?"

"Yes," she pants back. "Yes. Every word." Her mouth barely forms around the vow. She's breathing like we're sprinting, her hairline a gleam of sweat, her shoulders taut as she braces for my pounding, punching thrusts. "I love you, Reece. *I love you.*"

"And I worship you." My declaration is a growling rush against her lips just before I spear my tongue between them,

307

claiming the cavity of her mouth as ruthlessly as my cock invades her womb. "And now I'm going to fill you. Your entire exquisite cunt. All of it, damn it!"

"Yes!" She lurches her head up again, seeking my mouth with her own again, only not for another kiss. She bites at me like a leaping shark at escaping prey, taking any purchase she can get with brutal passion. And I let her. Dear fuck, we'll probably both look like we jumped off this boat instead of fucked on it, but the bruises will be worth it.

Emmalina Crist is always worth it.

"Yes," she echoes over and over again between her snappy sexiness. "Yes. Yes. *Yes!*"

"Take me," I moan, circling and swelling deep inside her.

"Yes."

"Clench me, Emmalina."

"Yes!"

"Now come with me, fuck bunny. *Hard.*"

"Ohhhhh..."

"Show it to me, baby. Show it all to me. *Give* it all to me." I decree it because I'm living it, exposing every ounce of my adoration as I spill every drop of my seed into her. Drenching her in the electric liquid only she can power this high, showing her the love I've never felt for anyone else in my entire insane existence. Nor will ever know again.

I ride her with that ferocity until she's nothing but softness and sighs beneath me, and then I yank free the ties and let her wrap her arms around my neck while her legs encircle my waist. The moment more of her skin contacts mine, I'm lost again—on a sea of stars this time. Nearby, the bells of Notre-Dame chime about the glory of heaven, but I'm already there. The paradise of this woman's embrace is the only deliverance

I need. The Eden of her love has made me a rebirthed Adam, ready to serve her lush beauty for eternity.

With all that I am.

With all I can imagine.

With all I can ignite.

"Reece!" It tears out of her on a high shriek as I rock back on my haunches, keeping her pussy wrapped around me throughout the motion. With one of my hands splayed on her back and the other gripping her waist, I set a new tempo for us that's steady but strong, tender but torrid.

"Now show me, Velvet." I charge it on serrated breaths, since the new angle of our bodies allows my cock into even deeper parts of her shivering tunnel. "Show me how you're not going to leave my side."

A wash of new desire covers her face, working its way across the sensual flow of her lips. She lowers her head, pressing that silken bow to my mouth as she wiggles a little, working herself around me until we're both groaning from the perfection of the friction.

Up and down. In and out. Plunging and retreating. I beg fate to wind its own laces around the two of us, binding us together like this forever, but soon our hormones have other plans. No longer can I resist how her channel squeezes me like a goddamned fist or how erotic her intimate lips are with the excess juices from her pussy smeared through them. She's my fuck bunny with extra features, and damn, are they worth the extra wait.

But not for too much longer. My cock, searing and sizzling its way into her, all but screams the confirmation at me now.

Still, as she pulls back a little and whispers, "Close enough?" I ram her tighter onto me with a King Kong snarl and a caveman glower.

"No." I claw into her hips, grinding our bodies until we both grunt in pain. "Closer."

She grabs the front of my shirt and tears the two sides until buttons are flying all over the cabin. In the same motion, she wraps herself back around me, crushing her breasts to my chest. "How about now?" she pleads into my ear.

"*Closer.*" I cup her by the ass, teasing at her back hole with little taps of my middle fingers while turning our fuck into a proper screw. While kneading her body in erotic tucks and rolls, I shove up only enough for her to feel how fully she's swelled my cock again...how thoroughly I'm going to blow for her again.

She gets it. Oh, God, how she does. As soon as her high, plaintive sigh warms the back of my neck, it pitches into an outright cry—reacting to the jolts of energy that pinwheel through my balls, shoot up my cock, and bang with impatient force against my jerking cockhead.

I'm going to blow.

Oh *fuck*, am I going to blow.

But for one last, gritted second, I hold the fuse at bay—long enough to ram my face against her neck and brace her hips astride mine, before ordering with scorching savagery, "Melt with me, Emmalina. *Burn with me*, baby."

And she does.

Her scream piercing the night.

Her thrusts rocking the boat.

Her orgasm ripping raw lightning through me. *All* of me. Every cell of my blood. Every inch of my skin. Every molecule of my air.

And then all the way out of me.

"Fuck. *Emma*. My *fucking* God!"

I've plummeted from heaven, dipped into hell, and brought the fire of Styx itself back with me, jetting it into this angel with skies in her eyes and stars in her touch and magic in her body. Using the magma to weld her to me forever. To fuse her into my marrow. To seal her into my soul.

To cherish her in every beat of my heart and breath in my body.

Many minutes later, I attempt to rearrange things so I can lie on my back and rest her atop me, but I refuse to give up my cock's seat in her body, resulting in whacking my ankles, knees, and shoulders against every piece of furniture in the cabin.

"*Not* helping, Miss Crist," I grumble as she fills in the spaces between my grunts with her soft giggles.

"But of course I am, Mr. Richards." As if I need clarification about *that*, she rocks her hips a few times. I groan and squeeze her ass tighter. She sighs and presses her cheek against my chest.

Heaven?

Hell?

I'm damn sure it doesn't matter. Wherever karma sends me at the end of this crazy ride called mortality, I want to make sure she's there too.

And with that thought, my psyche leaps to the next subject at hand. A conversation that can't be put off with any more kisses, jokes, or lovemaking star rides—no matter how many shivers she gives me with the length of her tunnel, hinting she'd be ready for a repeat whirl.

The important shit first.

Especially this *important shit.*

But there's nothing wrong with mixing at least a little pleasure with business...

"My, my, my." I growl it with soft wolfishness into her hair while changing up my grip on her backside. With my fingers making lazy circles across her firm spheres, I rumble on. "Guess my negotiating tactic worked."

Her delicate huff sends small shivers across my pectoral. "*This* time."

I curl my head down. Push gentle lips against her temple. "Well, they say three times is a charm."

She stiffens. Not by a lot, but by enough. "Which means what?"

An effort to soothe her tension, skating one hand up the little hills of her spine. "Which means there's one more term to go over."

"Also nonnegotiable?"

"For the sake of argument, yes."

"You mean *your* argument."

I have no intention of biting on that bait, an initiative supported by the universe itself as a lively jazz tune grows louder and louder in the air. Neither of us has a hope of speaking over the din as the large dinner *bateau* passes, with laughter and clanking dishes joining the band's bright song, prefacing a deafening silence in contrast.

In short, the perfect setting I need now.

"You have to promise me that if anything—*anything*—goes sideways during this dinner party, you will leave the Virage at once with Foley and will follow his instructions to the letter."

Emma jolts her head off my chest. Narrows her stare to such intensity, I wonder what the pattern of the brand across my face will look like. "What the hell does that mean? 'Sideways'?"

I steel my jaw. "Exactly what it implies, Velvet."

"Which, back on the bridge, you *implied* wouldn't be an issue. That Foley's already in the city, handpicking his secret Scooby squad, and—"

"And slow your roll, baby. That's all still happening. We're still one step ahead of the game, okay? We're running game plans and attack plans for every scenario Dad and Faline can think to throw at us. But unfortunately, that includes ones where we lose the upper hand."

"And you end up in their hands again." The last part of it is jagged, tearful, and as unsteady as her efforts to get away from me. Yeah, including a full break from our intimacy, which leaves me groaning for a couple of seconds—meaning she has the room to accomplish just that.

I center myself enough to roll up and slide onto the couch, where she's managed to crawl and tuck back into a ball. "That's not the plan, okay?"

Her form remains hunched and tight beneath my embrace. "But it could be—and by more than a few percentage points," she accuses in return. "Otherwise, you wouldn't be writing it into the terms."

"Which is what matters here," I volley. "Because it *is* part of the terms, baby." While I command her with my tone, I work for compensation with the tenderness of my touch. "If you're going to be a part of the squad on this, you have to be as prepared as the rest of us—and that means knowing what to do if all the hamsters fall off the wheel."

A weighted breath. A heavier exhale. But with equally determined purpose, she unfurls herself before tucking herself to my side. "Next, you're going to tell me that's a commendation, right? No guts, no glory?" She flashes a pondering glance. "And does that mean I get a cute hamster call sign like Reecy or Sally?"

Rough grunt. A tight tug to bring her closer. "You're already Bunny. And that stays the same."

"So the guys call me Bunny?"

"The guys call you by your *name*, or I'll deflate their balls with knitting needles."

She twitches as if tempted to laugh but instead takes my cue, snuggling closer. "All right, fine," she sighs, circling one of my nipples with a fingernail painted in a shimmery pink hue. "I agree to this term, as well, but"—she stops the caresses and lifts her head again—"only with *my* modification attached."

Now I'm the one tempted to laugh. Something in my gut already expected this. "You've already gotten an addendum, beauty. Now you're asking for a modification too?"

"Not *asking*." She adds a little snort. *Fuuuuck*. She knows I can't resist her adorable bunny snorts.

"Hell." I endure her light knuckle into my sternum before muttering, "Should I be afraid?"

She pushes all the way back up again. In her nude, proud glory, with her shoulders high and her gaze meeting mine, she doesn't hesitate before asserting, "If this thing does spin wrong and those monsters take you again, I claim every right, responsibility, and obsession to use every resource and weapon in the world to find you—and get you back." But a second later, with that scenario embedding itself into her head, her posture crumbles and her chin wobbles. When I beckon her to re-burrow into my arms, my killer rabbit eagerly accepts the offer. This time, she drapes half her body across mine, with her thigh against my cock and one gorgeous breast squished on my chest. "By the way, *that's* not negotiable either," she utters.

I chuckle, grateful for the concentration on something other than what the intimate smash of all her curves is doing to the corresponding parts of me. "I wouldn't dare think otherwise, baby."

"Damn right you won't." No more cute fingernail tracings. She goes straight for tunneling a hand in my hair and then twisting it with fierce force. All the incredible angles of her face are a karmic match, slamming me with the palpable rush of her love. "If it takes until the end of my days, Reece Richards, I will *not* let those cocksuckers keep you this time."

I let my stare flare with a touch of humor. Can't be helped. As intense as this subject is, her devotion flies my heart so high, it's in a stratosphere of nothing but light. "Cocksuckers, hmmm?" I drawl from the middle of that brightness. "You know, Miss Crist, you're kind of sexy when you have a filthy mouth."

"Sexy?" She pushes out a pout. "Damn. I was hoping you'd think I needed to be punished instead. Like, tied up with my shoes again...or something like that?"

Fuuuuuck.

Outwardly, I school my reaction to a sharp inhalation. As the little minx giggles, I murmur, "Enjoyed that, did you?"

She taps my jaw with a quick kiss. "You know, Mr. Richards, you're kind of sexy when *you're* filthy too."

I let a low hum vibrate up my throat. "They do say most superheroes have a dark side."

Her gaze glimmers. "That so?"

The backs of my eyes turn to lightning. My cock swells with thunder. "That's *very* much so."

Emmalina pushes up. In one smooth sweep of feminine grace, she's fully astride me, rolling and sliding along my erection again. My breath explodes out as my cock expands with renewed fire, and my senses confirm what my soul already knows.

I'm lost all over again.

Because of her and in her.

Drowning in her softness. Incinerated in her fire. Moved in her power. A willing sacrifice to her glory.

And as she leans in, bracing the side of my face in her tapered but mighty fingers, she curls up a slow siren's smile, accepting my consecration...and rewarding me with her pure, unhindered pleasure.

"Show me," she whispers from the center of that soft, smoky rapture. "Show me just how bad Bolt can really be."

Without hesitation, I lift her off my lap.

Without pause, I spin her around toward the empty bucket seat.

Without faltering, I shove one of her knees against one side and repeat the positioning on the other. *Fucking perfect.*

I'm about to tell her exactly that, but an echo of her demand takes over my mind. She wants Bad Boy Bolt—and that's what she's going to get.

"Lean over," I order in a low snarl. "Grab the edge of the bar, drop your head, and lift up that beautiful ass. I want a good view of everything, Velvet—every damn part of you that belongs solely to me."

Dear *fuck*. With just as much certainty, she complies with every syllable I've issued, down to the last wicked letter. For a long moment, I simply stand and watch as her pussy lips grab at the air, already greedy for my cock again. Finally, unable to take the torment any longer, I take myself in hand. Fist my shaft from top to bottom, over and over again, until precome rushes over my head again. The drops hit the carpet near her feet, instantly burning blue circles into the pile. Looks like I'll be telling Tristan to add new carpet for the cabin onto tonight's bill. Worth it. So fucking worth it.

"Not long now, beauty." I stroke the small of her back along with the reassurance. "I just want to be naked with you now."

Her impatient mewl makes me work harder to toe off my Pradas and push down my pants, practically freeing them from both legs at once...

Right before a distinctive sound comes from one of the pockets. The ringtone I've assigned to nobody else.

"Goddamnit." I've never meant every vicious syllable more.

"Reece?" Emma looks over her shoulder. "What is it?" As soon as she gets a full, fresh look at my size, she turns all the way around. "And why is your phone roaring?"

I give her knee a fast, apologetic squeeze with one hand while fishing the device out of my pocket with the other. "Because lions eat their young," I mutter. "And Papa Richards wants to play."

CHAPTER FOUR

EMMA

Three nights after Reece received that friendly but short call from Lawson, beckoning him to the Virage for the let's-all-get-along-again dinner, we're in a limousine on the Champs-Élysées, inching through traffic on our way to the stunning V-shaped tower about eight blocks away.

"Damn," the burly guy behind the wheel mutters. "That thing is impressive."

He's reacting, no doubt, to how the setting sun hits a fifty-story-high "waterfall" of crystals, which appears to be "flowing" out of one prong of the gigantic V. As my gaze widens at the sight, I murmur back, "I can't stand admitting you're right, but you're right."

"I usually am, princess."

The driver's chuckling comeback is quashed by Reece's growl. "Her name is *Emmalina*, my friend." I'm certain he uses the honorific purely out of respect to Sawyer and the fact that he—Max Brickham, another "buddy from the old days" Sawyer seems to have in every damn corner of the globe—has cut a Spanish vacation short to be on Team Bolt tonight.

If Max realizes that, he doesn't let on. The guy even jabs a thumb up from the front seat, nearly knocking free his fancy chauffeur's cap, before replying, "Heard and acknowledged, buddy."

Despite the blatant alpha-to-alpha respect, none of the tension leaves Reece's body. The leather seat beneath us creaks from his discomfited weight shift. He grasps my hand tighter and curls my knuckles against his chest. I don't attempt an escape, more than aware that he needs the contact of our clutch, though the man could likely use a tequila shot and a dozen deep breaths as well. But I can't help him with the former and I bite my lip from suggesting the latter, hesitant to highlight the tension he's already aware of.

Especially as Max drives us nearer to the Virage.

Another block.

Trimmed chestnut trees and happy throngs flow past our windows.

One more.

While we're stopped at a light, accordion music from a street performer drifts through the air. A smatter of applause follows.

Reece doesn't seem to hear.

As we roll forward again, he noticeably clenches his jaw—sending a small tine of power beneath his skin, back to the communications bud stuck inside his ear. The device is invisible to anyone looking at him, despite how he's pomaded his hair into a lush, formal style for tonight. It's a fashionable match for the charcoal suit he bought off the rack yet still fills out like a movie star in bespoke designer wear. Beneath the jacket, he's wearing a light-blue shirt with a silver-threaded tie—a special gift shipped express from Wade and Fershan back in LA. With the enthusiasm of twelve-year-olds who'd found a viable way to shoot humans to Mars, the guys had explained that in the right circumstances, the tie could be used as a special "Bolt Jolt" conductor. I'm not sure if Reece believed them, but he smooths the thing now while opening up a radio connection with the rest of the team. I know this because there's a matching comm bud stuck inside *my* ear.

"We're on final approach to the hotel," he states in a voice as pleasant as a tour guide's. "Everyone in place and ready to oo-la-la this shit?"

"Damn straight." Sawyer responds first, as I expected. "Everyone, remember the goals on mission. One: protect the fuck out of Chase Richards since he's still in the dark about all this. Two: assess and evaluate the team surrounding Papa Bear Richards for hints about their SOP. Number three, the big golden ticket: capturing one of them means we'll possibly have a lock to pick about this shit. Capturing two means we can play them off each other in questioning."

"Everyone roger that?" Reece jumps in again.

"Roger." As expected, the first response comes from a grim Tyce.

"Roger." From the driver's seat, Max adds a new thumbs-up.

"Roger." Mitch Mori's voice this time. "Everything's cool and calm so far in the dining room—though these waiter uniforms are uncomfortable as fuck."

"Roger." Loud clanks and hissing sounds punch the line behind Kane Alighieri's voice. "Kitchen's a beehive of nervous—but the waiters look fine as hell in those cutaway tux uniforms."

"Flattery will get you everywhere, asshole," Mitch grouses back.

"Counting on it, hot stuff," Kane returns.

"Ahhhh, the smell of young love in bloom." The next voice on the line takes me aback a little. I'm ready to hear

Alex Trestle, normally the third musketeer to Mitch and Kane, but as the most technically savvy of Team Bolt, he's stayed behind in LA to help Wade and Fershan get up to speed and—apparently, in his free time—help design an electricity-conducting necktie. In his place is Dan Colton, a mutual friend of Sawyer and Reece, who apparently likes leading a double life more than Reece ever did. In the eyes of the world, Dan's the dashing CEO of Colton Steel and a passionately devoted husband to his gorgeous wife, Tess. But in his guy-bonding time, he likes hanging with Sawyer and, in his words, "kickin' ass and taking names" of bad guys who eat their young. "And roger, by the way," he adds. "Quieter'n flat beer in the back of the lobby, though the banquet staff is bustling in and out of the ballroom. I expect we'll have some action back here soon."

"Good news," Sawyer responds. "Because that's where I'm headed with the tank."

Reece rolls his eyes. "It's just an SUV, man. A Mercedes, at that."

Before he's done, Sawyer's well into a resounding grunt. "I feel like Mother Hubbard driving a fucking oversized boot."

"Well, you sound like the whiny wench too," Kane cuts in, backed by more kitchen clangs.

"Says the guy who irons his socks?" Sawyer rejoins.

"*Guys!*" I'm the one who breaks in on them, channeling Mother Hubbard-meets-Natasha Romanoff in the same syllable. After their second of cowed silence, Reece speaks again.

"Foley, I need you in the rolling boot tonight, man," he reasons. "If this shit goes sideways and we need to cut and run fast, we can't all speed away on Ducatis—and you're our best driver."

"Hey!" Max throws a scowl over his shoulder.

"Because I usually ride a Ducati," Sawyer gripes.

"Make friends with the boot, buddy." Reece's hardened tone enforces his subtext. It's not a casual suggestion. "And stay alert and close to the back entrance, in case we all need to suddenly pile in on you."

"With our pretty ironed socks," Kane quips.

"Don't get those fuckers in my face, and we'll be good," Sawyer volleys.

"Yeah, that's what she said." Though Reece's one-liner earns him subdued chuckles from everyone on the line, he's still robot rigid next to me—an incongruity I wouldn't believe if not for sitting right next to him. For all anyone knows from his easy tone, he's simply escorting his woman out for a night of romance in the City of Light.

God, if that were only true. Though the two of us have seized every opportunity to get at each other for the last seventy-two hours, we've been more like animals than lovers, our mating more acts of desperate passion and urgent lust—as if recognizing our need to mark each other as much as possible before the inevitable...

I squeeze my eyes shut to block my musings from trailing into the realm of brooding, but when Max turns the car right, about half a mile short of the Place de la Concorde, I realize my effort isn't needed. The sheer magnificence of the building in front of us is reason to forget even my own freaking name.

"Fuck me to the moon and back." Max's exclamation about says it all—and thank God, because I'm still slack-jawed as we approach the Virage's entrance. It's lined by water fountains that are a breathtaking mix of classic and modern Paris, interspersed with crystal statues modeled after the dancing angels on the Palais Garnier's proscenium. Everything is lighted from underneath by gold, blue, and red LED bulbs. Just before the porte cochere of the lobby, there's a more modern sculpture in gold crafted by one of France's hottest young sculptors. The piece is called *Décalage*, which loosely translates to *Shift*. Everything is designed to support the hotel's bigger theme, representing the beauty of the city "then and now."

Wow. Just wow.

Get your shit together, Em.

I'm not here to gawk. More importantly, I'm arriving here with knowledge that arms me more than most against all this flash. No. Not knowledge. Awareness. A higher understanding of exactly what kind of "financing" is behind this magnificence. Money that's dripping in blood and bones and flesh. The lives of all three Richards brothers sold into a fate worse than slavery by their own father.

I swallow down bile from my normal nauseating follow-up thought to that. I actually let Lawson Richards help me set up the Richards Reaches Out organization. He stood in our New York offices and told me how proud he was of Reece and me for turning RRO into reality. That he was so honored to be part of a movement helping deserving kids break free from the shackles of their lives—when the whole time, he was planning to turn his own sons over to the Consortium and *their* shackles.

He's the worst kind of a human being.

No. I'm wrong again. And Reece is right.

Lawson's not a human being at all.

But there he is, strolling out to the Virage's main entrance like a damn king welcoming his cherished prince back to his castle.

Cocksucker.

I can practically hear the word roaring from Reece's mind as Max slows the car in front of the hotel's entrance. Though we're still holding hands, I compress my fingers around Reece's with a little extra force. When that makes him glance up, I openly wince—not at him but *for* him. Though he's still suave, sophisticated, and complete French *GQ* on the outside, I can feel the annihilation he's enduring on the inside. This open acknowledgment from his father, for which he's dreamed of for so long, is a sham. A "treat" waved like a dog bone in front of the stray son who's gotten nothing but his father's emotional scraps since he was a boy.

And this gleaming palace?

Welcome to the doghouse.

Okay, so it's a fancy doghouse. Both of the Virage's massive front doors are open, with the clear glass frame around them lit from within by LED lights in the same colors as the entrance fountains. Carved into those wide glass columns are designs in the ornate Beaux-Arts style. Beyond the entrance, the huge lobby looks like the inside of a swimming pool—not surprising, since the entire floor is clear and built on top of a manmade lagoon. Lights beneath the water act as projectors, making the whole scene feel otherworldly.

I'd even add enchanting and mesmerizing to that adjective—in any other circumstance than this. I'd be free to be dazzled instead of ordering myself not to vomit as Reece exits the car and then turns to help me out. We could be arriving here at the start of a thrilling date instead of my poor guy having to help me stay balanced as I rearrange the poufy layers of my tea-length skirt. And hell, I'm not even wearing crazy spaghetti noodle shoes tonight. I'm simply that nervous, even in a pair of conservative kitten heels. The navy satin shoes are an appropriate match to my vintage-inspired dress, with its square-cut neck accented by paisley-patterned bows and a wide, fitted waistline tapering into the full drama of the skirt.

"Emma!"

My world tilts for a second. I've been so ready to jump into the acting job of my life with Lawson, not the woman who sweeps me into her happy embrace. I have to pause and reset my mentality. Of course we've rehearsed every scenario in which Trixie could be involved with tonight's events; they were just all rehearsed with the contingency that she'd be inside, greeting us well after arrival. Yet weirdly, the twist helps me relax by a degree. Even if Trixie is complicit in Lawson's plans—and for the little it's worth, every instinct in my psyche protests otherwise—there's a good chance they wouldn't let the Consortium try a swipe at Reece out here with both of them present. So for the next two minutes at least, I'm free to sign my body's may-I-function-normally permission slip.

Too soon.

The second I allow myself a full breath, Lawson yanks Reece away for a hearty man-hug. The action aligns with Trixie's mama bear squeeze, meaning Reece and I have to let go of each other for a second.

It's only a moment.

I can live with that. I think. Or at least I order myself to while giving Trixie a solid return on her effort.

"*Bon soir*," I manage to laugh out. "You look *trés belle*, madame." And she does. Trixie's dark-green eyes have a perfect match in her refined sheath dress, which hits her just below the knee with a subtle hint of lace.

"*Merci beaucoup.*" She dips a demure curtsy. "But

honestly, you and I need to meet up for something that requires no heels, hose, or makeup."

"Agreed."

I tack a smile onto that, but it fades as soon as Lawson hooks an arm around Reece's neck to pull him into the hotel ahead of us, with his free hand waving through the air to point out how the soaring crystal "waterfall" from outside seems to penetrate the glass roof of the atrium and then "splashes down" into the exposed part of the lagoon at the far side of the lobby. Though I'm relieved to spot Dan Colton not too far back from that, still undercover as one of the extra security guards hired for tonight's "festivities," I'm not going to be even halfway back in my element until my hand is firmly back in Reece's again.

"I...ummm... Reece is holding on to my purse, so we'd better catch up." Not a lie. Reece *is* toting my clutch, having elegantly taken it off my hands while I stepped out of the limo. Like the stud he is, he rests the thing easily in his grip, as if it's just another part of *his* ensemble. Yeah, there really are some things only a true alpha stud can do. I have no idea how I got lucky enough to land one like him.

And right now, I'm determined to hold on to that goodness. In every damn way I can.

I won't leave your side, Reece. I promise.

"Dear heavens, how adorable you are." But damn it, Trixie has other plans. Determined ones. "But I promise you, the boys are going to be fine without us for a few minutes." She states it in that suggestion-but-not-really voice all mothers seem to have, linking her elbow with mine as if we're about to play Red Rover for the Olympic gold medal. "Besides, Tyce and Chase are already here. Brother bonding time is what the three of them need."

Bonding time. Shit. They're going to have lots of that if all the hamsters fall off the damn wheel tonight...

I won't leave your side, Reece...

Air starts sawing my lungs like they're a pair of nasty tree stumps. My balance wavers. My pores ice over. What now? *What now?*

Relief crashes in as Trixie pulls me past the huge check-in area—overlooking gardens that give Luxembourg a run for its money—and right past Mitch, with his lavender hair slicked back and his bright eyes boring into me. With one subtle motion, he motions a finger at his ear—reminding me of the communications node glued inside my lobe.

As soon as I push at my earlobe and hear the click that opens the connection to the guys, I prompt Trixie, "Wh-Where are we going?"

"Not far," she chirps. "I just know you really have to see the garden atrium that Law is having them put in. It's not done yet, so it won't be part of the tour for tonight, but I thought you might gain inspiration for your new place too. Atriums are such a smart idea for bringing more light into a home, don't you think?"

But by this point, I'm on autopilot with my *mmm hmmms* and head nods, because the reopened comm line—and my only link to Reece at this point—is where all my focus funnels. While my face feigns all the right awe in all the right places for Trixie, my head is still at Reece's side, listening to what's going on with him and Lawson—and now, with Chase and Tyce too.

"Well, there he is." Since the smooth baritone is the only voice I don't recognize at once, I attribute it to Chase. "Nice threads. Once again, little brother, you may step into some real shit piles, but you clean up real well."

Yep. Definitely Chase. The insult-couched-in-a-compliment technique is a trait he's picked up from his father—the asshole who now harrumphs out an uncomfortable laugh and sounds like he's moving in for the man-hug with his eldest. Though I'm just listening to the whole thing, my stomach painfully knots. This is like watching a horror movie, only worse. The psycho isn't in the woods or the closet—he's standing in a fancy dining room, now offering his victims pricey French aperitifs.

"Thanks, but I'll pass." It's Tyce this time, obviously morphed back into the mask of physical perfection everyone expects. I give him a mental high five, knowing he'd like nothing more than to drink some of his edge off, especially after leaving Angelique back at the apartment to haul the ditzy model-for-hire on his arm instead. Maybe *ditzy* is a little harsh. I only met her when we vetted her, but after the third time she asked us to be "more pacific" about our needs, I'd been really glad Reece and Tyce were conducting the interview.

"Same here." Reece's concurrence is delivered in his charming-as-hell-because-I-have-to-be voice. I'd know the tone anywhere after the countless reception lines and red carpets to which I've accompanied him, just as I know the gruff thumps that follow are his hand patting his torso. "If I'm compromising the clean regimen, I'll do it when my girl can indulge too."

A sarcastic grunt. I'm guessing Tyce again. "Little fraternal unit, isn't your girl *part* of 'the regimen'?"

I press my lips to hold in a snort. Yep. Typical asshole Tyce. Or, more accurately, *the asshole formerly known as Tyce*. Spending a lot of time near the guy over the past few days has shown me the real truth of the man—the hero he started to become even before the Consortium brought its truth out in the crucible of their torture. Fortunately for us right now, he still remembers a lot about being a jerk—and Reece still has the game for an appropriate response.

"Inappropriate as hell, party of one, Ricey?"

"Screw you."

"In your dreams."

"*Guys.*" Chase again, bringing it with his older-brother-law-enforcer boom. "Don't make me get out my own little Lucille."

As Trixie and I leave the half-finished garden, I let my gaze bug for a second. Perfect timing, because it's easier to let Trixie think I'm awed by the daffodils in fleur-de-lis planters instead of being horrified by the idea of Chase Richards, in all his Wall Street sleekness, with a spiked baseball bat in hand. No. Just *no*.

But an even worse *no*?

Following Trixie into the hotel's private dining room just as Lawson is informing Tyce's model and Chase's wife their men will be back right after he shows off the hotel's custom cigar room.

I won't leave your side...

Then wrenching free from Trixie and attempting to get across the room before they leave completely.

I won't leave your side...

Then failing at that because two more men are suddenly in my way. They seem like simple burly security members moving a pair of throne-like chairs, but I've never witnessed hotel security guards give off such daunting vibes. Their chests are like hangar doors. Their jaws are like engine blocks. They growl like a pair of revving plane engines.

Shit.

Jet engines.

Holy freaking shit.

Like at airports.

Like the one where these two followed the bidding of their bitch mistress, Faline Garand, to keep watch over Lydia and me...

Oh God, oh God, oh God...

"Reece! Tyce!"

Screw tapping on the comm link. I yell as loud as I can while lunging at the two goons, but these giants are shockingly agile for their size and machismo. They swing the chairs in and shove them together like rodeo clowns shifting corral fences. As I climb on top of one and shove its backrest to tip it over, my instinct screams with louder fear and my belly twists with darker dread. These jerks are working damn hard to keep me from catching up to the men, to the point that as I topple over with the chair and land on my butt in a puddle of fabric and crinoline, the other chair *just happens* to end up falling on top of me.

"*Ooofff.*" It's only a chair, but it feels like a baby elephant. For a long second, all I'm able to do is stare at the ceiling and attempt to regain the air that's been slammed all the way out of my chest. But as soon as it returns, I'm ready to use it all up again, screaming at the face that fills my vision—until I recognize kind, keen eyes and slicked-back lavender hair. Just as swiftly, Mitch's face is joined by a bigger visage. Kane's chunky face appears next to his husband's and is scored with matching grooves of apprehension.

"Fuck," Kane grunts, hurling the top chair away like it's a toothpick. "You okay, girl?"

"No." I'm fast and loud about it, especially because the hand I attempt to lift to my comm dot is a nonstop shriek of pain. "No!" Helpless tears tumble out as I stare down at my fingers, now bent at hideous angles. "And I can't get word to Reece." I dash a terrified gaze between them both. "I think they might be in trouble. I think the cigar room might be a tr—"

My own outcry is my interruption, as Kane and Mitch are taken down by a pair of brutal blows to the backs of their heads. A new sob escapes as I battle to comprehend what's happening. Have Faline's assholes really just sent two members of Team Bolt to la-la land using a couple of gaudy candlesticks?

"Holy *shit*." I grit it past the agony in my broken hand while swiping the good one up to my comm dot, jabbing it three times now. After using the team's signal for the hamster derailment code, I scream, "Code flash. Code flash. Reece, Tyce, you are in a trap. I repeat, you are in a—"

No yell of a cutoff this time. I crumple to the floor as the screech of electronic feedback fills my ear, joining the misery shooting up my injured arm. But I'm pretty certain Faline's goons don't care about any of that. My wails of agony might as well be a kitten's mewls as they grab me by the shoulders and begin dragging me the same direction in which Lawson just disappeared with his sons.

In my delirium, I entertain the weirdest thoughts—*this is ruining the toes of these cute kitten heels...is my left boob coming out of its cup?*—but I already concede them for what they really are. Stand-ins for the atrocity I'm really about to face. The nightmare I'm no longer able to shove away or have Reece kiss away for me...

Reece.

"Reece." I choke it out. Barely. A person needs air to

speak, and as of this moment, when I'm hauled to the entrance of the little room lined with racks of expensive cigars, air isn't a privilege I deserve or a gift I can take. I'm a ball of pain. A twist of remorse. A shell around vital organs, including the eyes blurred by two storms of miserable tears as they look down upon my beautiful man, now flat on his back on the polished wood floor. Unmoving. Unblinking. Unspeaking.

Unconscious?

No.

But one look into his eyes, thick with graveyard despair and battleground heartbreak, and I know he wants to be.

The same agony is stamped across Tyce's face—the good side *and* the mottled side. Somehow, he's no longer able to keep up the pretense of "Tyce." As I struggle with that recognition, I realize that while he doesn't move, he's not bound at all. The same is true for Reece, though his whole body is positioned as if another goon has come in and trussed him up with zip ties. There's only one captive in here with that kind of bondage, and it's Chase—who *has* been given the mercy of getting knocked completely out.

But he's not the only one.

I flash a fast glance back to the dining room. Sure enough, Trixie has joined Chase's wife and Tyce's date in the same kind of coma-state snoozes, their slumped forms surrounded by a few empty aperitif glasses.

"The drinks." I blurt it while snapping my sights around to Lawson. "You did something to the drinks. That was supposed to be the trap, wasn't it? But Reece and Tyce—"

"Were always the smarter two of my boys," Lawson supplies—with freakish, frightening calm. The stare he dips toward them could belong to any father bragging about the brilliance of his sons. With that same pride surging his voice, he continues, "Chase was always my loyal one, almost to a fault. He's my big Shepherd. But Tyce and Reece? They're my Dobermans. Smart as whips, both of them. And sturdy too. It was why I made sure this room was lined with special polymers designed for maximum electrical insulation." He pulls a palm-sized device out of his pocket, reminding me of a garage door opener. "And after one click of this modified EMP, the remaining pups were down for the count."

"Pups." I croak it while stumbling backward, until I'm planted directly in front of the men I'm ready to kill *this* man for. "In case you haven't noticed yet, asshole, those are human beings you've put 'down for the count'!"

Lawson flinches. For half a second. Then he's back to being as unruffled as a priest, even flowing his hand out with one finger raised, a la practically every holy man in the medieval paintings enshrined in the museums up the street. "You know, Emmalina, you're a pretty smart one too." A strange—and creepy—smile makes its way across his lips. "So you probably know that until recently, people bore children solely for the purpose that they'd serve the family name. Oh, of course you do. So you also know that whether it was increasing the productivity of the farm or expanding the clan's trade craft or being the centerpiece of an advantageous court marriage, children didn't receive their *life* until their *duty* was served."

I clutch at my stomach. "So this is *their* duty. Only you're making it their *life* too. Do *you* get *that*, asshole? Do you see that your sons, your flesh and blood, will now be Faline's matched set of trained toys for the rest of their lives?"

He opts for more of the Saint Lawson bullshit, pulling himself up as if wearing a cardinal's mitre. I wrap my arms tighter around my middle, debating whether to throw up or ignite one of these stogies and ram it into the center of his heart.

After a long moment filled with nothing but his quiet regard and my frantic breaths, he murmurs, "Hmmm. So Tyce did put all of it together."

"Damn right he did." I don't want to surrender an inch of my stance but know that I must, shifting back to stand between my man and his fallen brother. To stand *with* them and *for* them. "Why are you so surprised? Isn't he one of your 'smart ones'?"

I stumble back a few more steps when Lawson reacts by stomping forward, rage taking over his face. He stills as soon as I crouch into a battle-ready stance. I may not have all of Scarlett Johansson's moves, but I've got all of *my* fury and indignation, and I'm ready to unload both on this monster, henchmen around the corner or not.

Sure enough, as if giving the goons some mental space has magically summoned them, four figures stalk into the doorway behind Lawson, consuming the archway with their broad shoulders, tree trunk legs, and battle-ready bearings. I swallow hard, gulping down the icy sting of fear, muttering to Reece and Tyce, "I've still got this."

Because I am not *leaving your side again.*

"Damn right you do, girlfriend."

And in between one heartbeat and the next, my apprehension morphs into elation.

As the four figures step all the way into the room.

A grinning Dan Colton.

A glowering Max Brickham.

A scowling Kane Alighieri, with blood dripping down the side of his face.

A bloodier Mitch Mori—who still adds an arrogant-as-hell wink onto his one-liner. I'm damn sure he'd be embellishing with a saucy double snap as well, except that double snaps are difficult when a guy has a SIG Sauer aimed at the monster hell-bent on re-kidnapping his friend.

Max is the next one to move, sizing Lawson up as he saunters forward. The Richards patriarch is a strapping man but no match for a guy who's clearly taken out some nasty bad guys—and likely a few bulls, alligators, and aliens—in his time. I allow myself half a breath when Lawson's shoulders sag, seeming to accept the same inevitability. As I finally relax enough to drop to my knees next to Reece, imploring him to hang on with the connection of our gaze, Max drawls to Lawson, "We're just going to take what's ours, my friend—and maybe drop off a special delivery for the *Préfecture de Police* on our way out of town too."

"Ah, oui." Mitch keeps the SIG trained on Lawson as Max yanks out a pair of zip-tie handcuffs. "I'm sure they'll be kissing our fine, fine asses for the sweet prezzie—especially when they're informed it's a companion piece to the thumb drive that was delivered to them an hour ago, detailing every single one of the crimes you've committed both with and on behalf of the Scorpio cartel. From there, we've laid some bread crumbs that should lead them to the Consortium as well." He breaks into a huge grin. "So hey, win-win for everyone, man."

"Hmmm. Yes." Lawson returns the smile with an expression that swaps out his chill priest for an even more chill monk—which has me instantly holding my breath again. Though the man bows in submission as Max approaches, I trust the move as much as I would a dog with a side of bacon. The instinct worsens when Lawson murmurs, "Winning *is* what I'm best at, sir."

"Not anymore." I spit it despite my trepidation, vowing it's the last thing I'll ever say to the man before I turn to Max with a decisive nod. "Give that magic box a good click, Mr. Brickham, so we can break these two free."

But I battle lead in my throat again as Max answers me with a stunned gawk. "What magic box?"

"*Crap*," I rasp.

Because somehow, even throughout the handcuffing, Lawson Richards kept his magic little console hidden.

And now, with the thing still in his hand, he presses it again...

Triggering a sequence of events I should have expected but never imagined.

With a violent jolt, the room literally comes apart. I fall back to my knees, draping myself protectively over Reece. The floorboards splinter and separate and are then hydraulically pushed apart even farther, exposing several floors' worth of a black cavern below us—though as unseen motors roar to life, joined by whirring gears and whooshing pulleys, it's clear the cavity is actually an elevator shaft.

With horror, I realize that Tyce, Chase, Reece, Lawson, and I are on the moving side, getting ready to take a ride to the basement without a note of soothing Muzak. All of the Team Bolt guys are left to gape from the other side...

Except for Mitch.

Who's standing in the middle.

For one more second.

Before he's not.

"*Noooooooooo!*"

Kane's howl follows us all the way down into the darkness. It possesses the walls, claws at the air, and digs a place so deep in my soul, I know I'll never forget its terrible pain for as long as I live. It's consuming and wrenching and all-echoing, but I don't give up the fight to hear past it on the slim chance that Mitch might have survived the plummet...

But as the pseudo-elevator carries us deeper, that hope gets ripped from me in horrifying, agonizing chunks. We're fifteen to twenty meters down, and everything around us is dark, hard, unforgiving rock. Are we on our way to hell? It feels and looks a lot like what I'd imagine. No fire and magma; that would make everything too interesting. This is a freezing abyss, and there doesn't seem to be any way out—

Until...

Past the hiccups of my sobs and the grinding of the lift gears, I hear new sounds and feel distant vibrations, now trembling closer on the air. I lift my head a little more off Reece's chest, straining to identify the new presence down here with us. It rushes and fades. Again and again. Powerful rumbling and then anticipating silence. And beneath it all, the return of a constant hum. *Electricity.*

So Lawson's nifty little clicker didn't penetrate down here. I see that much by looking over as the man again maneuvers the thing in his handcuffed grip, clearly knowing the buttons well enough to operate it in a blind spot. After a tap of his thumb, the lift starts to slow. After another, the rocky chute is illuminated by a blast of light from below, though all I can see is more dark rock. Nothing to explain the sounds and vibrations I'm noticing...

Though enough to silhouette a hand, noble and familiar and strong, closing around my wrist. Barely muting my joyous gasp, I close my other hand over his and hang on for everything I'm worth. Tears come bursting out of me with silent intensity.

I swipe them from his face while kissing him with open apology. Reece forgives me in the same wordless way, lifting his other hand to stroke into my hair. He's still as weak as a wraith but forms his lips into answering kisses for mine, punctuating with heavy breaths that convey their ultimate cost on his shorted-out system.

We waste valuable seconds just confirming the mutual beats of our hearts and the precious mix of our air before he stops and pants harder, seeming to summon every shred of his sparse strength before rasping, "Tyce?"

"He's right here." I glance over, noting his brother's fresh twitches of movement. "He's alive."

"Chase?"

"Also here. And alive."

He nods, though the gaunt tension in his face doesn't diminish. "Mitch?"

There's a fresh burn behind my eyes. "Gone, I think." As the platform bumps to a surprisingly smooth stop, I have to clutch back another gasp. To our right, splayed against the rocks, there's an eerily inert form sprawled facedown—with slicked-back lavender hair. "Gone," I repeat and am unable to hold back a couple of hiccupping sobs.

Strangely, I'm relieved to see my grief doesn't faze Lawson at all. Relieved but not stunned. I don't want to think of him as a man again, in *any* way. Right now, he's disconnected from everything that makes him human, and that includes the ramblings from upstairs about "the good ol' days" of the freaking Middle Ages. Does he think that justifies any of this? Does he think that if the ghosts from those times were resurrected, they'd be *applauding* him?

Don't go there.

It's insanity—*his* insanity—and this moment has to belong to the only lucidity down here for me. The man I hold right now. The light in my darkness. The love in my spirit.

"Emmalina." His whisper, stronger now, surges me with hope despite the deep shadows in his eyes. I compel myself to keep looking, no matter how hard I yearn to shake him and rekindle the storms I'm so used to seeing there. Irony has never laughed harder than in this moment. If Lawson's bioelectric zapper shorted out Reece's powers for good, he's out of contention as a pretty plaything for Faline—but never have we needed his Bolt Boost more to get out of a hole. Pretty damn literally. "Emmalina, listen to me."

I lean over, brushing a thumb against his temple. "I'm here," I pledge in a fervent grate. "I'm listening." Though I have a damn good idea of what he's going to say, which is why I dip down farther, spreading fingers against his skull before amending, "And I'm *not* leaving your side."

My assumption was right. I see it across his face as he waits through the interminable minute it takes for his father to walk past us and then cover the short hop off the platform, kicking at the edges of what used to be the cigar room's floor as he goes. I'm still trying to comprehend that the man had a trap door built into his polymer-lined cigar room, attached to an elevator with an express trip to the bowels of Paris. But the man has also been in bed, professionally and probably personally, with a crime cartel that funds fringe scientists who are infusing human DNA with electricity. One good strand of lunacy deserves another.

As Lawson leaves the lift, new lights flick on to show a tunnel attached to the cavern. It's actually lined with cement block walls and possesses right angles. If we're still in hell, it's now a manmade version, complete with six new henchmen materializing out of the darkness to greet the man. One yanks the snipper feature out from a Swiss Army knife, readying to cut his boss free from the zip ties.

My attention is jerked back down with Reece's commanding grasp. Though all his strength still isn't fully back online, the effects of the EMP are fading faster now. With any luck, Lawson isn't aware that Reece's blood cells have hit the Boost Star on the regeneration lap. Has he even tried this thing on anyone else before? And do I really want to know the answer to that?

"Velvet." Though he keeps it to a heavy rasp, the electric authority returns to his voice too. "We don't have much time. You have to listen to me."

I settle higher over him, vertically aligning our gazes. I frame his face with matching purpose, my hands deep in his hair, though everything beyond my right wrist throbs even worse now. I gladly endure the injury for this second of basking in his paradise. Even now, defeated and down and damn near depleted, he's the most beautiful person I've ever seen. My superior man. My perfect hero. "As long as it doesn't involve me leaving your side, I'm all ears."

His jaw flexes. And, thank *God*, there are now tiny sparks at the backs of his eyes. "Goddamnit," he rumbles. "You agreed to *all* the terms, woman."

"And you agreed to my amendment," I counter. "*And* my modification. No negotiations." When those sparks flare brighter, I want to scream with joy. Instead, keeping my resolve firm, I finish, "The monsters have you again—and I'm not stopping until I have you back. Only difference is, you're along for the ride now. Deal?"

He doesn't get even a second to answer—which under normal conditions might be a damn fine thing. But I'd gladly endure an hour more of his arrogant growls over watching his father pivot back around, truly and clearly ready for the next phase of kidnapping his own sons. The sight of Lawson Richards with his hands free and half a dozen armed men in tow only slams one awful icicle of a conclusion through me.

I have no idea what *this* ride is going to be like—except freaking bumpy.

CHAPTER FIVE

REECE

The maddening woman and her fucking contract changes.

And I agreed to all of them...why?

All too clearly, my memory sends out that reminder. She was naked when she issued them. Naked and dewy and glorious and irresistible—which meant I wasn't anticipating, with even a sliver of an inkling, that Dad would have thought through his plan like this. Building an entire room in the Virage for the express purpose of disabling Tyce and me like this. Then capturing Chase along with us and smuggling us out of the city in tunnels below even the Métro itself...

Like nothing more than a commodities shipment.

A drug run.

A gun hoard.

Cash-bearing goods.

That's all we are to him.

Was that all we ever *were* to him? Were all those years of my young adulthood, so desperately seeking his approval, just a sham of time and a waste of my heart?

The questions are flames inside me, spread by the gasoline of my bile and the tinder of my heartbreak...

And the forest of my fury.

I really *am* going to kill him.

One exchanged glance with Tyce, and I see he's more than on board with that plan too. The second purpose of my look meets with equally outstanding results. He's recovering from Daddy Bear's electronic paw swipe as rapidly as I am but is opting to play opossum about it as well. More than likely, Dad got his magic little box from the gang back at the Source and was told to use it in experimental mode until learning how much of a hit we could really take.

Goal one? Don't give him another reason to try to find out.

The thought blasts through me, at once alarming and exhilarating. Never again will I be able to laugh at a zombie joke after actually being one for close to thirty minutes. *Brains are friends, not food.* And now, mine spins up to full mission mode again, locking down the coordinates of all the prep that still needs to happen before Dad sets his goons back into motion.

"All right." I add a definitive nod to my rasp up at Emma, communicating that I'm taking the reins back on this plan, even if it's from flat on my ass. "You want to be helper girl here?"

Despite biting the inside of her lip, she barely contains her answering grin. And there's nothing she can do about the eager sapphire gleams in her gaze.

"Good. Then kiss me."

The sapphire shards turn to steel. "Excuse me?" she seethes from locked teeth.

"You want to be on the team, you follow orders. *Kiss me,* goddamnit—and as you do, pretend you're easing the agony of my paralysis by loosening my tie."

At once, understanding flashes across her face. "Your *tie.*" She already starts in on yanking at the knot. "You're freaking brilliant."

"Kiss. Me."

I've never issued a command that sounds more desperate, more demanding, or more asshole.

I've never been kissed by a pair of more entrancing, erotic goddess's lips.

Jesus. Christ.

It's all I can do not to moan—or let the pure power of her passion sizzle all the way down to my groin. Paralyzed captives aren't supposed to have raging erections. At least I don't think so. Accurate or not, I'm not about to give Dad pause for doing a double-take in my direction at all. Too much of this made-up-as-I-go strategy depends on staying inconspicuous.

And stockpiling the lightning.

As much of it as fucking possible.

Emma makes short work of pulling my tie free and laying it against my side. As she pulls her hand back in, I lift my head to capture her fingers beneath my lips...

Until she winces out loud.

And I pull focus on my vision.

To take in the red, blue, and purple mangles of her fingers.

"What the *fuck*?"

Emma gulps. Works her lips together.

Tyce rolls to his side. Spears me with a questioning glare.

"What. The. *Fuck?*"

Dad whips around, handing me my nightmare of a double-take. His expression has already bypassed curious for a full facial DEFCON alert. I'm beyond caring. And yeah, that includes any shred of careful strategizing now. The sight of Emmalina's fingers—the beautiful, creamy tapers custom-made by God for my kisses, my adoration, my clasps, my partnership—now battered and bent because of *this fucker*'s evil, is the final click in the circuitry of my reborn rage, my unthinking vengeance.

My stockpiled lightning.

Driven by my stockpiled pain.

All of it.

The horror of my captivity. The mire of being an escaped mutant. The grief for my normalcy. The shock of *Tyce's* truth. The loss of my friend, Mitch Mori.

The loss of my father...the man I always, desperately, tried to be.

No more.

No more.

"No more."

I'm beyond regulating even the words from my throat, so it's no shock when their echo is like a cannonball on a gong along the high walls around us. The cacophony jerks Chase out of his stupor, at least enough to try to look around, wondering where the cigar room went. But he'll be no use for another hour, at least. This shit is going to be up to Tyce and me.

I'm ready.

Tyce pops to his feet along with me, his version of a high sign. He's ready too.

"No. More!"

I just hit the gong with the whole cannon. And it feels fucking *good.*

I release a wicked grin from the victory. I spread it even wider as Dad's shock makes him drop the magic remote box.

And as long as everyone's trying out new toys...

I wind my necktie once around my right fist. Grit my teeth, focusing a pulse of energy down from my shoulder, through my fingers—and straight into the threads that blaze to life, turning my mild-mannered accessory into a sizzling, snapping weapon of raw electric power.

"Fuck!" Chase and Tyce shout it together.

"Wh-Whoa," Emma stammers at the same time.

"No!" Dad roars as they're all catching their breaths—at the same moment I sweep the lightning rope out with a low, fast, scorching crack, hooking the flaming tongue right beneath the magic clicker. With another flick, again just following my instinct on how this damn thing is going to work with me, I send the device flying into the air, over everyone's heads, deep into the broad brick tunnel beyond the lift platform. "Don't stand there, you morons," he yells at the henchmen. "Go get that damn box!"

Only he's already short by a superhero and behind by twelve steps—the dozen strides of a head start Tyce has already gotten on the walking lumps of bread dough. And counting. My former lacrosse player of a brother sprints even farther into the tunnel, disappearing from view as Dad bellows again at his lackeys.

As thoroughly as my gut churns, knowing Tyce has half a dozen pachyderms stomping his direction, I take a second to fully acknowledge my newfound respect and admiration. I can't give him an ounce more of my love, because he and Chase have always had that, but the giant neon sign reading *Tool* over his head has been shattered now. The guy's more than capable of holding his own now.

I can't say the same thing for Emmalina—or for Chase, who's now gotten to his feet but looks like a frat boy on a bender about the whole thing. *Fuck.* The observation, made with lightning assessment skills that come back as easily as riding a bike, forces me to realign my priorities between one breath and the next.

And in doing so, to chuck the fantasy of putting my father out of everyone's misery.

"Wh-What the h-hell?" Chase grates it while slamming a palm to his forehead, using his other hand for balance. "What is this place? What's going on?" He peers over, blinking as if clearing his vision—a very real possibility. "D-Dad?"

"Wouldn't call him that if I were you, C." I send a new jolt of energy down to the rope, cracking it in warning at our asshole sperm donor.

"Reece? What the *fuck*? Why are you all—what's going on?"

Emma sends my brother a supportive look, eyes soft and lips compassionate. "We're beneath the hotel. The aperitif you drank was spiked."

"*What?*" Chase bunches his brows. "Spiked? Why? By who?"

Dad sucks in a breath as if prepping some lame explanation. I snap the lightning rope with twice as much force. "By our fun-loving paternal unit, who thinks our 'use' to the Richards family legacy hasn't been fulfilled yet."

"Huh?" Chase stumbles forward, heading for Dad. "What's he talking about? Does somebody want to tell me—" But he skids short, jetting his brows back toward his hairline, upon sighting Mitch's still form. "Holy *shit*. Isn't that the waiter from upstairs? Is...he—"

"Oh, for fuck's sake. *Yes*, Chase. He's *dead*, son." Dad explodes with it, causing both Chase and me to flinch for two seconds. Even now, our father's I've-had-it-with-you snarl reverts us back to duck-and-cover-he's-on-a-rampage mode, even if we're only doing it mentally.

And fuck me—that's what the bastard has counted on.

Because in those two seconds of my distraction, he gets the chance to sweep a hand up to his ear—and visibly slam on a comm dot of his own.

And from his opening words, sends a freezing rain into my blood, mixing in sickening ways with the lightning that already carries my loathing for him. "*Buenas tardes, mi bonita* Faline."

And for her.

That woman.

The only person on this planet I'd love to kill more than him right now.

"Yes. I know. We're still on our way, but there's been just a slight hiccup in the tunnel. You'll need to be on standby with the pods, darling."

"The pods of what?" Chase interjects then. "And who the hell is Faline? And where the hell is Mom?"

"Still upstairs," I bark. "And probably still asleep from that shit in the drinks." Just having to form the words causes a brushfire in my blood, completely canceling out the ice. *Thank fuck.* I send a solid flow of it into the lightning rope before whipping the length out and wrapping it around Dad's legs. As the heat sears through his pants, he goes down in a screaming, steaming heap. At once he rolls into the fetal position, clutching his ankles where I've branded him with the fiery length. "You'd better thank Emmalina for being here, cocksucker." I lean over him, practically spitting it on him. "Otherwise, you'd be clutching your sorry dick."

"The dick he's been putting into someone besides Mom?"

I chuff at Chase, who really does spit on the man—though I'm cleaved about how to take his arrival at the big wake-up-your-dad's-a-prick party. "Didn't need that visual, C—but we can cover that in debrief."

He glowers. "Debrief?"

"After we get the fuck out of here."

With timing I couldn't have coordinated better—thank Christ something finally meshes tonight—there's noise and movement from the darkness of the hallway again. I seize Emma by the shoulder, thrusting her behind me just in case Tyce hasn't been successful with the hoard of henchmen.

I release a huge breath when my brother's two-sided face comes into view.

"Tyce!" Emma yells, adding a little jump of joy.

"Tyce?"

Chase's echo is drenched, understandably, in confusion. I clap a hand around his shoulder. "I'll tell you in—"

"Debrief." Chase nods. Sort of. He's past looking like a deer in headlights about all this. Right now, he's more like a vampire in the daylight—a strange but fitting metaphor since our half-fried brother remains on one hell of an approach, covering the last twenty feet before the lift like a goddamned puma—

Being chased down by blood-thirsty game hunters.

Christ.

Somewhere in that darkness, the henchmen have actually secured rifles. The only reason they haven't fired them is the obvious. Tyce has outrun them—only now that he's reached a point where he has to slow down, the goons have time to stop and line their shots up.

We all drop to the platform as the first rounds crack the air. With Chase's profanity in one of my ears and Emma's scream in the other, I'm amazed I keep my head up to keep track of Tyce—but I owe it to him. *I owe it to him.*

He beams his finest asshole grin and then circles the air

with a fist. "Bet your sweet ass, Cheesy Reecy."

Only then, he's not waving that fist anymore.

Or calling me shit-tastic boyhood nicknames anymore.

Or running anymore.

He's grimacing as blood sprays from one leg and then the other, the hits taking him all the way down...

And making him lose grip on the magic remote he's just raced into the darkness to retrieve...

A box he lifts his head to watch arcing through the air, a fly ball of our fatality, lobbed with such excruciating perfection...

Back into our father's grip.

"*No!*" Emma shrieks. I think I roar the same thing but I'm not sure, since all my cells burst like that glass in the old stereo commercial, splintering and surrendering, preparing themselves for the vast, awful zombie palsy again. I'm numb, only I wish I were *more* numb—especially as I watch Dad hover over the damn thing like Gollum with his Precious, working fingers over the dial on top, clearly cranking the settings higher for the next pulse he'll punch into Tyce and me. He isn't deterred even as Emma lunges down on him, scratching and biting and snarling like a harpy. Before I can toss aside the lightning rope and yank her away, Dad's already thrown her off like an asshole chucking a puppy onto the freeway, uncaring where she rolls or how she's hurt.

And even then, my stunning, alarming little fool of a Team Bolt beauty scrambles right back to all fours and goes after him with even more vehemence.

"Enough!" I bellow, plummeting to force her back. "Emma, damn it! He'll kill you without thinking twice!"

"Damn right I will."

As soon as Dad growls it, Chase releases his own unhinged

roar—and rushes in to take Emma's place on the attack. Now *this*, I will support. Even in his half-sauced state, Chase has seven inches and at least sixty pounds on Emma.

But more importantly, as of this second, he now has Tyce.

Our astonishing, unyielding brother has somehow regained his feet and has stumbled to a spot just beyond the platform. He stands there in a puddle of his own blood, his skin pale and his stance swaying—but his gaze still drilling hard at Chase as he lifts an arm and wiggles the tips of his fingers.

"Here, C," he orders. "Send him out here."

"What?" Chase's bafflement is real and understandable. He slept through the entire opening chapter of this horror story.

But I didn't.

And now, the ending Tyce wants to give it is unfolding like a seriously shitty spoiler. "Fuck," I mutter. "*Fuck*," and then I shout, while rushing over to rip at the back of Chase's neck. But I only end up with a handful of his hair as Dad kicks at him and Chase throws several solid, furious punches in return. He's even grunting in satisfaction, finally able to unleash his own growing gall at all the evidence of all the bullshit Lawson Richards has fed to us and the world throughout the years.

"No!" I turn and snarl at Tyce. "Goddamn you, Tyce! I won't let—"

"Shut the hell up," he yells back. "This isn't your decision anymore."

"And it's not yours!"

"No." The sudden dip of his volume makes me angrier than his asshole-like shouts. Because it terrifies me three times more—especially when he shucks his thousand-dollar Prada jacket, exposing the dress shirt underneath. "No, it's not my decision either."

"Oh." Emotion robs Emma's voice of any volume past her gasp. "Oh...my God." Now it's just a series of sobs. Bursts of grief that echo through me as well, bombing the fuck out of the chasms and canyon in my chest and heart, turning my system into nothing but a wasteland as I struggle to keep standing, to keep seeing, to keep breathing...

Because Tyce's entire right side is nothing but a bloom of bright crimson.

"Fuck," I rasp. "Damn it, Tyce. God*damn*it."

The asshole shrugs. *Shrugs*, like the hero that I never can or will be, before shivving my soul even deeper with his bullshit by kicking up one side of his mouth in his classic rogue's grin. "Hell doesn't pick favorites, brother," he drawls. "But I promise you, I'll make sure those demon dickwads give Papa Bear Richards some extra special attention."

And with that, his smirk vanishes. Watching his grimace take over, conveying the extent of his true pain, wastes whatever's left of my heart. Now I'm running only on instinct and adrenaline, watching him shuffle a couple of steps over, fists balled as he screws together the courage to do what Chase still can't wrap his head around.

He drops to the edge of the platform, leans in, and grabs Dad by the ankle.

With one swoosh of astonishing strength, he hauls our father off the platform.

With one determined jab at the remote box, he powers up the lift again.

"No!" I roar, scrambling to the edge of the rising platform. "You asshole! You *asshole!*"

But the fucker just cracks a grin that's so defiant and brilliant and insolent, I'm stripped of words. He's ripped every single one of them from me with this act and drives his goddamned point home by giving the remote a huge, defined twist, pegging the needle into the red on the thing's power output.

Just before rolling himself all the way atop our father's prone form.

And detonating the Consortium's version of a grenade between their bodies.

I know this because I can hear it. Because I *know* it. Because as fast as the platform's gears and pulleys work around us, they're not laboring hard enough—ensuring that I'm a sobbing, choking, heaving witness to my brother's last seconds of mortality. Of humanity. Of bravery.

As we rise back into the shaft of black rock and dark silence, I plummet my head down to my crumpled knees... whispering a desperate prayer for the soul of that arrogant, brilliant dickwad of a hero.

And in broken, spurting snarls, pray that my father is screaming in a hell just like the one he nearly sold us into.

EMMA

Five days after we've returned to LA from Paris, exactly a week after the most awful night of my life, Reece and I are spending our first night back in bed at home. Okay, so anywhere I'm with him is truly home, from the Brocade's penthouse to an apartment on the Hudson to a little walk-up near the Seine, but when I think of a forever *home* with this man, it's up on this bluff north of Malibu, with the Pacific in the distance, the smell of night jasmine in the air, and the whisper of wind through the wildflowers and sage scrub down through the valley. Just by walking in the door, I can feel my psyche sloughing off layers of tension. I listen to the evidence of the same as Reece releases a long, mellow sigh.

Sometime in the middle of this week's scourge of shock and grief and comprehension and recovery, we've turned our new routine into a nightly tradition. With him settled against the bed's headboard, I nestle between his legs and lean back into the solid plane of his chest. Our phones are off, the windows are open, and we rest together in the peace of simply existing, silent and sublime with each other for long minutes, until one of us feels the compulsion to whisper...

"You still here?"

Tonight, the words come from him. Doesn't really matter, since my follow-up is the same. With a full sigh, I tug at his left hand with mine—my only option, since my right is still encased in the cast that's helping my three mangled middle fingers to heal—and then press tender kisses to the backs of his knuckles, confirming that I hear everything he's saying. That *here* doesn't just mean "here." That it means I'm present not just with the proximity of my body. That my heart is still beating with every throb of his. That my spirit still hears the call of his. That my soul still reaches for every special spark of his.

That we're *here*. Alive. Together. And ready to take on the future we've decided to face as one...

No matter how terrifying that vista looks.

Thoughts for another moment. Not this one. In *this* moment, I finish the ministrations to his skin before murmuring, "Right here, mister. By your side. And I'm never *ever* leaving."

And I'll never get tired of saying it, either.

Damn good thing, since I now know how much he needs

to hear it. Probably as intensely as *I* need to hear it. "Are *you* still here?"

The pressure of his lips in my hair, then snuggling down to my neck, is better than the warmth of the early summer wind filtering in from the ridge. "Always, Velvet. And forever."

I let out a long sigh against the bulging goodness of his bare bicep. He's wearing only his black track pants tonight, and it's a delicious change. He's been staying covered up over the last week. First he used the blustery Paris weather as an excuse, and then after we returned, he's kept up his Reece Richards version of swaddling, even when we've been intimate in just about every position possible.

I've given him what he needs in full because it's been what I need too—if the shrinks want to tag us as substituting one of the grief stages with sex, let them—but have *really* missed getting to touch all of him at the same time. The gleaming ropes of his arms. The hewn planes of his chest. And best of all, getting up close and personal with the steady beat of his heart.

But this isn't me complaining. Not by a long shot. Because while my hero has kept his armor on physically, he's been unspeakably brave about keeping me with him emotionally, right here at the center of his heart. Letting me see every moment of the horror and the heartache, the burden and the confusion, the love and the loss of every second, minute, and hour of the last seven days. The magnitude of not just mourning his friend and his brother but his father too. Not the monster we all discovered at the end. The man Reece idolized before that. The ideal he aspired to.

The hero he's had to become for himself now.

The husband he already is...in my heart.

Especially after today.

Yes, I know that in so many ways, we're just at the beginning of this journey—but a milestone is a milestone, and this moment can be about celebrating that. About acknowledging where we were when we got up this morning compared to the difference of where we are now...

Using that silent segue, I tuck my head against his arm with the same tentative softness of my new prompt. "So...you ready to do this?"

His deep groan is followed by the distinct conk of his skull against the headboard. "Can't I distract you with something involving the new hot tub and my hotter cock?"

Somehow, I manage to rein my reaction back to a guttural chuff. "Humor isn't going to earn you a hall pass, Mr. Richards."

A chest-deep growl vibrates into my hair. "There's nothing humorous about what I want to do to you with my cock, Miss Crist."

With an insistent huff, I scoop up the TV remote and tap the green button, and the monitor in the cabinet flares to life. "You need to watch this, baby. To know you did it. And to know we're all behind you too."

Another gruff grumble from the depths of the torso behind me—though now the sound sends primal pulses right through my knit tank top, turning into a million enticing tremors through my body. My nipples pebble and punch at the stretchy fabric, and I nearly brain myself for putting him off about the hot tub. But there's one thing about being here to help the man cope with his grief, and there's another about avoiding the feelings altogether with a hedonistic romp in the pool...

Thank God for the TV, jerking my thoughts out of that conceptual gutter. I refocus on the screen—most specifically on the image that fills a corner of the national news feed.

An image of him.

His face clean-shaven and somber. His shoulders tight beneath a custom black Brioni suit. His posture noble but tense and then stiffening even more as the anchorman gives an introduction to the piece.

"Reece Richards, also known to the world as superhero Bolt, spoke out publicly today for the first time since the horrific events of last week at the family's newest luxury hotel, the Virage Paris. Many have speculated that an elevator in the as-yet-unopened building was to blame for the tragedy, resulting in the deaths of a security staffer as well as Tyce Richards and the family's patriarch, Lawson Richards—but today, the most notorious member of the family was also the bearer of their most shocking news to date. We now bring you a recap from the press conference today, which was held at the Hotel Brocade in Los Angeles, California."

As the news anchor speaks, her key headline words are summarized in the text crawl beneath the feed:

Richards Family in upheaval:
Lawson Richards, Tyce Richards dead

Reece Richards reveals father's ties to Scorpio crime cartel

The truth behind Bolt: Reece Richards now on the offensive

The headlines, along with the grief so evident in Reece's eyes on the feed, succeed in fully sobering me. The man of my heart and soul is striking and strong as he raises the microphone on the podium by another inch. Trixie, Chase, and I are behind him, putting his grief—and his new determination—into courageous words for the entire world. These moments are why I'm coercing him to watch right now. He needs to see this too. To believe he did this. To see the fortitude and leadership with which he did it. To know he's more than what Lawson Richards ever gave him full credit for.

"The incident in question occurred last Friday night, a week ago today. It involved my father, Lawson Richards, luring my two brothers and me to what was supposed to be a celebratory dinner with the opening management team for the Virage."

The onscreen Reece pauses, pulls in a deep breath, and looks as magnificent as a king, suit or not. Here on the bed, I pull his arms even tighter around me, hoping like hell he feels the pride and love that swell through me. And we haven't even gotten to the hard part yet.

Yeah.

Shit.

The hard part.

"Shortly after we all arrived at the event, nearly every attendee at the party drank some spiked drinks, making it easier for our father to put a greater plan in motion—to hand over my two brothers and me to a criminal organization called the Consortium."

The onscreen Reece exhales and then inhales again, his breaths coming in sharp spurts. Clearly, he's debating whether to go on. Tears blur my eyes as he pulls his shit together—and does.

"None of you have heard of this group before because they've remained top secret, protected by the illegal money and corruption of the Scorpio crime cartel. But they do exist. I swear this to you. I know this because they're the scientists who captured me, tortured me, and turned me into the mutant you all now know as Bolt. They did much of the same to my brother Tyce as well—and last Saturday night, to save me from being recaptured by these lunatics, he sacrificed himself so that my brother Chase and I could escape from the trap our father had cleverly laid out for us. During the incident, my father was also killed, along with another man—a brave member of the tactical team who also tried to stop him. The operative's name will not be released upon request by his family and friends."

I take a moment to let my heart pang once more for Mitch and Tyce—and also for Kane and Angelique, working through their grief in their different ways. Kane's off the grid somewhere in Tibet, the place on earth Mitch loved more than any other. And Angelique, ignoring Reece's vehement argument, has dived right back undercover with the Consortium, promising us a complete blow-by-blow of the bastards' reaction when Reece outs them to the world.

My musing for them both is well-timed, since the footage of the press conference now includes a shot of the whole room exploding in a deafening, buzzing, outraged, excited, scandalized, terrified din. I watch the onscreen Emma give in to a widening stare, remembering how I'd started wondering who'd dropped a hive of confused bees in the room.

I duck my flushing face back into Reece's bicep. "Holy crap," I mumble. "What a dork."

Reece leans over, brushing affectionate lips over mine. "My *adorable* dork."

Onscreen Reece holds up his hands, taming the bees again. "Let me be clear about this, everyone," Reece proclaims. "Because this is the most important reason why we've called you all here today. Number one, the Richards Family

Companies and all their diversified brands, are stronger today than they ever have been. My brother Chase and I are ready to guide this massive ship, and its valuable crew members, into a lot of success for a long time to come."

On the bed, I melt a little as my real-life bee tamer caresses the curve of my ear with his warm, adoring mouth and then skims his softly glowing fingertips along the side of my ribcage. My body starts humming at a higher frequency for him, though the arousal is a slow, blissful burn instead of our usual rocket launch of desire. And right now, in this lingering twilight that's just a tiny start of our healing, that's completely right. And absolutely perfect.

"Number two," states TV Reece now. "We're not only going to keep succeeding, but we're going to do it *right*— because we are dedicated to fighting every corner of every *wrong* we see in this world. That begins here, and that begins today—with the promise we are openly, publicly making to find and shut down every shred of the Consortium and their barbaric scientific practices."

As TV Reece pauses to let the press cheer and snap and get lots of juicy B-roll, my personal Reece gently kisses his way to the place where my neck meets my collarbone while spreading his magic touch across my stomach. The heat of his fingers and the softness of my tank are like the first breeze of a summer storm: heated but mellow, dusky but melancholy. Quickly, I fall into a fugue state between reality and fantasy... into the ripple that's a little bit of both, possible only with him.

Somehow, I'm still able to rasp, "Errrmmm...Mr. Richards?"

"Yes, Miss Crist?"

"You're distracting me."

"And that's a bad thing why?"

"Because we're getting to the best part."

"Hmmm." He turns his head, following my gaze back up to the monitor. "You're right."

TV Reece scales back on his glower for the faintest glimmer of a smile, although the look is edged by the ferocity only he could bring to a basic hotel ballroom in front of a horde of rabid reporters. "I'm done with living in the shadows," he declares, forming his hands into fists on either side of the microphone. "And I'm done with living in shame about who and what I am. I can't promise you all that I'm going to get it right all the time—but I promise you I'm going to try, and with the help of this woman"—he uncoils one hand to reach back for me, yanking me up to the podium with him—"who has graciously and generously agreed to be my wife, we're going to take down the Consortium and make this world a better place, damn it."

On the screen, the reporters break out into stadium-level applause.

In our bed, I turn so I can curl up against the man of my dreams. Listening to the throbs of the heart he's gifted to me in return—despite knowing we're likely headed for the hardest part of our journey together.

But we're doing it *together*.

Rejoicing in our love. Blinded by our future. Ready for our challenges. Prepared for our fight.

Ignited by our destiny.

Together.

Always together.

And always forever.

"You're right," I whisper into the center of his chest. "This really *is* the best part."

Continue the Bolt Saga with

Fuse

Available November 27, 2018

ALSO BY ANGEL PAYNE

The Bolt Saga:
Bolt
Ignite
Pulse
Fuse (November 27, 2018)
Surge (Coming Soon)
Light (Coming Soon)

Honor Bound:
Saved
Cuffed
Seduced
Wild
Wet
Hot
Masked
Mastered
Conquered (Coming Soon)
Ruled (Coming Soon)

Secrets of Stone Series:
No Prince Charming
No More Masquerade
No Perfect Princess
No Magic Moment
No Lucky Number
No Simple Sacrifice
No Broken Bond
No White Knight

Cimarron Series:
Into His Dark
Into His Command
Into Her Fantasies

Temptation Court:
Naughty Little Gift
Pretty Perfect Toy
Bold Beautiful Love

**For a full list of Angel's other titles,
visit her at AngelPayne.com**

ACKNOWLEDGMENTS

The Bolt Saga journey would not be this exciting or amazing without the diligence and dedication of so many amazing people.

As always: thank you to the magnificent team at Waterhouse Press, especially my beyond-talented editing team. Scott Saunders and Jeanne De Vita, none of this would be the jewel that it is without you both helping me to polish it to an amazing shine! I am beyond grateful! And David, Jon, and Meredith: you three have believed so strongly in this crazy world from the start, earning you such deep and heartfelt thanks from the bottom of my heart. And absolutely everyone else on this epic team: Robyn, Yvonne, Haley, Jennifer, Amber, Jesse, and Kurt—you are the ultimate superhero squad! Thank you!

Special gratitude and thanks to Martha Frantz for continuing to keep me sane on so many levels.

My "Passionate Payne" gratitude to all the gods and goddesses in the Payne Passion Nation across the social media platforms. You are all so incredible and bring such joy and light into my life on a daily basis!

Meredith Wild and Victoria Blue: thank you for talking me down off all the ledges, all the time, and for the writing sprints to keep me chugging along and inspired!

A special thank you to all of the bloggers and reviewers, in the romance and superhero fandoms, for reading and loving and chatting up the books all the time! You guys and gals are so awesome and generous, and I appreciate you so much.

ABOUT ANGEL PAYNE

USA Today bestselling romance author Angel Payne loves to focus on high-heat romance starring memorable alpha men and the women who love them. She has numerous book series to her credit, including the popular Honor Bound series, the Secrets of Stone series (with Victoria Blue), the Cimarron series, the Temptation Court series, the Suited for Sin series, and the Lords of Sin historicals, as well as several standalone titles.

Angel is a native Southern Californian, leading to her love of being in the outdoors, where she often reads and writes. She still lives in Southern California with her soul-mate husband and beautiful daughter, to whom she is a proud cosplay/culture con mom. Her passions also include whisky tasting, shoe shopping, and travel.

Visit her at AngelPayne.com